Dark Wars

by

Nicolas Brentano

Copyright © Nicolas Brentano 2017

No part of this book may be reproduced in any form or by any means electronic or mechanical, including recording or by any information storage and retrieval system without permission in writing from the author. Sole exception is in the case of brief quotations embodied in critical articles or reviews.

The Author asserts the moral right to be identified as the author of this work.

Paperback ISBN: 978-1-910088-18-0

Ebook ISBN: 978-1-910088-42-5

Bret PV46

DARK WARS

is available in all Ebook formats from Amazon, Smashwords, Ibooks and most other retailers

DARK WARS is the second book in the DIRTY WARS Trilogy

Also by Nicholas Brentano

DIRTY WARS

DEEP WARS

The social, political and economic events which form the backdrop to this account are based on reality. The opinions expressed about these events are however those of the protagonists and any similarity with real events or persons living or dead is purely coincidental. Those who might detect such resemblance may be either flattered or offended. The author hopes that, in the latter case, since no offence is intended, he will eventually be forgiven.

Cover photo by kind permission of *mpicsmedia.com*

To my beloved wife – *por aguantarme...*

On Sunday, 18 January 2015, the body of judge Alberto Nisman's was found collapsed in the bathroom of his apartment in the Le Parc condominium in the Puerto Madero, a .22 bullet in the head. Some 24 hours before he was due to appear before the Argentine Congress in response to a summons to explain the reasons for which he had launched a formal indictment of President Cristina Kirchner and her Foreign Minister, Hector Timmermann, for having conspired to sabotage the investigation into the role of Iran in the 1990s bombings of the Israeli embassy and the headquarters of the Argentine-Israeli Mutual Association (AMIA), which delivered a combined death toll of nearly 100. In particular, Judge Nisman had cited the memorandum signed between Buenos Aires and Teheran in (DATE), whereby Iran would agree to the Argentine investigation being pursued in Iran, including the interrogation of a number of leading figures suspected of having been involved in the original decisions.

The announcement of the existence of this Memorandum had been almost universally condemned, and in particular not only by the Jewish community in Argentina, but also by leading figures in Israel and in the United States.

From the moment of the discovery of his body, the investigation showed every sign of manipulation and cover-up, even from the first mismanagement of the crime scene by the Argentine security forces. An initial immediate statement by President Kirchner suggesting suicide, was, not more than 24 hours later, overtaken by her conviction that this was no longer the case. Subsequent instalments consisted of thinly veiled attempts to discredit Nisman both professionally and with regard to his private life.

In the ensuing, confused investigations which continue until this day, a number of theories were advanced regarding the reasons which might underlie not only the death of Nisman, but also the whole question of Argentina's relations with Iran. Among many theories cited, reference was made to the possibility that all this might be a cover-up for

Argentine collaboration with Iran in the development of its militarised nuclear capacity.

This theory provides the backdrop to Dark Wars which, in its first edition, appeared some six months before the death of Nisman, who is cited by name on a number of occasions in the book.

Breaking News

BUENOS AIRES — President Vladimir V. Putin of Russia and his Argentine counterpart signed deals on nuclear energy and other projects on Saturday in an effort to expand his country's influence in Latin America. Russia will help build the third reactor of a nuclear power plant in Argentina, Mr. Putin said after meeting with the Argentine president, Cristina Fernández de Kirchner, here on Saturday.

(The New York Times, July 12 2014)

DARK WARS

April 2008

Wednesday, 30 April 2008 (AM) – GRAND' PLACE, BRUSSELS

A waiter, on his way to set out the tables and chairs at Le Roy d'Espagne, almost stumbled over the body, spread-eagled on the cobblestones near the point at which Rue de la Tête d'Or enters Grand' Place. The head crushed by the fall, dark red blood against grey cobbles.

An hour later, once Inspecteur Principal Jean Michel Leroy had satisfied himself there was no further evidence to be obtained on the square, the body was taken by ambulance to one of the Institut National de Criminalistique et de Criminologie laboratories.

At around 7.30am, Leroy got through to the duty officer at the Argentine diplomatic mission in Brussels as he was having breakfast in a cafe round the corner from the embassy. Juan Carlos Moreno, a thirty year-old second secretary, caught a taxi and met him at the entrance to number 3 on Rue de la Tête d'Or. Leroy handed him the wallet they had found in the back pocket of the dead man's trousers. It contained a diplomatic carnet, identifying him as Luis María Sanchez.

"He's a First Secretary in your embassy, I believe."

Moreno nodded. "Yes, arrived about six months ago from Buenos Aires."

"I understand from the concierge that he occupies the top flat alone. Are you aware of any family?"

"Señor Sanchez was a bachelor. I guess he has family in Buenos Aires. We will inform the Ministry. I presume you will require someone to identify the body."

"Yes, he has been taken to the Institut National out on the Chaussée de Vilvorde. I'd be grateful if someone could accompany me there at some point today to identify the body formally. These keys were attached to his belt. One of them is, I assume, the entrance to his flat. But, given that he's a diplomat, I would prefer someone from your embassy to accompany me there too. From the condition of the body, it's clear that he fell from a height. What's strange is that, as far as I can tell from here, the windows of his apartment appear to be closed."

"The wind? There was rain last night."

"Possibly. There are also some matters of a more delicate nature, which I would like to discuss with you at some point."

Moreno could see the Belgian policeman did not propose to elaborate. He pulled out his cell phone and dialled the ambassador for the second time that day. Leroy, not speaking Spanish, made no effort to listen in. The conversation was brief. Moreno folded his cell and turned back to Leroy.

"My ambassador insists that our legal adviser accompany me. He should be with us in about five minutes, if traffic allows."

"I understand. Of course, we will wait a little, but you will appreciate that the sooner we can get access to his flat, the quicker we can establish what happened. I'll be waiting in my car over there."

Moreno gazed around the square. He had come here often, usually accompanying some visiting Argentine official or businessman keen to see the sights. To respond to their curiosity, he had made himself at least minimally knowledgeable about its history. The mixture of architectural styles was extraordinary, though not, as far as he could remember, the result of a progressive build-up over time. The unique product of the burgers's determination to rebuild what the armies of Louis XIV had destroyed in a massive bombardment of the city in the last decade of the 17th century. He wondered how Sanchez had been so fortunate as to find somewhere to live in this beautiful setting.

A pale sun was bathing the square, reflecting in the leaded windows, the southwest side dominated by the Hôtel de Ville. A few tourists had begun to appear at the cafe tables on the far side.

Much to Leroy's irritation, he could see that a two-man film crew, perhaps tipped off by the waiter, were preparing to film the scene of the crime.

"The body has been taken away," Leroy called out. "We may have something to report later in the day. That's all I have to say at the present time."

With a look of frustration, the reporter signalled to his cameraman to switch off his equipment and the pair soon disappeared. Early arrivals at the Hôtel de Ville threw only a passing glance in their direction.

It was nearer fifteen minutes before a taxi finally parked on the edge of the square, disgorging the embassy's legal adviser. Moreno greeted him and led him to the police car. Leroy and the lawyer shook hands, quickly establishing that since they were both Walloons, their common language would be French.

"The body was discovered by one of the waiters here on the Place at about 6.30. Lying where you see the chalk mark."

The adviser nodded, squinting at the cobblestones.

"We know it had rained at some stage since the body fell. The back of the body was wet, but the ground underneath dry. So we estimate the time of the fall, if it was a fall, at around 4am. That tallies with the temperature of the body. Death was certainly instantaneous, damage to the skull significant. Post-mortem will establish whether there are traces of alcohol, drugs or anything else. But our initial examination indicates the fall was certainly not accidental. Señor Moreno has kindly agreed to accompany me upstairs to examine the flat, and I understand that you, Maître Dubois, will also be coming along."

Turning to Moreno, Leroy continued.

"We will obviously need to speak to his colleagues at your embassy. And anyone else you may suggest, who might have had contact with him yesterday and especially during the evening."

"We'll put together a list. We should have his diary. I'll speak with his secretary."

Moreno paused, seeing that Maître Dubois was making a furtive signal not to say more.

"Just a minute, Inspecteur, I need to speak to Maître Dubois."

The two walked a few metres away.

"Señor Moreno, you need to be very careful. Remember that you and most of the senior members of the embassy have diplomatic immunity.

This is a criminal investigation and we need to bear that immunity in mind. Under the Vienna Convention, Señor Sanchez's flat enjoys the same immunity as the embassy offices, so the Inspecteur has no right to enter the flat unless the ambassador expressly allows it. Senior members of the staff need to be briefed on what they can and what they cannot say, for which your ambassador will almost certainly need guidance from Buenos Aires. So, please don't make promises in that direction."

Moreno thanked him and they turned to the Inspecteur.

"I need to make another phone call to the ambassador before we go up to the flat, if you don't mind."

After five minutes, Moreno and Dubois confirmed that, until instructions had been received from Buenos Aires, it would not be possible to enter the flat.

Inspecteur Leroy smiled as though he'd heard it before.

"I understand. But we will need access sooner rather than later if we are to throw any light on Señor Sanchez's death. Please convey this to your ambassador. I hope to be hearing from you soon."

Moreno promised to come back with a reply as soon as possible.

They shook hands and Moreno and the lawyer set off in search of a taxi to take them back to the embassy.

Leroy watched them as they made their way across the Grand' Place, then turned back to his team.

"This isn't going to be an easy one, *les amis*."

May 2008

Thursday, 1 May 2008 (PM) (PM) – GRAND' PLACE, BRUSSELS

After a series of exchanges between the Argentine embassy and the Ministry of Foreign Relations in Buenos Aires, involving consultations with other organs of government and even the President's office, permission was finally granted to Inspecteur Leroy to examine the crime scene. But not before a member of the embassy had paid a brief nocturnal visit to make sure that nothing too incriminating would be found. Inspecteur Leroy, having mounted discreet surveillance on the building, was well aware of the intrusion.

The ambassador had sent Moreno and Maître Dubois along. They again met the Inspecteur on the Grand' Place in front of Sanchez's building.

The concierge let them in and the three of them, now joined by four forensic experts in protective clothing, made their way up the old, winding staircase. At the fourth floor, the Inspecteur identified the keys on Sanchez's key ring. He asked Moreno and Dubois to put on overshoes, putting on a pair himself, before opening the door.

Leroy could not resist the temptation to hint at what he knew.

"We must hope that things are pretty much the way they were left on the night of the crime," Leroy said, casting a glance at Moreno.

Moreno said nothing. Although not officially privy to the decision, the forceful discussions between the ambassador and a member of the staff known to have connections to SIDE, the Argentine intelligence service, had not gone unnoticed.

The flat consisted of the sitting room with its spectacular view over the square through two large leaded windows, two bedrooms on the inner side of the building, each with a bathroom, and a small kitchen. Seemingly a peaceful bachelor flat, through which the investigating team proceeded to move, each taking a room, with Leroy watching and occasionally giving instructions.

It looked as though Sanchez had hung his jacket over a chair in front of an 18th-century inlaid desk. His tie, from Hermes, had been tossed onto the sofa. A copy of a 29 April edition of Le Soir lay open on the floor beside the chair. On the side table, an almost empty cognac glass. The forensic team, with cameras and floods, began to photograph and film the scene. On the Inspecteur's instructions, Moreno and Dubois had remained in the hallway, to allow this first photo record to be made.

"Please, gentlemen, you can come in now. Señor Moreno, is there anything that you might be able to tell us about the lifestyle of Señor Sanchez? Any friends or acquaintances you might know about?"

Moreno looked at Maître Dubois for guidance.

"I believe that Señor Moreno is under no obligation to make any comment at this stage, Inspecteur. I see our role as essentially to ensure that you undertake whatever investigation appears appropriate, whilst respecting the privacy of the deceased. Unless you object, we will remain here while you do your work. It is not for us to contribute directly to that process."

Leroy had little choice but to acquiesce, though the look on his face betrayed his true feelings.

"I understand, Maître, and will respect your wishes."

With his team, Leroy, occasionally looking over his shoulder at his two observers, began a systematic but discreet search, removing drawers or shifting books on the shelves. The fingerprint expert went about his business, examining glasses, bottles, any shiny surface, the doors, the windows.

"Señor Moreno, I would draw your attention to the fact that these windows are all closed from the inside."

Watching them at work, Moreno wondered how a similar investigation might be conducted back in Buenos Aires. The corruption of evidence, so often attempted by someone well-placed to divert an unwelcome investigation, probably started even earlier, through careless or inexperienced crime scene management.

The four specialists had now been joined by a woman, also wearing protective clothing. Moreno walked out into the hall, followed by Maître Dubois.

"Complicated, I would say," the Belgian muttered.

Moreno nodded. "Not much we can do. What do you think?"

"I agree, but we should stay here just in case."

Finally the Inspecteur joined them on the landing.

"We know that Señor Sanchez was not alone, although we're having some difficulty in finding any trace of his visitor. And we're certain he was dead before striking the pavement. The initial examination of the body shows marks of a ligature, some kind of narrow wire around the neck. There are also signs of a struggle, scuff marks on the carpet in front of the armchair, and scratches on the window sill. It looks as though somebody strangled him before throwing him out and then cleared up afterwards."

Moreno couldn't think of anything to reply. He wondered what Sanchez had been up to. His intelligence connections had been common knowledge in the embassy. Not an easy man to get close to, a loner. Rumours from the secretaries he might even be gay.

"Is there anything more you require from us?" he asked Leroy. "I presume that when you're finished, you will be sealing off the flat. Though as soon as possible, we will require access to pull together Señor Sanchez' personal possessions."

"Very soon," Leroy replied. "In the meantime, please advise your ambassador that we wish to call on him and speak to certain members of his staff."

At this point, the woman came out onto the landing and took the Inspecteur aside, leading him a couple of steps down the stairs. Moreno watched as she handed him a small pile of photo magazines, which the Leroy did not even bother to study. He turned to Moreno.

"I think I mentioned some additional, more troubling aspects to the death of Señor Sanchez. Firstly, as you know, he was strangled and his wrists were handcuffed behind his back. And now these," handing Moreno one of the magazines, "appear to add a certain texture. My assistant found them at the back of a drawer in the desk."

It was one of the more garish and violent examples of specialist literature of a kind to be found in the gay section of sex shops anywhere in the world. The nocturnal visitor had been less than diligent in searching the flat.

Moreno tried to convey a look combining disgust with the curiosity of someone who might have never seen such a publication. Which was not necessarily the case, Moreno not being a total stranger to the kind of shops to be found behind the Gare du Nord in the Belgian capital.

"This is most troubling, Inspecteur. Obviously, I know nothing about this side of Señor Sanchez's private life."

"Of course," Leroy said. "But you should be aware that we will be pursuing this line of enquiry as well. We will attempt to do so with maximum discretion."

Sensing a delicate conversation, Maître Dubois had walked to the window at the far end of the landing.

"I believe we can leave now, Maître," Moreno called to him.

Moreno turned on reaching the far side of the square to look back at the elegant building he had just left. What was all this about? There had obviously been more to Sanchez than met the eye. A flat in the Belgian capital's most spectacular setting. Handcuffed! Strangled! Those magazines!

Secretaries often knew far more than one imagined.

Tuesday, 6 May 2008 (PM) – 2060 ANTWERP

"As-Salāmu 'Alaykum."

"Wa alaikum salam. You're late!"

The visitor sat down on the other side of the octagonal inlaid table, placing his two small travel bags on the floor next to him. The older man studied him discreetly. Fit, slim, the baggy jeans and loose hooded tracksuit concealing a strong physique. Handsome as well. Early thirties? He had chosen to avoid the popular combination of shaven head and beard, which usually provoked the curiosity of the security forces in this part of Antwerp. This might be an area of the city frequented for many years by a migrant population of Middle Eastern origin, but profiling still led to random searches and too many questions being asked. The younger man would probably pass unnoticed in any neighbourhood.

Strict security meant he knew little about his visitor. From his Arabic, he detected Moroccan or Tunisian origins. His instructions had been to grant the visitor safe passage for the next leg of his journey. On balance, the less he knew the better, though for some reason he suspected that press reports of a diplomat's mysterious suicide in the Grand' Place might have some connection with the man sitting opposite him.

The courier from Baghdad, who had passed through a month earlier, had made clear that the operation formed part of a wider strategy against the Iranian apostates, the fruit of decisions taken at the highest level. A campaign to disrupt the nuclear ambitions of their Shia neighbours, no less.

"Apologies. I decided to take extra precautions at the station in Brussels. Quite a lot of police around. I've heard the investigation is beginning to look towards the Middle East."

"I see. And how do we know?"

"We've heard that the Politie have been showing a photofit of someone with Middle Eastern features to some of their contacts. Presumably, it's me."

He laughed.

"Let's hope it's not too accurate," the older man replied.

The two were sitting in a small cafe on the Handelstraat, a thoroughfare in the immigrant quarter of Antwerp commonly referred to by its postcode, '2060'. The cafe catered almost exclusively to the local community, unlike one or two of the upmarket restaurants on the street, which had acquired a reputation for Oriental cuisine which now attracted foreign tourists. A part of the city which was starting to see a measure of ethnic unrest and consistent attention from the police as a result. Precautions were called for.

The visitor was also observing his contact. From his accent, almost certainly Iraqi. Well over fifty, overweight, unshaven, he looked like any one of the middle-aged men he had passed standing in front of their shops and stalls as he made his way down the street. Average. Anonymous. Better that way.

The waiter approached with a small engraved glass in one hand and the traditional long-spouted silver-plated teapot in the other. He began to pour, raising the pot high above the glass to generate the desired froth on the surface of the liquid.

"I hope that your mission was a success," the older man returned to the charge.

The visitor merely nodded.

The older man could see that little more would be forthcoming. A change of tack.

"Have you been to Latin America before?"

"No, but for various reasons, I know Spanish. I learned it as a child."

None of the other man's business, but his father had worked in an import-export company in Casablanca, specializing in bulk olive oil exports, for which a number of major clients were Spanish. Aged ten, when the family had moved to Cadiz, he had attended school for three years, before returning to Morocco. He fully expected the older man to have spotted that he was Moroccan from the way he spoke. The fact that he also spoke fluent English and French was, along with the rest of his career, no concern of this man.

"I've never been to Latin America either. Though of course, many of our brethren moved there when the Empire collapsed. I believe I have some distant cousins in Buenos Aires, but we've never been in touch."

The visitor could see that his contact would have loved to hear more about what had happened in Brussels that night. A pleasure to be savoured alone.

Sipping his tea, he recalled the image of Sanchez, slumped in his armchair, losing consciousness as the wire round his throat slowly shut off the supply of oxygen to his brain, eyeballs almost invisible as they rolled up into his skull. In the minutes leading up to his final collapse, as he had pulled the wire tighter, he had repeated the same questions slowly, relentlessly.

"To whom do you report in Buenos Aires? Names."

Sanchez, just sufficiently lucid to hope that an answer might save his life, had nodded in the direction of his desk. The visitor could see a file open on the fold-down top of the bureau. A final twist of the wire. After which it was only the work of a minute to roll the lifeless body onto the floor, pull the arms into the small of the back and apply the handcuffs. Opening his briefcase carefully on the carpet, he took out the small selection of magazines he had bought that afternoon in one of the city's sex shops and placed them at the bottom of one of the desk drawers. Finally, with his digital camera, he took a couple of shots of the lifeless Sanchez, face down, wrists bound. Proof of mission accomplished.

A quick search through the folder enabled him to photograph one or two documents with names and addresses in Buenos Aires. Also a couple of letters from a certain José Ramon Hernandez in Caracas. From the tone of one, as he later studied them, it looked as though Sanchez might have been his predecessor in the Venezuelan capital.

Dragging Sanchez to the leaded window, after a quick look to see that the square was empty, with a sweeping movement he propelled the corpse out onto the cobbles below.

A final clean-up to remove any possible trace of his presence and he was gone. The investigation would inevitably establish that Sanchez had not been alone. But, hopefully, that would be as far as they could take it.

The visitor could see from the look on the older man's face that he was suppressing his natural curiosity, perhaps to reassure himself that he was part of something important, taking risks for a worthwhile cause. As the visitor had made his way to Brussels, passing through Marseilles, one or two contacts along the route had not been so reticent, prepared to question him point blank about the purpose of his mission. He had told them to mind their own business and reported back to Baghdad that some of their European representatives should be reminded of the need for discretion. The operations commander had asked him to alert them to any security breaches he might detect along the way.

March 2008 – BAGHDAD

It was one of the last instructions at the end of the meeting some six weeks earlier, in the Sha'ab neighbourhood of Baghdad. There had been four of them in the room, the operations commander of the Sons of Ibn Taymiyyah terrorist group, its planning commander and the special operations leader of the cell, as well as the visitor, arrived that morning from Lebanon. He could hear the guards moving around in the stairway outside and on the flat roof above their heads, the safe house being under constant guard to prevent any risk of eavesdropping or sabotage from the numerous Shia groups operating clandestinely in the same neighbourhood.

Assassinations by followers of the charismatic cleric Muqtada al-Sadr, coming in the wake of unconfirmed rumours that he might have returned from his exile in Iran, were on the rise. The campaign by government forces against his Mehdi army in Basra was showing only mixed success. With the departure of the Americans iminent, the field was increasingly thrown open to such groups fighting each other for territory. Nearly every day, bodies turned up in an alleyway or on waste ground, a bullet in the back of the head or throats cut, with traces of torture or gratuitous mutilation.

"First of all," the planning commander began, "thank you for coming. I hope your flight was comfortable and your arrival discreet."

"Thank you."

"Good. Our battle continues. As you can hear..."

On cue, the sound of gunfire from the nearby Shia bastion of Sadr City, southeast of where they were meeting, could be heard through the windows.

"Let me explain. The reason for your mission is complex. As you know, we are doing everything possible to stop Iran getting its hands on nuclear weapons. Which means we must also find a way to strike at those who are helping those dogs in Tehran. It's clear that, whatever the pressure the Americans - may Allah banish them also - are trying to place upon those apostates, it's only partially working. Sanctions are making things uncomfortable for the Iranian population, but the mullahs are still finding ways to speed up their enrichment capabilities.

And we know they're not doing it by themselves. There are other countries helping them. If we cannot do enough about things inside Iran, then we must think of attacking their allies and friends." He looked hard at the visitor. "We need you to undertake a mission for us."

The visitor bowed his head, appreciation for the honour. Not to mention the fee he would extract in the process.

"You will go first to Europe and then to South America."

In the ensuing briefing, the planning commander, with occasional input from his colleague, outlined the mission. Much of the evidence of which they now disposed pointed to the fact that, whatever the apparent state of bilateral relations between Tehran and Buenos Aires, seemingly mired in the Argentine investigation into Iranian involvement in the Hezbollah bombings in the 1990s, all signs pointed to collaboration in matters of uranium enrichment, secretly conducted on separate channels, possibly passing through Venezuela.

"This is typical *taqiyah* of these two-faced Shia dogs. Misleading. But we know they're working with these fools from South America. Not just the Argentines, also the Venezuelans. Somehow, we need to break this link. We need to frighten the Argentines into realising there is a high price to pay for working with these infidels. In the process, we may also be able to stir up relations between the Argentine government and its Jewish community. Collateral benefits. As everywhere else, the Jews dominate Argentine business, the financial sector, as well as their intellectual elite."

The visitor had wondered where all this information was coming from. Argentina seemed a long way off the map for a terrorist group embedded in the middle of Baghdad.

"But how do we choose the targets? If it's as secret as you suggest."

"We have information – I'm not saying any more than that - as to the identity of one or two of the people involved on the Argentine side. Diplomats. We have selected two of these. You will apply your usual techniques, to ensure they are eliminated in the most visible – and embarrassing – fashion possible."

His usual techniques. Not for nothing had they nicknamed him 'The Director'. A man who specialised in elaborate scenarios around the elimination of his victims, calculated to add additional layers of outrage, of embarrassment, of provocation. That was what they hired him for and paid him well. He had once overheard someone referring to him as 'Tarantino' and suspected they used it as his codename. He rather liked the title 'Director'.

"For the first of your targets, an attaché at their embassy in Belgium, we have prepared a cover identity for you. How you deal with him after that is your affair. Once that is done, you will go to Argentina. Obviously, you must take advantage of your contact with this Argentine in Belgium to identify other possible targets. Reliable information. You will also be receiving the support of our representatives in those countries. Otherwise, the less that is known about your presence and your mission, the better. We want to make sure that the message is clear. We are giving you free rein to cause as much damage to their discussions as you can. You chose your targets but they must all be clearly involved in the nuclear dialogue. We want you to operate as independently as possible."

That suited him. He'd always preferred to rely as little as possible on the local members of such groups, the quality and reliability of their operatives being, to say the least, variable.

The operations commander, having up to that point sat fiddling with his cell phone, a bored expression on his bearded face, leaned slowly forward.

"One of the problems the Argentines are examining at the moment is transport. Transport for the equipment the Iranians are planning to buy. We have reason to believe this man in Brussels is handling that question."

Next day, the Director had been provided with an email address, along with the identity of a Lebanese forwarding agent specialising in the shipment of arms and equipment between some of the terrorist groups in areas where Hezbollah was active. Once back in Lebanon, an exchange of communications between the forwarding agent office in Beirut and the attaché in Brussels, offering transport services for unspecified shipments, had led to a rendezvous in a restaurant on the outskirts of Rome in the middle of April. Sanchez had shown interest in the services this agency might provide. The requirement was to ship certain items, possibly from Buenos Aires or alternatively from La Guaira, the main port of Caracas, to somewhere in the Gulf. The need for complete discretion, most of all to avoid the surveillance of the Americans and Israelis, had been a precondition. The Director had been asked to come back with a plan and a price.

This he had done two weeks later in Brussels, at the dinner they'd shared at Aux Armes de Bruxelles. The Argentine had appeared sufficiently excited by the proposal to suggest celebrating with a visit to a strip club, L'Intime, and had subsequently invited him for a brandy at his flat on the Grand´ Place. He had fleetingly wondered whether Sanchez might be gay, but his host had done nothing to confirm the suspicion. Rather the contrary, judging by the way he'd fondled the girls at l'Intime. He had seemed in a mood to celebrate the solution his bosses in Buenos Aires were looking for.

After about an hour of savouring Sanchez's excellent cognac, he had visited the bathroom to slip on a pair of surgical gloves. Returning with his hands in his pockets, he made as if to look out of the window onto the square below, standing behind the armchair in which Sanchez now slouched, the brandy glass warming between his fingers. It had been child's play to step up behind him and whip the garrotting wire round his throat. Protected by the back of the chair, he had avoided Sanchez's initial punches as he tried to extricate himself from the thin cable compressing his windpipe. Slowly, Sanchez's movements had become feebler as he had begun to lose consciousness.

After the search for documents and a clean-up of everything he had touched, he had closed the windows and silently made his way down the narrow staircase to the ground floor. A quick glance through the front door was enough to see the crumpled body in front of him. Rain was falling and the vast square was empty. He stepped out and walked a couple of blocks through the pedestrian area, before finally picking up a taxi on Boulevard Anspach. First a hotel, then on to Antwerp.

The older man signalled to the waiter for more tea.

For a few minutes they drank in silence.

"And the timing for the next target?"

"I thought you were to give me that," the visitor replied.

"I received the instruction that it should be as soon as possible. You are to make your way to Buenos Aires through Venezuela and Brazil. You will be smuggled into Argentina by our representative in Foz do Iguaçu. He will give you the Buenos Aires contact. I have the itinerary and the name of your first contact in Venezuela. He will provide you with details for your onward journey. Where are you staying?"

"I would prefer you to suggest something."

Tossing some euros on the table and signalling to the waiter, the older man stood up.

"Come. I will take you there now."

Tuesday, 13 May 2008 (PM) – CALLE PERÚ, BUENOS AIRES

They had pushed aside the remains of a couple of large *bifes de lomo* and were savouring the last glass of a cabernet sauvignon from Mendoza.

"Interesting place," Leandro said, looking round.

The black and white decor of Querandí, one of Buenos Aires' more traditional restaurants, in Calle Perú, had preserved the sculpted woodwork, bevelled glass doors and windows, and elegant brass fittings of a bygone age, the waiters dressed to match.

"Not bad," Juan Carlos Grunwald said. "The tourists like it too. They give a tango show in the evenings. You should take it in sometime. They say it's quite good. Though perhaps a little acrobatic for my taste."

"I know what you mean," Leandro replied. "That's globalisation for you. Anyway, there's no chance I could tempt my girlfriend to come here. She hates tango."

"You're a bit of an exception yourself, Leandro. I don't know many Anglo-Argentines, particularly of Scottish origin, who like tango."

Leandro Flemming laughed. "I can't explain it. The transience of life. All that betrayal, unrequited love, corruption. I can see why it depresses people, in spite of the sensuality. Two people pressed close, bodies swirling round. Somebody - I can't remember who - once described it as the dancing of a sad thought. But I agree with you. It's lost its simplicity. I love the old masters, Julio Sosa, Edmundo Rivero, Anibal Troilo."

"Might have been Ernesto Sabato, who wrote that," Grunwald murmured.

It had all started at the end of January in the discreet Mayfair headquarters of Frobisher, a private intelligence-gathering boutique set up in the aftermath of the Cold War by specialists from the British intelligence community. As the priorities for intelligence collection had begun to move away from the Soviet bloc and international Communism towards terrorism and drug trafficking, some of the more experienced agent-running and security-trained experts had seen a growing market in corporate intelligence. The services they provided included negotiation in hostage-taking situations and tactical intelligence for corporations, particularly those seeking to operate in more exotic markets, such as Central Asia, Africa or Latin America. Like so many activities previously jealously guarded by the state, intelligence gathering had gone private. Organisations of this kind had flourished, even behind the old Iron Curtain.

In spite of Leandro's Scottish origins – his ancestors had come to Argentina from Aberdeen in the 1820s - he had made it very clear to Frobisher from the outset that there would always be some areas in which he would not help them. Anything he consideded Argentina's true long-term interests were off-limits. Coming close to being killed during the Malvinas campaign, when British ground fire had shot down his Pucará fighter-bomber in the wake of the San Carlos landings, had served to clarify this boundary between where his Scottish ancestry stopped and his homeland's long-term interests began. To his relief, Charles Colson, his Frobisher case officer, had understood completely.

As he had explained to Leandro back in January, Charles was now interested on behalf of one of their clients in a particularly sensitive area of Argentine foreign policy. The possibility that Argentina was supporting Iran's nuclear ambitions with technology or hardware. If this was the case, it would be in almost certain violation of the numerous United Nations resolutions and other sanctions imposed by the international community in an attempt to forestall a particularly risky case of nuclear proliferation. Leandro had almost immediately reached the conclusion that Argentina's best interests would not be served by fostering the ayatollahs's ambitions. A regime many thought responsible for the terrorist attacks in Buenos Aires in the early 90s. So, a month earlier, he had confirmed to Charles he would see what he could find out.

The picture was confusing. Argentina's nuclear activities were far from his traditional area of expertise and heavily ring-fenced. The industry was geographically dispersed, the division of government responsibilities obscure. Whether by sloppiness or design, it was hard to tell. By dint of much searching on the web, and the occasional phone call to a close journalist friend dealing with the energy sector, Leandro had finally been able to pull together some of the pieces.

As far as he could detect, Argentina was no longer suspected of attempting to create a militarized nuclear capability of its own, though there was no doubt that a major focus of its R&D related to the fuel cycle. Argentine scientists had apparently devoted efforts to a technology called SIGMA, based on gas diffusion, which seemed to offer lower costs. He could not tell the extent to which this particular technology might be of interest to the Iranians in taking low-grade uranium to the first stages of uranium 235 enrichment.

In his search for links between Argentina and Iran, he had discovered that Argentine scientists had made up a large part of the foreign technicians employed by Iran in the early days of their nuclear programme under the Shah. For all he knew, some of the relationships established at that time might have survived. His research also showed that some twenty years earlier, the Argentine research institute, INVAP, had boasted an international collaboration agreement with Iran. A collaboration which had been brought to a close by President Menem in the early 90s, a decision seen by some as the pretext for the subsequent terrorist attacks on the Israeli embassy and the Israeli Argentine Mutual Association, generally referred to as AMIA, in Buenos Aires.

However many bridges might have survived between Argentine and Iranian scientists from many years back, it was hard to see how such collaboration could be reconciled with the fact that the Iranians were now prime suspects in those attacks. Was it possible that relations between Buenos Aires and Tehran were being conducted on two quite separate levels, the apparently hostile investigation providing a measure of political camouflage for a secret nuclear alliance?

The more his research progressed, the more he realised he must familiarize himself with the broader context of Argentina's political dialogue with Iran. Research into the nuclear side could not ignore the long-running saga of the bombings.

He had done a round of his favourite bookshops to discover what might have been written on the subject. Research on the internet and the available archives of major newspapers helped too. But there were also contacts who might be able to add something.

He looked across the table at Juan Carlos Grunwald, a Jewish journalist and political commentator whose opinions he had long respected.

Leandro knew he was also active in the internal politics of his community. Well placed to follow the endless saga of the bombings.

Most of the lunch so far had been devoted to talking about the government's problems with the *campo*, as the nation's farming sector was commonly called. It had dominated the economic and political scene over the last two months and looked set to continue a couple more. The government's decision to brutally increase the percentage withheld on exports from the key soya and sunflower agricultural sectors, already standing at what many would regard as a punitive 35%, one of a number of emergency measures instituted following the financial crisis of 2001, had provoked widespread resistance. Rumours were beginning to circulate that President Cristina Kirchner might soon double the ante by sending a draft law for approval by Congress and the Senate as a way of imposing her wishes. The fight was set to continue and the outcome would be messy!

"Knowing the mentality of the Kirchners, they won't back down," Grunwald said bluntly.

"I think you're right. Changing course isn't a part of their vocabulary." Leandro poured the remains of the wine into Carlos' glass. "Here, have the last drops."

Leandro looked at his watch.

"You were going to give me a crash course on the AMIA bombing. I don't want to take up too much of your time or your kindness. Perhaps you have another meeting?"

"Relax, Leandro. You've helped me in the past. Obscure corners of the financial system. Just returning the favour. The least I can do."

"Well, I know the basics. The AMIA car bomb in '94 took eighty-five lives and injured some three hundred. In '92 it was the Israeli embassy, killing twenty-nine. I think a jihadi organisation in Lebanon claimed responsibility."

Leandro sipped his wine and visualized the mountain of collapsed masonry in Calle Pasteur, people digging desperately in the wreckage of the AMIA building in search of survivors.

"300 kilos of ammonium nitrate concealed in a Renault Trafic pickup van," Grunwald sighed. "They traced them through the sale and repair of the vehicle. Four Iranian diplomats."

"That trail then mysteriously abandoned, as I recall?"

"In favour of the arrest of a number of military and police. Among those detained, one Carlos Telleldín, responsible for the transfer of the van to the bombers. A central player in the farce to follow."

"Telleldín - son of the head of police in Córdoba before the military coup of '76, wasn't he?" Leandro said.

"Exactly. Tough guy, the father – to put it politely!"

They both knew Córdoba had been the test bed for so many of the repressive practices used during the 1970s 'dirty war'.

"You were going to say something about the way in which the investigation had been handled. All the signs of deliberate political manipulation. Key documents and tapes disappearing. Bribery by the prosecutor leading the investigation."

Carlos nodded. "When they began to lift the lid, it turned out that Telleldín had been bribed four hundred thousand dollars by none other than the investigating prosecutor, Galeano. Funds provided by our intelligence gurus at SIDE. Bribed to produce a story that'd deflect attention from the Iranian connection."

"Wasn't the ploy attributed to an agreement between Carlitos Menem and his top ministers? I seem to remember something about them persuading him that there was little to be gained pursuing the Iranian connection. Except the risk that Tehran might launch a third attack in retaliation."

"And the fact that Iran had become a major trading partner for our beef and cereals was not entirely irrelevant. And if that weren't enough, Menem's soft-pedalling was later attributed to his having received a ten million dollar bribe from Tehran."

"Which he denied, of course."

"Of course. Except that subsequent investigations by the Swiss indicated he probably received it. There's still a case outstanding against him for covering up. But then there are so many against him, for one thing or another…"

Leandro shook his head.

"Yet here we are again. They say that the level of corruption makes Menem's pale into insignificance. How long will we go on tolerating this kind of thing?"

"I suppose we ought to be grateful. It gives us journalists something to write about."

"Careful, you're becoming cynical."

Grunwald chuckled.

"The investigation went nowhere. Then, in 2003, Kirchner lifted the embargo on testimony from SIDE operatives. They began to let out that Telleldín had been bribed to fabricate a story to conceal the truth. The finger was finally pointed directly at the prosecutor in charge of the case since the beginning. At the end of October 2004, the judges concluded the public hearings with a statement that the Argentine state had deliberately built up a case on the basis of fabricated evidence. Which led to a general acquittal of virtually all the previous suspects, including the members of the Buenos Aires provincial police force. So you can imagine the impact on my community, on the Jewish families of the victims. After ten years waiting to know the truth, it was the ultimate insult!"

"Yes, I remember the outcry."

Nearly two hundred SIDE operatives had been sacked on Kirchner's orders in the years following his inauguration.

"A new prosecutor, Alberto Nisman, was put in charge of the case. He began to reassemble the threads of the investigation. He found that a first piece of the jigsaw puzzle was the arrival in Buenos Aires as far back as August 1983 of a certain Mohsen Rabbani, brother of a member of the Iranian revolutionary government with links to Hezbollah. Rabbani arrived on a tourist visa, ostensibly to promote bilateral trade.

A couple of years later he was granted permanent residence. He used his commercial activities as a cover for his Shi'ite proselytising, preparing the way for direct action in Argentina. He seems to have regarded Argentina as a land of opportunities for the kind of attacks we were to see. This came in parallel with a strengthening of the Iranian intelligence service presence in the embassy and cultural section. Even today, Rabbani is still apparently involved in terrorism in Latin America."

"I'm bound to say, it had never occurred to me that Arab immigrants did very much more than make money. They're usually a successful part of the business community in the provinces. Menem was of Syrian origin. But I wouldn't have put anti-Semitism particularly high on their agenda."

"You're right. That's not to say that, as in so many other countries round the world, you won't find Islamic fundamentalism on the increase in Argentina. As 9/11 showed, it only takes half a dozen to kill a few thousand. That being said, it appears that the driver of the AMIA van had to be imported from the Middle East to blow himself up."

"Which would suggest this Iranian had some difficulty in finding a local candidate for the job."

"It probably takes growing up in a refugee camp in Lebanon or Palestine to create the right mind-set for suicide. But the truth may lie elsewhere. What's been called the local connection. A strong undercurrent of anti-Semitism flowing through the far right of the Argentine political spectrum. There was talk of links with right-wing extremists, some of whom had been involved in the failed mutinies in the Armed Forces at the end of the 1980s. Which, as you'll recall, Menem, unlike his predecessor Alfonsín, was quick to put down. Then of course there's the old Plan Andinia conspiracy theory."

"What was that about? I've heard about it, but I've no idea what was involved."

"It goes back a long way. Crazy stories about the Jews wanting to set up a Jewish state somewhere in the south of Argentina. Take over the place. The kind of idea being talked about at the end of the nineteenth century. A Jewish homeland, for which some of the large Jewish landowners, Hirsch, Dreyfus, Bemberg, Bunge and Born, were alleged to be paving the way. You may remember that East Africa was another candidate. But Balfour put an end to all that! Mind you, the theory was still doing the rounds at the time of the *dictadura* in the 1970s. Zionist theories never die completely in this country."

"I suppose, given the size of the Jewish community in this country, Argentina was an obvious target. Even before bin Laden came along to preach *jihad*."

"Absolutely," Grunwald said. "We forget that these terrorist attacks took place nearly ten years *before* 9/11. We can only guess what Osama must have thought watching Argentina do nothing. A lesson in the total failure of our society to respond to concerted aggression, whether it comes from outside - or even from within, when perpetrated by our own leaders."

In August 1993, Grunwald explained, Rabbani and another member of the Iranian embassy were thought to have been invited to a meeting in Mashad, attended by some of the highest members of the Islamic revolutionary leadership. The target of the AMIA, the Argentine Israeli Mutual Association, had apparently been approved at that meeting, one of the principal motives being ascribed to Menem's decision to suspend all nuclear collaboration with Iran. At about the same time that Menem had decided to halt the development of the Condor missile in cooperation with a number of Arab states.

"As I said, an additional reason given for choosing the AMIA as a target was Argentina's muted reaction to the destruction of the Israeli embassy two years earlier. So then finally, thanks to Nisman's hard work, you have a formal accusation of Iran, with Hezbollah as the perpetrator. Ali Khamenei named as directly responsible. Interpol warrants obtained for the detention of eight senior members of the Tehran power structure. Rabbani was on the list."

"As far as I can recall," Leandro said, "the press coverage seems to have played up the link between the bombings and Argentine backpedalling over the transfer of nuclear technology to Iran."

"It was cited as one of the pretexts for the bombing. Although it's been disputed by some."

"And does the fact that there hasn't been another bombing indicate that we may have changed our minds?"

The turn of the conversation had finally given Leandro the apparently innocent opening he was looking for.

Carlos didn't reply at once. He sat looking out of the restaurant window at the queue of cars piling up in the street.

"They're going to have to do something about the traffic one of these days," he murmured.

He had clearly heard the question, but Leandro detected an expression in his eyes which had not been there before. Anxiety? Caution?

Carlos looked back at him, his gaze steadier behind the thick lenses of his glasses.

"That's not an easy question to answer, Leandro. In fact, I think I would need notice of it. Don't misunderstand me. I'm not trying to be unhelpful. But, as you can imagine, it's a very delicate subject. One, in fact, that I've been researching for a while. Will I ever be able to publish my thoughts on the matter? I don't know. I just don't think I can go into any detail today."

He paused and finished his wine.

"Something is happening, I believe. Rumours that Kirchner might be offering to stall the investigation in exchange for more bilateral trade with Iran. I can't tell whether there's any truth in this, though I'm told our agricultural exports to Iran have started to rise. But soya oil is one thing, nuclear technology something else. I can't say more than that. Sorry, *che*."

Carlos looked out of the window again. Leandro could see he was unhappy at not having been more forthcoming.

"Don't worry, Carlos. I certainly wouldn't want to pressure you. You've already been most helpful and I'm grateful for that. Saved me a lot of reading and research. And you've put things in perspective. Let me get the bill."

"It all makes one wonder how long we can remain immune from everything that's going on in the Middle East. Whether we like it or not, even way down here in the South Atlantic, we could get mixed up in it all."

Leandro looked surprised at the afterthought.

"Not sure I understand what you mean…"

"Can't say any more. Sorry. But I've a nasty feeling that we've been on the side-lines longer than we deserve. Particularly with everything we've done – or rather not done…"

Leandro detected that that was as far as Carlos intended to go.

They emerged onto the pavement, where Carlos waved down a taxi.

"Can I drop you somewhere?"

"No, I can walk home from here. It's only a few blocks on the other side of 9 de Julio. Thanks again for answering my questions. It was good to see you. And if there's anything I can help you with, just let me know."

Carlos put his hand on Leandro's shoulder.

"I still owe you one answer. Be patient. And thanks for the offer."

He climbed into the taxi and wound down the window. "And for the lunch."

Leandro set off against the flow of traffic to cross Buenos Aires' widest thoroughfare, more than fifteen lanes of traffic.

Once again he wondered when to bring Sam into his confidence. For the time being, better to remain as unobtrusive as possible in his research, and savour the freedom from Sam's enthusiastic interference – however well-intentioned - a while longer. Not that he enjoyed her absence since she had disappeared off to see Carla in Zürich. An absence more painful than he had expected.

Back in the flat, Leandro found an email from someone he had never seen before. A certain cmholland9T6@yahoo.com. The title was simple: 'A lead worth following'. The mail provided a link to a short article in

La Nación, about three weeks old, which he vaguely remembered having glimpsed on the day of its appearance. The apparent suicide of an Argentine diplomat in Brussels. As far as he could remember, the story hadn't lasted more than a day or two, swamped, like so much recent news, by the smouldering confrontation between the government and the agricultural sector.

The message appeared to be steering him in the direction either of Belgium or the Argentine diplomatic service. Why?

On impulse, he rang the Ministry of Foreign Relations, asking to speak to a career diplomat with whom he had played rugby a few years back. The Ministry switchboard put him through to a secretary, who informed him that Señor Consejero Morales was on mission out of the country, but returning the following week.

"Would you be so kind as to tell Dr Morales that an old rugby friend, Leandro Flemming, called?"

He left his cell phone number.

Friday, 16 May 2008 (AM) – RICHARD-WAGNER-STRASSE, ZÜRICH

"How's your man? Your Oscar Wilde?"

Sam looked up from the soft boiled egg she was decapitating.

They were sitting on the first floor terrace of Carla's house in a secluded part of the Enge residential district of Zürich, looking out across Conrad-Ferdinand-Meyer-Strasse towards the park on the other side, its fruit trees in full blossom. It was a beautiful mid-May morning, the sun finally beginning to shed warmth on the city. Carla's mass of flaming blonde hair fell over her white towelling robe, her cheekbones catching the light, her wide, sensitive mouth smiling, almost shyly. Large dark eyes, now filled with softness. Eyes which Sam knew could change in a flash.

'She's really amazingly beautiful for her age', Sam thought to herself.

From the moment Carla had sat down next to her at a party at the end of the Argentine polo season some six months earlier, Sam had been mesmerised by her. What had initially been a purely physical attraction had given way to something much more profound. In the process, she had got to know Carla's story, although the descriptions of her torture at the hands of the Argentine military dictatorship, when she had first met Dávila, had been recounted dispassionately, in only the briefest detail. As if Carla had found a way to defuse that episode in her life. Dávila had interrogated her, tortured her, yet, in the evenings, she had accompanied him to restaurants in Buenos Aires. She had not been the only good-looking female prisoner to receive such extraordinary treatment.

In Zürich in the '80s, where both had sought asylum before the final departure of the military, Carla's relationship with Dávila had continued. When, during the '90s, Carla had launched her escort service, now one of the most exclusive agencies in Europe, Dávila had hovered in the background, providing support and protection, an evil presence from which she had been unable to escape. Until, less than a year ago, as if seeking tangible confirmation of the sinister bond which linked them, Dávila had tried to compromise her in the sadistic murder of an English polo groupie in a Buenos Aires boutique hotel. The spell had snapped and Sam had found her own solution. Dávila's body had washed up on a riverbank in the Delta north of the Argentine capital.

The agency of Lady Blast, Carla's exotic pseudonym, specialized in elaborately orchestrated escort services of the five-star variety. A product targeted specifically at men – but also women – with a taste for strong sexuality, fantasy, exhibitionism, a luxury lifestyle and the transmission of a 'power image'. A very high net worth market, populated by hedonists not averse to spending a lot of money to be seen in the company of strikingly good-looking women, provocatively arrayed, exuding an image of the darker side of sex, of control.

"In Russian you see, the B is pronounced like a V. So to a Russian, it reads like Vlast. And in Russian, 'vlast' means power," Carla had explained on one of their first evenings together, as she had shown Sam her web page. "Works well with the new clientele."

As their relationship had progressed, Sam had become aware of Carla's ability, in spite of everything that had happened to her, to show compassion and, at the most human level, true affection. Sam knew that, unlike the majority of dominatrix, Carla would have nothing to do with inflicting pain on her clients. Not for her the verbal or physical humiliation of submissive men. She had once described her vocation as providing the pain of pleasure, not the other way round.

By the look on Carla's face this morning, Sam could see that the release from Dávila's control had restored to the older woman much of the tranquillity she sought. Her expression was softer, her eyes gayer. Gone the haunted look which had, on occasion, darkened them.

"My Oscar Wilde?" Sam asked. "Who do you mean? I have two men in my life. Three, if I count my father, God bless him. Oscar Wilde is certainly one of them. You've never read anything by him or about him, have you?"

"I must read him someday."

"Did I ever tell you that L'Hôtel, the name of the place where Janet Williams was murdered, was taken from the little hotel in the Latin Quarter where Oscar Wilde died in Paris?"

Carla shook her head. Sam detected that Carla wasn't quite ready to think about that night.

"Sorry, my love. I didn't mean it. But you're right, Wilde has often been an inspiration to me. In a number of ways, although they were tragic for him, his passions have shaped mine. My willingness to take risks, my sexuality, my taste for artifice. He once wrote that the first duty in life was to be as artificial as possible. Typically, he then added that he still hadn't discovered what the second duty was."

Carla smiled distantly.

"So unless you were asking about father, I presume you mean Leandro."

"Of course, you idiot. So, how is he? Yesterday, in the car, I detected a certain hesitation. Nothing serious, I hope. You're so lucky to have him."

Sam saw no reason to share with Carla Leandro's mixed feelings about the relationship between the two women.

"I told him I'd be going to Switzerland."

"He seemed to approve of the suggestion when you came to stay with me, after your ordeal."

"I think he takes my dictatorial ways as a sign of my recovery."

"He knows opposition to you, Sam, only makes you more determined. Giving in gracefully is usually the only option."

Carla had met Sam off the Swiss flight at Kloten. The end of spring, with the last of the cherry blossom sprinkling the fields, was a welcome contrast to the grey of autumnal Buenos Aires. Carla put down the hood on the Porsche, enjoying the attention en route.

"So, how's Leandro?" Carla had asked as they drove out of the airport car park.

Sam hadn't expected this to be Carla's first question. Yet here she was, next morning, returning to it.

"Fine, sends his love," she had replied as they drove along.

Carla had shot her a sideways glance.

"Send him mine in return."

Changing down with the steering wheel-mounted shift, Carla streaked past a large truck on the carriageway into the City.

"Everything okay between you?" she asked, her eyes fixed on the road ahead.

"Certainly."

Carla had dropped the subject. But last night having re-established their intimacy, she was coming back to it over breakfast.

"Come on, how is he? Why the mystery?"

Sam sighed. In the same way she knew she had to conceal something of her relationship with Carla from Leandro, she was reluctant to be wholly transparent with Carla. On that evening in the Sanctuary back in February, deep in the basement of Carla's house, Sam had made it clear to this woman that Leandro was emotional territory onto which Carla should not trespass.

"You're right, I'm lucky to have him. But it's not as simple as that. You're way ahead of him in terms of what you can accept about me." Sam paused. "Don't worry, I still love him. And I think he loves me."

"He's a man, I'm a woman," Carla replied. "There's the difference. Somehow, women have always had to make room for others. Usually for another woman. In the case of you and me, Sam, I make room for Leandro. Why? Because I know you love him, because he can give you things I can't, because somewhere you need a man to keep you under control."

Carla leaned back in her chair.

"You may think I'm a dominatrix," she laughed, "but I sense I can't even begin to control you. Nor would I want to. You have such passion, such idealism, such a taste for risk. As I once told you, somewhere I'm reminded of myself. Though I was ten years younger at the time. And much more confused than you are today. As I think back, I realize that our idealism was so naive. We had fallen in love with violence. A violence that plunged me into El Hoyo. And from there to Dávila."

Her laughter had faded. Painful memories. Then after a moment, the smile returned.

"I'm reassured about Leandro. Here, have the last croissant. Did you sleep well? You look rested."

Sam took the patisserie.

"I slept wonderfully, after last night," she said, smiling.

Thursday, 15 May 2008 (PM) – RICHARD-WAGNER-STRASSE, ZÜRICH

The pleasures of the night had begun when, stopped at a traffic light ,Carla had placed her hand inside Sam's thigh, stroking it softly. Oblivious to the mesmerized gaze of the tram driver alongside.

"I've got a welcome home dinner planned for you with the girls tonight. They've all been very busy since you were last here. There's also a new one. I look forward to your views on her. She's Russian. A relative of Viktor Alexievich. She's very pretty. And very, very wild."

As the soft top had turned into the yard in front of Carla's house, a tall, powerfully-built man in his mid-thirties had stopped watering the flower beds and come over to the car. Sam could not fail to admire the physique showing through the tight T-shirt.

"This is Ivan," Carla said.

From his flat face, slightly slanted eyes and high cheekbones, Sam guessed this was one of the Russians, who had now replaced Dávila's Argentines as Carla's 'minders'.

"*Здравствуйте!*" Sam smiled. "Hello."

After her rescue, she had retained a soft spot for Russians – at least for Russian men.

Ivan bowed his head and, without a word, lent over to extract her two suitcases from behind the seats of the car.

As they followed him into the house, Sam turned to Carla.

"You haven't got either Sergei or Tolya looking after you, have you?"

"No, sorry, they stay close to the boss."

"Pity, would have loved to see them again. To thank them."

Naya, Carla's Bolivian maid and shadow, greeted Sam with far more warmth than she had ever shown in the past. Sam wondered whether the story of her ordeal had made its way to Carla's retinue. Possibly.

Naya showed Sam to her room, the same she had occupied in February, looking out onto the quiet street below, and set about unpacking her things. But Sam soon waved her away. She badly needed some sleep.

"Please tell Madame Carla that I want to get a couple of hours rest and that I will see her for drinks."

Naya bowed and slipped silently from the room. Sam switched off her Blackberry, following a quick message to Leandro to say that she had arrived safely. Within a minute, his reply came in.

'Not too much Dalal, if you please. *Beso.*'

She smiled.

'Don't worry. I've become too expensive, priced myself out of the market. Love you too.'

A few hours later, rested and showered, she wondered what to wear. The competition from Carla's girls downstairs would be fierce. She must hold her own in every sense of the word. Opening the closet into which Naya had placed her clothes, she found Carla had been shopping on her behalf. A beautiful trouser suit by Jean Claude Jitrois in Paris, in the softest tobacco leather. Must have cost Carla a fortune! She obviously wanted to spoil her. Still, with a squad of ten girls, each pulling in three or four thousand dollars a day, she could probably afford it. Hanging beside it on the rail, a selection of shiny latex dresses and accessories.

Sam loved the powerful sense of arousal that certain materials transmitted to her body. Since her early twenties, her passion for lingerie of the purest silk or satin was one of these, absorbing what even she regarded as a disproportionate share of her clothes budget. Admittedly unlimited, thanks to the allowance provided by her father. Boots were another passion, the higher and softer the better. Alongside dresses and suits from London or Paris, or from her favourite Argentine designer, a rising star called Fabian Zitta, her cupboards boasted items of expensive, highly stylised leather clothing, usually from Italy. Chosen for their softness and elegance, but above all for their sensuality. And certainly for their sexiness. If such clothes played to her inner passions or heightened her sexuality, she was fully conscious of the effect they could also have on other women, not to mention men, Leandro was no exception.

"You could call me a sensualist. In the old days, Leo, it was called 'fetishism', with overtones of dark perversion. But all that's changing. Many of the fashions from that hidden underworld have now become street wear. Look at couturiers such as Jean Paul Gaultier and even Yves St Laurent. And what about all those sexy superheroines you drool over?"

"No doubt it all began when you fell in love with Diana Rigg… What did you say? When you were 16?"

"Exactly, Steed."

On her last visit to Zürich, Carla had taken her to meet Amadeo, the designer of some of Carla's more spectacular outfits and a disciple of Jitrois. And during those days, she had also introduced Sam to the extreme enclosure of latex. A sensuality playing to every inch of Sam's body.

The labels of Westward Bound and Atsuko Kudo. The delicate ensembles coming out of the diminutive Japanese designer's north London boutique could be seen on supermodels like Kate Moss or Naomi Campbell. She had even worked with some of the leading fashion houses, including Cerruti and Fendi. Carla seemed to be saying that what was good enough for the stars was good enough for her lover.

Spreading them out on the bed, Sam made her choice. Carefully she inserted herself into a tight fitting dress in a deep purple rubber, sleeves puffed above the elbow, a laced cleavage running from a high ruffle collar down to the waist. Carla had obviously bought it to show Sam's breasts to maximum advantage! Carla, whose breasts were nothing if not imposing, had always lavished particular attention on Sam's.

Pulling on black long sleeved opera gloves and stockings with a purple seam up the back of the same material, she slipped into a matching pair of stiletto-heeled pumps. Carla had thought of everything. High-gloss. Strong make-up. A final glance in the mirror. A sensuous embrace over her entire body. A new look, which she thrilled to test in public. The kind of sartorial extravagance of which Oscar would have approved. She wondered what Leandro would make of it. One day she would show him.

She went downstairs in search of the party. The drawing room was empty. She found Naya in the kitchen.

"Where is everyone?"

"Down in the Sanctuary. You know the way. Well done, Señorita, you look wonderful."

"Thank you, Naya. Good to see you again," she added. "And thanks for unpacking my things."

Sam had learned early on that it was vital to keep on the right side of Naya.

She stepped down the hall and passed through the sliding door, which gave onto the small lift. She pressed -2. Silently, the lift descended and stopped at the foyer to the Sanctuary. The black lacquered door with its silver hinges and fittings was two steps farther down. She pushed it open.

Images of the erotic 'torture' to which, with Naya's assistance, Carla had subjected her after her night with Leandro at the Baur au Lac in early February flashed before her eyes. The gleaming black lacquer walls of this crypt, mirrors on the ceiling and walls, a vast couch sheathed in shining black PVC in the centre of the room, on which Carla now reclined propped up on satin cushions, brought the memories flooding back. A session during which Sam, shackled and gagged, had been forced to watch Naya's loveplay with Carla. An experience which had finally sealed their relationship.

Tonight, the large white sofas, contrasting sharply with the darkness around, were crowded with Carla's girls.

"Welcome home!"

A chorus of voices greeted her. This time, the reception was warm, friendly.

The girls were in flamboyant form, their assets and contours flagrantly displayed in a variety of provocative uniforms.

Looking around, Sam recognized Arabella, the diminutive but spectacularly proportioned English girl, who had approached Carla straight out of finishing school in Lausanne. So much for the money her father had poured into that establishment to set his daughter up for a career in banking.

Helène, a former dancer from the Crazy Horse Saloon in Paris, waved to her. Her 'bourgeois' parents, as she had described them, were proudly telling their friends in Lille that their daughter was training for the Paris ballet. Sam was surprised to see her, given the fact that a Corsican millionaire had been relentlessly pursuing her since first setting eyes on her at Le Crazy.

Sam's eye was caught by a newcomer, who was undisguisedly studying her. The girl must have been over a metre eighty, a wasp waist cinched in leather below spectacular breasts, uncovered. At least a triple D, Sam guessed, wondering whether there wasn't something more than genetics behind them. Gleaming patent black thigh boots with vicious stiletto heels, near fifteen centimetres. If she had been sent by Viktor Alexicvich, Carla had been slipped a winner!

Yet there was something about the look in those eyes that instantly put Sam on her guard. She would have to watch this one. For now, she went straight up to her.

"Hi, I'm Samira."

"Yes, I know," came the frosty reply. The eyes hadn't softened an iota. "Call me Tatyana."

"Such a pretty name," Sam smiled, kissing her and receiving the faintest caress of the other girl's lips in return. The scent was overpowering. Russian women were rarely subtle in their choice of perfume.

Alert as always, Carla had detected the stand-off.

"Let's drink to your return to the team, Sam. Welcome back!"

Sam sat down beside Carla. Leaning forward to kiss her, she whispered, "My God, you've spoiled me. You're mad!"

"But look at the result! You're fantastic!"

Carla passed champagne to Sam and the girls raised their glasses and toasted her. Again, she wondered how much they knew about events in Argentina. The Russian might well be the best informed.

As she listened to the chattering, it was apparent the financial crisis had made no dent in their business. They had clearly all been on client assignments in the greatest luxury, whether in the most expensive ski resorts, on safari or on yachts in the Indian Ocean. Demand for the personalised services provided by Carla and her squad remained strong.

Arabella sat down on the opposite side from Carla.

"So, Sam, where've you been? We missed you. Certainly Carla did," she whispered.

Sam was unprepared for the clear signal that her relationship with Carla was public knowledge. Not surprising, perhaps, in a group of women as intimate as this.

"Had a rough time, we heard," Arabella went on. "Not that Carla said anything about it, but the new girl, Tatyana, mentioned something."

So Tatyana did know.

"Nothing too terrible. As you can see, I'm in fine form."

"You certainly are," Arabella murmured, lightly stroking Sam's breasts with the tips of her fingers. Sam flashed her a look.

"Don't worry, Sam," she hissed, "I know you're Carla's. You're a lucky girl. Very lucky, what with that handsome Argentine in the background as well."

They really did know a lot about her emotional life. She would have to tread much more carefully.

Naya appeared to announce that dinner was ready out in the conservatory at the back of the house. Given the neighbourhood, Carla had taken the precaution of installing frosted glass, allowing her girls to unwind unobserved in their more extravagant outfits. The Swiss were ever-curious neighbours.

"Take only your glasses with you," Carla instructed. "There's plenty more champagne upstairs."

She allowed the girls to lead the way, slipping in last behind Sam.

"Don't let Tatyana get to you," she whispered. "She's a gift from you know who and I have to accommodate her. Viktor Alexievich is keeping an eye on his investment. Tell you more about it later."

Friday, 16 May 2008 (AM) - RICHARD-WAGNER-STRASSE, ZÜRICH

Later had come in the early hours. The rest of the girls had left by limo for the large apartment in town, which Carla rented for them when they were not on assignment. The two women were reclining on the first step of the large *jacuzzi* at the far end of the conservatory. A few candles were still burning amid the debris of dinner and a pale glow from the lights of the town filtered through condensation on the glass overhead. The softly swirling water was warm, faintly perfumed, caressing their bodies.

Carla lay beside Sam, her breasts pressed against her, her blonde hair caressing Sam's face, her scent heightened by the warmth of the water. Sam had removed only her stiletto pumps. The slippery caress of liquid and latex on her skin.

"You've been away too long, my love. I've missed you. I've needed your touch. The feel of your skin, the taste of you."

Slowly unlacing the front of Sam's bodice, Carla inserted her hand and cupped the globe of each breast in turn, her fingers grazing the nipples.

"You know, after your ordeal, they seemed to lose some of their fullness, as you had, my poor love. But you're the old Sam again."

Having stretched the cleavage of Sam's dress to lay bare one breast completely, Carla began to tease its taut nipple with her tongue, her teeth pulling, biting. Forcing their way under the tight hem of the purple dress, her fingers plunged into Sam's vagina. Sam's fingers released Carla's thong and found their way to her clitoris. Locked together, their lovemaking increasingly passionate, they slipped into the warmth of the pool, coming to rest on a wide shelf in the shallows, Carla straddling Sam. Whilst her tongue explored Sam's clitoris, Carla lowered her cunt onto Sam's face.

Their lovemaking in Punta del Este in December and January had introduced Sam to the strange addiction of breath control. During their time together in Zürich, in response to Sam's relentless determination to explore new forms of sexual arousal, Carla had cautiously taken her farther down this dangerous path, a path on which even death was not a stranger. Given Sam's dualistic response to sex, Carla wondered how much the death of Janet Williams, suffocated in a ritual of breath control, had fuelled her curiosity. Now she enveloped Sam's nose and mouth, pressing Sam's face level with the surface of the water, cutting off her air. As the seconds passed, feeling Sam begin to writhe, Carla lifted her cunt off Sam's face just enough for her to snatch a lung-full of air, before pressing down once more. The hunger for oxygen began to power a crescendo of sensations flowing from between her thighs. The high she was seeking. An explosive orgasm.

The ritual was prolonged until Carla determined that Sam might be losing the will to call a halt, that she needed to be saved from herself.

"You're certainly back on form, my love," Carla murmured, releasing Sam, her orgasm subsiding.

As Sam lay beside her, Carla caressed her gently, allowing her to rebuild the level of oxygen in her bloodstream.

Sam's heart was beating too hard to respond. Her fingers slipped between her thighs to calm the exertions.

The candles had gone out.

Once upstairs, Carla kissed Sam softly as they parted by her bedroom.

"Welcome back."

Sam woke around noon. Out on the terrace, she found Carla reading the Neue Zürcher Zeitung.

"I need to keep up with the world of my clients," she said, without looking up. "They make their money by reading this kind of newspaper. Did you sleep well, my love?"

Sam nodded and smiled.

"So did I. How could I not?" Carla replied.

"So, tell me about Tatyana," Sam asked, greedily dipping a croissant into her coffee.

"She's quite something, isn't she? But I detect some tension there. Am I right?"

"Not from my side, but I would say from hers. Has she been so cold with all the girls?"

Carla thought for a minute.

"Not all of them. But I suspect your reputation precedes you."

"What reputation is that?"

"If nothing else, you and me."

Carla stretched out her hand and placed it gently over Sam's on the table.

Sam looked out over the city towards the lake shimmering in the distance. Her thoughts turned back to the days she had spent with Carla last winter. As to what Carla felt for her, she had no worries. But would this new girl, by any standards an unknown quantity, come with a different agenda?

"Perhaps we need to be careful, Carla."

"To survive, I've always had to be careful. It's you who should be more watchful."

There were times when Carla came close to transmitting a level of concern for Sam which verged on the maternal. For someone who had lost her mother at an early age.... There were already enough people showing apprehension for her well-being.

"So, tell me, Carla, how's the new regime? How's it working out with Viktor Alexievich?"

A couple of months had passed since Carla had accepted the patronage of the dynamic Russian businessman as a replacement for Dávila.

Carla hesitated.

"Fine, really. Like everything, these relationships have to be run in. Although he's clearly following my every move, what with his redhead and the two blonde musclemen downstairs, at the same time he's promised me complete freedom. How much does he see it as a business proposition? Hard to tell. It seems obvious I'm just another tool in his empire, to be deployed as and when necessary. But so far, apart from no doubt having someone go through the files on my clients, it hasn't been too intrusive."

"But the musclemen. They must be driven out of their minds with your girls. How do they cope?"

Carla laughed. "Somehow they do. Though I suspect that Tatyana may have something to do with that."

Sam remained silent. Not only was Mossad using the unique platform provided by Carla's escort business, but now the Russians were on board as well. The decks were getting crowded. However, that was her problem, not one to be shared with Carla.

"Well, I suppose that's reassuring. So, my love, how are we going to spend these few days? I'm afraid I'll be leaving on Monday. Paris."

"Ah, your other masters…"

Carla, not disguising a certain *tristesse* at the brevity of Sam's visit, had got up from her chair and now stood next to her. She undid the belt of her towelling *peignoire*, revealing the perfect contours of her nakedness beneath.

"Some of the time, well… I'm sure we'll think of something. For the rest, it's May, a lovely month for two beautiful women to take an open Porsche into the mountains."

Sam smiled.

"As usual, Carla, you've thought of everything."

Friday, 16 May 2008 (AM) – PARIS

Never one to miss an opportunity to keep her tan in perfect order, Sam spent the rest of the morning stretched out on the white sun mattress on Carla's balcony, naked but for a tiny triangular *cache sexe*. Her Syrian skin, always a beautiful pale bronze, never had any problems with sunbathing, but she was careful. As she lay there, she allowed her thoughts to drift back to the previous night. And forward to the days she would spend in Paris.

Carla's guess at the reasons for Sam's visit to Paris had been only partially correct. Sam did have a meeting with her Mossad case officer to provide her with a new brief. The choice of the French capital had been hers. Yet for Sam, there was someone even more important she wanted to see. Someone she felt an overwhelming need to engage with once more, with whom to recapture the cerebral intimacy and stimulus she'd found during those six months in Paris. They'd been one of the most formative periods of her life. In the wake of the last three months, the emotional wounds still healing, just as she was now rebuilding her sexual and emotional confidence with Carla, so she needed time with Sophie to rebuild her intellectual edifice. Time to lay aside for a while the purely physical dimension of her life and regenerate the stimuli of the mind.

One autumn evening, nearly five years earlier, she had been sipping a *kir* at Les Deux Magots across from the church of Saint Germain des Prés, watching *les Parisiens* stream down Rue Bonaparte to the Seine, her senses tuned to that special cocktail of perfumes - Gauloises and Balenciaga or Dior - as well as the particular crackle of Parisian French, but also of all the other tongues on the planet. Her eye had been caught by a diminutive figure at the table next to hers. Sam had been idly trying to conjure up the black and white photographs of Sartre and Simone de Beauvoir as they had sat at these same tables in the early '50s, surrounded by intellectual adepts and rivals, when the couple had reigned supreme in the French intellectual firmament. Both were now dead and few of their theses had survived undamaged into the 21st-century. Yet, in that uniquely French love affair with *'l'intélo'*, their names and words still resonated. Perhaps not so unique after all. Argentina also boasted an intellectual caste, its attitudes and postures not dissimilar from those of their European role models. Sartre, de Beauvoir, Michel Foucault, Gramsci, Régis Debray and many others of similar persuasions. Not altogether surprising, given the number of writers and artists who had migrated to the French capital from Buenos Aires. Some to escape the military dictatorship of the 1970s, but many just drawn to the fountainhead they detected in the *quartier latin*. Affinities included a general inclination to the left of the political spectrum and shared hostility to all things American, even Anglo-Saxon, a love-hate relationship which often betrayed similar inconsistencies. Argentina, like France, could boast a library of writings devoted to *'l'anti-Américanisme'*, sitting comfortably alongside McDonalds.

The woman at the next table might have come straight out of one of those photographs. Petite, almost anorexically thin, her hair cut short *'en brosse'*, a Gauloise drooping from the corner of her mouth. Discreetly dressed, yet unmistakably displaying that sense of style that only a Parisian woman could convey. Probably over fifty, dark eyes, almost disproportionately large in a finely chiselled face, the complexion nevertheless, in spite of expert make-up, not entirely concealing the ravages of nicotine. Rimless glasses, strangely unfeminine. She was reading Le Monde and, in the most natural manner in the world, had turned to Sam beside her.

"These terrible Americans are destroying our world. Piecemeal. First Europe, now the Orient."

The American invasion of Iraq was some six months old.

The woman had - of course - addressed Sam in French. No self-respecting Frenchman – or woman - would ever stoop to using a foreign language if it could be avoided. Nor could she really be blamed for assuming that Sam would understand. To Sam's dark Mediterranean features had now been added, after three months in the French capital, the evidence of her innate ability to assimilate the best of French fashion. Not any fashion. Only that which enhanced her natural elegance and extreme femininity. Not for Sam the slashed jeans or shapeless grunge favoured by so many of her age and sex. She preferred to shop at watering holes such as Emmanuelle Khan, Chloë, Max Mara or Azzedine Alaia, her boots from Kurt Geiger.

"I couldn't agree more. They're destroying our world, our culture. In fact, my world, my culture. And the worst thing is that they think they're doing us a favour."

Sam's companion had put down Le Monde and was studying her neighbour more closely.

"Your world? Where are you from? You speak excellent French."

Thanks to her father, but no thanks to her teachers either in the convent or at St. Mathew's, she had been subjected to long hours of private tuition. With her photographic memory for the written word, her vocabulary and reading in both languages was broad. On arrival in Paris, a month at the *Alliance française* had given this grounding the final touches. Helped along the way by a passing affair with one or two young men, including one of her teachers at the *Alliance.*

"I'm from Argentina, but my family is from Syria," Sam said simply.

The woman nodded. "Argentina. The land of so many great writers and intellectuals. I've never been there, but I've read so much of Borges, of Bioy Casares, Victoria Ocampo. Her wonderful publication, Sur. And many more. I also knew Cortázar well. As you know, he spent much of his life here. One day, I would love to go there."

"And I would love to be your guide."

Sensing a strange magnetism emanating from this little woman, Sam had responded sincerely.

Her companion smiled quietly.

"And what is your name?"

"Samira Haidar - but my friends call me Sam," she replied.

"You'll forgive me if I think that sounds rather American. I'll call you Samira."

She folded her newspaper and placed it on the chair beside her.

"Why don't you join me, Samira?"

Sam picked up her half empty *kir* and moved across to the next door table.

"And your name?"

"Sophie. Sophie Colbert." They shook hands. "And what brings you to Paris?"

Over the ensuing three months, Sophie had become Sam's mentor, introducing her not only to a side of Paris few tourists could penetrate, but also to the fascinating labyrinth of her mind. In the little apartment in one of the elegant buildings overlooking the Place des Vosges, with its contrast of red brick and cream stonework over shaded arcades, Sam had become Sophie's research assistant and archivist, vainly trying to bring a semblance of order to the piles of books and journals which, as much from a lack of the necessary physical stamina as anything else, Sophie had allowed to accumulate in unruly piles. In return, when not writing on her computer, Sophie had talked. Incessantly. The Gauloise never far from her lips.

In the evenings, she had taken Sam to meet friends, writers, journalists, painters. Not only French, but often uniting intellectuals from the former French colonies. Sam discovered that the notion of culture, of erudition, coursed through the veins of this race in a way so many other parts of the world could hardly begin to understand. Argentine intellectuals might pride themselves on the role they played in society. But their's was but a pale shadow, an all too self-conscious emulation, of their peers in France.

In *cafés* and *bistros* on both sides of the Seine, or in the decaying 18th or 19th century apartments of her friends, Sophie had, not just figuratively, led Sam by the hand. For Sam, aged twenty-five, the experience of being taken so seriously, solicited for her brain rather than her body, had been stimulating, opening up a world the existence of which she had only dimly suspected.

Sophie had explored Sam's sensibilities, almost clinically, recommending writers, philosophers, political commentators, as if they were part of a medical process. It hadn't taken Sophie long to detect, beneath the veneer of a girl who had for too long been neglecting her brain in favour of her body, the untapped potential crying out.

"My dear, you mean to say you haven't read Aron? There's a copy of his 'Opium of the Intellectuals' somewhere in that pile over there."

Sam would dive into the labyrinth, finally, with a cry of triumph, extracting the volume, if possible without causing the total collapse of the precarious edifice. Sometimes, she would find that Sophie hadn't even bothered to cut the pages.

"I know, that's a more recent copy. I had already read it over twenty years ago."

Many nights were spent reading Sophie's latest recommendation in the spartan *chambre de bonne*, one of the old servants' bedrooms under the roof of her 17th century *hôtel* on the eastern side of the Place. An unshaded lightbulb giving the only light. There were times when her ability to survive with so little sleep surprised even Sam. As if expecting no less, Sophie would remorselessly quiz Sam about the book, as they sat at breakfast on opposite sides of a small table in the window looking out onto the stone and brick elegance of the beautiful early 17th century square founded by Henri IV. Each with her thick china cup of bitter French coffee, into which Sam dipped a *tartine au beurre* fresh from the *boulanger* round the corner, the crust brittle, the butter salted. Sophie already with a cigarette between her fingers. Looking back, Sam suspected this experience had finally led her to give up smoking. Though she had always regretted the passing of smoking on film. Her favourite actresses of the 40s and 50s had somehow made it look so sexy.

But for the single vice that'd been expelled, a multitude had been implanted. Contact with the cut-crystal mind of this diminutive Jewess – her father was descended from Odessa fur traders who had come to Paris in the second half of the 19th century – opened up, alongside many other subjects, the domain of comparative religion. As a girl, Sam had almost involuntarily acquired an interest in Catholicism and Islam, but it wasn't as if the nuns had achieved much more than to leave her critical of the institution controlled from Rome. Sophie could not be termed a practising Jew. But, through countless facets of her lifestyle, she had transmitted many of the contradictions of her exiled race, its unique genius, its sufferings, its amazing survival.

Over one weekend they'd sat through the nine hours of Lanzmann's 'Shoah'.

"Fascinating," Sam said. "Nine hours on the 'final solution' with not a Nazi uniform in sight!"

There had been times when she wondered how much her later decision to work with Mossad had been influenced by Lanzmann's film.

"You met Lanzmann the other night," Sophie said. "At one time, he was Simone de Beauvoir's lover. Although, they say Sartre had Lanzmann's sister as a mistress. Quite an arrangement. But then, they had so many lovers between them…"

Sam was fascinated by Simone de Beauvoir. She had read a number of the French philosopher's works since her arrival in Paris, including *Le Deuxième Sexe* and *Pour une morale de l'ambiguité*.

"I detect you're very interested in Simone de Beauvoir," Sophie said. "Existentialism is heady stuff."

She observed Sam.

"I suspect you're the kind of woman who could be captivated by it," she added.

"You're right. I am. By the idea of creating your personality. Even – though it sounds extreme – your gender. And a radically different approach to ethics, it seems to me. Is that right? Have I understood it correctly?"

The idea of creating a new Sam, a different Sam, was thrilling. In some strange way, she sensed a certain commonality with her other icon, Wilde.

Sophie had enjoyed explaining the ideas of Sartre's lifelong companion, albeit warning Sam that it was very hard to implement most of them.

"You're right. For an existentialist, there are no predetermined concepts of good and bad. Just as you can determine your personality, who you are, what you are, so you can also determine your values. Your ethics. What you have made yourself, who you have become, and the circumstances in which you find yourself - these to a large extent determine whether your actions are good or bad. According to the scale of values which you have chosen to adopt. And in making that choice, you accept full responsibility for the consequences of your actions."

Sam sat there, trying to think this through.

"In some ways, that's even more constraining than, say, abiding by the 10 Commandments. You're free to make your choices..."

"...but you're constrained by the results. Exactly. You are what you have made yourself and in the process you may do things which, however good the intention or even the action, may bring negative results for which you are entirely responsible. Results for you – but more crucially, for others. An existentialist is responsible for all his actions. No-one or nothing else to shift the blame to. Responsibility for who you are and what you do lie at the heart of it."

A challenge Sam felt she wanted to test in her life. Perhaps had already been testing, but without the intellectual and emotional framework of a Simone de Beauvoir....

"'On ne naît pas femme : on le devient.' I find that such a challenging idea. And so right."

"But also so much more. You can become so much more. I sense that you, Sam, can. But be careful, Sam. Be careful."

On other evenings, sitting over an Armagnac - Sophie's cellar almost rivalled her library – she had taken Sam back to different episodes in the history of her people as, persecuted, ostracised or even simply murdered, they migrated across the face of Europe. She talked about how many of them had only found tolerance and acceptance in the Ottoman Empire following their expulsion from Spain by Ferdinand and Isabella, though never enjoying again the equal status granted in tenth century Córdoba and Toledo. Sam had been dipping into kabbalah, reading Jewish thinkers like Maimonides, Spinoza or Moses Mendelssohn, but also Marx and Engels. Hannah Arendt and Arthur Koestler had seen many a light bulb give out in her tiny attic bedroom.

Not that Sophie proselytised. She was equally prepared to point Sam in the direction of Christian or Islamic thinkers. Amongst others, she had dug out translations of Sayyid Qutb, spiritual mentor of the Moslem Brotherhood, executed in jail on the instructions of Nasser in the 60s. Sam had vaguely heard of the man, but never read him.

Sophie was sitting cross-legged by the fireplace, her bowl of Castarède vintage Armagnac in one hand, a Nicaraguan Padrón cigar twirling slowly between the fingers of the other. Thank God she only came round to cigars after a good dinner!

"I used to start the day with one. Like Churchill. But I stopped a few years ago. I was growing old."

They had come back from a dinner with a couple of Sophie's journalist friends at La Coupole.

"Far too many tourists these days," she had muttered on pushing through the swing doors.

"*Vous êtes combien ce soir, Madame Colbert?*"

Sophie had raised four fingers and the *maître d'* had swept them past the queue of waiting Americans to a table in the centre of the enormous restaurant.

"He's been here for years. It may have become fashionable, but I come here once in a while. Good memories. Many a revolution planned here which never happened."

Sam had pursued her new taste for oysters - October was after all a month with an 'R' - before demolishing a classic '*entrecôte frites*'.

"Surely, my dear, that can't rival your Argentine steaks," Sophie had tutted. A small '*poireaux vinaigrette*' seemed to be all she was proposing to eat that evening, having already switched to her Gauloises.

"Perhaps not, but it's different. And I need my ration of calories."

Sophie had merely smiled.

"You really must come to Buenos Aires some day, Sophie. We don't have any restaurants as large as this, but a number of them go for the same atmosphere. I think you'd enjoy them."

"I'll use you as my guide. Some day. I promise."

Two journalist friends had finally arrived before the coffee.

"Jacques used to work on Le Canard Enchaîné, until he began to think it rather tame," Sophie offered. "He won't tell me who he works for now."

"It's too embarrassing," Jacques had laughed.

Much of the rest of the evening had been devoted to a lament of the demise of revolutionary fervour in France's younger generation.

"Back in '68, when we were all much younger, even Cohn Bendit came here. Now he's so respectable. Iraq would've had thousands of us out on the streets when we were young. But then, Chirac himself condemned it all along. It was never fashionable to protest against something if the government had already done so."

By the time they came out onto Boulevard Montparnasse, it was starting to rain, and they had gratefully accepted Jacques' offer of a lift back to the Place des Vosges in his acrobatic Citroën 2CV.

"The Armagnac is fabulous," Sam said after a pause.

Sophie placed another log on the fire. "Help yourself whenever you want. But your reading may suffer."

"Tell me more about Sartre and de Beauvoir's and their entourage."

"Dear Samira, I know the two of them fascinate you, but I'm not as old as your question might suggest. By the time I came on the scene, their heyday was virtually passed. In May '68, I was just 18."

Sophie's gaze seemed to wander. Not for the first time, Sam asked her to tell her stories of that moment in history when the world's youth appeared set on changing the course of history.

"We were dreamers. We thought we could do something. And what have we got to show for it now? They call us - or perhaps we call ourselves - *'les soixantehuitards'*, the generation of '68. Some of us still carry a tiny flame, a flame of illusion. Unwilling to recognise that the forces of change are so different. We were a hiccup, nothing more. Look at France today."

"I suppose also because the left got disillusioned with communism, with any new world being built in Moscow or Peking?"

"They've been replaced by the new intellectuals like Bernard-Henri Levy. More media oriented, more TV. *Les nouveaux philosophes* as he likes to call them. Not the same rigour, I would say. Easier positions – anti-Americanism, the failure of Marxism. Populist causes and a handsome face. It makes good headlines."

"France seems to be one of the few bastions prepared to resist all that neoliberalism and commercialism."

"In spite of our fascination with so many things American – supermarkets, the cinema, *'le Macdo'* - there are still forces. Preservers. And doing it quite well, in my view. Just walking down the street in Paris or in the provinces, the small shops still thrive. In England or Germany they would have been eaten them up!"

"It's the same in Argentina," Sam said. "Buenos Aires is filled with little shops that never change. There's an iron monger every five blocks. How do they make ends meet? And the specialists. Four or five blocks of guitars or saxophones. Or kitchenware. Another similarity is the number of small restaurants which survive. Little room for Starbucks or Kentucky Fried Chicken. Though sadly the food bears no comparison with Paris," she grinned.

"You think too much about food, Samira," Sophie warned. "Though I have to admit that you somehow manage to keep that elegant figure of yours."

As close to a personal remark about Sam's beauty as Sophie had ever come.

Tuesday, 20 May 2008 (AM) - BRUSSELS

Inspecteur Leroy invited Juan Carlos Moreno and the embassy legal adviser to take a seat opposite his desk. Nearly three weeks had passed since their first meeting on the wet paving stones of the Grand' Place.

"Thank you, Señor Moreno, for coming. And you, Maître Dubois. I wanted to bring you up to date with our investigation. We are grateful for the cooperation we have received from your Embassy. Though, to be quite frank, our interviews have sadly not added very much in terms of leads."

Leroy had detected a fleeting discomfort on the face of some of those interviewed whenever he brought the subject round to the role of Sanchez in the embassy. A look at the dead man's curriculum, backed up by what he had been able to find on the Internet, suggested that foot and mouth disease probably didn't mean very much to the late 'agricultural attaché'.

"The case is far from simple. The circumstances of the murder, the magazines I showed to you, Señor Moreno, suggest a possible crime of passion. But our search of the rest of the flat has added nothing to that thesis. No fingerprints belonging to Señor Sanchez on either the magazines or the handcuffs. In fact, hardly any fingerprints at all! Whoever handled them must have been wearing gloves."

Photographs of Sanchez shown to members of the gay community had only produced a shaking of the head. No one had seen him. It was always possible that Sanchez had conducted his homosexual affairs elsewhere, afraid of the risks of being seen in the capital to which he was accredited as a diplomat. Leroy had been struck by the level of homophobia which even the mildest line of questioning appeared to provoke among the male members of the embassy. One of the secretaries, however, had hinted that Sanchez's private life had not held so many mysteries for her. And homosexuality had not been one of these. Leroy was definitely keeping an open mind.

"We have continued to try to build up a picture of Dr Sanchez's last hours. It has not been easy. We have a name. A certain Abdul Al-Jaffar. It appears in his business diary for the day of his meeting. His secretary was not able to tell us anything more about this person, other than a suspicion that Dr Sanchez might have gone to Rome on one occasion in

April to meet him. We are trying to trace the name with our Italian colleagues, so far without success. As to the murder itself, our team has been able to find a few pieces of evidence on which you might be able to comment. With your permission, I'll ask my assistant, Jean Marc Forestier, to give you a briefing."

"Of course," Moreno said.

They were joined by a young man, unshaven, in an open shirt and jeans, carrying a couple of thin folders. Leroy made the introductions.

"Jean Marc, please tell these gentlemen what you have been able to piece together to date."

The young man cleared his throat and glanced down at his notes.

"On that evening, on the 29th of April, Dr Sanchez left the embassy at around 21.00 hours. We believe he picked up a taxi and went to dinner at Aux Armes de Bruxelles in the Rue des Bouchers, where he was joined by another man. So far, unfortunately, we have failed to identify that person. Our enquiries in the restaurant, particularly with the waiter who served their table, suggest someone possibly of North African origin. The waiter was able to put together an identikit portrait of Dr Sanchez and of the person dining with him. May I ask you to take a look at them?"

Forestier passed over the two portraits, which Moreno studied, before passing them to Maître Dubois.

"A good likeness of Sanchez, so the other may also be fairly accurate," Moreno commented.

"Thank you, Señor Moreno, that's very useful," Leroy said.

Forestier placed the two portraits in his folder and went back to his notes.

"Dr Sanchez and his guest - I say his guest, since we know that Dr Sanchez paid for the meal with a Visa card - left the restaurant at approximately 23.30. A taxi was called for them by the restaurant and we have been able to track down the driver, who confirms he dropped his passengers at Club L'Intime, in the Rue Saint Michel, about fifteen minutes later."

"I've heard of it," Moreno said. "Popular, I believe."

"Popular among those looking for the wilder side of Brussels. Pretty girls, that kind of thing. They appear to have spent about two hours there. Dr Sanchez paid for the drinks. We were not able to establish whether they did anything more than just drink and watch the show. Again they called a taxi and this time were dropped near the Grand' Place. It would have been around 02.00 – 02.15. At this point, we have to rely on what we were able to discover in the flat itself."

Forestier opened the second file.

"Have you any comments so far? Any questions?" Leroy asked his visitors.

Moreno looked across at Maître Dubois, who shook his head.

"No, Inspecteur, not so far."

"Carry on, Jean Marc."

Again the young man cleared his throat.

"Although both men served themselves a drink, there are few traces of the other person. Not that the circumstances of his death leave any doubt on that score. We have been able to find only a single item, which has provided us with DNA. To date, we have not been able to establish a match."

"Time of death?"

"We estimate somewhere around 04.30 – 05.00. For some reason, nobody appears to have seen the body until an hour or so later, which is perhaps surprising given the number of people who usually frequent the square, even at night. But, it was raining, which could explain it. On that basis, the two men might have spent up to three hours together in Dr Sanchez's flat. Obviously the most important evidence that he was not alone is the fact that the windows were closed from the inside. And, of course, the handcuffs and the traces of strangulation. Inspecteur

Leroy, I believe, pointed all these out to you on the day the body was discovered."

Moreno nodded.

"The focus of our investigation," said Leroy, sitting foreward, "is obviously the person who accompanied Dr Sanchez to dinner and subsequently to his flat. It is vital that any piece of information, which may serve to identify him, is passed to us. My question to you therefore, Señor Moreno, is whether such information may be available in your embassy, from his colleagues or from his correspondence, which has still not been shared with us."

"You saw his diary?"

"We were allowed to see the week in question, which provides no clues. I must ask you to discuss this with your ambassador, to see if there is any way we can collaborate more closely on this. Have I made myself clear?"

Moreno and Maître Dubois exchanged glances. The Argentine diplomat got up from his chair, followed by the legal adviser.

"Inspecteur Leroy, you have made yourself perfectly clear. I cannot, of course, respond directly on this occasion. But I will do as you say and consult my ambassador. And no doubt we will need the agreement of Buenos Aires."

"Jean Marc, please accompany these gentlemen to the exit," Leroy said, showing them to the door. "Good day, Señor Moreno, Maître Dubois, and thank you."

He watched them from his window as they crossed the street and stopped a taxi. A minute or two later, Forestier tapped on his door.

"Come in, Jean Marc. This is going to be slow. You were right not to reveal the possible Tehran connection at this stage. Let's see if they come back with something that confirms it."

"At least we have the CCTV."

"Sanchez at the Iranian embassy, yes. Not that the photofit of the other appears to match anybody working there."

"We don't know whether he was Iranian, either. Or maybe Arab. Both the restaurant and the club have insisted he came from that part of the world. There's also a suggestion from one of the waiters that he may have spoken French. On the other hand, everyone agrees that they spoke Spanish together, which might indicate Morocco. The *garderobe* girl said something about him having thanked her in French. She also added that he was rather good-looking. We are going through the immigration files, it's quite a trawl. So far, nothing."

"Many Iranians spoke French or were educated in France at the time of the Shah. Farah Diba almost spoke better French than farsi, as I recall."

"I'd forgotten that."

"He may also have been travelling on a European identity. Are we picking anything up in the Middle Eastern immigrant community?"

"One of our informers mentioned that, in the period running up to the murder, there was - I don't know how you would describe it - a sort of vibration in the system. A suggestion that somebody special might be coming through. But, so far, nothing more precise than that."

"Which immigrant community in particular?"

"He thought it might have been among the Iraqis, but he couldn't be sure. We'll try and put flesh on the idea."

"It was obviously a contract killing, Jean Marc. So we need to think who might be interested in that kind of operation."

"Yes, Inspecteur."

"I do detest these diplomatic cases. So many ways they can slip through our fingers."

Thursday, 22 May 2008 (PM) – BARRIO CONSTITUCIÓN, BUENOS AIRES

What with his concentration on the Frobisher assignment, as well as dealing with Sam and the aftermath of the Dávila saga, too much time had passed since he had last attended to his family. His mother, in her battle with cáncer. He would have dinner with her. Take advantage of Sam being in Europe.

The other candidate for his attention was Elena.

"Hey, stranger, where have you been? Or shouldn't I ask?"

"How is it, after our years apart, you still know exactly how to tease me?"

"Don't worry, I'll never lose that. It's too easy. But I'm serious. Amicable and transparent, that's our rule, isn't it? For the sake of Alejandra. So! Haven't heard from you in a while. Hope nothing's gone wrong with that Arab lady."

"No, everything's fine. What about you?"

Somehow, he couldn't bring himself to refer to her 'man'.

"Fine, fine," she said. "So, what's the problem? Got no-one to cook for you?"

Leandro laughed. "Am I that transparent?"

"Well, your stomach - as well as another part of your anatomy not a metre south - quite often condition the timing of your calls. Now that the latter is out of bounds, that only leaves your stomach! Dinner?"

Leandro detected she was enjoying this. And so in fact was he. It wasn't just the fact that Sam was away in Europe. He needed to touch base with a part of his life that'd brought him happiness and stability for so many years. In fact, Sam had once said as much.

"When it comes to Elena, Leo, I never want you to think that I'm jealous. Or that I wouldn't want you to see her. I'm not like those girlfriends who cannot bear their men keeping up old friendships or relationships. I detect that Elena is good for you. Not to mention the fact that your relationship with her is the basis for your relationship with Alejandra. And I suspect that, when you can't stand me anymore, you'll need someone else to run to."

Sam's insight was at times unnerving.

"Dinner would be great. Tomorrow evening? I'm seeing my mother tonight. Or do you want me to invite you someplace?"

Elena hesitated. "No, I'd prefer to have it here. Perhaps some of your favourite pasta. More like old times. I wouldn't like to be treated like one of your girlfriends, needing to be impressed by some expensive restaurant. That was never our scene anyway. Maybe the Arab lady likes it, but…"

Leandro had ignored the minor sideswipe.

"I'll be there by nine. I've just come across a very good cabernet sauvignon from a small vineyard in Mendoza. Belongs to a Frenchman. I'll bring a couple of bottles."

Having taken his coat, Elena served him the remains of a bottle of Glenmorangie.

Elena sat down opposite him with a glass of red wine.

"How's business treating you?" she said.

"Very busy, what with all this nonsense with the farmers."

"Yes, I'm getting quite a lot of it at first hand."

Since Leandro had not the slightest doubt that Elena would not be sharing her bed with someone from the Kirchner stable, this suggested that her man was in farming. Worth a try.

"Spending time out on somebody's estancia, are we?"

"As a matter of fact, yes. And that's as much as I'm telling you. So let's change the subject. Anyway, I've got to go back to the kitchen. I know I promised pasta, but then I found this great farmyard chicken at my butcher's this afternoon."

"I didn't dare ask, but the smell was killing me."

"Come and help yourself. And pour out some more wine. I'll light the candles."

She had prepared roast chicken, deep fried potatoes, even something faintly reminiscent of a Yorkshire pudding. Argentine culinary licence.

"My God, this is delicious. Your potatoes are out of this world. One of the great secrets you brought back from London."

Perhaps she hadn't been so wrong on the phone when she had identified his stomach and his libido as two of his main drivers. He had to admit that, irrespective of her innumerable talents, cooking was one department in which Sam was terribly deficient. He couldn't recall a single occasion on which she had even attempted to boil an egg. Three star restaurants and delivery were the sum total of her culinary skills.

The remains of the chicken cleared away, Elena sat back and studied Leandro.

"So, am I right in presuming that the charms of the Orient are being deployed elsewhere?"

He hoped that her phraseology wasn't anywhere near the truth.

"She's in Switzerland. Or, to be more precise, probably on her way back. Went there for a week. Maybe Paris. Should get in tomorrow."

She looked at him. Switzerland. Something had happened in Switzerland back in February.

"Well, you look less worried than the last time she was there. I trust that's a good sign."

She needed Leandro to be in a stable relationship. On his own, he might begin to explore the possibilities of their coming together again. And just for the present, that wasn't what she wanted.

He nodded.

"Good. I'm glad." Seeing the quizzical look on his face, she added, "Truly I am." Then, after a pause, "Alejandra met her the other day. At your place. Said she was very kind. You need that kind of woman."

Again Leandro nodded. He wondered whether Alex had finally told her mother about her problems with Nouria.

"Yes. Alex was a bit down that evening."

"I know, she told me about it. And she also told me the reason. Which I think you've known for rather longer than I have. Not that it matters. The important thing is she confided in one of us. And now both of us."

"I'm glad she told you. I advised her to. She just took her time."

"I'm very sorry for her. As we all know, Argentine men are a complicated lot. And I think the new generation even more so. Somehow, things seemed easier when you and I were going out. More black and white."

"Though tougher in those days for gays and lesbians. Now, there are so many different shades, so many options."

"And as a result, I think they're all very confused. They don't necessarily think so. Or maybe some of them do."

"You're right. Sexual inclinations now come in many flavours."

Leandro knew what he was talking about. Not that he had the slightest intention of sharing his concerns about Sam's bisexuality with Elena.

"I'm rather afraid that Alejandra's flatmate Nouria is going to end up marrying. We'd better prepare ourselves to pick up the pieces."

"Which means you'll probably have her back on your doorstep."

"Or perhaps yours."

The look on Leandro's face left little doubt as to how this would be viewed, however much he might love his daughter.

"Let's face it when it happens. You never know, she might stay on in that flat in Barracas. She's told me it's very beautiful. One of those wonderful 20s houses. Very well restored, apparently."

"You're right. Let's wait and see."

Saturday, 24 MAY 2008 (AM) – CAFÉ IBERIA, AVENIDA DE MAYO, BUENOS AIRES

"So, good trip?"

They were taking a late coffee at one of the tables inside Café Iberia on Avenida de Mayo. The elegant avenue laid down at the turn of the last century to provide a grand link between Plaza de Mayo in front of the Casa Rosada, the nation's presidential palace, westwards to the imposing building of Congress. That tangible symbol of Argentine faith – in those far-off days – in strong institutions. Today, little more than a talking shop, a rubberstamp for the presidential couple.

In spite of the cold, the streets were full on the first day of Argentina's Independence Day holiday. Although many *porteños* had already taken advantage of the long weekend to get out of the city, Leandro had preferred to remain in town rather than confront the suicidal driving of his countrymen, whether in their cars or motor launches up in the Delta. They had decided to stay in town.

"Fine," she said, somewhat noncommittally. "Except that my overweight was very expensive."

Sam had returned the previous day from Europe. Leandro suspected she might have been somewhere else as well, but was reluctant to press her on this.

"The usual extra suitcase?"

"Carla's gifts," she said, rolling her eyes. "And of course a little shopping in Zürich and Paris."

"A new set of Italian leathers for your Harley, Mrs Peel?"

"That bastard of a customs official must have paid his salary for the month with what he took off me in import duties! Hate their bloody radar machines."

She seemed in no mood to provide details about her days in Zürich or Paris. And certainly nothing about her meeting with her Mossad handler.

He went back to his newspaper. The farmers had agreed to talks and had called off their strike, though a major demonstration was planned for the following day in Rosario, to coincide with the *25 de mayo* national holiday.

"Do you realise," he said, folding his paper, "we first met here, at one of the tables outside, almost a year ago?"

Sam relented.

"How could I forget? And all the fault of bloody Oscar Wilde."

A year earlier, as Sam had sat down at the table next to his, he had spotted her reading a copy of the Irishman's collected plays. Although he had never read Wilde, to start a conversation with this striking girl, he had asked her what she was doing reading so unusual an author.

"If I'd known where that question was going to lead me, I'd have gone on reading my paper. Kept my stupid mouth shut."

Wilde was her fetish culture icon, even a form of role model. She was fascinated by the man. In that first half hour together, she had given Leandro what almost amounted to a twenty-minute doctoral thesis on the subject of the playwright.

"*Hijo de puta!* How dare you? Just think. You would have missed out on everything we've done in the last twelve months. You'd still be sitting at your desk writing those boring economic reports. Thanks to me, all that belongs to the past."

Leandro smiled. She was right of course. His life had changed and, looking back, in spite of the tensions and danger they'd lived through, he would not have wished it otherwise.

"So, you're not going to tell me anything about your trip."

"Not just yet. Be patient."

He wouldn't want to hear much about her time with Carla anyway. And as to Paris…

She had found Sophie remarkably unchanged in spite of the five years since they'd last been together. Perhaps a few Gauloises less per day.

"My doctor finally convinced me," had been her only explanation, as she stubbed out a cigarette at Café Flor, eyes twinkling in the afternoon sun.

Sam doubts had been confirmed at a dinner party with some of the old crowd of *6ème arrondissement* intellectuals.

"She's looking better," one of them had confided. "She probably didn't tell you. And she won't. But she had a nasty scare. They seem to have caught it in time. Two years ago."

Wherever the disease had struck, it had not been the brain.

Sam's five days in Paris had allowed her to plunge back into the world of the abstract, of mature ideologies, a world in which politics was seen as serious business, not a populist charade. On returning to Buenos Aires, she sensed her critical faculties had been recharged.

Leo knew nothing of Sophie, so there was nothing to tell. He might even jump to the wrong conclusions about another woman in her life.

"But you still love me, don't you? Nothing on your trip might have changed that?" Leandro interrupted her thoughts.

"*Que boludo,* Leandro."

She shivered, in spite of the long fur coat she was wearing.

"I'm beginning to feel cold. Pay for the coffees and let's get back to your place. Ten days is too long for abstinence. I want you to fuck me all weekend! Fortunately it's a long one."

How to resist such a subtle invitation? Almost as subtle as the day she had picked him up the first time, he thought. Or had it been the other way round?

"As your friend Eric Clapton so ably puts it, 'I wanna make love to you'."

He smiled. The look on her face gave nothing away.

Saturday, 24 May 2008 (PM) – PASAJE DE LA PIEDAD, BUENOS AIRES

She threw her coat on the chair in the hall of his flat. The floor length red leather coat she had worn as Dalal, Carla's high-class escort, that evening back in February in Zürich. An evening filled with painful memories for both of them. Wearing it today almost a provocation. Why did she enjoy this?

Tucked into her trademark stiletto-heeled boots, Sam was wearing pleated jodhpurs of pale grey leather. A voluminous roll neck sweater of soft alpaca in a darker shade of grey.

She was stunning as always and Leandro whistled in admiration.

"You're the second man to see me wearing them," she told him. "Guess who else?"

"Your fucking Saudi Prince, I presume," he said.

"Quite right!"

He studied her. He had missed her. Her dark hennaed hair framed the strikingly made-up eyes and large mouth. As always, a veneer, different from any Argentine girl he had ever known.

"Anyway, now that we're here, what's next? Before I fuck you. Though before that, I need a rest. A touch of jetlag. And some champagne might be nice after all that coffee."

Leandro disappeared into the kitchen and re-emerged with a bottle of Baron B rosé and a couple of glasses.

He found Sam scrolling through the notes he was writing for the monthly bulletin.

"Leo, explain something to me. What's this government's trying to do? They already take thirty-five percent from what the farmers earn. And now they want fifty? Nobody can sustain that, right? Our agriculture pulled us out of the 2001 recession. Why do they want to screw them?"

Sam was by far the most politically astute girlfriend he had ever had. It had struck him the first day they had met, when, over lunch a year ago down by the river, their conversation had ranged over an unusually wide spectrum of topics. Not just Argentine politics, but also the Middle East, the Iraq war and the role of the United States since the fall of the Berlin Wall. The depth of knowledge and insight she had shown had taken him completely by surprise.

"It's a barefaced grab for cash," he said. "The way the Kirchners run this country, they need as much as they can get. But there's another reason. An old bias linked to their unreconstructed left-wing ideology. Anyone living off the land must be a *latifundista*, a multimillionaire driving around in a Toyota, in cahoots with imperialism. It's an old tradition in Argentine politics to think that *estancieros* are some kind of fifth column for the imperialists and colonialists. It runs very deep."

"Haven't they ever met these people? A few hectares and a twenty-year-old truck at best."

"For a start, they have little contact with ordinary people. The truth doesn't fit the kind of social antagonism between the poor living around Buenos Aires and the middle class, which this government would like to foster."

He filled their glasses.

"Anyway, for God's sake, stop talking politics and get your rest. I've got a bit more work to do."

He sat down at his worktable, having placed a glass beside her on the couch, where she stretched out, a book resting in the folds of her trousers. Oscar Wilde. No surprise. As for Wilde, there were so many occasions when Sam seemed to operate on the basis that conventional moral labels were inadequate to capture the complexity of human behaviour. Especially her own.

The last rays of the afternoon sun were dying in the west. He looked out of the drawing room window at the Italianate mansion opposite, blessing the day he had found this pretty corner flat, on the second floor of the central block in Pasaje de la Piedad. Off Calle Bartolome Mitre near the corner of Paraná, a couple of blocks from the Argentine Congress building, it was one of the city's rare '*pasajes*'. Little gated streets, accessible through a locked wrought iron gate at both ends, no traffic and no more than two hundred metres long,.

He got up and refilled their glasses and sat down once more at the table to read through some of the notes he had made in his research into the nuclear industry.

Some ten minutes later, Sam broke the silence.

"What are you up to, Leo? I detect something. You've got a look in your eye which tells me that your little brain is busy with something. It might be sex or some new perversion, but somehow I doubt it. If it were, I suspect you wouldn't be quite so secretive about it. Unless of course, the perversion is so unspeakable."

Sam chuckled before continuing.

"And if it's that unspeakable, then I really do want to know about it!"

"You are *such* a bitch. Why do you always think so badly of me?"

"Who said that? When I got back from Zürich last time, before the…"-- she hesitated--"before the events, your internet browsing history was very revealing."

"What do you expect, given your new profession? High class escort. I have to keep up with your areas of interest. if that's the word. Bondage, fetishism….There's no-one to guide me in these matters."

"You're trying to side-track me. If it's not sex that's keeping you focussed, what is it?"

"Nothing!"

"Don't you lie to me, Señor Flemming. Your body language is far too shifty."

Leandro sighed. "I'm sorry, for the time being I can't answer your question. You'll just have to be patient. You once asked me to be patient. Now it's my turn."

From the expression on her face, Sam had clearly not expected this reaction, nor the level of importance implicit in his reference back to their parting in Zürich. On that occasion, her refusal to explain her decision to work with Carla had come perilously close to destroying their relationship.

"That's not like you."

He had been anticipating this. Her relentless desire to know everything about the man she loved, above all his work for Frobisher, his London contacts, could be controlled no longer. Not for the first time, his attempts to conceal his work seemed to have failed. She seemed to read his mind.

As he pursued his research into the Iranian – Argentine nuclear dialogue, Leandro knew the time would inevitably come when he would have to share something of all this with Sam. But he didn't feel ready to do so yet, not tonight. Until he could get a clearer idea of how he was going to pursue it himself, he was reluctant to add the pressure of an enthusiastic Sam throwing suggestions at him…. or worse, leading him off in unpredictable directions. For the time being, things would be quite complicated enough without the added stress of having to save Sam from herself.

The search for the killer of Janet Williams, an English polo groupie murdered in a Buenos Aires boutique hotel in July of the previous year, had put Leandro and Sam on the trail of Carla, the mysterious woman who had apparently assisted Williams in the course of that fatal session of sadomasochism and erotic asphyxiation. From that investigation had blossomed Sam's relationship with Carla.

Perhaps he should not have been surprised. Faced with a choice between a safe and a risky option, Sam could almost invariably be relied upon to choose the latter. She wasn't Argentine for nothing.

As she buried herself once more in her book, he could see she was annoyed. As if to convey it more forcefully, she sighed and rolled over on the couch, turning her back to him.

"Don't be childish, Sam, just trust me."

She looked at him over her shoulder. Was there a glimmer of amusement in her eyes?

"Had you worried there," she murmured. "Thought I wouldn't love you any more, didn't you? Well, you're right. I won't! But, since I'm giving it up, one last fuck can't do any harm."

She dropped her book on the floor and rose from the couch. With one smooth movement - the stiletto heel passing perilously close to his face - she straddled his lap and, resting her breasts on top of the papers on his worktable, pressed the soft folds of the leather pants covering her butt upwards into his face. Slowly caressing his lips with a sideways motion of her hips, she looked over her shoulder to gauge its effect. The provocation was classic Sam.

The scent and caress of the leather beginning to take effect, Leandro pulled her thighs closer, pressing his face into the cleft of her arse, which he could feel through the leather.

"Enjoying that, are we?" she purred. "But I want you inside me, not just giving your fetishist instincts free rein. Look carefully, Leo. The way in is between your lips."

Her hips stopped swaying.

Leandro pulled his face back to discover that the soft pleats of the jodhpurs concealed a long zip, which ran from her waist at the front, between her legs, to the centre of the waistband in the small of her back. He slid the fastener along its length, and with both hands parted the folds to reveal the full beauty of her anus and shaved genitals, their arousal only partly concealed by a minute *cache sexe* of black silk. He stood up, and, as she bent her knees slightly to line up with his penis, thrust it deep inside her, forcing her against the table.

"Be careful with my pants," she murmured. "They cost Carla a fortune. And by the feel of your dick, worth every last Swiss franc! Come on. Harder! Harder!"

His hands around her waist, he impaled her. After a few minutes, she slipped off the table onto her knees, resting her face sideways on the carpet, her eyes seeking his, her butt thrust upwards towards him. It took her only a second to unbutton her waistband, the jodhpurs falling away on either side. Below the fissure of her anus, her glistening vagina hung like a ripe fruit.

"God, who designed that?"

"Fool! I did, of course. What d'you think?"

He closed his mind to the possibility that the Saudi Prince might also have been ahead of him in discovering the jodhpur's secrets.

"You're the first to find your way in," she whispered, reading his mind again.

He knelt behind her, his penetration rewarded with a slow crescendo of viscous contractions. As he fucked her, she began to lubricate her anus with fingers covered in saliva.

"Now, Leo, now!"

He pulled back, then slid slowly, brutally, into her, forcing a loud moan from her lips. As he arse-fucked her, her fingers worked her clitoris, until finally she came with a massive orgasm. Unlike most of his previous lovers, who had only seemed to accept anal sex as some kind of male imposition, Sam loved it.

An hour later, Sam was lying on her back beside him on the bed, submerged under a large fox fur rug, a wedding present he had somehow slipped out from under Elena's vigilant gaze at the time of their separation.

She could feel his fingers softly stroking her vagina.

"What news of Carla?"

The question, seemingly innocent, caught Sam by surprise.

The discovery of Sam's bisexuality one morning in late November following an unannounced visit to her flat seemed, to his own astonishment, to have heightened the fascination of the girl's powerful sensuality. In the months that followed, he had watched Sam develop a powerful relationship with the beautiful Carla, a woman some fifteen years her senior. It had taught him that Sam could be irresistibly attracted by a certain class of woman, intelligent, endowed with a strong personality, sexually forceful and invariably very good-looking.

One evening, as they had sat together in Punta del Este around New Year, Sam had tried to explain her complex emotional psychology.

"You see, Leo, ever since I was a child, possibly since my mother's death, I've seen my emotions and affections as in some way compartmentalised. It's rather like a mental apartment, in which people I love occupy different rooms," she had explained. "I like moving from one room to another. And at the same time, to stand back and observe myself."

Sam always insisted that he occupied what she called the master bedroom. But it was obvious to him that Carla, albeit an occasional visitor, enjoyed very privileged residential rights.

Although he had come to accept Sam's relationship with Carla, the mention of her name invariably provoked a mild sense of disquiet. Not to mention, if he was being honest with himself, a strong dose of old-fashioned jealousy. The more he thought about it, the less he could make up his mind whether he was mad to accommodate such a situation. Or whether, in some strange way, this affair was uncovering some new emotional dimension within himself. Ninety-nine percent of Argentine males would think him out of his mind.

His attempts to rationalize Sam's relationship with Carla had explored many possible interpretations. Among them, the possibility that the older Carla might in certain ways, by bringing the lessons learned from the harsh experience of her own life, fill part of the space of the mother that Sam had lost when she was twelve. Not that he would ever confront Sam with that version.

Somehow, Sam sensed all this and was surprised by his question. Leandro did not usually take the initiative to ask about Carla.

"Fine. Why do you ask?"

The tone cautiously noncommittal.

"I know how important she is to you. I can't just ignore her."

Sam stretched out her hand and found his between her thighs.

"Poor Leandro. What a problem this girlfriend is for you. What with her multiple emotional relationships, her bizarre sexual inclinations."

"Not to mention her professional ones," Leandro added quietly.

"What do you want me to say?"

"I suppose," he hesitated, "I just want to hear you say it."

She placed her hand over his. A minute passed before she replied.

"First and foremost, Leo, as I've said time and again, it's you I love. Yesterday, today and tomorrow. Will that be the case in ten years time? Who knows? I'm not sure we want to know. We both live for the present."

She watched him out of the corner of her eye.

"How many times have I told you, Carla is a welcome guest in my emotional apartment. You, Leo, are in permanent residence. I know she loves me, perhaps more than I love her. And I'm convinced it's genuine."

She must choose her words carefully.

"Given the fact that I have room for love and passion with both sexes, Carla is somehow the ideal other partner. For those moments when my love, my need for sexual stimulation is not focused solely on you. When I need something else, she brings it to me. A different love. Different sex. Sex you probably wouldn't understand."

Now was certainly not the time to elaborate on sex with Carla. Sex Leandro would find difficult to contemplate, let alone experience.

"Is that what you wanted to hear? Or have I got it all wrong?"

She paused, studying him in the half light. His face remained expressionless. Usually a sign he was troubled.

"There's also what she can bring to my work for Mossad. Though I suspect you still don't understand that either, given my Arab origins."

He still said nothing.

"Answer me!" she snapped.

He stared at her, shaken by the change of tone. The reaction seemed totally unwarranted. Yet, on reflection, probably evidence of the fact that, although her ordeal with Dávila, the psychopath who had kidnapped and then tortured her, was now some two months in the past, not all traces had disappeared. Stress could still break the surface.

He looked at her, a look of sorrow more than anger.

"Sorry, Leo. I didn't mean it," she finally whispered.

He studied her.

"Apology accepted."

He lay back, his hand straying once more between her thighs. Again she placed hers over his.

"Yes, Sam, I suppose it's what I wanted to hear. Not that the message is one of pure solace. But I'll focus on the good side. What you feel for me. It's also true, our days with Carla in Punta, the three of us together, demonstrated the depth of your relationship with her. She clearly loves you. In some ways, I think she needs you. There's a level of understanding between you two, which I would be a fool to try and destroy. But I can't deny the escort business causes me pain. I seem to be just about able to accept another woman touching you. But another man?"

He paused, but Sam was silent, as if waiting.

"Is that so strange? I don't think so."

Still she said nothing.

"Remember, we once discussed one of your cult films. *Les Liaisons Dangereuses*. You preferred the older version by Vadim. With Gérard Philippe and Jeanne Moreau, as opposed to Malkovich and Michelle Pfeiffer. I found a copy the other day. You're right, it's far better. Destructive, forceful promiscuity. Each partner telling the other what's happening. It's that which scares me. They don't manage it in the film. Can we, Sam?"

After a minute's thought, she leaned over him, taking his face in her hands.

"Leo, I want to believe we can. I'm not religious, but I pray we can. Trust must guide us."

Saturday, 24 May 2008 – CARACAS

José Ramon Hernandez never saw them come up behind him as he was opening the door of his BMW on Avenida Eugenio Mendoza. María Isabel, on the other side of the car, cried out as she saw the men stop their motorbike just behind her husband, but too late. Above the noise of the traffic on this tree-lined artery of central Caracas, she heard the single shot which sent José Ramon crashing to the street, yelling in pain, his cries drowned in the roar of the bike as it pulled away.

For half a minute or so, she crouched on the pavement from where, under the car, she could see her husband clutching his leg. A few seconds later, another car pulled up alongside and its occupants, two girls, jumped out. One of them stood waving her coat to ensure the passing traffic gave a wide berth, the other bent over her husband, trying to calm him. Sensing the danger had passed, María Isabel rushed round to the other side of the car. Although it appeared that José Ramon's injury was far from life-threatening, he was clearly in great pain, the bullet having shattered his knee-cap. The girl beside her had already dialled for an ambulance, which, given the evening traffic, would take some ten minutes to arrive, about the same as the police car.

A small crowd gathered almost immediately. A young man, with the help of one of his friends, lifted José Ramon and carried him round to the pavement. A medical student, he was tying a tourniquet of strips from his T-shirt around the thigh and the knee itself.

Later that evening, at the Sanitas Medical Clinic, fortunately only some ten blocks away on Castellana, José Ramon was lying in a small private room befitting his diplomatic status, his knee having received the attentions of the emergency team. As María Isabel sat beside his bed, stroking his hand, she could see that the painkillers were doing their work. She tried as best she could to answer the embassy Counsellor's questions. He'd rushed over from a party to celebrate Argentine National Day at the Caracas Country Club not far away.

"We'd been with friends at Leon, the bar on Castellana, you know, by the big circle. Nothing special, just a few drinks. We walked back to the car to go home. José Ramon was unlocking his door, I was standing on the pavement on the other side. Then this motorbike arrived, two guys. Can't have been more than ten seconds. They shot him and drove off at full speed. What with their helmets and everything else, I never saw a face. And José Ramon had his back to them anyway. I'm sorry, that's all I can tell you."

"No motive? They weren't trying to steal the car? It doesn't seem to make sense."

María Isabel began to sob quietly. The Counsellor put his arm round her shoulders.

He wasn't entirely surprised that something of this kind should have happened. He knew perfectly well that José Ramon wasn't a career diplomat and suspected that, as such, he might be involved in matters which he, the Counsellor, would prefer to know nothing about. Knee-capping was a practice usually reserved for terrorist organisations or criminal gangs. From the little María Isabel had told him, in the absence of any attempt to steal anything, it looked like a settling of scores. He would have to wait until José Ramon could be questioned in safer surroundings. In the meantime, there was little to be gained by further questioning here in the clinic.

Once María Isabel had calmed down, he went out into the corridor and asked to speak to the doctor who had treated José Ramon. Dr Mendoza sounded none too optimistic about José Ramon's chances of returning to football.

The embassy team had lost its star player. The Brazilian embassy, their greatest rivals on the Caracas diplomatic football pitch, would never go to such lengths!

The inter-embassy league was likely to be the least of their worries. Worse would be the diplomatic fall-out, given that this episode would almost certainly provoke a phone call between the Argentine President and her good friend Hugo Chavez, to whom she had little compunction in speaking very bluntly when, in her sole estimation, the occasion warranted. What, in diplomatic parlance, was known as a 'frank and constructive discussion'. And somehow he would have to explain things to his ambassadress, another lady not averse to speaking her mind.

June 2008

Sunday, 1 June 2008 (PM) – PUERTO IGUAZÚ, ARGENTINA

"How much longer, do you think?"

The ageing white Mercedes 220 had been waiting some two hundred metres back from the Brazilian – Argentine frontier post for nearly half an hour, the queue of cars stretching behind them towards the long span of the bridge crossing Rio Iguaçu, the boundary between Brazil and Argentina. In spite of the fact that the central panel of the rear seats had been removed to allow the air conditioning to circulate into the boot, the build-up of humidity in this climate was unbearable. It had been raining for nearly three days non-stop since his arrival.

The driver at the wheel turned and spoke in the direction of the dark hole between the seats.

"Not long now, they come on duty in about five minutes. Ramón has just signalled to me that our two friends will be on the same shift. Be patient."

The Director did his best to relax.

He had arrived in Foz do Iguaçu a couple of days earlier, spending much of the intervening time coordinating his clandestine transfer into Argentina with the help of the local representative of the Sons of Ibn Taymiyyah's and fine tuning the details of his arrival with his contact in Buenos Aires.

Confirmation had come through that the attack on the Argentine embassy attaché in Caracas had been successful.

On arriving in Caracas, it hadn't taken him long to track down Hernandez, Sanchez's successor at the Argentine embassy. But with time at a premium, not to mention the presence of the attaché's wife and family as complicating factors in the design of the kind of exotic scenario in which he specialised, he had finally opted to subcontract the hit. In a city as dangerous as Caracas, there was no shortage of candidates for the job. Through the group's local representative, and for the modest outlay of a thousand dollars, a couple of motorbike *sicarios* had rapidly snatched up the assignment. Given the banal level of violence to be found daily on the streets of the Venezuelan capital, he had insisted on a style of attack which would more readily be interpreted as something other than a carjack gone wrong. Throughout the terrorist world, kneecapping was a recognised form of retribution, having most notably made the headlines during the troubles in Northern Ireland, but also practised in those days by the Italian Red Brigades and now more recently by Hamas in the Occupied Territories. Hernandez's colleagues would certainly draw the appropriate conclusions.

For his onward journey, his movement in and out of Argentina should go unrecorded. His itinerary to date had already been long and wearisome enough. A first stopover in Caracas, from where he had made his way by bus to Ciudad Guayana to reach the Brazilian frontier at Santa Elena. An exhausting nine hundred kilometre coach journey had brought him to Manaus, followed by a flight to Foz do Iguaçu, one of the three towns making up the notorious 'Triple Frontier', lying at the point at which Argentina, Paraguay and Brazil meet.

Long considered by drug enforcement and anti-terrorist agencies around the world as a 'hotspot' for the clandestine activities of many criminal and terrorist organisations, living alongside a flourishing contraband trade, the Triple Frontier towns were close to being a 'no-go' area. This in spite of a formal agreement between the three countries to set up a joint intelligence centre on the Brazilian side to monitor the situation. The Director knew that Argentine intelligence had established a major presence in this border area ever since the terrorist attacks of the 1990s in the Argentine capital.

Argentina had, almost since independence at the start of the 19th century, considered itself somehow a member of the developed world, but happily immune to its problems. Observing events from a distance, Argentina had grown rich on two World Wars and only declared itself against the Axis states a few months before the end of hostilities in Europe in 1945. In much the same way they saw themselves as part of the Latin American family. Perhaps geographically a member, yet clearly a cut above the rest. So when the bombs had exploded in Buenos Aires, the country – and its main intelligence service, SIDE - had found themselves catapulted into a world from which they had believed themselves somehow quarantined. In a speedy response to these new threats, SIDE had flooded the Triple Frontier with agents.

Given that, even many years later, the intelligence effort remained significant, the Director must cross the frontier undetected. On the

Brazilian side, the lagre Arab population in the area had made it easy for him to merge into the background. And now he must enter the target territory invisibly.

The driver started the engine and the car began to edge forward towards the large frontier plaza. From inside the boot, the Director carefully replaced the central panel of the backseat, giving the car the appearance of containing only the driver. Concealed in the space behind what looked like a large LPG tank of the kind found in the boot of taxis, he pulled the dark blanket up over his face, covering himself completely. The plan foresaw that the border official on the Brazilian side would open the boot of the car, appear to look in and see nothing, before closing it once more. It had nothing to do with invisibility and everything to do with the size of the envelope. Everything would depend on the border officials on both sides respecting the deal. He had been told that, in exchange for a percentage of the profits from the contraband regularly run across the border, they would not be too curious.

The volume of cross-border traffic was anyway expected to be larger on a Sunday and the formalities more perfunctory as a result, if long queues were to be avoided.

He sensed the car slowing down again and finally stopping. The muffled sound of the driver's voice speaking to someone outside the car. The car door being opened. As expected, the official on the Brazilian side had only checked the documents. Now for the Argentine. He could hear the sound of voices around the car, probably the passengers off the tourist bus which had been ahead of them in the queue. The car tilted as the driver got out. As agreed, he heard the light tap on the bodywork indicating that they would be coming round to the boot. He froze. The sound of the lock being turned and the lid lifted.

This time the voice was much clearer. A brief exchange between the driver and whoever was with him. Suddenly, the Director felt a hand moving over the blanket which covered him. Then the hand was gone, a brief exchange and the lid slammed shut. The contents of the envelope had clearly been satisfactory. The car tilted and the engine revved, as they moved off into Argentine territory.

"It's okay, you can open," he heard the driver calling.

Carefully, the Director pulled the central panel back into the boot, allowing some of the coolness from the air conditioning to reach him.

"It's okay, we're through. But stay where you are. I'm going into a parking in the town, where you can get out."

Some ten minutes later, the boot lid was opened and, unfolding his aching joints and with a helping hand from the driver, he climbed out.

"Your overnight bus leaves for Buenos Aires from the terminal in about three hours. I'll take you there, and you can buy some food on the way to take with you. Here, I was asked to give you this envelope. And to tell you that it's genuine."

At just after five in the afternoon, the coach pulled out of the bus terminal. It had started to rain again, the heavy grey clouds of autumn hanging low. In about eighteen hours, he would reach the Argentine capital.

He stretched out on one of the sleeper seats, making sure that the small bag containing his beloved SIG Sauer 229 9mm pistol remained within easy reach. A couple of heavily worn travel bags had been squeezed into the rack above his head.

Opening the envelope, he studied the Argentine identity document it contained. Mario Azoulay, born Rosario 1972, a photo likeness of a man of about his height, black hair, dark eyes, a thick beard. The finger print obviously would not match, but then only in an extreme situation was that likely to be put to the test. Sufficient to pass idle scrutiny. He had been warned that these long-distance coaches might be stopped and the identity of passengers checked somewhere along the way. He would have to explain that his latest girlfriend was allergic to beards!

As he dozed, he almost felt remorse that his driver had had to pay so high a price for transferring him into Argentina. The man's back momentarily turned to tidy the boot of the Mercedes, a spin of the head between right and left head and neck grips, the soft crack of the vertebrae. Tipping him into the boot of the car, where only minutes earlier he had suffered heat and humidity, seemed almost poetic justice. A small bag of marijuana hidden in the wheel well. Just another drug run gone wrong.

No loose ends for his entry into the country.

Monday, 2 June 2008 (AM) – AVENIDA DE MAYO Y PERÚ, BUENOS AIRES

"So, Eduardo, how's your mother?" Leandro asked his son, as they sat at Leandro's usual table in London City bar on the corner of Avenida de Mayo and Calle Perú.

Avenida de Mayo was blocked with cars, taxis and buses outside the cafe, the pavements crowded with the mid-morning throng always to be found on the edge of the financial district. The fallen leaves from the plane trees whirling in the late autumn gusts, there was a feeling that winter was round the corner, passers-by pulling up the collars of their coats as they lent forward into the wind. Leandro loved these days of transition. There was something boring about the heat of summer, when the women had little option but to put on jeans and T-shirts. Autumn and winter forced women to reveal their personality through their choice of clothes. Perhaps another reason for his fascination with Sam. And like the women, the city he loved took on another look.

Eduardo was sitting opposite, Sam beside him, the remains of breakfast waiting to be cleared. The tables around them full of chattering secretaries and young dealers.

"She's fine, Uncle. Busy with the guesthouse."

Inspector Eduardo Falcioni, a young detective at the *Comisaría 17a.* in Barrio Norte, the upper-middle class part of Argentina's capital, had taken advantage of the Independence Day holiday to travel up to the north-western province of Salta to spend a week with his mother. The twenty-fifth of May was close to the anniversary of the death of his father at the height of the Malvinas campaign, a day he tried, not always successfully, to spend with her. Flying low over the advancing British forces, his father's Pucará fighter bomber had been struck by ground fire. Killed outright, he lay buried on the islands. The man sitting opposite him had survived, ejecting just in time. His mother had never remarried.

She had inherited a small, colonial-style hotel with four guestrooms in the village of La Caldera, lying north of the city of Salta. An old coaching inn with a pretty courtyard of plants and roses, on which his mother lavished relentless attention. A décor of comfortable sofas and hammocks, local handicrafts and textiles, and good local cuisine.

"It's so pretty," Leandro said. "Is she still getting good business?"

"Seems to be holding up. Probably having a website helps as well. Mainly Europeans, on the way up to the Quebrada de Humahuaca or salt flats and deserts near the Bolivian and Chilean borders."

"We really must get up there sometime," Leandro said, turning to Samira.

"I've been. I love that whole area. Let's take a trip there someday soon with some 4x4s," she replied.

Her kidnap by Dávila had never been revealed to Eduardo, her absence having been disguised as a solo trip to that Andean region.

"Of course, I'd forgotten. You've just come back from there. When we get a moment's peace, let's do it."

Sam scowled at Leandro for nearly destroying their cover story.

"How about ordering some more of those *medialunas de grasa*? They really are so good here," she quickly changed the subject.

Leandro pointedly eyed her waistline, before calling over his waiter and asking for another half dozen of their delicious croissants. *Medialunas de grasa*, a crispy, unsweetened croissant, an Argentine speciality, which he had found nowhere else on his travels.

"Let *me* look after my figure," Sam muttered, catching his look.

"Has your boss Fonseca said any more to you about how Dávila died?" Leandro asked.

"Frankly, I've had far too much to do since Davila's death. It's not as if murders didn't happen every day in this country. That and planning the wedding."

"When's that for?" Leandro asked.

"We're thinking of early December. Than we can get away on holiday. Maybe Punta del Este. If I can afford it. After all the expense which Florencia is planning…"

"Argentine's love weddings," Sam muttered, her tone of voice less than enthusiastic.

Leandro shot her a glance to keep her thoughts to herself. Sam entertained a pretty cynical view of the institution of wedlock in Argentina.

"Though that's not entirely correct," Eduardo began. "We were talking about something else the other day and the conversation came back to the Williams case. The 'polo groupie', he calls her. I naturally asked if there was news. He said consideration had been given to identifying whatever assets Dávila might have had in Uruguay and also in Switzerland. But given a high-level political reluctance to dig much deeper into what Dávila might have been up to, the legal advisers had finally recommended no further action."

"There must still be files."

"Taken by SIDE and apparently locked away. I acted disappointed, but like last time, Fonseca was pretty emphatic that this was a hot potato that no one was keen to handle."

"That's probably good news for Carla," Sam commented.

"On balance, yes," Eduardo said, turning to her. "Though one can never rule out the possibility that someone in SIDE may try to dig deeper. Unofficially. There may be some kind of stand-off between those inside SIDE, who would like to know more about what their colleague was up to, even try and get their hands on his offshore funds, and others, probably high up in government, who would much prefer to see the name of Dávila completely forgotten."

"For all our sakes, let's hope the latter win the day. Presume you've seen no more sign of anyone taking an interest in you?" Leandro asked.

"No, whatever attention there was seems to have stopped pretty much around the time that Dávila died. And my ribs feel almost normal," Eduardo added with a smile.

"I would hope so. After all, its at least 9 months since he sent his thugs round to beat you up and make you drop the case. And as always, where you're concerned, it had exactly the reverse effect. Stubborn bastard. I've lost count of the number of times I was invited to discuss your attitude to school rules with one or other of your teachers."

Eduardo chuckled.

"Anyway, thanks for the coffee, Uncle. Got to be getting along."

Eduardo got up and, having kissed Sam, put his arms around Leandro's shoulders.

"Take care of yourself, Uncle. Particularly, given the company you keep," he whispered, looking in the direction of Sam. Although serious by nature, Eduardo was not above the occasional flash of humour.

Leandro waved as Eduardo climbed into a taxi.

"He's a good lad," he said. "Not an easy career he's chosen, but for some reason, he set his heart on it between school and university. It's a dirty profession in this country, but I don't need to tell you that. More coffee?"

Sam shook her head.

"Do you think Carla's safe?" she asked. "I didn't much like that remark about people in SIDE still having an agenda of their own."

Leandro thought for a moment.

"To be frank, I don't have the answer to that one. I can imagine that, what with Dávila's blackmail operations and the little private army he was running on the side, a number of people may have wanted to get to the truth."

"SIDE are a vindictive lot. My friends at Mossad tread carefully with them."

"So should Carla. I wouldn't recommend any visits to Buenos Aires in the near-term, unless she travels on one of her false passports. You say she's good with disguise, so who knows."

"I don't think she's any immediate plans. As to Uruguay, she has a good lawyer. I don't know his name, but she said he was sweeping up any evidence of Dávila's ownership of the house over there. He certainly didn't have it in his own name and it's even possible - in fact probable - that it was in the name of some company in which Carla was also a shareholder."

"Did she ever tell you how Dávila died?"

Sam hesitated for a second. "No. Why do you ask?"

"Curiosity."

Sam stayed silent for a minute or two, watching Leandro skimming the headlines of La Nación.

"You know, Leo, I was watching you two. You have certain mannerisms in common, you and Eduardo. Little things, uncanny. His father died with you in the plane? You looked after him during his school days. No wonder he feels close to you."

Leandro detected she was studying his reactions. He continued to read the editorial, almost as if he hadn't heard her. Only Elena knew the real truth about Eduardo. For a brief instant, he contemplated bringing Sam into his confidence.

He looked up from the newspaper.

"Sorry, I missed that. What were you saying?"

She looked at him in a way that left him far from confident he'd fooled her. But in the breathing space he'd gained, he'd realised there was little benefit in bringing Sam into this particular secret.

"I think you heard me. I was saying that you and Eduardo seemed so similar in a number of ways. In your ways of thinking, for instance. The way you scratch behind your ear when at a loss for words. That innocent look you can put on – usually when you're anything but."

"Do you think so? You may be right. After all, with his mother so far away, Elena and I were his stand-in parents. Let's hope the similarities are good ones. Including not allowing himself to become a victim to predatory females."

"Did you have anyone in mind?"

Leandro shook his head.

"Of course not, why should I?"

Sam kicked him under the table.

"Fuck you!"

He might have gained a temporary respite.

"Clearly you have a guilty conscience," he teased, rubbing his shin. "Anyway, what are we doing today? The weather's foul. Back to my place?"

"We've just come from there. And I'm sure we can find something more attractive than this place. Can't see why you love it so. What's the time?"

"You know I don't wear a watch. As to this bar, I know it's not as smart as some of the others, but it has some interesting ghosts. Did you know Julio Cortázar wrote *Los Premios* here?"

"Never read it."

"You see, your education is far from complete. Some important gaps still remain. One day, you'll have to dedicate time to the culture of your own country. Not just nineteenth century England. You can't claim to love the country the way you do and ignore its icons. In literature. In music. Even in the tango."

Sam wrinkled her nose.

"Not tango!"

The waiter told them that it was nearly eleven.

"You can buy me a copy. For now, I want a good lunch somewhere. One of those exclusive places all you ex-bankers go to dream up new ways to screw the country. Where women are rarely seen. I've just got enough time to get changed."

Leandro thought for a minute.

"All right, see you at New Brighton in Sarmiento at one-thirty. It's something like number 650. I'll get us a nice table. You'll like it. Used to be a shirt-maker's emporium. It's still got all the old wood panelling."

He waved to the waiter and settled the bill.

Helping Sam into her taxi, he decided to walk the ten or so blocks back to his flat. Crossing the wide expanse of 9 de Julio, the wind howling up from the south, bringing the colder air of Patagonia, was more chilling than expected.

Monday, 2 June 2008 (PM) – SARMIENTO 645, BUENOS AIRES

Some two hours later Leandro was back in the heart of the capital's overcrowded, unkempt financial district, pushing open the elegant *art nouveau* doors of New Brighton. He knew from experience that Sam would arrive later than agreed, mainly so that she could make him witness the impact her appearance was calculated to make on any assembled males. He was not disappointed. No sign of her The waiter led him to the table he'd reserved for two.

"Can I bring you some champagne, Don Leandro?"

Leandro nodded, but even as he did, he sensed a ripple of silence making its way down past the bar towards the main body of the restaurant where he was sitting. Sam was making her *entrée*, the effect rather like the Mexican Wave in a football stadium.

"What kept you?" he asked, as the waiter helped her out of her voluminous fake fur cloak.

The girl would stand out at a fashion show. The slightest hint of an audience seemed to bring out a desire to knock any woman within a few kilometres out of the contest. She rarely failed. Reasonably handsome in his own way, he was used to attracting some attention from the opposite sex, but a measure of shyness inclined him to avoid the limelight. The proximity of Sam seemed invariably to mobilise the attentions of predatory males and jealous females alike.

"What do you mean? What about all this?"

She spread her hands to allow him a clear view of her anthracite pinstripe trouser suit, impeccably tailored to her silhouette, worn over a pale golden yellow silk blouse with a heavy, loosely tied cravate of the same material, held in place by a small gold and enamel star. A thin black leather corset cinched her hourglass figure, long black leather gloves and patent leather pumps with perilous heels completing the ensemble. As usual on this kind of occasion, her wardrobe must have cost the equivalent of twice his monthly salary!

"The Druze star, I see," Leandro said. "It's back."

"It never left. Anyway, is that all you have to say? After all this effort?"

"Of course not. You're so beautiful you take my breath away. No words are sufficient to convey my admiration."

Leandro adopted a look of abject devotion.

"Don't give me that shit, Dr Flemming. If you don't like the result, I'm sure I've got the pick of any one of the tables here."

Judging by the fact that conversation had virtually come to a standstill in their part of the restaurant, filled by bankers and their clients, Leandro was in no doubt that she could instantly make good on her threat.

"Please, Sam, sit down. You're attracting attention."

"I should hope so!"

"Actually, with that cape and the thing around your neck, you remind me of one of the photos of your dear Oscar."

"Quite right. Clever of you to spot it. Exactly what I had in mind. You see, you do occasionally pay attention to what I try and teach you."

The photograph had been on the cover of a biography of Wilde, which she had given Leandro for Christmas.

She lowered herself carefully into the seat, which the waiter had been patiently holding for her. Taking them by the tips of her fingers, she began to pull off her long black leather gloves in a motion reminiscent of a film from the 1950s. So many scenes played by any one of her favourite actresses, Katherine Hepburn, Gene Tierney, Ingrid Bergman or Lauren Bacall. Maybe, he wondered, even Charlotte Rampling in *The Night Porter*. In Sam's darker moments, the ultimate version of the Stockholm Syndrome to which Carla had introduced her.

"If you're thinking of Rita in Mullholland Drive again, you can forget it," she said.

The waiter brought their champagne.

"Would you do me the favour of removing those unattractive glasses? There really isn't much sun in here and anyway, I want to see your eyes," Leandro suggested quietly.

With a smile, she slipped the dark glasses onto the top of her head.

As they raised their glasses, he looked into her eyes. Her pupils, normally a pale green, had turned to a golden yellow!

She laughed at the look on his face.

"Do you like my new lenses? Remind you of anything?"

"Not really…."

"No marks, Dr Flemming. *'Sette uomini d'oro'*? With Rossana Podestà and Philippe Leroy? Mid-60s. She has the same hairstyle in the movie as mine and wears golden lenses. I rather like them. Do I detect that I embarrass you?"

"Yes … and no," he replied. "There are just times when…."

He shook his head in disbelief. Roleplay unlimited.

"So, what are we going to eat?" he asked. "Let me tell you, the *bife de lomo* is particularly delicious here. I know its traditional Argentine cuisine, but their steaks are in a class of their own. By the way, what do you think of the place?"

Sam surveyed the room. Highly-polished wood panelling covered the walls, one side still showing the range of display cabinets with which this former shirt-maker's emporium had catered to the sartorial taste of its well-heeled patrons in the surrounding financial community. Large mirrors reflected the light of the overhead chandeliers and antlered stag trophies looked down from the walls onto the heads of the new clientele.

"Old world," she said. "Older than yours, even."

"30s I think. The Brighton, it was called. When elegance and masculine fashion parted company, probably in the 80s, it became a restaurant called Clarkes. That was the *'uno a uno'* heyday. Now it's the New Brighton."

"We'll add it to our list of places where I show you off," she said.

Leandro laughed.

"Funny, I thought it was the other way round."

"You know your problem, Dr Flemming? You're too modest. Anyway, let's concentrate on ordering before we go any farther."

She hid herself behind the tall menu, but after a few minutes, laid it down beside her.

"Oh, why all the effort? I'll have the *lomo* as you suggest. Very rare."

"Good."

Leandro signalled to the waiter, who had been watching them from the far end of the room.

"Very simple, Fernando. Two *bifes de lomo,* both rare. And when I say 'rare', I mean it. Please make sure the message gets through to the kitchen. With that, some *papas paille* and a salad."

"What kind of salad, Don Leandro? Lettuce, tomatoes, spinach, avocado, watercress, arugula, radish? With olive oil and balsamic vinegar?"

"Avocado and watercress, for me," Sam said. "Oil and balsamic."

"Make that a big one for two," Leandro added. "We'll have a bottle of the Catena merlot. And a couple of San Pellegrinos as well."

"So this is where you used to come to plot the economic downfall of the country. Making life impossible for the Central Bank. Robbing pensioners."

Leandro looked around the room.

"In today's business climate you have to look after yourself first and foremost. Argentina's always been like that. With no economic policy, which is the present situation, you've little room for worrying about your neighbour. Anyway, let's talk about something else. I'm getting bored with finance…"

Sam was silent for a minute or two, sipping her champagne and looking around the room. Bored with finance, was he?

"Did I mention I got into an argument at the gallery?"

"No. What gallery?"

"I went to an exhibition in Arroyo last Friday evening. A gallery owner I know invited me. A new Brazilian abstract sculptor. Not the kind of thing you'd like. You're such a Philistine when it comes to art anyway."

Leandro did not contest her remark.

"One of those dinner party leftists who flourish under this government. Old guy, sixty or more. Strong *cordobés* accent. Tried to fill my head with the change in society, the peaceful revolution."

"Hope you told him it's all cheap populism?"

"Exactly. And a facade for corruption. I even suggested that they appeared to have corrupted his mind. He didn't like that!"

"What was he saying?"

Sam downed half her glass.

"Said he'd been a supporter of the Montoneros in the early 70s. Went on and on about the horrors of the dirty war. But now, thanks to the Kirchners, what his generation had failed to bring about through armed revolution, they would achieve through the ballot box. Human rights, the work of the Madres de la Plaza de Mayo, bringing the military to justice, an equitable distribution of wealth across the nation."

"Did he actually fought for the Montoneros or did he just sat on the sidelines? Quite a lot of armchair Montoneros have emerged since the arrival of the Kirchners."

"He didn't say."

She paused, before continuing.

"You know, Leo, there are times when *Kirchnerismo* seemes closer to a religion than a political movement. If you don't agree with them, you're a heretic, banished to outer darkness."

Leandro nodded.

"That's extremism for you. The generation your man comes from suffered from the same distortion, that black or white view. And Córdoba, you say? Makes sense. Córdoba was the birthplace of most of these guerrilla movements in the 60s. Che came from Córdoba – or just outside."

"I used to have a T-shirt. All black, with his face in gold," Sam murmured.

"Typically proletarian of you."

An image of Sam's breasts encased in the face of *el Che* momentarily deflected his train of thought.

"What was I saying? Oh yes… For every thousand drawing-room followers of Che, a few took it seriously enough to put their lives on the line. That's how the Montoneros and ERP were born in Argentina, Tupamaros in Uruguay and others. Except that a country like Argentina could never be a Cuba. Though they certainly tried hard enough, they probably never stood a chance. Córdoba was the heart of it."

After a pause, he added "Ever been to Bologna?"

"They say the food's fantastic. What's the connection?"

"'*Bologna la grassa!*' Bologna the fat. Because of its cooking. But also '*Bologna la dotta*' and '*Bologna la rossa*'. One of the oldest universities in Europe. And the heartland of the Italian left. Although no one would accuse Córdoba of being a gastronomic fireball, it's often known as '*Córdoba la docta*', with one of the oldest universities in Latin America. As for its politics, it's definitely left-wing and revolutionary. The Cordobazo in 1969 was a real left-wing uprising. Set the scene for everything that led to the '*dictadura*'. So you could also call it '*Córdoba la roja*'."

"How do you know all these things, Leo?"

"Remember I was a kid when all these movements were in full swing. And then the military came along. Ironically on the initiative of old Perón himself."

"As Carla found out to her cost."

"Yes, sadly. I'm interested in the Kirchner family's political origins. Or at least the ones they lay claim to. The way they surround themselves with so many who can trace their origins back to the terrorist left and the 'dirty war'. Many of their key advisers are ex-guerrilleros. Take Zannini, her legal adviser, for example. Not called '*el Chino Zannini*' just for the shape of his eyes. A Maoist *guerrillero* in his youth. Member of the Vanguardia Comunista. If you don't understand where the Kirchners are coming from, you won't understand where they're going."

Sam nodded.

"Some of the things Carla used to tell me are making sense. She tried to help the Montoneros in a small way. To speak out against the dirty war."

"By the time she got involved at the end of the 70s, it was all over for the Montos. The army had total control. But somehow, somewhere, that left-wing fervour lived on and, because of the unacceptable excesses of the dirty war, gained new vitality when democracy returned '83 after the Malvinas war."

"The war that nearly took you," Sam whispered, pulling his hand towards her side of the table.

"Yes. Nearly. But it didn't. And that's why you're fortunate enough to have me sitting opposite."

She blew him a kiss as the waiter arrived with their *bifes de lomo* and salad and poured the wine.

As usual, the food captured all Sam's attention for the next ten minutes, that special sweetness of only the finest cuts of Argentine beef.

"That's delicious, Leo. Nothing like it in the world."

"It's the grass. Our farmers don't seem to realize that moving over to feedlots is going to kill that."

Leandro's hopes that, with the arrival of the *bifes*, the discussion of Argentine politics might be over, were dashed as soon as she pushed her empty plate away. Sam was a fast eater.

"But, going back to our discussion, surely, how can these people believe that they can shift society in the direction they wanted to forty years ago?"

"Our middle class has been so abused by our politicians that they've lost their critical faculties. They can't – or won't - see what's coming. As long as they can spend the summer in Punta del Este or St Tropez, have the latest Mercedes or go out to flashy restaurants, they're not fussed who's running the country."

"Reluctant to get their hands dirty?"

"Exactly. To be in Argentine politics, you have to have a strong stomach. Our lady President has a favourite political guru, a man called Ernesto Laclau, who preaches the virtues of constant antagonism between different forces as a way of revitalising politics. Which explains why the Kirchners always need enemies."

"Some people are just built that way."

"One day it's the military. Then it's the press. Or the big corporations. Now it's the farmers. They thrive on confrontation. Promote it. It's no longer about class. It's not the old Peronist trade union class against the rest. Kirchner followers are to be found right across the board. When the Kirchners finally go, that'll be one of the hardest things to eradicate. It's very worrying."

"But if you're living in a *villa miseria*, a slum on the outskirts of this city, all you see are subsidies and hand-outs, millions of pesos of social programmes and cheap housing administered by the Madres de la Plaza de Mayo. Whilst, oblivious to it all, Madame President spends piles of her money on clothes and jewels."

"Our money to be more precise! That's part of the dream. Evita came from a very poor background. A third rate film actress until she married Perón. The more lavishly she dressed, the more the poor adored her. Cristina Kirchner plays a similar game."

"And now this fight with the farmers? Where's it going?"

"To hold onto power, to dictate, they need cash. The problem is, they have so little clue about what running the economy of a complex country involves. The level of mismanagement, waste and corruption is unparalleled. To ignore all that, you have to be a believer in the myth they peddle. *El relato* as they call it. You're right, it's a religion."

Leandro was silent for a moment, looking for an idea.

"The more I think about it, the more it strikes me that there's something very critical about the fact that Cristina is a woman."

"Not the kind of woman that Argentine men are used to," Sam smiled.

"She's not an icon, not an Evita, something to be looked up to. Nor is she a fool, like Isabelita was. No, she's far more dangerous than that. In fact she has all the determination, the cunning and the commitment of a man. She's a tough male politician disguised as a woman. And most of our opposition politicians haven't got their brains round that one. Which is why she catches them out. In a strange way, she's our Margaret Thatcher..."

"I hadn't seen it that way, but I think you're right."

Leandro poured the remains of the merlot.

"I'm beginning to think we drink too much," Sam murmured, though doing nothing to deter him.

All of a sudden, Leandro switched the subject.

"Since we have the whole day in front of us, there's another subject I wanted to discuss with you. We can get another bottle of Merlot."

"Why are you looking so serious, Leo? You frighten me."

He ignored her remark.

"You and Mossad. It's been business pending for too long. You owe me an explanantion. I don't understand why you work for them."

Sam sighed. The time had finally come to convince him. She pulled on the hem of her corset. It was a tick Leandro had occasionally detected, as if the marshalling of her thoughts and her clothes somehow needed synchronising.

"Is that thing uncomfortable?" Leandro asked.

"On the contrary," she replied firmly.

"Pour me some more of that good merlot."

She drank some more.

"Some of it, you already know, Leo. How Mossad approached me, following my interrogation by the Israeli woman intelligence officer in the Occupied Territories. The whole experience left me with a feeling of waste, of frustration. That male aggression and religious intolerance should apparently always lead to violence as the only option."

Leandro nodded.

"You know what I think about the way the religions of the Book have perpetuated the second-class status of women," she continued. "Even Christianity still has a long way to go. In the case of Judaism, I detect rather less of the kind of discrimination, enslavement and prejudice which you find in parts of Islam. Just look at the Taliban in Afghanistan or that women still can't drive a car in Saudi Arabia!"

Her eyes flashed. One of her deepest passions.

"Even before the Enlightenment, at least Christianity did allow a few women occasionally to play a leading role in religious life. A small one, I grant you. But some women did gain prominence in the Church. Teresa of Avila for example. Interestingly, her grandfather was a Jew converted to Christianity. Others, Hildegard of Bingen or St Catherine of Siena, key figures in their day."

Where did this girl get all this from?

"I've heard of St Teresa. But the other two?"

"It doesn't matter. The interesting thing is that in mediaeval times, there were exceptional women who shaped religion, who had political influence from inside the Church. Take another example of what I'm talking about. Heloise, banished to a monastery from which she corresponded with Abelard. They were actually married and had a child. Before he had his balls cut off."

Leandro grimaced.

"Perhaps that's the solution," Sam laughed. "We'll have you castrated. Then we can just concentrate on this kind of discussion. Like they did. Writing letters to each other. Would have to be emails today."

"For that to work, we probably would have to be locked away in a monastery," Leandro commented dryly. "Though I can't see you remaining faithful to a eunuch."

She blew him a kiss.

"That day you came to my flat, you spotted my photograph of the Italian journalist, Oriana Fallaci. Did you ever find her book, 'The Rage and the Pride'?"

Leandro shook his head.

"She was an amazing journalist. Never afraid to speak out, whether on Vietnam or the Islamic revolution. In an interview with Khomeini, she told him exactly what she thought about the way in which women were treated under Islam. And in that book, which she wrote after 9/11, she spelt out the risks we run by being afraid to face up to Islam and its excesses. I admired her enormously. I was very depressed when she died a couple of years ago."

"I must try to find a copy."

"Don't worry, I'll order it from Amazon for you."

She drained her wine glass. Leandro refilled it.

"In the Occupied Territories, and what with everything I'd read, I felt I had to get involved. I couldn't simply sit on the side-lines any longer. The way we Argentines have always done. Just think, here in Argentina, we allowed Hezbollah to kill over a hundred people – mainly Jews - with complete impunity. We even fabricated a false trail for ten years, whilst the relatives waited for justice. In vain."

Leandro nodded. But the key piece of the puzzle was still missing.

"But the final step? To work for Mossad? I'm sure that's an organisation this woman Fallaci would have despised."

"I gave it a lot of thought. With people out there denying the Holocaust – the Iranian Ahmadinejad just the latest example - or wanting to destroy their nation, is it so surprising the Jews, after centuries of oppression under Christianity, resort to methods that could be condemned in isolation? We Christians have treated them abominably since the days of St Augustine. Who invented the ghettoes? You could even argue it all made the death camps possible."

"But couldn't you have seen a way to contribute, whilst still remaining in the Arab camp? Without having to make the wholesale switch to the Israeli side? What would your father say?"

"He must never find out. It's the biggest secret I keep from him. I thought hard about the Arab option, but there are fewer and fewer voices of moderation. Islamic extremism is taking over, the Moslem Brotherhood in Egypt, Al Qaeda-inspired groups in Somalia, Yemen. I wanted to make a difference and I wanted to make it in a hurry."

"But Israeli policy in the Occupied Territories. How can you agree with that?"

"I don't agree with it. I can't. But don't confuse short term Israeli measures, however unacceptable, with the long term threat of Islamic fundamentalism. To enslave the Arab world under the law of Shari'a. And not just the Arab world. And while they're about it, wipe Israel off the map. And it's getting worse. Now that the battle is shifting to the Arab states themselves."

"You're right. Islamic fundamentalism risks tearing those states apart. The American invasion of Iraqi took the cork out of that bottle."

She paused. Perhaps a little trap to get him to come clean on his research.

"Finally, add the nuclear ambitions of Iran. To recover their leadership of the Middle Eastern world, which they see as having slipped to Saudi Arabia."

Leandro spotted the trap and ignored it.

He sometimes wondered where she found the time for all this. Was it being fed to her by Mossad as part of her indoctrination? Perhaps. Though the reference to Israeli vulnerability didn't sound that way.

"I can't fault your analysis," he said "although not everyone would agree with all of it. And it still doesn't answer my question. How can you reconcile Israeli policies in Gaza and the Occupied Territories, which you admit to condemning, with working for Mossad?"

"Oh dear, I thought I was doing a reasonable job to explain that. Apparently not. Give me some more," and she pushed her glass across the table towards him.

"I'll put it another way. I support the Palestinian cause for nationhood. On the other hand, I can't live with the possibility that Islamic fundamentalism takes over. In my view, it's possible to disagree with Israeli policies in the Occupied Territories without necessarily supporting the cause of Islamic fundamentalism. I made that clear to Mossad. Areas in which we can work together and others in which we can't. They understand. I can help them to undermine the broader, aggressive agenda of Islamic fundamentalism, but will do nothing to strengthen the Israeli grip on the Occupied Territories. The two problems are not mutually exclusive."

He said nothing.

"Not unlike what you agreed with Frobisher. Certain areas are off limits."

She leaned forward and took his hand in hers.

"Have I made myself clearer, Leo? I really hope so."

He looked up and smiled.

"I think so. It's a problem, which has defied the world for fifty years. Or perhaps two millennia…"

Risk. Adventure. A double personality. A secret life. For a girl brought up on a cocktail of Oscar Wilde, the Avengers and James Bond… heady stuff! Probably no wonder she had gone to work for Mossad. To make a difference? Time would tell.

He kissed her hand.

"Since I can never doubt your sincerity, all I can do is plead with you to be careful. Very careful."

He might have a better understanding of her motives. But that was not the same as agreeing with the risks they implied.

"Anyway, before we wreck this lunch any further," he signalled to the waiter. "Let's order dessert and coffee."

"I think I saw some kind of thin pastry with apple."

An idea crossed his mind. Could some of this be harnessed to his assignment? Which he would inevitably have to share with her one day soon.

"Whilst we're on that subject, and since you clearly know so much about it, perhaps I should make you my Middle Eastern expert. Or, to be more precise, my comparative religion expert."

Now she was really paying attention. Thanks to Sophie's indoctrination, comparative religion was one of her favourite subjects.

"Go on," she replied slowly.

"Islam versus Christendom. I need a quick guide to some of the issues. And you're the cheapest and most accessible teacher I've got."

"How could any girl resist such a testimonial?"

"I know you've got a lot of books on the subject. For various reasons, I need to understand it better."

"Not unconnected to your work, presumably?"

He ignored her question.

She pushed back in her chair and again adjusted the position of her corset. He watched, but made no comment this time.

"I assume I don't have to go back to Muhammad, the angel, Medina and the Koran. All that's presumably known to you."

"Yes, you can skip that. The general picture is broadly familiar to me. It's a better feel for some of the drivers of the present confrontation that I need. What's changed? Since 9/11 or even before."

Sam thought for a minute and smiled.

"A fundamental difference is that, unlike Christianity, Islam isn't based on the concept of original sin, from which the human race has to be redeemed in order to get to heaven. So for a serial rapist like you, Leo, Christianity was always going to be a tough option."

"I want a serious contribution. Not just another way for you to make fun of me."

"Sorry, Leo."

Another tug on the corset.

"Islam believes that eternal life will be achieved by the creation of a society which puts into practice God's wishes for humanity, which can only be achieved by submission to God's will. As you know, the word Islam means submission, or surrender, so a Muslim is one who submits his or her entire being to Allah."

"Hence the position they adopt when praying?"

"Quite. On the positive side, a powerful sense of social justice, equity, compassion, charity - so-called *zakat* - are key. Rampant terrorism couldn't be farther from the truth. Or more precisely, *shouldn't* be. It's a distortion."

He sat back in his chair, eyes half closed, studying her as she warmed to her subject. Sam's body language was beginning to betray a level of passion which Leandro loved to watch, a spectacle to be savoured.

"There's the 'myth' of the religion and then there's the 'logic'. In the case of Muhammad himself, through his dialogue with the angel which brought him the revelations, that level of submission was feasible. But the subsequent historic turmoil has come from transposing an ideal, which was designed for one man and his group, one tribe, to a complex society of many races."

"We faced the same challenge in the West. When we discovered that religion couldn't provide the answers, we looked for secular solutions. Hence the Enlightenment."

"But Islam didn't. Or at least, their attempts generally failed. The clash between modern reality and their nostalgia for the 'golden age' of that first period. The period of Muhammad himself and the four caliphs that succeeded him. You might say that it's the 'myth' of their religion, the moral construct to which so many want to return, an orderliness enshrined in *shariah* law. An ideal at odds with science, with democracy, with the internet."

She looked across at Leandro.

"You with me so far?"

He nodded.

"It's a myth so powerful that, after the first centuries, they stopped questioning it. What they called closing the 'gates of *ijtihad*', the gates of independent thought. The reverse of what we did with the Enlightenment."

"Christianity no longer has room for myth."

"Well, up until the late 17th and 18th century it did. Until about then, Islam and Christianity were on a similar wavelength. After that, never again."

She was interrupted by the arrival of the apple tarts, but for once she ignored her plate.

"Arab leaders did try to emulate Western progress in the nineteenth century. Muhammad Ali in Egypt, for one. But he, like most of the others, soon discovered that the modernization of his country merely left him at the mercy of the Europeans, especially their bankers. A modern army, modern industry, the trappings of Western progress, all were rejected. Like hostile cells, by a society which could not see progress the same way. Opening the way for people like Khomeini and ultimately the Islamic Revolution."

Fernando arrived with their coffees. In five forkfuls, Sam now demolished the tart before downing the coffee.

"That was very good."

She wiped her mouth carefully and pushed her empty coffee cup towards Leandro. He signalled to the waiter.

Leandro tried not to betray his admiration. If there were moments when her focus on sex and artifice seemed all-consuming, behind it lay a depth of interest in subjects totally at odds with her outward persona. To get this kind of dissertation from a professor as beautiful, as well dressed as Sam, in a restaurant like New Brighton, a glass of merlot in one hand – that was given to few men on this planet!

"Where did you get all this? You never told me you studied this kind of thing."

"You never asked. I didn't actually study it, but - as I think I told you - I was fascinated by my Druze origins, and that led me to read more and more about my region."

Not to mention her months at the feet of Sophie.

"Yes, I saw books on the subject in your flat."

Sam nodded.

"And I've got more packed away. A girl like me can't afford to scare her boyfriends away by appearing too intellectual."

"Well, now that you've got me, you can relax. Anyway, I'm not worried about you being intellectual. I'm far better educated than you are."

Sam threw him a glance which unmistakably conveyed her doubts.

"I didn't like that look. Although, deep down, I've always suspected you might be more *intelligent* than me," he added quickly.

"That's better," Sam muttered. "My friend Oscar once wrote that the only thing that sustains one through life is the consciousness of the immense inferiority of everybody else. A feeling I've always cultivated. And perfectly applicable in our case."

"*Por Dios*, you're insufferable."

Sam sat thinking, stirring the remains of the sugar in her coffee cup. Memories of late night conversations with Sophie. The life and works of Qutb had been one the more fascinating lectures.

"Have you heard of the Egyptian, Sayyid Qutb?" she asked.

Leandro shook his head.

"To understand where Osama bin Laden and his followers are coming from, you need to go back to this man. Amongst others, the spiritual mentor of the Moslem Brotherhood."

"I've heard of them."

"Not a mullah locked away in a *madrasah* pouring over texts. Although devout – he learned the Koran by heart as a child - Qutb was also a lover of English literature and spent time in the United States, even went to Stanford. But he ended up hating American values. In many ways, Qutb was the inspiration of today's Sunni fundamentalism. He was convinced that the kind of secular society which Nasser wanted to introduce was incompatible with Islam as a religion."

"A return to the Stone Age?"

"Not quite. But a way had to be found for the values of Islam to preserve their full and essential place in society. There was nothing the matter with progress, if it could be interpreted as reflecting the perfection of the intentions of Allah for mankind. If materialism had no place for the sacred or for the moral, then there was no place for materialism. It's not surprising Nasser locked him away. And finally had him killed."

Sam drank the second cup of coffee.

The restaurant was almost deserted. Not that she wanted any audience other than Leandro. But she sensed a certain impatience in the body language of some of the waiters. She looked at the wall clock. Four. The lecture would have to be continued some other time. Leandro stirred in his chair.

"Thank you, Professor," he said. "That's helpful. But where does it go from here? Are we ever going to bridge the gap between our two views of the world? I mean, Israel, Sunni and Shia, Iraq... And now all this talk of Iran and a nuclear bomb... It's a nightmare scenario."

Sam was nodding her head in agreement. She pretended not to notice he had let slip a reference to Iran's ambitions. So was she right?

"Let's have the bill and get back to *La Piedad*. You've worked me too hard. My turn to get a reward. By the way, did you light the fire?"

"What do *you* think?"

As they were leaving and shaking the *maitre's* hand, Leandro booked a table for 1 o'clock next day.

"Two days in a row? Not sure I can take that much cholesterol," Sam objected, "however delicious."

"No, I'm lunching with an old rugby friend. Counsellor in the diplomatic service. Made contact again a week or so ago. Haven't seen each other for years. We agreed to meet."

"Diplomat? Not your usual milieu?"

"No. I got a rather strange mail the other day, from someone I've no recollection of ever having contacted."

"What did the mail say?"

She knew perfectly well. Cmholland9T6. A fictitious email address she had invented for herself. None other than one Samira Haidar, hiding behind the name taken by Oscar Wilde's wife after their separation. Plus the year of her death - 1896. Leandro had obviously not made the connection. Why should he?

"Something strange. A reference to a story about a diplomat committing suicide in Brussels. Whoever seent the mail seemed to think I should take a look."

"And that's the purpose of the lunch tomorrow?"

"Yes. Anyway, I'll tell you more if I find out anything. Let's grab a taxi and get back to the flat."

Half an hour later, back in Pasaje de la Piedad, he helped her out of her cloak. Twirling in front of him, she dropped her jacket to the floor after a *revolera* worthy of a Manolete or Dominguín. Perhaps she saw herself as a successor to the Peruvian Conchita Cintrón, the world's most famous woman bullfighter?

"So, Señor, what do you think of my figure?"

Sam had once claimed she had a waist of sixty-five centimetres which, cinched into some of her corsets, she could bring down a further ten. He'd had his arm around her often enough to believe it.

The elegant black leather corset confirmed the hourglass silhouette.

"Irresistible."

Monday, 2 June 2008 (PM) - BOEDO

At about the time that Leandro and Sam were leaving New Brighton, the Director climbed out of a taxi at the address he had been given in Foz do Iguaçu. The bus having arrived early in the morning at the Retiro terminal, he had first dropped off his suitcases at a hotel in the Once district. The Argentine identity document had easily withstood the cursory glance of a bored duty manager.

"That's quite a beard you had."

"I know. My girlfriend didn't like it. Had to go. Last week. Got to change the DNI soon. Unless of course I grow it again. Maybe change girlfriends instead."

He was relieved to see that the manager appeared not to notice that his Spanish accent was more reminiscent of Iberia than of an Argentine province.

In the *barrio* known as Once, its pavements crowded with small stallholders and lined with Jewish emporia specialising in everything for the rag trade in Argentina, he'd merge easily into the scene. Before catching the taxi, he had spent an hour wandering around the area. Serried ranks of shops with bolts of every kind of textile in endless colours, whether for clothing or interior decoration, jostled alongside little boutiques of cheap ornaments or plastic toys from China. The pavements seethed with young men and women, touting for business or unloading more wares from double-parked vans and lorries. As he had strolled amongst them, one or two people even stopped him to ask the way.

In contrast, Boedo, where he now found himself, was more a working-class, largely residential district, which had suffered less than others from the predatory inroads of cheap real estate. Tree-lined streets, one or two-storey colonial-style houses of the kind that had originally characterized so much of the Argentine capital, windows and doors surrounded by an ornate cartouche. A general air of being out of the mainstream, out of the rush and bustle which characterised Once. Pavements nearly empty, cars parked on both sides of the street under the trees. In the distance, the hum of heavier traffic from one or two main avenues, San Juan or Caseros, but most loudly from the 25 de

Mayo flyover, which cut through all these *barrios* down towards the river.

Pushing open the outer door, he found himself in the large central courtyard of a *conventillo*, its four sides rising several floors all around, each outer walkway lined by the doors of apartments. A wrought iron bridge at each level spanned the central space. Checking the apartment number he had been given and which he had encoded as a number on his cell phone, he looked up. A young man was leaning over the railing of the second-floor walkway, looking down at him. He betrayed no sign of interest, let alone of recognition.

Shouldering his small bag, the Director made his way to one of the spiral staircases set in each corner of the long inner courtyard.

Passing a number of children rushing up and down, he was reminded of the atmosphere in the medina in Fez in which he had spent part of his early childhood, its back streets full of children playing ball, the smell of spices and the noxious fumes of the nearby tanneries hanging heavy in the air of the narrow passageways. As he came out on the second level, he followed the cast-iron railing round the outer edge, checking the numbers on the doors. The one he was looking for turned out to be adjacent to a suspended patio, complete with wilting plants and a couple of wrought iron benches. The young man he had seen looking down had moved over to the opposite side and was watching him. As he was about to press the bell, he approached cautiously.

In Arabic, in which he detected a Syrian accent, the young man gave him the agreed password, to which he replied that his grandmother was indeed in good health, thanks be to Allah.

"Hamid," the young man introduced himself.

"Ahmed," he replied.

"Please, come this way."

Hamid opened the door and led the Director inside. Compared with the damp cold of the outer courtyard, the small gas fire made for a reasonable temperature. The same kind of stove he remembered being used to combat the late winter damp and draughts in his parent's house in Casablanca.

"Please, sit down. Did you have a good journey?"

"Yes, thank you."

"And have you found somewhere to stay? I provided your contact in Foz with the address of a couple of hotels. I hope they were useful."

"They were, but I am staying somewhere else. For obvious reasons, the less you know about where I am, the better."

Hamid nodded.

"Of course. Is there anything else you need from me? Support or getting round the city."

"No, I thank you. I'm sure I'll be able to manage. Though I believe you have certain things for me."

"Indeed. But first forgive me, I'm a very poor host. Can I offer you something to drink? Some tea, some coffee?"

"Perhaps a coffee."

Hamid disappeared into the kitchen, embarrassed at having failed in such minimal courtesies.

Left alone, the Director looked about him, trying to build up a picture of the young man, seeking any sign that might confirm his reliability. In his business, rotten apples could prove disastrous. The young Syrian enjoyed the reputation of being a reliable contact - but the operations officer in Baghdad had made it clear that he had full discretion to ensure that his own security was paramount.

"People like Hamid are replaceable. People like you, my friend, less so. You know what I mean."

The Director hoped he would not have to cover more of his tracks by disposing of Hamid at any stage.

The small collection of books on a narrow shelf next to the TV boasted a couple of copies of the Koran, one in Spanish. Otherwise, nothing of any particular interest. Hearing Hamid still busy in the kitchen, he pulled open a side drawer of the dresser a couple of centimetres. With the tip of a finger, he pushed aside some of the papers inside and found what looked like a copy of the Argentine Playboy magazine, well thumbed. Young Hamid might be succumbing to the temptations of Western society. Not such a good sign, though probably inevitable at his age.

The sound of crockery in the kitchen having suddenly ceased, he turned, leaning against the drawer to shut it quietly, just as Hamid reappeared with two cups of coffee.

"So, Hamid, how long have you been here in Argentina? As far as I know, you were not born here."

"I arrived with my father about ten years ago, during the period when the Syrian Menem was president. My father was an engineer and, thanks to contacts, was offered a good job here. Certainly better than the limited opportunities back home in Latakia. I finished my education here."

"And your parents are still alive?"

"My father died of a heart attack a couple of years ago. My mother died back in Syria."

"Brothers or sisters?"

Hamid shook his head.

"Girlfriend?" the Director added, smiling.

"Until about a week ago, yes. However, she claims to have found someone better."

"Was she also Syrian?"

"No," he replied with a bitter laugh. "Argentine. Italian origins."

The Director pointed questioningly towards a small framed photograph on top of the TV set.

"Yes, I suppose I should get rid of the photograph."

"One always lives in hope," the Director said by way of consolation."However, women are sometimes a distraction in our business. Even, at times, a danger."

Hamid looked slightly uncomfortable. He did not reply.

The Director sat down on the worn sofa, having first placed his empty coffee cup on the dresser. Hamid pulled a wooden chair out from the end of what appeared to be an all-purpose dining and worktable.

"So, my friend, have you been able to find me some assistants? I was told to discuss this with you."

Looking at him, the Director wondered whether this young man could really be expected to have the kind of contacts he needed. The delicate business of contract killing was usually organized by men older than Hamid. Except in the case of the growing fraternity of young *sicarios*, willing to kill for a pittance in exchange for a motorbike and a gun. Like the ones he had used in Caracas. But for what he had in mind here, to be avoided at all costs.

Hamid shifted on his chair.

"I believe I have someone who can introduce you to the right kind of person."

"What kind of person is that?"

"The man was a friend of my father's. Used to belong to the Provincial Police in La Plata. Has now retired. Just before my father died, he told me that this man could arrange anything. That I could trust him, as his grandparents also came from Latakia back in the 1920s."

The Director studied the young man silently.

"You think that your father meant that we could go to this person even with the kind of request which I have to make?"

"My father made it clear that I could ask this man anything."

"Did he give any reason for that?"

"My father lent him money, to do with some problem he had. At the time of the financial crisis in 2001. Many people lost money. He never repaid it because he couldn't. But, apparently, he promised he would help my father in any way that he might need. Even if it was illegal."

"And you think this man will honour his debt to you in the same way?"

It was clear to the Director that this lad was far from having broached the subject to his father's friend. This might in fact be an advantage. Perhaps the people in Baghdad had been naive to think that Hamid could deliver the kind of introduction he needed. However, this was a business which he, the Director, knew all about. And could certainly handle more professionally. And securely.

"Do we know anything about this man's family back in Latakia?" the Director continued. "Do we need to check out that end?"

Hamid shook his head, though with a visible lack of conviction.

"Well, Hamid, I think it would be best if I dealt directly with your father's friend. I presume you can arrange this and also ensure that he understands that, by helping me, he will be paying his debt."

Hamid looked relieved.

"I can certainly arrange it. I spoke to him a few days ago and said that the time had come to repay. So he will be expecting something. I can introduce you to him whenever you like. See whether he will be coming to Buenos Aires or whether we need to go to La Plata."

"I think the less contact you have with him the better. You must ring him and say that he will have a visitor coming in the name of your father, to whom the debt should be paid. No more than that."

The look of release on Hamid's face was unmistakable.

"Certainly, I can do that immediately if you like," he offered enthusiastically.

"Please, do it now."

Hamid picked up his cell phone from the table and placed the call. The Director listened.

The call lasted only a minute or two, sufficient for the person at the other end to confirm that he would be pleased to receive the visitor at his home in La Plata a week from now, at two o'clock in the afternoon.

"Well done," the Director said, concealing his concerns. "I think from now on, there should be as little contact between you and me as possible. I will take your cell phone number just in case I need to make contact, but I do not expect to have to do so."

Again the look of relief. The Director found this worrying. They would need to think about Hamid for the future. And he would need to try and discover how he had been recruited in the first place. Perhaps not the best choice made by someone.

Hamid opened another drawer and produced two cell phones, a couple of sheets of paper and a rubber immigration stamp.

"I was asked to have these ready for you. Here are the numbers. And after you've put the stamp in your passport, you need to fill in the date and something to indicate a stay of ninety days. Here are a couple of photocopies for you to imitate."

The Director slipped the phones and other items into the small bag he was carrying.

Then, thanking Hamid, he made his way back out onto the patio and down the spiral staircase to the ground floor. Looking up, he caught a glimpse of the young man watching him as he left. He would need to think through whether Hamid represented a risk or not. So far, he had delivered. Just about.

Tuesday, 3 June 2008 (AM) – CALLE ARENALES, BUENOS AIRES

Leandro announced himself at the reception desk of the towering block of concrete and glass, annexed alongside the 19th century palace which housed the Argentine Foreign Ministry. Like many of the city's older government buildings, designed in the early years of the last century, the main Ministry had clearly been modelled on a French provincial prefecture or major *mairie*. Both buildings stood on the corner of Plaza San Martín, one of Buenos Aires' many squares, a favourite haunt of young lovers in the spring with its *ombú*, magnolia and linden trees, grassy slopes dropping down towards Retiro railway station. Though today, in a cold late autumn, any lovers were noticeably absent. Farther down the hill, the sober monument to the 649 fallen of Malvinas, with the usual honour guard provided by one of the armed forces.

Within a couple of minutes, Luis Miguel appeared. Although he had put on some weight since their rugby playing days, he was still a handsome man.

"*Hola*, Leo, you seem to be looking after yourself better than I am," Luis Miguel joked, patting his stomach. "Though a couple of weeks in Brussels and Paris don't help. Great idea, getting together again after so long."

"It struck me that we hadn't seen each other in a long time. Must be over ten years. I've recently taken to making amends, calling good friends I've allowed to drop out of sight. Thought a lunch would allow us to catch up. I've reserved over on Sarmiento."

"If you don't mind, can we stay around here? I haven't all that much time."

Luis Miguel led the way out onto Calle Arenales and they walked a short distance to a small restaurant, where he was greeted as a regular.

"Most of the Ministry eats here at some point during the week," he explained, almost apologetically.

"What table would you like, Señor Consejero?"

Luis Miguel looked at Leandro.

"How about that one over in the corner. A bit quieter?" Leandro suggested.

One of the waiters took their coats and led them to the table.

"I had it reserved for one of your colleagues, but I'll fix that," the owner whispered to Luis Miguel.

"Suggest we do the hard work first," Luis Miguel said, passing Leandro a menu. "They do a mixture of oriental, some Indian, Thai, but you can also get a steak if necessary."

Their orders placed, a good bottle of Lagarde cabernet sauvignon on the table, they began to catch up with their news. Luis Miguel asked about Leandro's consultancy work.

"I've seen it quoted a couple of times in the press," Luis Miguel said. "Professional stuff. It must be frustrating, trying to write something sensible about the economic situation in this country. What with the statistics being fudged and so little in the way of a solid economic policy. I can imagine your clients appreciate any light you can throw on the situation as it really is, as opposed to the way the government tries to project it."

"Do I sense you're not part of the regime's legion of ardent supporters?"

"Still," Luis Miguel laughed, sidestepping the question. "I imagine the battle between the farmers and the Kirchners gives you some fairly lurid material to report just now. My reading of the international press is that no one can understand why the Kirchners seem so keen to kill the goose that lays our golden egg."

"From what I can tell, reading the papers, our foreign policy isn't any too easy to project either," Leandro added, watching Luis Miguel's reaction. He noted a slight shifting of position and a brief scan of the room.

"To be frank, it's a disaster. We're slowly being invaded by a new generation of Kirchner fanatics, members of their terrible youth movement, La Cámpora," Luis Miguel almost spat the words.

Leandro was surprised by the vehemence.

"The kind of ideology that went out of fashion with the fall of the Berlin Wall. Inexperienced young men and women brought up on a diet of unreconstructed leftism and visceral hatred of anything smacking of the United States or liberal capitalism. There are signs some of my colleagues are being kicked out, or jumping ship. We've hardly got any foreign policy left, apart from an uncritical alignment with people like Chavez in Venezuela or others who fall into that camp."

"Correa in Ecuador or Morales in Bolivia?"

"Exactly. Gone are the days when we could earn ourselves a measure of respect in fora such as the UN or the G20. Depressing. Particularly with all these young idealists rushing round, telling us what to do on the basis of zero experience."

As if to emphasise the point, Luis Miguel stabbed a roll in the basket of bread which had been placed on the table.

"Anyway, enough of that. What do you think of this wine? I visited the vineyard a year or so ago, with a delegation of Arabs. I always thought they weren't supposed to drink. Well, let me tell you, another fiction."

Leandro had been listening carefully, waiting for an opportunity to bring the conversation round to the death of the Argentine attaché in Brussels.

"You certainly don't make it sound reassuring. Do you think you're going to stick around?"

"I don't know at the moment. At least I don't have a wife and family to worry about. As a lawyer, I can probably slip back into that line of business. I've got plenty of friends running large law firms, but even they're finding it increasingly difficult. What with a combination of legal uncertainty and some early signs of an economic downturn, business for the profession may well get tougher. So I'll probably hang in here a little bit longer. I'm also due for a foreign posting fairly soon. Not that that's certain. Quite a large number of ambassador posts haven't even been filled. I tell you, the mood inside the Ministry is depressing."

Leandro finally saw an opening.

"So depressing that some of your colleagues are taking their own lives?"

Luis Miguel looked up at him sharply.

"Not sure what you mean? I don't think we've got that far yet."

"Oh, I don't know, wasn't there something about an attaché in the Brussels embassy throwing himself out of the window the other day? I thought I read it in La Nación. Maybe I got it wrong."

Again Luis Miguel shifted in his chair and took a sip of his wine, as if to gain time.

"Oh, Luis María Sanchez. Poor guy. Though I'm not so sure it was suicide."

Luis Miguel took another look around, before lowering his voice.

"Between you and me, Leandro, he wasn't a career diplomat. Came from that tall building next to the Casa Rosada. You know the one I mean. Complicated. Not at all clear it was anything as simple as suicide. I probably shouldn't be talking about it."

Luis Miguel drained his glass. At that moment, the waiter appeared with their first course, a kind of Thai spring roll. Leandro wondered whether to keep the conversation on the same subject or conceal his curiosity. On balance, he decided to take the risk.

"I'd heard that SIDE sometimes posted people to our embassies abroad. But surely there can't have been much for him to do in a place like Brussels. Practically nothing is secret in that place. I know that agricultural exports are the lifeblood of our country, which is why the President is currently doing her utmost to get even more money out of farming. But is that really the kind of thing SIDE works on?"

"No. I don't think he was interested in the price of beef. He was a scientist by training, a physicist. Anything I can tell you is largely hearsay anyway and certainly off the record. All I know is that, when they scraped him up off the pavement, alarm bells were sounding. In fact, they were sounding in some rather strange places, like Caracas, which is where he'd been before getting posted to Brussels. He'd only been in Belgium about six months."

"And you don't think it was suicide?"

Luis Miguel was clearly in two minds about how to proceed. He raised his eyebrows and shook his head, as though to say that it was more than doubtful.

"The press don't seem to have picked up on that."

"No. And it didn't stay in the press for more than a day. Telephone calls were made. Not that La Nación usually pays much attention to that kind of pressure. But I can tell you, there was a lot of interdepartmental to-ing and fro-ing over that one. And, what's more, the Middle Eastern desk was involved. I should know, as it's my area."

"I didn't know you were a specialist in Arab affairs? Were you ever posted there?"

"Four beautiful years in Morocco, between 1998 and 2002. Loved it. I'm not saying the Arab world is easy, but compared to many of the others, Morocco is really very civilised. Not like some of the places I have to deal with now."

Leandro said nothing, allowing him to continue.

"By that I mean those mullahs in Iran!"

The depth of feeling was unmistakable. Leandro's heart leapt.

"I can imagine. No doubt you're involved in the business of the attacks on the Israeli embassy and the AMIA."

Far too soon to raise the subject of Iran's nuclear ambitions.

"Up to my eyeballs. Never-ending story. The Jewish community here never lets go. If we aren't on top of it daily, veiled accusations of anti-Semitism are trotted out. Don't misunderstand me. They have all my sympathy, not only because of what happened in the Shoah, everybody has that. No. It's because I think we've seriously let them down in pursuing the case."

He paused to allow the waiter to bring the main course.

"You probably know, Leo, that the Jewish question in Argentina has always been a complex one."

"Yes, I now. And we do have a large Jewish community."

"About as many as in Russia and certainly the largest third world concentration. Surprising when you remember how much Perón was accused of having made entry easy for ex-SS and concentration camp people. Mind you, the Catholic Church played a very important part in that one too. Not one of their finest moments. I'm a fairly devout Catholic, but there are times I have my concerns about the institution."

"Their behaviour in the 70s at the time of the military also left something to be desired," Leandro said. "Easier for me to say that. I'm an agnostic."

"Yes, not one of their best chapters. But getting back to the Jewish community, as you know, they're pretty vocal. And on top of that, they are not insignificant contributors to the family of Argentine intellectuals. During the 1960s and 70s many of them swelled the ranks of the left-wing. A surprising number of them were even members of the Communist Party."

"They're pretty well represented in psychiatry, too. Can't all be descendants of Freud."

"Somebody was commenting the other day on the link between some of our left-wingers and our predisposition for psychoanalysis."

"There are times when I feel that all our politicians should spend time on the couch."

Luis Miguel's face clouded a little. "Perhaps you want to be a bit careful what you say," he murmured.

"Really? Has it got that bad?"

"Probably not, but a significant level of paranoia is seeping into large parts of the administration. Frankly, better safe than sorry."

"Should we talk about the weather, then? Or perhaps our favourite sport? By the way, I didn't see you during the World Cup last year."

"Actually, I was one of the fortunate few at the Parc des Princes, at the semi-final. Fantastic! Atmosphere incredible. We really did very well coming third. It's Pumas against Scotland next Saturday, isn't it? Should be a good game."

"I'll be torn down the middle, as you can imagine."

"I'll bet."

Luis Miguel looked around the room again.

"No, don't take me too seriously. There are times I'm more jittery than others. It's actually very interesting to deal with the Jews. I have a lot of admiration for them. I'm not a fan of the way in which the state of Israel runs its affairs, but then again, it can't be easy. Complicated race. As the Romans found out. That's why they kicked them out."

"And then the British sent them back. A conditions for the return of the Messiah."

"Could also have had something to do with keeping the French a bit farther away from the Suez Canal. Motives were very mixed. So perhaps we shouldn't be surprised by the results. Looking after the Middle East has taken me back to the history books."

"It's a fascinating subject," Leandro said. "For various reasons, I've been doing the same."

He could thank Sam for that, he thought, sipping his wine.

"But why so little progress?" he asked. "After all, the bombings were nearly fifteen years ago. I mean, you can't put it down to anti-Semitism. Not here, in Argentina. It used to be strong fifty years ago, but now? Is it just our judiciary? There was talk of Menem receiving a payoff from Iran to stop the investigation moving forward."

Luis Miguel thought for a minute.

"Hard to say. We all know he was one of our more corrupt presidents. After all, he was of Syrian origin. Frankly, I don't know. The present government has said it will pursue the AMIA case more enthusiastically than their predecessors. That remains to be seen. We all assume that both the Israeli embassy and the AMIA bombing were the work of Hezbollah, or at least of some group associated with them. With over a hundred people killed, it's quite natural that the Jewish community should be pressing for some kind of result."

He signalled to the waiter to clear their plates.

"A dessert?" he asked Leandro.

"Just a coffee will be fine for me."

"We don't expect much from either Syria or Lebanon, so the finger is pointing firmly at Iran. That was made clear in Nisman's indictment last year. He even went so far as to name Khamenei as directly involved in the decision. You can imagine that that didn't go down too well in the corridors in Tehran. It was suspected at the time that, because we hadn't been prepared to play ball with the Iranians over their nuclear programme, the bombings were a way of getting back at us."

"Do you believe that?"

"I can't say I've seen any direct evidence, but it could make sense. Anyway, it keeps me busy. Between you and me, it was the main reason for my trip to Brussels, to visit our embassy, and Paris to see Interpol. Something will be coming out on that soon enough."

The waiter brought the coffees.

"They were good, those spring rolls, don't you think? Not sure about the main course. I've no idea what nationality the chef is. Probably been no closer to the Orient than the beach at Mar del Plata, but nowadays, thanks to the Internet, cuisine has gone global."

"They were good," Leandro agreed. "But how did we get onto Iran? Oh yes, that man's death in Brussels. You think there's some link?"

Luis Miguel put a finger to his lips, but nodded his head.

"I've no idea," he said, still nodding his head. "Anyway, I get enough of all that sitting at my desk. I thought we were going to have a pleasant lunch, which would allow me to forget the papers I have to read."

"You're right. It's my fault. However, let this lunch be the first in a series. We can't allow another ten years to go by."

He thought for a moment.

"Tell you what, Louis, perhaps you'd like to come along to one of our Thursday lunches."

He used the French version of Luis Miguel's name, an affectation common to a certain upper strata of Buenos Aires society, for whom all things European had always carried extra prestige.

"Mostly the gang from university. And a rugby man or two. But they're fun...and cheap! Doctors, lawyers, some engineers. Strong opinions on every subject. Politics, economics, a little sex. On second thoughts, quite a lot of sex."

Leandro laughed, Luis Miguel too, although Leandro detected something less than total conviction.

"By the way, wives are never invited."

"I'm not married, anyway."

"I have some recollection of a beautiful girl cheering you from the touchline. Wasn't there?"

"There may have been," Luis Miguel hesitated. "Can't offhand think who that might have been."

"I seem to recollect that she was pretty. That's all I can remember."

"So you're also leading a bachelor life now, as I understand?"

"If you call having a girlfriend who runs my life for me being a bachelor, then the answer is yes. But it's almost back to monogamy."

"You make it sound terrible. But by the grin on your face, it's obviously not so bad."

"You're right. I love every minute of it. She's of Middle Eastern origin, *turcos* from Syria originally, with very definite ideas on the whole

Middle Eastern question. She'd probably give you a run of your money."

"I'd be delighted to meet her someday."

Some ten minutes later, Luis Miguel pleaded the need to get back to his desk for a phone call with Brussels.

"It's actually to do with Sanchez. A number of loose ends to be tied. Not that it's me that's doing the tying. Messy business. No, this is my territory, I'm inviting," he added, seeing Leandro producing his wallet.

He waved to the owner, writing in the air.

"I settle up the account at the end of the month. Anyway, Leandro, it's been really good to see you again after so long. And if business allows, I'll take you up on that lunch with your friends. Sounds fun. Here's my cell phone. Probably better than coming through the switchboard."

He handed Leandro his Ministry card, having first scribbled a number on the back.

"Don't forget the game next Saturday. Take care, Leandro."

Leandro remained at the table and ordered another coffee. He wondered again about the mysterious cmholland, who had pointed him in this direction. Luis Miguel seemed very close to the subject of Argentina's relations with Iran. That didn't mean that he would necessarily step out of line. But it was also clear he was not a fan of the present administration. How much he might not be a fan remained to be tested.

Tuesday, 10 June 2008 (PM) – LA PLATA, PROVINCIA DE BUENOS AIRES

The Director had caught a bus from the terminal at Retiro to La Plata, the capital of the Province of Buenos Aires. Like so many provincial cities, life in La Plata moved at a different pace, even though it lay only 60 kilometres east of Buenos Aires.

He now found himself standing outside the gate of a single-storey house on the southern outskirts of the town. A dog lying on the small, untidy lawn found the all-consuming battle with its fleas more critical even than barking at this stranger, who now pushed open the gate and walked up to the front door. He pressed the bell and waited. He pressed again and this time detected the scraping of a chair somewhere inside. A shuffling of feet and then the door was opened as far as the security chain would allow.

"Hamid called you, I believe. We agreed to meet today."

Through the crack in the door, he could see a man grown prematurely old, unshaven, hair grey, clothes dishevelled, hesitating as if trying to recollect.

"Ah, yes. One minute please."

The door was pushed shut again. The sound of shuffling receding. Then lowered voices.

He turned round on the doorstep and surveyed the street. The house was one of a line of modest suburban villas, most in an advanced state of disrepair, the vintage of the parked cars indicative of the fact that Argentina's economic recovery had not filtered through to every layer of society. The street was practically empty, other than the inevitable dogs, one even lying in the middle of the road. A pale sun was making little impact on the temperature.

He turned back towards the door, hearing the sound of shuffling return. The clinking of the safety chain as it was removed and the door opened.

"Come in please," the old man grunted.

Judging by the temperature, a gas-fired stove, visible through a door into what appeared to be a small sitting room, was the only source of heat.

As his eyes became accustomed to the semi-gloom of the place, the Director could see that everything was rundown and shabby. A curtain half hanging off its rail allowed a little daylight to filter in. A couple of deformed arm-chairs, the springs showing through in several places. And everywhere an overpowering smell of sweat and cat's urine, which combined with the odour of stale food from the kitchen, almost had him retching.

"You have come from Hamid. A good boy. A true son of his father. To whom I owe a great deal. So how can I help you?"

He could see the old man was studying him closely.

"Thank you for receiving me, Señor. Yes, I believe Hamid spoke to you a week ago. There is a service you can render me and so pay some of your debt to his family."

The old man was nodding.

"Please tell me what I can do."

"I understand from Hamid that you may have contacts with certain skills. Skills of a less pleasant nature."

The old man thought for a minute.

"That is correct. I served for many years in the Buenos Aires provincial police. One meets many interesting people in that job. I retired about five years ago. As you can see, my pension does not take me very far. I must apologise for the poverty of my hospitality."

"Please. No need."

He waited for the old man to install himself in one of the armchairs, not without some difficulty - arthritis probably - and draw a frayed blanket over his knees.

"Depending upon what you plan to do, I would make different recommendations. I would need to know a little of what you had in mind."

A reasonable request.

"I'm afraid that I need to take someone to the limit - if you understand what I mean."

"Would this person have some kind of bodyguard to overcome?"

"No, they have no protection."

"Is it to take place in town, or in some more favourable environment?"

"The town where the person lives. So whoever you suggest might also need break-in skills."

"What is the approximate date?"

"I would like to get it done in the next ten days."

"And will the final act involve a swift execution or a more prolonged process?"

"It might involve either. I would prefer to have two people."

"And - though of course I will not share this with them - are the chances of being caught high or low?"

He thought for a minute.

"Probably low."

"Obviously I need to consider whether, if they are caught, all this will come out."

"Of course."

The old man pointed in the direction of a small pile of notebooks on the dresser.

"Please, could you just pass me those?"

He got up and handed the old man a couple of children's exercise books, the first of which he began to consult, turning the pages slowly. Now and again he would lift his eyes and stare into the middle distance, as if trying to visualise whether the name he was looking at matched the requirement. The process lasted some ten minutes, in total silence. Finally, he looked once more at his visitor.

"I have a couple of names which may suit you. What's more, they often work together in this kind of situation. They are still serving in the force, but that is no obstacle. I know they have undertaken this kind of work before and, apparently, have never been caught. However, they will expect to get paid. Well."

"Naturally. Have you any idea of their rate?"

The old man was thinking, presumably calculating a figure to include himself. Perhaps there was a way of getting round this.

"Before you reply, let me suggest that you and I reach a separate agreement. In this way, you can be more confident you will get your share."

The old man paused in his calculations.

"I would normally take ten percent for the introduction."

"Depending upon what you suggest for them, that would be perfectly in order."

The old man closed his eyes. "Ten thousand dollars for each of them."

'And no doubt your second ten percent is in there also', the Director thought to himself.

"Fine. I would not want to go higher. Which means two thousand dollars for you. I would give you one thousand for setting up my meeting with them. Could we do that today?"

"I can try and call them now. Though, if that fails, I may have to try later. In the evening when they come off duty. Could you pass me that cell phone?" he said, pointing at a Nokia on the windowsill, which was well on the way to becoming a museum piece.

He dialled the first number, but from the look on his face he was not getting through.

"Let me try the second number."

Again he dialled. This time he nodded. The ensuing conversation appeared to be conducted around the subject of how best to dispose of a rabid dog. The old man was recommending two people, one to control the animal, the other to dispatch it. A number of other coded messages were exchanged, until finally the old man pressed the 'off' button.

"I will have final confirmation later tonight when he's been able to speak to his partner. I indicated the price, which seemed acceptable."

"I am most grateful to you."

Handing the old man a slip of paper, he continued.

"This is the number of a cell phone you can use once - but only once - to confirm their agreement this evening. I would wish to meet them either tomorrow or the day after in Buenos Aires. This evening, I will give you the time of that meeting. If they agree, I will need the cell number of one of them to confirm the address. But I will confirm that only on the day of the meeting. Is that clear?"

The old man slowly repeated the main points.

"Good. I will now give you half your commission, the other half when the job is done."

From the inside pocket of his jacket, he produced a small clip of ten one-hundred dollar bills. The old man accepted them gratefully.

"Please remember, that the number I've given you can only be used once. If necessary, I will give you another number this evening when you call me. Please, do not trouble yourself," he added, standing. "I will let myself out. And thank you. I will tell Hamid that you have paid your debt when the job is done."

The old man shook his hand.

There might have been someone else in the house when he knocked. But of that person, there had been no sign.

A minute later, having replaced his knitted cap and dark glasses, he was closing the garden gate. With so little action in the street, curious neighbours behind net curtains were almost certainly a fact of life. Nothing had changed, not even the dog lying in the middle of the road.

Thursday, 12 June 2008 (PM) - ALMAGRO

The Director was sitting in a cafe. He had been there for nearly an hour, the two previous hours spent on public transport, switching from buses to taxis since leaving his hotel. There had been no sign of anyone following him. Nor had he seriously expected it, having given no clue as to where he was staying.

Since his arrival some ten days earlier from Misiones, apart from his visit to La Plata, he had spent most of the time in his hotel bedroom, only occasionally visiting the shops near his hotel or taking a quick meal at one of the small restaurants around Once. A whole day had been spent getting to know the area in which the target lived. And the occasional evening being ministered to by Sonia, the physiotherapist.

When he'd asked the hotel manager one evening where he might be able to find someone to give him a massage, the man had smiled and written down a number on one of the hotel visiting cards.

"You will find that Sonia can provide everything you need."

Somewhat to his surprise, it turned out that Sonia was actually a very good *masseuse*, although her other talents, weighing in at a modest ninety kilos, had proven perhaps less irresistible. Fine in small doses, particularly if the need was great.

In five minutes, they should be arriving. The choice of cafe had been communicated to them only two hours ago, as agreed with the old man in La Plata. From his position close to the large window, he could look straight across the street at the cafe opposite, watching arrivals and departures. The less fashionable neighbourhood of Almagro, which he had selected, meant that he and those he was to meet should blend in easily. A group of workmen from a nearby building site emerged from the cafe, causing the two men approaching from the corner to pause just long enough for him to see that one of them was carrying a blue and orange rucksack over his shoulder. The identification he was to look for. He watched them go into the cafe. Calling over his waiter, he paid for his coffees and sandwiches.

He got up. No one else moved. Turning right out of the cafe, he stopped briefly to look into the window of a shoe shop. Out of the corner of his eye he checked that no one was leaving behind him. He walked up to the corner, crossed the street and made his way back along the opposite pavement.

Simple wooden tables, a tiled floor, a long bar down one side with two men behind it. Three of the tables occupied near the entrance. The blue and orange rucksack propped against the leg of a table at the rear. The table preferred by anyone wanting to monitor arrivals. Or make a quick getaway out the back. Only one man at the table.

He moved in his direction and placed a copy of that day's Clarín next to the rucksack. The man hardly looked up, but pointed in the direction of an empty chair. He sat down, placing both hands flat on the table. At that moment, the second of the two men emerged from the back of the cafe and joined them.

"All okay? *Todo bien?*"

It was the first who asked the question.

He nodded. "*Todo bien.*"

They ordered coffees, nothing else said until the first man spoke again.

"Have you got the envelope?"

The Director pulled it out from the inner pocket of his jacket and placed it on the table.

"Please check that you understand it."

The larger of the two men slit it open with his coffee spoon. Carefully, he pulled out a sheet of paper and three photographs held together with a paperclip. On the paper, a name, an address and a single telephone number.

"Ten thousand dollars now, the same amount when the job is done."

The two men looked at each other.

"Now that we know who it is, the price goes up!" The larger of the two men had spoken.

He had been expecting that. Although Argentines were well known for renegotiating every contract, in this business they were little different from their breed anywhere around the world. He wasn't too worried, since he had genuine doubts as to whether they would live long enough to enjoy the money. The life expectancy of people like the two men who sat in front of him, however much they might be moonlighting from the Buenos Aires provincial police force, the infamous *Bonaerense*, was low. He had made contingency plans which might save him the second payment, but giving in too easily might alert them.

He reacted angrily, keeping his voice low.

"That's not what was agreed," he retorted.

"Maybe not. But that's what it is today, here, now. Now that we know enough. An extra ten thousand."

He looked doubtful. "I may have to consult."

"No you won't. We leave with a deal. Or we make it just that little bit harder for you to leave at all."

He pretended to be impressed by the threat and adopted a look of frustration, before finally giving in with a bad grace.

"Very well, fifteen now. I haven't got twenty here."

The two men looked at each other. The second man nodded. He should perhaps have been surprised that it had been so easy.

"*Está bien.*"

From inside his jacket the Director extracted a second envelope.

"Here's ten."

From the back pocket of his jeans he produced another wad of one hundred dollar bills, divided into thousands, held together by a rubber band. Shielded by his hand, he counted out five and slipped them across the table. The risk that they might take it all was small. They probably suspected that he knew more about how to get to them than was actually the case. Not that he wouldn't find a way to get it out of the old man in La Plata if necessary.

The first man slit open the envelope and with the tips of his fingers checked that it contained ten folds of ten one-hundred dollar bills. He nodded to his partner.

"What's the deadline?"

"You will take the person on Friday of next week. Ring the number at the bottom of the page to indicate that the job has been done and that you are holding him at his flat. I repeat. At his flat. As of Friday night. We will meet there. You will stay with me until we've finished. Do not make contact with that number more than once. The person who replies will also tell you how and where to collect the balance. Is all that clear?"

The larger man nodded.

"I'll be going now. If necessary, I'll contact you via our intermediary in La Plata. Do not leave for another five minutes"

Without shaking their hands, he got up from the table and walked out onto the street, turning left and left again at the corner. He stopped the second taxi coming past.

Although he could not exclude the possibility that the two men had not come alone, it was unlikely, given the assignment and the fee he was paying, that the circle would be much larger. Another hour or so covering his tracks should suffice to get him back to his hotel undetected.

Friday, 13 June 2008 (PM) – CALLE LEVENE, BUENOS AIRES

"And another thing. We've got to do something about upgrading your social life. A girl like me can't simply be hidden away."

"Impossible. Nobody could hide you away."

"I was thinking of an audience slightly more sophisticated than the pizzeria round the corner. And, more importantly, I want to show *you* off."

"But I don't want to be shown off!" Leandro snapped.

"What you want and what you'll get aren't always compatible. For some strange reason, I received an invitation to dinner at the Russian Ambassador's residence. Can't think why. Don't think I've ever met anyone from there. I suppose it's possible that Carla's new *patrón* might be behind it. Anyway, the invitation specifically asks for you as well. So I'm going to parade you. It's tonight."

"How the hell would he know about you and me? Though you're probably right. It must be Viktor Alexievich. But why? Formal dinner? I hate that kind of thing."

The look on Leandro's face showed that being paraded was certainly not high on his agenda.

"And there's no point in putting on that face. It's an order!"

"Anyway, as you say, I've got nothing to wear."

"Not quite. Your blazer will be back from the cleaners this afternoon."

"Bitch! I wondered where it had got to yesterday. I'm not master in my own home. Even the decor is being changed."

"And don't you just love it!"

Just before her departure for Zürich, Sam had appeared with a huge photograph by Helmut Newton. A wasp-waisted brunette in a silken corset, sexy suspenders and long opera gloves, looking wistfully skywards in front of what appeared to be an unfinished block of flats.

In the middle distance, a man in a black suit and dark glasses, stretched out on the pavement. Dead?

"Christ, what will my clients think? Do I have to?"

"You only bring lovers here. And, given your new inclinations, you might as well give them a foretaste of what's in store," she had thrown back, as she steadied herself on a chair to remove his wall map of Argentina.

"Somehow, those images look so much better in your flat," had been his final weak riposte.

With Sam away in Zürich, he had caught himself more than once studying the photo on returning from the office, a whisky in one hand. Perhaps a matter of getting acclimatised.

The Russian ambassador's flat was located not far from Recoleta cemetery, a part of town which housed a number of upmarket executive residences. An elegant building dating back to the mid-1940s, entirely renovated to command monthly rents of many thousands of dollars. Out of respect for their host, Sam and Leandro arrived more punctually than would usually be the case. In Argentine society, where guests could easily arrive an hour late, to arrive on time was usually referred to as '*hora inglesa*', in recognition of a stronger tradition of punctuality in the Anglo-Saxon community. Few hosts wasted their time suggesting it.

A servant showed them into the spacious drawing room, which, alongside the comfortable modern furniture, displayed a collection of icons and modern art on the walls.

"Ah, Miss Haidar, welcome. And you too, Dr Flemming."

Their host greeted them warmly.

"The ladies will be with us in a minute. What can I offer you? We naturally have a large selection of excellent vodka. Maybe some champagne? Or whisky?"

He focused on Sam.

"You are most elegant tonight, Miss Haidar. Indeed, if I may say so, quite beautiful. Or may I call you Samira? Please call me Mikhail."

Sam was wearing a pleated black silk dress, in the style of the 1920s couturier Fortuny. The work of Fabian Zitta, Sam's Argentine 'fetish' fashion designer, it had the unquestionable virtue of partially revealing her breasts, from which the ambassador appeared to have some difficulty in detaching his gaze. Black patent leather stiletto-heeled pumps and virtually no jewellery completed the picture. With the exception of the Druze star pendant.

"Ambassador, I give you my full permission to say so. And please call me Samira. I'd love some vodka, ice cold, no rocks."

The Ambassador turned to Leandro.

"I'll have the same, thank you, but with rocks."

The ambassador gestured to the waiter, who reappeared within a minute with a tray of drinks.

"You have some very interesting paintings, Ambassador," Sam said. One or two from the early 20s, a great period in Russian - or should I say Soviet - art. That looks like a Tatlin drawing. And perhaps a Rodchenko on that wall? Before he gave up painting?"

Leandro didn't know whether to feel proud or embarrassed by yet another flagrant display of his girlfriend's erudition.

"I'm most impressed, Samira. Your knowledge of Soviet art does you credit. You're quite right. The drawing is mine. However, sadly, the Rodchenko is provided by our ministry. Not even our salaries would have been sufficient."

The three of them were joined by the ambassador's wife, Galya. If perhaps a little overweight, she was nevertheless a handsome woman, a good example of the new Russian middle class.

"We've discovered that Samira is not only elegant, but also very knowledgeable about Soviet art," he said. "What about those girls? Are they going to keep our guests waiting for long?"

"No, Mikhail, they'll be with us in a minute. Finishing touches. Yes, Manuel, I'll have some champagne."

At this point, a handsome, dark-haired man of about forty was ushered into the room.

"Ah, Vladimir, good to see you. Samira, may I introduce Vladimir Mikhailovich Kuznetsov, a new arrival at our embassy. How long is it now? About three months? Vladimir Mikhailovich, this is Señorita Haidar."

Vladimir Mikhailovich made a slight bow.

"At your service, Señorita Haidar. Nearly four months," he added, turning to the ambassador.

"And this is Dr Flemming, one of this country's most astute economic observers. And, I believe, at one time a banker."

They must have been doing their homework.

He noted that the new arrival was observing Sam closely. Physically fit, well-cut suit, Hermes tie. The look of a ladies' man.

"Vladimir Mikhailovich is on our political side. He's something of a Middle East specialist, so he'll have a lot of learning to do to get used to Argentine ways. Your last post was Amman, if I'm not mistaken?"

"Yes, Ambassador, I spent two most interesting years there. Very different, you're right."

"Leandro – may I also call you that? We'd welcome your views on where this agricultural confrontation is going. Madame President seems determined to force it through," the Ambassador went on. "I'm told she's going to send it to Congress any time now."

These diplomats never seemed able to relax.

"I think it's going to be a matter of who blinks first. Not something you can accuse the Kirchners of doing often. What is true, however, is that the *campo* is getting the support of the Argentine middle classes. You're seeing it with sporadic *cacerolazos*. Though, unlike in the 2001 financial crisis, all this banging of pots and pans from the rooftops isn't going to bring down this government."

The Ambassador nodded his agreement.

"Galya, please go and get those girls. The party's too small for half the group to be absent. What can I give you, Vladimir Mikhailovich?"

"I see a good single malt on your bar, Ambassador."

"You've picked up some un-Russian habits, I see. Not very *kulturny* as they used to say in the old days," the Ambassador smiled.

The door at the far end of the drawing room was thrown open as the Ambassador's wife returned with two beautiful young women in tow, one blonde, the other a redhead.

Samira gasped.

"Tatyana? What are you doing here in Buenos Aires? You never told me you were coming!"

"So you know each other?" the Ambassador beamed. "That's wonderful. She's a great friend of my daughter, Larissa, they studied together at Moscow University. Larissa, this is Samira." he added.

In spite of their embrace, Sam once again detected that same cold hostility in Tatyana's eyes. Larissa on the other hand seemed more sincere, although not going much beyond the traditional Argentine light kiss on the cheek.

Galya, following in the wake of the two young women, was making a gesture of helplessness behind their backs, as if to transmit her disapproval at the way the girls had got themselves up. Sam, having seen Tatyana performing in Zürich, was not in the least surprised by the chasm of the décolleté, the tightness of the black skirt, and the length of the red patent boots. All this surmounted by that voluminous mane of red hair cascading over her shoulders. Vladimir Mikhailovich's jaw clenched visibly. Sam took another mouthful of vodka to disguise a smile, throwing a sideways glance at Leandro to watch his reaction. Tatyana might have overplayed her hand as far as her own man was concerned. She knew from personal experience that he was susceptible to sexy women in boots. She had taught him that. But she also knew that his youthful browsing through Vogue and Elle, to which he had confessed one day as a means of looking at pretty girls with a clear conscience in his teenage years, had shaped his eye in matters of style and elegance. Perhaps not quite the terms applicable to Tatyana's display this evening.

Larissa was more discreet. A simple black silk dress off the shoulder, cut loosely in such a fashion as to show off a fine figure. Her long blonde hair elegantly piled up on her head. Of the two, she was probably the more dangerous to a man with taste. Russian womanhood had certainly been transformed since the day that Boris Yeltsin had climbed on his tank in front of the White House!

Watching Leandro, she could see he was giving nothing away.

So what was going on?

The coincidence of Tatyana's sudden arrival in Buenos Aires with the invitation to the Ambassador's private residence, in what looked to be a very small and select group, all suggested something rather more than a simple increase in the ambassadorial entertainment allowance. That Larissa and Tatyana might be friends from Moscow University seemed plausible enough. But, Sam wondered, to what extent did Larissa have any idea of Tatyana's foray into the world of international escorts as part of Carla's team in Zürich? And what about that shadowy figure in the background, Carla's new *patrón* , Viktor Alexievich? As she had discovered from Carla in their conversations after her rescue, it was clear that Viktor Alexievich was completely plugged into the new Russian power structure, having mobilised the resources of at least two embassies, in Brazil and Uruguay, to facilitate the operation which had rescued her. The *siloviki* network no doubt. Could the Buenos Aires embassy simply be added to the list? She guessed that Viktor Alexievich and the Ambassador, Mikhail, might belong roughly to the same age group. Anyway, if Viktor Alexievich was as powerful as Carla made out, Mikhail would certainly know who he was.

But she had no time to reach any conclusions, as the wife of the Ambassador signalled that they should go through to the dining room. A quick count of the places showed that one guest was still missing. Although the Ambassadress placed Leandro on her right, as old-fashioned protocol would have it, the left remained empty. Sam was on the right of the Ambassador. She was relieved to note that Tatyana was not next to Leandro. With that bitch, who could tell?

"Well, my friends," the Ambassador began, "a small toast to all our guests. To you, Samira, for bringing such beauty to this table," and he toasted her directly, his gaze once more having some difficulty in rising above the level of her neck line, "to you, Tatyana, for having come so far to find your friend," this time looking at Tatyana and his daughter, "and to you, Leandro. We are honoured to have so prestigious an observer of the Argentine scene at our table."

He looked down the table towards his wife.

"And of course to you, *дорогая моя*, as always."

The toast had hardly finished, when the door to the dining room opened to a small, energetic-looking man of around fifty.

"Viktor Alexievich! What timing!"

So Tatyana *had* come accompanied!

Having greeted the Ambassador and his wife like old friends and embracing their daughter, Viktor Alexievich paused behind his empty chair. An almost imperceptible nod to Tatyana, before turning to Sam.

"And you are Samira. We meet at last. As you can imagine, I've heard a lot about you."

For once, Sam was confused as to how best to react. That this man had orchestrated her rescue from Dávila was highly unlikely to be known to any of the guests with the exception of Tatyana and Leandro. Nor likely Viktor Alexievich's sponsorship of Carla's escort agency. Prudence dictated. The less said the better.

"And you are...?"

Playing it safe.

"Viktor Alexievich. I believe we have a close friend in common in Zürich. I passed through there on my way here and she asked me to make sure to look you up. So I asked my old friend, Mikhail, to invite both of you," he added, smiling at Leandro, and also clearly playing it cautiously.

"Viktor Alexievich! I have so much to thank you for," Sam said, "May I kiss you?"

"I would be blind to refuse," Viktor Alexievich replied, embracing Sam.

Leandro detected that, other than Tayana, the others were having difficulty following the exchange. What could this girl Samira possibly have to thank Viktor Alexievich for?

He sat down between her and the Ambassadress.

"You were just making a toast, Mikhail. May I make one?"

The Ambassador indicated his consent.

"To more intimate relations between Russians and Argentines. And most of all to the beautiful company around this table."

Viktor Alexievich raised his glass in the direction of the four women, who acknowledged his words with smiles and raised their glasses.

He had better not be referring to Tatyana and Leandro, Sam thought to herself.

"To Russian-Argentine relations," they echoed.

The Ambassador, having said a few words about how he and Viktor Alexievich had got to know each other many years earlier, finally turned to his friend.

"Tell us, Viktor Alexievich, how have your meetings been going? Any progress with our friends at INVAP?"

So Viktor Alexievich was also in the nuclear business! Leandro kicked himself for not having done more research into Carla's *patrón*. All this was getting way beyond a matter of simple coincidence.

"Not too badly."

But the look Viktor Alexievich threw the Ambassador indicated the subject was closed. Sam detected fleeting embarrassment on Mikhail's face. He immediately changed the subject.

"Leandro, have you ever been to Russia?"

"No, I'd love to go sometime."

"Capitalism perhaps at its wildest. Wouldn't you agree, Viktor Alexievich?"

"Certainly. I should know."

The Ambassador raised his glass.

"Viktor Alexievich, I drink to your continued success."

Another round of vodka disappeared. At this rate, Leandro was wondering whether he was going to make it to the first course.

Mikhail turned back to Leandro.

"I will have a word with my Economic Section. Might you be interested in an invitation to speak at a conference in Moscow?"

"I would be delighted."

"How long are you here for, Viktor Alexievich?" Sam asked her neighbour.

"Probably another week. Maybe two. Not much more."

Sam looked across at Tatyana.

"And you, Tatyana?"

"Oh, my stay is open-ended."

No shit, Sam thought. She wondered how the Viktor Alexievich - Tatyana duo would perform. Coming together in Buenos Aires was no coincidence. Perhaps he was using his niece's undoubted skills as part of his negotiation. Not a bad idea. Half the male population in Buenos Aires would sell their grandmothers to get alongside Tatyana. Luckily,

Leandro belonged to the other half. Or should do, if he valued his safety.

They were back in the drawing room, Sam, Tatyana and Leandro standing in front of the fireplace.

"I told you about Tatyana, whom I met in Zürich."

Sam had shared her concern about the true intentions of this dramatic redhead who now towered before him, only in part due to the ten centimetre stiletto heels she was wearing. If anything, Sam had perhaps understated the air of dangerous malevolence this girl exuded. He had no difficulty in imagining her standing over some hapless male, who would be paying way over the odds for the privilege of being maltreated by her.

"Yes, of course, what brings Tatyana to Buenos Aires?"

They were speaking English, Spanish not appearing to be one of Tatyana's talents. She didn't wait for Sam to reply.

"So, you're the Leo we've heard so much about."

Larissa threw a quizzical glance at her, again wondering quite what the link might be between her Moscow friend and these two Argentines.

"Only good, I trust," Leandro responded.

Tatyana had the good grace to allow a faint smile to cross her lips.

"Oh, certainly, you have many admirers."

The look on Larissa's face suggesting she was losing the thread completely, Leandro steered the conversation into safer waters.

"But you haven't told us why you've come to Buenos Aires. Is this your first visit?"

"Larissa's father has been posted here for a few years already and she has been inviting me to come down for far too long. She seems to think there might be some Argentine men I should meet. Now I can see why."

Sam's eyes flashed. The incursion was brazen. Her first instincts had been correct.

"If you're here for a few weeks, we must show you some of the sights," Sam replied smoothly. "Tell you what. Let me give a dinner at my place in the coming weeks. If by then you and Larissa have already found some of these Argentine specimens, please bring them along. Otherwise, I'll dig some out of my address book."

"I thought I'd burnt it," Leandro muttered to her.

"What's all this I hear about dinner parties?"

Larissa's father had silently joined the group.

Tatyana had now placed herself next to Leandro, on the other side of Sam. He detected her hand caressing the top of his thigh. This wasn't the kind of behaviour Sam would tolerate for an instant. If there wasn't to be a full-blooded diplomatic incident here and now, a discreet exit was in order.

"Sam, don't forget we've promised to drop in on my mother. It's her birthday, Ambassador. You want to fix an evening for your dinner party now?"

"Why not?"

Sam looked at Larissa and Tatyana.

"I'll get back to you with a date for the dinner."

"Give us plenty of warning," Tatyana replied.

"Fine," Sam confirmed. Leandro thought he detected a slight edge in her voice.

The lift doors had hardly closed when Sam exploded.

"Fuck that girl! Did you see what she was doing?"

"I didn't actually see it, but I felt it," Leandro replied, with a grin. "Quite enjoyed it, in fact."

"Then fuck you, Leandro Flemming! What are you doing, even allowing that bitch to get within a metre of you? What game is she playing? I know that your reputation as my lover has made it as far as some of Carla's squad, but this is a step too far. I knew that cow was bad news when I first set eyes on her in Zürich. She's Carla's *patrón's* spy in the camp, Carla knows that. But I wonder whether Carla knows she's down here."

On the pavement, she pulled out her cell phone and dialled Zürich.

"Come on, come on, Carla, pick up!"

When no one answered, Sam left Carla a message to ring back at the earliest opportunity.

"I'm pretty sure she's in Zürich, she's only just come back from somewhere in the Mediterranean. Some huge yacht! She sent me a photo. I need a drink.

"Even after all that vodka?"

They picked up a taxi on the corner of Pueyrredon.

"Where are we going? To my knowledge we don't have another party. All that business with your mother," Sam said.

"It was the only way I could think of getting out before you turned nasty!"

"Thanks. For that you can take me to Ferona. It'll just be warming up at this hour. I feel like something different. As long as you've got cash, since I'm told they don't accept cards. And lots of it. Which is all you deserve, after your behaviour with that Russian bitch."

The taxi driver had by now switched off the engine and was patiently watching them in the rear-view mirror, a broad grin slowly spreading over his face.

"I haven't got the cash, Señorita, but if you need an impartial arbiter, with twenty years in the business, I've seen most things."

Sam's look of fury faded and she and Leandro burst out laughing.

"You're very kind, Señor, but it's not serious. This man knows when he's defeated even before the battle has started. Don't you, Leo?"

Leandro looked at the taxi driver and shrugged his shoulders.

"Have you got a good response to that?" he asked the driver.

"Señor, there is no response to that. Particularly when it comes from so beautiful a woman …"

"Maybe I should be going to dinner with you," Sam threw in the direction of the driver.

"Perhaps, Señorita. But el Señor looks a bit too strong for my taste. And the club sounds as though it's more than I've taken in a week. I thank you, nevertheless, for the invitation. I'll go to sleep smiling tonight."

Sam lent forward and placed a resounding kiss on his unshaven cheek.

Leandro pretended to be jealous.

"For that, Señorita, I would drive you to Chile for free. Fortunately, however, it's only as far as Palermo Hollywood."

He started the engine with a flourish and pulled out into the traffic. Judging by the blaring of horns and the squeal of brakes behind them, a glance in his side mirror might have been a minimal precaution.

"They should look where they're going," was his only response.

Sam and Leandro leaned back in the seat. Silently, her hand found his crotch and began softly to stroke it. A peace offering? Not that war had even come close to being declared.

"So, what do we make of all that?" she finally asked.

"Hard to tell. Mikhail's little *faux pas* seems to have told us why Viktor Alexievich is here. Interesting."

"And where do you think Tatyana fits in?"

"Part of the marketing effort?"

"Almost certainly. All this talk of finding some Argentine *macho*. All in all, rather a strange party. Though the vodka was delicious. And what about that guy Kuznetsov? What's his role?"

"I thought you were going to tell me," Leandro replied. "Didn't he give you his card as we left?"

"As a matter of fact, he did. Rather discreetly, I thought."

"My impression as well. You don't trust Tatyana. Not sure I trust *your* friend Vladimir Mikhailovich. That makes us square."

Saturday, 10 June 2008 (AM) – FERONA BAR, HUMBOLT 1445, BUENOS AIRES

Although there was the usual queue at the entrance as befitted one of Buenos Aires' most fashionable night spots, the wait for a table was short.

"I wonder what's brought that bitch down here. Carla has the impression that she's Viktor Alexievich's spy. At the same time, it's my guess that her arrival has something to do with me - and perhaps with you. This isn't tourism or looking up an old school friend. What do you think, Leo? And I'm not interested in your views on her body."

Leandro smiled. "Before we get into that, what do you want to drink."

"Evading the issue, as usual, I see. And I thought my attentions in the back of the taxi might have made you more compliant. Anyway, you're right. What do you suggest?"

"A couple of pisco sours, no sugar around the rim of the glass. They do them very well here."

"How do you know? Been here before? I thought you didn't do that kind of thing."

He ignored her minor fit of jealousy.

Sipping the pisco, they studied the assembled company. Even in the worst economic crisis, Argentine bars and restaurants usually came out well. With the money now flowing out of the agricultural sector and the country growing, Ferona was full, the crowd young and elegant.

"We should come here more often," Sam said. "It's got a good atmosphere."

She looked around the room.

"Though some of the men look a bit Mafiosi to my taste. That pair over there, for instance."

She nooded in the direction of a nearby table. Leandro followed her eyes, but shrugged his shoulders.

"Not one of the cheapest in town. So more than likely to have the odd unattractive customer. It's a worldwide trend. Anyway, you're paying. My consolation for Pumas beating Scotland a few days ago. You can't imagine how I suffered."

"Enough to give any man schizophrenia, I would imagine. Anyway, nice try. However, after your behaviour with that bitch Tatyana, the bill is firmly coming to you. I thought I made that clear in the taxi!"

"I don't know what you're talking about," Leandro said.

"Don't give me that. She was touching you up and you were enjoying it. Don't you dare deny it."

"For Christ sake, it must have lasted all of five seconds."

"With that girl, that's five too many. Anyway, I don't want to give her any more of my precious time. But what *do* we make of her sudden arrival? There's got to be a reason."

"Give me some guidance. Tell me a little more."

"She's Viktor Alexievich's niece or something. She arrived in Zurich a couple of weeks after my rescue. Aside from her vulgarly obvious talents, she doesn't quite fit in with the rest of the girls. She's much tougher and more aggressive, and I suspect they don't really trust her. I also detect that she told them quite a bit about what happened to me, which means at the very least that Viktor Alexievich took her into his confidence. Up to now, I would say that Carla merely suspects her of being sent to keep an eye on the business."

Sam's cell phone began to vibrate. She looked at the incoming call.

"It's Carla. Ringing back. With all this noise, I'll have to take it outside."

The call lasted well over five minutes before she returned.

"Interesting! Carla didn't know Tatyana had come to Buenos Aires. She simply disappeared one day, saying nothing. And apparently hasn't been answering her cell either. She couldn't offer any reason why Tatyana might have come down here, but like me, she doesn't think that it's just to look up an old school friend. Carla apparently asked Viktor Alexievich if he knew where she was and thought his response rather evasive. So, in the words of the English playwright, the plot thickens!"

"Which English playwright?"

"Haven't a clue, but I like the expression. Anyway don't change the subject? Why is she here?"

Leandro paused to consider the problem.

"I agree with you, this isn't a social visit. Not with the sudden invitations to you and me. And on top of that, you're becoming inseparable, if they've also accepted an invitation to your place. It's not as if you're bosom pals."

Sam let out a bitter laugh.

"From the moment we first met, we were bound to be enemies. I think I told you that."

Leandro nodded. With his usual clinical approach, Leandro presented the options.

"It's hard to tell whether her visit is connected to something that's happened in the past, something current, or even in the future. One way and another, I rather doubt it has much to do with past events. Alexievich must have done his research into Carla's relationship with Dávila and anyway he knows full well that it's history. That there may be some loose ends down here relating to the way in which they rescued you or killed Dávila can't be ruled out, but it's not someone like Tatyana he would send to handle that, I would have thought."

Leandro sipped his drink.

"Perhaps he thinks you or I, or both of us, are some kind of weak link in a chain," he continued. "Though I don't know what sort of chain. But then again, that would hardly warrant involving the embassy. Anyway, he almost certainly knows how important you are to Carla. Not that that would necessarily prevent him from trying to move you out of the way. But, I can't see why he should want to do so."

"Except to make way for Tatyana. For the rest, so far, I'm with you," Sam said. "I agree, I don't think it has much to do with the past. And I wouldn't rule out the possibility that Tatyana, at a personal level, would be happy to see me off. Hardly likely to endear her to Carla, nevertheless. In the same way the girls all seemed to know that something had happened to me, they also seemed fully aware of my relationship with Carla. As Arabella put it, 'I know you're Carla's girl'. So presumably Tatyana might be interested in displacing me. And possibly, she might be under orders to Viktor on that front. But somehow, I don't think it's about that. There's something else."

Another round of piscos had arrived, Sam made short shrift of hers.

"Feeling better? With all those vodkas as well…"

Sam's ability to hold her drink never ceased to amaze Leandro.

"Yes, much. Go on with your analysis."

"So, if we assume that it's not connected with the past, nor perhaps do we give much importance to the possibility of simple rivalry between two sexy girls—"

Sam interrupted him.

"I'd prefer you not to put me in the same bracket with that bitch! Frankly, she's a whore! And anyway, I'm far sexier than she is. At least, for a discerning man as opposed to just a walking penis."

"So I presume that you've decided that I don't fall into the latter category either. At least that's reassuring."

"Fortunately, although there's nothing the matter with that part of your anatomy, you've also got one hell of a brain. And anyone with a brain would discover limits to Tatyana."

"Brains can be switched off, the other less easily."

"Don't give me that, Leandro, you're not seriously telling me that girl impresses you. At the slightest hint of that, I'll be gone. Never lose sight of that."

The look in Sam's eyes told him that the conversation had moved from simple teasing into more perilous waters and he would be wise to remain in his depth. He reached across the table and took her hand.

"Sam, it's you I love."

"And don't you forget it. Now, back to business. You're playing hard to get with your ideas tonight."

"Okay, so let's focus on what's current."

"And when we've finished with the subject of Tatyana, you're going to tell me what you're up to. Somehow you've managed to evade most of my attempts to find out exactly what you're doing for Frobisher."

Sam's eyes lit up with a look of anticipated triumph. Leandro hesitated. Somehow, Ferona didn't seem to be the right setting for a discussion of that kind.

"Listen, Sam, the subject is a very complex and this isn't the place. Suffice to say that, as you've probably discovered through checking out my computer, it's to do with Iran."

Sam seemed not in the least embarrassed to have had her forays into his computer detected. Her eyes flashed.

"I knew it! Go on."

"Sam, you heard me. Let's talk about it later. As to Tatyana, perhaps when they come to your dinner, whenever that is, we'll get a better idea of what's going on. Now let's enjoy this, for Heaven's sake."

Short-lived enjoyment, as it turned out.

The two men who had caught Sam's eye earlier rose simultaneously from the table they'd been occupying near the centre of the bar, a small automatic in each hand. While one moved swiftly to the entrance and, knocking the doorman aside, opened the door to let in two more men, also armed, his companion had moved over to the bar from which he could cover most of the restaurant.

Silence descended as everyone struggled to grasp what was happening. One of the two men coming in took up a position near the entrance to the kitchen to control any movement there.

Without having to raise his voice, given the silence of fear which now gripped the room, the man by the bar made their intentions clear.

"Anyone using a cell phone will be shot."

This announcement visibly paralysed a number of people in the room, and a small scream rose from one corner. Had anyone had time to begin typing a message out on their phone?

"Everyone puts their hands on the table, where we can see them. Now!"

Hands appeared as if by magic, in many cases quivering.

"Watches, cash, credit cards, jewellery, cell phones. Nothing else. Get them out now! No suspicious movements. We want it all and we want it within the next two minutes. Put it all together on the side of your table."

Sam looked across at Leandro, as if to ask him what they were to do. He merely nodded and began to remove his wristwatch, an old gold Rolex Oyster Perpetual he had inherited from his father. An expression of sadness came into his eyes as he began to undo the black crocodile leather strap. He had been wearing it the day he had been shot down over Malvinas, his father having given it to him just before he had set off for the islands. He did not wear it often, preferring to keep it for more formal events like the evening's dinner party. On the rare occasions he wore a watch, a Swatch was fine and less likely to tempt the minor criminals to be found on many a street corner in the tourist areas of town.

The sight of the bulbous Rolex always brought back memories of those moments when, as a small boy, his father had allowed him to take the watch off his wrist, wind it, or use the second hand to time something. Though the last man to be superstitious, his father had, on strapping it round Leandro's wrist the day before he left for Malvinas, muttered something about it having seen him through good times and bad.

"Do as they say, Sam, this is no time or place for heroics," he murmured.

She appeared outwardly very calm.

She nodded. In fact, she wasn't worried, as she had deliberately taken no jewellery that night. Only the gold and enamel Druze star which always hung at her throat. That wasn't going anywhere. As discreetly as possible, with one hand she undid the clasp in the nape of her neck under her hair, allowing the necklace to drop between her breasts into the waist of her dress. Leandro, watching, faintly shook his head as if to suggest that this might not be a good idea, but she ignored him.

With the leader of the team covering the room, his three companions had begun to move swiftly between the tables, raking the growing piles of jewellery, cell phones, credit cards and cash into the small bag each one of them carried. Watching, Leandro spotted that each man's gun - seemingly of small calibre, possibly a .22, adequate for killing at short range - was equipped with a silencer. They might not be so reluctant to use them. Even though, in this part of Palermo, policemen were to be found on most corners, their role too often one of deterrence rather than intervention. Over the noise of the traffic and the other restaurants and cafes, a silenced shot was unlikely to carry far. Even assuming their attention could be distracted from their cell phones.

"Come on, get it off."

One of the trio moving between the tables was growling at an elderly man, who seemed reluctant to hand over the massive gold watch on his wrist. The gun's barrel was pressed against his forehead.

"I'm going to count to five."

The tone of voice was low.

Leandro watched with a sinking feeling in the pit of his stomach, as the man's wife pleaded with her husband to comply with the instruction. The trim of the older man's hair, the small moustache, the old-fashioned double-breasted blazer he was wearing, with its polished brass buttons, but most of all the arrogant look on his face, all suggested someone more used to giving than receiving orders. Someone not easily intimidated by a minor delinquent. Leandro sensed this confrontation was going to end badly.

"Go to the devil!" the older man spat at him.

A short crack was the only sound as a small red hole appeared in the centre of his forehead and the old man pitched back on his chair into the space behind his table, dead before he hit the ground. The woman screamed and threw herself onto his body.

"Anyone else feeling like being difficult?"

The killer turned towards the rest of the room. What had started off as a tide became a flood, as jewellery, watches and cash poured onto the tables.

One of the three bagmen had reached their table.

"Is that all? Are you sure?"

Leandro nodded.

"Nice watch. Collector's piece? Thank you."

The man smirked and made as if to admire it on his wrist. Leandro's fixed stare concealed his fury.

Their small contribution disappeared into the bag and the man moved on to the next table. In the terrorized silence of the restaurant, the only sound was the sobbing of the woman as she rocked the bleeding head of her husband in her lap.

Then suddenly, it was over. On a signal from the three that their work was done, the fourth joined them at the door and, with a final bow to the petrified company, disappeared into the dark street. Pandemonium immediately ensued, people cursing or screaming as terror and tension were released. No one seemed in a hurry to go through the front door, perhaps fearing the killers might still be on the scene. A man from another table, claiming to be a doctor, was bending over the victim, but, shaking his head, turned his attention instead to the hysterical wife. The owner of the restaurant was already on the phone and within less than five minutes, spinning blue lights announced the arrival of two police cars out front.

Leandro looked over at Sam. An expression of quiet triumph on her face, as she toyed with the Druze star necklace, back in its usual place just above the valley of her breasts. She smiled back.

It was well past midnight before they were finally able to leave, having given their names and addresses, which the four policeman had laboriously taken down in their notebooks. An ambulance had arrived within ten minutes to collect the body and take care of the widow, who was accompanied to the hospital by the doctor and his wife.

Leandro and Sam picked up a taxi which took them back to his flat.

"God, after all that, I need the best brandy you've got," Sam announced, collapsing onto the sofa. "Nice country we live in. That poor man! But, to be frank, he was a fool!"

"'Fraid so. And it happens a lot. Whether it's a case of stupid heroics or that our materialist society has so distorted our values that we're prepared to risk our lives for a watch, I don't know. Though the loss of my father's Rolex really pisses me off. Not to mention the hassle getting back all the cards and documents."

He turned towards her with two glasses of brandy. She got up from the sofa and, taking both glasses out of his hands, pulled him into her arms.

"I know. I'm sorry about your watch. But don't be superstitious. It's more than a Rolex that saved your life that day. My father used to collect watches. Spent fortunes at auctions. Maybe I can find one like it. I'd love to give it to you."

Leandro shook his head and kissed her.

"That's a lovely thought, but little episodes like tonight teach us where our true values lie. The old man, sadly, learned that lesson the hard way."

There was no point in arguing with Leandro, but Sam knew she would need to find the time to go through her father's auction catalogues. She vaguely remembered him mentioning an Italian specialist in Geneva from whom he had bought some of his most valuable pieces. Perhaps, on her next visit to Carla, she would drop in and see him.

Leandro was relieved to detect that the events of the evening had apparently taken Sam's mind off the question of Iran.

Thursday, 19 June 2008 (AM) – EXUMAS, BAHAMAS

The single-engine, high-wing seaplane touched down on the glassy surface of the bay and taxied slowly in the direction of the two yachts lying at anchor farther out from the shore. The larger of the two, over eighty metres in length, its lines sleek and harmonious, painted from stem to stern in the purest white, was lowering a small cutter with twin outboard motors. Sam noted the helicopter on its pad near the stern. She looked towards the beach where a group of people were relaxing on the sand, children splashing in and out of the warm sea.

The seaplane taxied to a large buoy where the cutter was now waiting, with two sailors on board. One of these took a line to one of the seaplane floats and attached it to the ring of the mooring.

"Welcome, Miss. Can you manage? Here, let me give you a hand."

The pilot had opened the side door and was helping Sam to lower herself onto the float. With the help of the sailor, she stepped into the cutter. The pilot passed her two suitcases to the man at the stern, who placed them carefully on one of the cross seats.

"Thank you so much," she said. "That was a wonderful flight."

"My pleasure, Miss. Any time."

The call had come to Sam's cell three days earlier. It was late on the Monday evening and she was reading in bed in her flat.

"Hello? Is that Samira?"

"Yes, who's that? Isn't it rather late?"

"Oh, I'm sorry. This is Aziz. I must have got the hours muddled up. Perhaps I should have subtracted rather than added. You know, we lawyers are not very good at numbers."

Except when it comes to totting up your timesheets, Sam thought.

"No problem, Aziz. It's a pleasure to hear from you. Are you well? Does this call mean you're coming to Argentina?"

"No, sadly, it will have to be another time. I'm phoning on behalf of His Royal Highness. First of all, he sends his best regards and hopes you are well."

"Please thank him and return my best regards."

"He has asked me to extend an invitation to you to join him."

"That would be a great honour. May I ask where?"

"Of course, how stupid of me. He's in the Bahamas, on board his yacht."

It being a few days before the official start of winter in Buenos Aires, Sam's heart leapt at the prospect of some Caribbean sun.

"How wonderful. I am most honoured and delighted. When?"

"It's Tuesday today. I presume it's Tuesday in Buenos Aires?"

"Actually it's still Monday. Although late in the evening."

"He would like you there by Wednesday evening, or possibly Thursday lunchtime. Of course, all flight arrangements will be made as soon as you let me know if this possible."

Although the deadline left hardly any time to prepare, she knew it was out of the question to do anything other than comply. Carla would never forgive her. Let alone her masters in Tel Aviv.

"I'm sure that'll be possible. There are one or two flights every evening from Buenos Aires to Miami. From there no doubt it's just another flight to the Bahamas. Should I see about the tickets?"

"No, no. His private office in London will see to that. They will get back to you within the hour. So I can confirm to His Royal Highness?"

"Yes of course. And please tell him how much I look forward to meeting him again. To being with him."

Sam felt that a little message of intimacy would not be out of place and that she could rely on Aziz to transmit it faithfully. She was pretty certain that Aziz would give a lot to be with her. But he would never dare to trespass.

"Excellent. Good night, Samira. I hope to see you again someday soon."

"Good night, Aziz. Thank you and take care."

Sam lay back against the pillows. At last, the mission had arrived. The mission for which her Mossad handler had briefed her at their meeting in Paris in May. She picked up her laptop and went on the web.

"Order has been placed for delivery before the weekend," she wrote.

Separately, she sent a quick mail to Carla.

"Aziz has made contact on behalf of his client. Off to Bahamas tomorrow night or Wednesday. Wish me well. Love you. Sam."

Within the hour, she had received two responses. One from the Gmail address asking for the destination, which she returned in simple code. The other from the Prince's London office. They must work some terrible hours. Seats had been booked first class on American Airlines, departing just before midnight the following evening from Ezeiza, arriving very early morning in Miami. Onward flight by American Eagle to Nassau, where she would arrive around midday. For various reasons, the Prince's private jet, a Challenger 300, would not be available until the following morning, Thursday, so she was to spend the night at the Ocean Club on Paradise Island, where a room had already been reserved for her. She was to present herself at Nassau airport at 0900 hours on the Thursday morning, in the section reserved for private aircraft. She was given the name of the person in the administration office to ask for. The return flight would be 'open'.

What to take? What to wear? She regretted not having asked Aziz if he could tell her any more about what to expect, who would be there? And how long would it be for? An open return. A week? Longer? One thing she could be certain of. If His Royal Highness had asked her to join him, she had better look her most beautiful and very certainly her most sexy.

She picked up the phone and dialled Leandro. From his muffled voice, it was clear he had been asleep.

"*Mi amor*, sorry to wake you. You all right? It's a bit early for you to be asleep."

"Yes, I'm okay. Hard day and felt the beginnings of a cold coming. Took some aspirins and climbed into bed. What's the matter?" He paused. "I miss you."

"I know, it's been at least twenty-four hours since you made love to me. And I'm afraid it's going to be a bit more before you can hold me again."

"What's happening?"

"The Prince has called. Or rather Aziz. I have to be in the Bahamas the day after tomorrow."

"Bahamas? Not all bad. Though I don't need to tell you what I think about it."

"I know, *amor*. Let's not start that discussion again."

"Good night, Sam. Sleep well. See you tomorrow."

By the morning, there was a mail from Carla in her inbox.

"Wonderful news, Dalal. Remember to take all the right equipment! Love you too. C."

Sam was amused to see that Carla had addressed her by her professional *nom de guerre* as a member of Carla's escort service. Right equipment? Did she know something about the Prince that she hadn't shared?

Leandro's cold showed every sign of having disappeared by the time they had finished lunch and returned to his flat. As if determined to compensate for her coming absence, he made love to her for the rest of the afternoon.

At the airport, she bluntly asked him not to accompany her to the check-in desk. As usual, she had her choice of porters. A last wave, as she followed one of them pushing her luggage through the sliding doors. He felt a strong sense of anti-climax as he drove towards the exit. This was the first case of Sam responding to a call from one of Carla's clients. He knew perfectly well that in Sam's mind, it was above all connected with the role which Mossad wanted her to play. But it didn't help.

Seated in first class, surviving the ministering of the American Airlines' hostesses, Sam recalled Leandro's parting words, as she got out of the car.

"Take care of yourself, won't you?"

Adding after a slight pause, "and take care of us."

The message could not have been clearer, however delicately expressed. He was deeply worried that her activities might ultimately destroy the love between them. She was as conscious of this as he was, and could find no words at that moment to reassure him. She would have to prop up the partitions in her mental and emotional apartment.

At Nassau airport, a handsome Bahamian driver was waiting with her name prominently displayed on an Ocean Club board. As the black Mercedes Benz drove up to the pseudo-Palladian entrance of the Club, she recognised it from the last Casino Royale movie with Daniel Craig. Waiting for the receptionist to finish her registration, she texted Leandro.

"Dateline. Ocean Club, Paradise Island. Missing you, James. Your ever-loving Solange Dimitrios."

The reply came swiftly.

"Try and do better than she did. Like staying alive. James."

A bottle of Dom Perignon and two hundred grams of caviar, with a bouquet of roses, had greeted her in her suite. A small card, marked simply with a green star, was pinned to the bouquet. Roses. Perhaps not the most original. Never mind.

After a nap, she decided to stay and dine in her room, sitting on the small balcony, looking out over the sea. Tonight was a night to herself, a night to enjoy some simple luxuries to the full. No man or woman to intrude on her lazy thoughts.

The wake-up call came at six thirty next morning and, emerging from the shower, she found breakfast laid on the terrace. Perhaps next time, come with Leo. At eight o'clock, she made to check out, but was told in no uncertain terms that all this had been dealt with.

"We hope to see you again soon, Miss Haidar. And perhaps see more of you," the elegant blonde behind the Louis XV-style reception desk had added, smiling. "You were very discreet last night. And missed by not a few gentlemen who saw you arrive…"

Sam smiled. She hadn't quite expected this level of complicity between the staff and the guests. She would have to watch her step next time. Assuming there was a next time.

By nine ten, she found herself on board a twin jet Bombardier Challenger 300, the Prince's personal aircraft. Interior decoration by a disciple of Starkey. On the other hand, the hostess who greeted Sam at the top of the steps might have been chosen by Hugh Hefner in person.

"What can I get you for breakfast, Miss Haidar."

The velvet voice and silhouette went together. Sam wondered whether this hadn't been laid on by Carla as part of her exotic travel packages. Maybe Carla had some kind of service contract with the Prince.

"You're very kind, but I've already had breakfast. Maybe an espresso?"

"Before or after take-off? The flight is very short."

"After. Thank you."

Some twenty minutes later they had landed at Exuma International airport, where the Challenger taxied alongside a high-wing seaplane on the edge of the runway. Both aircraft were painted pure white with just a single green star on the tail fin. The colour of Islam.

As she was about to step down the retractable stairway, Sam turned to the girl.

"What's your name?"

"Joslyn. May I give you my card?"

An act of recognition between professionals? Sam tucked it into the case of her Blackberry. You never could tell.

The last lap had been a mere ten minutes, flying low over the clear waters along the string of cays stretching north from Exuma, small bars of golden sand breaking the surface, each island more beautiful than the last.

The side companionway was lowered from the larger yacht as the tender came alongside.

"After you, Miss. I'll bring your cases."

She reached the top of the stairway. There was no one to be seen. She stopped, uncertain what to do or where to go. The sailor carrying her bags came past her.

"This way, Miss."

He showed her through a side door into the luxurious living quarters of the yacht. The air conditioning was ferocious, but welcome after the heat and humidity of the bay. The Saudi concept of energy saving! At the far end of the passageway, he led her down a companionway to the next level, apparently the private quarters.

"Your room, Miss. Hope you like it."

She gazed around her suite. Through the door of the small living room she could see a well-lit bedroom, with bathroom and dressing room giving off the connecting passage. Pale greys, beiges and whites. Here and there a flash of colour, the deep red of a lampshade matching the curtains falling in front of the rectangular windows, through which she could glimpse the far shore, the yellow sand and palm trees. She stepped cautiously into the bedroom, dominated by a massive bed, the sheets of pale satin below a mound of red and grey cushions.

The sailor had remained by the door, watching her, having already placed the suitcases on the trestles.

"Everything alright, Miss?" he asked.

"Beautiful. Thank you."

"His Royal Highness has asked me to tell you that he looks forward to your company at drinks before lunch, at one thirty sharp."

"Of course. I'll be there."

"There will be certain other guests. They're away diving at the moment, but are due back at about twelve thirty."

"Tell me," Sam said, "how formally should I dress? These other guests?"

"His Royal Highness asked me to tell you to make yourself beautiful. Nothing more." And he smiled. "Don't worry, I don't think you'll have any difficulty in complying with that. Drinks will be served on the small rear deck behind the lounge. Is there anything else I can do for you, Miss?"

Sam looked at her watch. She had about an hour before the drinks.

"Thank you. You've been very kind. What's your name?"

"Malcolm, Miss."

"Thank you, Malcolm."

She noticed he had discreetly avoided asking hers. He probably knew it anyway. There was bound to be a daily programme brief circulated to the crew.

He smiled once more and left, closing the door behind him.

She threw herself into the pile of cushions on the bed, breathing out the tensions of the flight. This promised to be a good adventure. She lay back and studied the room. On the bedside table, an internal phone with about fifty numbers. International calls also available. She was tempted to ring Leandro. Perhaps not wise. Who knew whether the calls weren't monitored. Her eye was caught by a small white envelope propped up against the phone. A green star on the rear flap. With a fingernail, she slit it open. A small crisp note on handmade paper. Unsigned. Only the embossed name of the vessel.

"The pleasure of your company is requested at lunch today on board White Lady. Given the presence of other guests, you are requested to dress conservatively and to assume the role of one of HRH's personal assistants from the Beirut office. Drinks will be served as of 1300 on the rear quarterdeck."

Personal assistant? Conservative dress? She hoped she had brought something that would meet that criterion. She opened her suitcases and began to hang her clothes in the cupboards lining the passageway between the sitting room and bedroom. She had brought two large cases, one of which was divided into two layers, the lower containing her more exotic pieces. Some of these had been chosen with Carla on that afternoon back in Zürich, when she had taken Sam to a tiny shop also specialising in beautifully handcrafted lingerie - a subject on which Sam already considered herself more than a connoisseur. Sam's selection had only partially been guided by the 'wish list' which Aziz had filled out as long ago as February on behalf of the Prince. At that time, none of Carla's girls had been assigned to His Royal Highness, but Carla had forecast his choice.

"There's not the slightest risk, Sam, that the Prince won't ask for you. Aziz has already given me feedback. But you'll have to be patient. His call will come some day. And when it comes, you had better be ready. So, what are you going to choose?"

She had made numerous choices, trying them on in the small rear boudoir of the shop. Carla had sat, fur coat spread wide over the armchair, guiding Sam's fittings. A long, close-fitting evening gown in a dark shade of pink, the little black cocktail dress without which no girl could survive. Some more exotic items too. And accessories. Lots of accessories.

She picked out a simple off-white linen skirt, not too short, with a very pale grey silk shirt, safari cut, as befitted the tropical environment. Dark burgundy red belt, matching grey pumps, heels low. Make-up understated. Nobody could take exception to this.

She looked at her watch. Still fifteen minutes before she needed to make an appearance. She sat down by the small desk near the window. Time to run through the instructions she had received at Miami airport.

On finally emerging from the lengthy immigration and customs procedures which had become an inevitable part of the process of visiting the land of the free, she had rechecked her two suitcases at the American Airlines transfer counter and made her way, as instructed, to the Barnes and Noble near Concourse D. Positioning herself in the fiction section, the little Cuban-American woman standing next to her had provided the agreed password.

"Such a fascinating writer. Have you read his books on the Middle East?"

"I'm not sure *she's* ever been there," Sam had replied, as instructed.

She settled herself at one of the tables in the lobby of the Miami International Airport Hotel in Concourse E, where the little woman joined her. Sam had briefly outlined the little she knew about the context of her contact with the Prince.

"It sounds as though he's invited me to spend up to a week on his yacht, anchored somewhere in the Bahamas. I've no idea who else is going to be there nor what he has in mind."

The woman, who only gave her name as Ruth, indicated that she was aware of the fact that Sam had been invited essentially to give the Prince a good time and therefore that opportunities for more valuable information-gathering might be limited.

"This is your first assignment with him, isn't it? In that case, we should play it long. Don't take risks. Afterwards, give us as full a rundown as possible on his personality, his interests, his lifestyle, the people you meet, anything you think might be relevant. This is the first time we've ever had anybody get so close to him and we wouldn't want to jeopardise that with too intrusive a brief. Here's my email, in case you need it. I don't see any need for us to meet up again on your way back. Take your time. Play it by ear."

Ruth smiled, adding, "And enjoy yourself!"

Sam had taken to this little woman. Probably aged around forty-five to fifty. Clearly, from her accent, of Cuban extraction, but, with a name like Ruth, possibly also Jewish. Just the kind of unobtrusive operative that Mossad would use in a place like Miami.

"Fine. That's useful, and, as you say, not too ambitious. It's up to me to ensure that the invitations keep flowing. Which might not be so bad..."

Sam laughed. She sensed Ruth slipping something into her open handbag on the floor beside her.

"It's a cell phone registered in the US. If you need to call me, you're my niece, Rachel. But only in an emergency. If there's something really important."

Ruth gave her a friendly kiss as they parted. Sam made her way to the American Eagle counter.

"Play it by ear, Sam," she muttered to herself, as, with a final look around her suite, she set off to find the drinks party on the after-deck.

"Ah, there you are, my dear."

The Prince, dressed in a pair of slacks and short-sleeved T-shirt which did little to conceal his athletic build, stepped forward from a group to which he was serving champagne. He took her by the hand, a light pressure not unnoticed by Sam, and led her over to the group.

"This is Samira, a very valuable assistant from my Beirut office. She has come to join us for a few days, so that I may get some business done. Let me introduce you. My wife, Farida, the mother of my children. Those wild animals you can see playing on the beach over there," he said, pointing towards the shore, where a small group could be seen under parasols, two children leaping in and out of the waves.

Sam bowed her head as she shook hands with Her Royal Highness. The last person she had expected to find! A very good-looking woman. Sam had Googled her. Of Jordanian extraction, some ten years younger than the Prince, educated at the Sorbonne, they had been married about fifteen years. Even in the restricted environment of Saudi Arabia, she was known to be pushing the boundaries of what women were allowed to do, having set up a small foundation to help some of the nomadic communities in the Empty Quarter, where medical facilities and education were scarce.

A second glance brought back the evening in the dining club in London a few months earlier, when Aziz had taken her to meet the Prince. As they had stood around chatting, sipping champagne, Sam's eye had been caught by a small group of very elegant women at a corner bar. She now realized that Her Royal Highness had been one of these. She remembered noting that the Princess' eyes had been quietly fixed on her. Perhaps her interest in this girl brought to meet her husband was more than idle.

Although Saudi men and women were rarely seen together on social occasions in the Kingdom, no sooner had they left the Wahhabi heartland than a much more visible proximity and socializing became the norm. Add to that the fact that the Princess, as a Jordanian, was even less likely to accept the kind of purdah which Saudi social mores reserved for their women. So, on reflection, Sam was not really surprised that Her Royal Highness, elegantly dressed in a silk *pareo*, her jet black hair falling over her shoulders, should be one of the party on the yacht.

The Princess flashed a warm smile at Sam.

"Welcome, Samira, trust you had a good flight."

Sam found the friendliness slightly unnerving.

"And these are some friends from Washington," the Prince went on, walking her towards two couples. The women somewhat vulgar, showing too much bosom and sunburnt flesh, the men red-faced, both of them with the kind of tough look which put Samira instantly on her guard.

"James and Katherine Watson, and Bill and Jean Lauder. They've kindly joined us for a few days, but are sadly leaving tomorrow."

"Hi, Sam, glad to have you along," the man identified as Bill greeted her. "You missed some fantastic scuba-diving this morning. Barracuda, even some dolphins. And the lobster, well, you'll see at lunch. His Highness never stopped picking them off the bottom." Turning to the Prince, he continued. "Pretty soon they'll be asking you to move along for overfishing."

The two men laughed.

After a couple of glasses of champagne, the party moved to the stern of the yacht, where a long white canopy shaded the luncheon table. Two waiters, in white slacks and a simple T-shirt bearing only a single green star, were positioned behind the chairs at the centre of the table on each side, clearly reserved for the Prince and Her Royal Highness. The Prince placed the wives of the two Americans on his left and right, their two husbands on either side of Her Royal Highness. This left Sam near one end of the table, between James and Jean.

She decided initially to concentrate on the wife nearest to her, calculating that a combination of American familiarity and a desire to ensure that any listener would be duly impressed by their presence at a royal table probably meant she might learn something from that source. Her bet paid off quite quickly when Jean almost immediately confirmed that her husband was a senior executive at Raytheon, the US defence industry giant.

"I probably shouldn't be telling you", she whispered, "but there's a very big air defence contract coming up. Everything's riding on Bill's shoulders. The bonus will be fantastic! I'm getting so excited."

"I can imagine," Sam said.

"Of course it all depends on His Royal Highness. That's why we're here. And he was so kind to invite us, the wives, along as well. You see this bracelet? It was on my night table, the evening we arrived. Solid 18 carat gold!" She allowed her left wrist to rest next to her plate, so that Sam could admire the gift.

"It's beautiful," Sam whispered. "I'm so sorry you're leaving tomorrow," she lied.

"I know, it's a shame, just when I was beginning to get a bit of a suntan."

Sam suspected that Jean would probably require hospitalisation if she gave her skin any more exposure.

At this point, Her Royal Highness having turned her attention to her other neighbour, James Watson struck up a conversation.

"So, Samira, you work for the Prince," said Watson."A wonderful job, I'm sure. Not only the lifestyle," and he spread his hands as if to embrace everything around him, "but also the fascinating business he deals in. As one of his personal assistants, no doubt you see a lot of it crossing your desk. Do you understand anything about the armaments industry?"

Sam had the distinct impression that Mr Watson wasn't just passing the time of day. She needed to fend him off fast, before his CIA credentials became too intrusive. Or whatever part of the US intelligence family he also worked for.

"Sadly not, I look after His Royal Highness' social engagements. He has many much more competent advisers and assistants for those affairs. But I'm sure that the defence business must be a very exciting one."

"You're right, it is. Big bucks, and very, very competitive."

Watson proved to be much more discreet than his colleague's wife and Sam was careful not to give away that Jean might have said a little too much. Perhaps, in the remaining twenty-four hours or so before the Americans left, Jean might prove even more loquacious. The supply of champagne to fuel this was clearly unlimited.

Watson, having apparently come to the conclusion that Sam was nothing more than a good-looking social secretary, his conversation running dry, for the rest of the meal he regaled her with stories of his peripatetic existence, rushing backwards and forwards between one big deal and the next. She displayed respectful interest in his adventures in First Class on every airline on the planet. But she noticed that he managed to tell the stories without revealing what company he worked for.

Towards the end of lunch, His Royal Highness raised his glass to thank the assembled company for having done him the honour of joining him on his 'boat'.

"And may our conversations prove fruitful," he ended, toasting the two Americans. Their wives chimed in with gusto. Sam noticed that Katherine Watson, as she raised her glass, shook her wrist where a large gold bracelet was also much in evidence.

"And to you, Samira, on this your first visit," the Prince added."I'm sure it will not be your last."

She was surprised by the personal attention, wondering whether his other secretaries and personal assistants got the same. She modestly lowered her gaze. At the same time, she felt that her neighbour, James Watson, was watching her out of the corner of his eye. He almost certainly knew that social hierarchy in the Kingdom usually separated employers from their staff except on very rare occasions. On top of that, the presence of a woman was even more unusual. And not just any woman. In his vernacular, a possible pressure point. Sam would try and make sure she got a photograph of these two Americans. No doubt the boys in Tel Aviv would have files on them.

Lunch over, the royal couple excused themselves, pleading the heat of the mid-afternoon as time for a siesta.

"James, Bill! Feel free to ask any one of the crew, if you want to go back to the beach or snorkelling. But until about four thirty or five, you may find the sun far too strong."

With that, the Prince gave a low bow and, taking Her Royal Highness by the hand, led her back into the area of the state rooms.

The Americans, having treated the champagne with little reticence, took the hint and headed for a side lounge. Sam remained on deck, finding a comfortable chaise longue to lie on under the awning.

She felt instinctively that someone was watching her and opened her eyes.

"Oh, hi Malcolm. That was a delicious lunch."

"Glad you appreciated it, Miss. The chef's French, he has a whole team down there. Can't understand half of what he says, but who cares when he cooks like that."

"But you're..." she hesitated, "English?"

"That's right, Miss. From London. The Captain and most of the crew are British. Often the case on these luxury yachts. The Captain commanded a frigate in the Navy until about ten years ago. Got to know the Prince sometime when his ship was on station, can't remember where, perhaps the Red Sea or the Gulf. No doubt got an offer he couldn't refuse. But he's a bloody good Captain. Runs this place like clockwork. Anything I can get you, Miss?"

She liked Malcolm. And she suspected that he wasn't entirely immune to her either. Although she'd heard stories that, as in the airline business, male crewmembers on these luxury yachts were often gay, that wasn't the feeling she got from Malcolm. Quite the contrary.

"No thanks, Malcolm, you're very kind. I think I'll just take my siesta here. Everybody else has gone inside, so it should be quiet."

"Just as long as the children are kept on the beach. When they get back, pandemonium will break out again." And he laughed. "They may have a couple of English nannies looking after them, but frankly, it would take Hitler to beat them into shape. Though I shouldn't be saying so, of course. In fact, they're good kids. Just a touch spoiled...."

With the help of the two waiters, Malcolm finished clearing the table.

"I'll leave you to your rest, Miss. If you need anything, the buzzer is over there. Otherwise, high tea at around six in the nursery. And drinks at eight, same place as lunch."

He pushed up a foot rest, which Sam gratefully accepted.

Thursday, 19 June 2008 (AM) – CALLE PEÑA, BUENOS AIRES

From across the street, they watched the target leave his apartment building and, hailing a taxi, head off towards Plaza San Martín. Unawares. Luis Miguel had been alerted by his secretary that the head of the Middle East department had been looking for him. A second-rate ambassador, unsure of himself, and particularly unprepared for the wholesale politicisation of the Ministry by the young acolytes of the lady President. Unused to an environment in which political manoeuvring had become more important than professionalism. Palacio San Martín had never been completely immune from such power games. No Argentine Ministry ever was. But the current regime had taken it to new heights and his boss was regularly flailing around to adapt to this unfamiliar context. He wondered what kind of genuflection the older man would be looking for this time. How to ingratiate himself further.

The two men followed the taxi on their motorbike, confident they knew where it was going. The rest of the day would be spent making a final check of his movements, confirming the pattern they had sketched out over the previous days. The times he left in the morning, the times he came back at night. Any other commitments during the day. Not a particularly social animal. In the time they had been following him, he had only gone out one evening, apparently to a dinner party round the corner from where he lived. His manservant - or was it his lover, or both? - did the shopping, usually in the early evening. He didn't appear much during the day. Once they thought they'd detected an even younger man coming to the flat, whilst Morales was at the office. Did the lover have his own lover?

As they sat in the corner cafe, having 'housed' Luis Miguel at around eight thirty that evening, they agreed they had everything they needed to make their move the following day. They were just within the time limits set under the contract.

Friday, 20 June 2008 (AM) - EXUMAS, BAHAMAS

The departure next morning of the two American couples seemed to raise everybody's spirits. They had bid an effusive farewell to the Prince at around ten o'clock, before the tender carried them with their matching sets of designer luggage to the waiting seaplane. The Prince and a couple of the crew dutifully stayed by the rail, waving to them as the aircraft gathered speed over the light chop in the bay and finally lifted off. The pilot, perhaps to give them an extra thrill, performed a tight circle and came in low above the sea behind the two stationary yachts, dipping his wings in salute. Sam, through her cabin porthole, caught a glimpse of one of the two blondes waving.

She emerged onto the deck and was warmly greeted by His Royal Highness.

"Good morning, Samira, now at least we can relax a little, without our friends from the North. It's just another beautiful day. The boys are organising a lunch on the beach. Would you care to join us?"

"Of course, Your Highness, I've come here to be at your command. That kind of a command is pure pleasure. I feel very honoured."

"Let's just concentrate on the pleasure. We're delighted to have you with us for a little while."

Sam wondered how long 'a little while' might turn out to be. Now was not the time to be too curious. She was also struck by the Prince's courtesy.

"I'm sure you've brought some beautiful swimsuits with you," he continued. "I asked Aziz to make sure of that. Did you speak to him?"

"Yes, he rang me in Buenos Aires. He didn't go into very much detail, so I permitted myself to use my imagination."

"And from what I've heard about you, that should be more than adequate," the Prince said with a slight smile. "I also gave it some thought. With the help of the lady Carla, we did a little shopping on your behalf. I believe the purchases arrived with your flight yesterday."

Carla's reminder to take all her 'equipment' with her. Rather more preparation had gone into this trip than she had imagined.

"What time would you wish us to leave for the beach, Your Highness?"

"Oh, around eleven thirty or twelve. Has anybody taken you on a tour of White Lady?"

"Not yet, Your Highness."

"Well then, allow me to be your guide."

For the next hour, the Prince strolled with Samira round the vessel. She had seen the saloon on the previous evening, but now the Prince took her through the state rooms, including a glimpse into his own bedroom, with a matching dressing room and bathroom for him and for Her Royal Highness, separated hermetically from the guest quarters. From there, they passed through what was clearly his office and administrative backup, with its wall of computer screens following stock markets, currencies and streaming news. A couple of young men were hunched over their keyboards, managing the Prince's positions.

"They're Palestinians," he murmured. "Some of the best. Along with the Indians, great head for numbers."

From there they passed up into the command area. The English Captain, who had been sitting at the far end of the dining table on the previous evening, greeted Sam warmly. The Prince briefly described the Captain's career in the Royal Navy.

"That was before I tempted him away from Her Majesty's Service. Have you regretted that, Bill?"

Bill gave a deep laugh, patting his stomach.

"I fear that my waistline provides the answer to that. Too much good living on board White Lady. Have to spend more time in the gymnasium."

The Captain gave Sam a rundown of the equipment he had at his fingertips on the bridge.

"Perhaps not quite so much hardware or comms as my frigate, but almost. With a range of about eight thousand miles, I can take this lady anywhere, wherever His Royal Highness wants to be. She's a beauty. Best German engineering."

The Prince smiled.

"I paid for it all, but you have the pleasure of making it work. Times when I'm jealous. We do have a small navy in Saudi. Perhaps I should have done my military service there, instead of in the cavalry."

Turning to Sam, he asked.

"Are you at all interested in mechanics? You don't look that kind of girl."

"In Buenos Aires, I've a Harley-Davidson. Perhaps I don't know exactly how it works, but I certainly get a thrill from the feeling of its power. One day I should take a course in how to repair it. Probably a wise precaution."

The Prince and the Captain laughed.

"The men of Buenos Aires must be very fortunate to have a girl like you cruising around town. Anyway, the Captain will take us down to the engine room, won't you, Bill?"

"My pleasure, Sir. This way."

A discreet lift carried them down into the engine room. Almost everything was, like the outer skin of the vessel, painted pure white and kept spotlessly clean by the two engineers on duty. Even for someone as unaccustomed to heavy machinery as Sam, the massiveness and brutal aesthetic of the diesel turbines conveyed an impression of power.

"Perhaps a little more horsepower than my Harley," she murmured.

"Only about thirty times," the Captain said. "Five thousand plus, to be precise."

Friday, 20 June 2008 (PM) – SARMIENTO Y MONTEVIDEO, BUENOS AIRES

"The Thursday lunch has been postponed to Friday," Leandro had told Luis Miguel when the latter rang through a few days earlier. "Still interested?"

"Yes, suits me better, in fact. I had a lunch on Thursday, which I wouldn't have been able to get out of. Remind me of the address?"

At about one fifteen, on the first floor of the restaurant near the corner of Sarmiento and Montevideo in which they had been congregating for the last five or six years, Leandro's university friends gathered to shoot the breeze. Lawyers, engineers, a doctor or two, even a retired detective, but no one connected in any way with a political party. As he had already told Luis Miguel, the topics varied, politics of course, football inevitably, their sex lives, however fictitious, a permanent feature.

Oblivious to the followers on the motorbike behind his taxi, Luis Miguel arrived last. Leandro introduced him to the assembled company.

"Ah, a diplomat indeed!" Francisco, one of the engineers, exclaimed. "Perhaps you'll be so kind as to explain the foreign policy of our highly esteemed government."

Luis Miguel momentarily looked embarrassed.

"Don't worry, Louis, no tape recorders here, everyone a trusted friend. Things said around this table never go any farther. Otherwise the divorce rates would double," Leandro assured him.

"That's right, Luis Miguel. You can say virtually anything you like. There's a house rule. Anyone repeating something heard around this table to a third party has to pay for lunch for a year. Probably wouldn't break the bank, but it's a reasonable deterrent. Never been applied, so far," Alfredo, one of the engineers, explained.

"Well, Señores, I am most honoured to have been invited to join this august company and I fully accept your assurances."

"First of all, let's fill your glass. And then you should order. The *bife de lomo* is particularly good, not even this terrible wine can do it any damage," Francisco added, filling Luis Miguel's glass.

"So, for your maiden speech, tell us all about our great foreign policy," one of the others repeated.

Luis Miguel took a mouthful of the wine.

"Perhaps not quite up to the Premier Cru I was drinking in Paris a couple of weeks ago," he began, but was immediately howled down.

"No, Señor, no-one around this table is allowed to suggest that anything might be better outside Argentina."

Again they all laughed.

"Well, gentlemen, which particular area of our foreign policy would you like me to comment on?"

"How about Malvinas?" Jaime suggested.

"Our policy towards the United States?" someone else.

"I'm not really a specialist in either, but I'll do my best."

He took another mouthful of the wine.

The table fell silent. A maiden speech deserved respect.

"I don't think there's a lot to be said on Malvinas. It's our territory, it belongs to us, along with all the oil and fisheries. But sadly, the *dictadura* screwed things up back in '82 when they invaded the islands. It was a noble but foolish attempt, and certainly set our case back five decades at least. Some of you may have fought there, so I don't want to offend anyone. Menem tried to change things by opening up relations with London again. Too soon, and the kelpers weren't in a mood to listen. But on balance, I can't see it doing any harm."

Turning to Leandro, he said, "I know you fought there, I don't know what you think."

"No, I agree with you. It was always going to be a long process."

"But now, we're terminating the agreements signed by Menem and generally turning up the volume. It's a different approach. Will it work? Off the record, I rather doubt it. The official position is that the wishes of the kelpers are irrelevant. Whatever the legal merits of that position, I'm personally not sure that two thousand people can simply be ignored in this fashion. Perhaps, not everyone would agree."

Francisco was the first to reply.

"I don't see why we should pay any attention to that. The kelpers are an imported population, not native to the islands. They weren't there when the English threw us out back in 1833, and now that the British government, after the war, has finally begun to take an interest in the place, giving them autonomy and protection - things they weren't prepared to give them before the war - the population has doubled. But that shouldn't deter us. The islands are ours and that's the end of it. Now it's up to diplomats like yourself to find a way out of the problem. United Nations, Gibraltar, Hong Kong - all pieces of a jigsaw puzzle for you to play with."

Leandro detected that, as was so often the case, an Argentine reaction on Malvinas was as much visceral as intellectual. It would be a shame to allow this to spoil Luis Miguel's first lunch. He waded in to the rescue.

"I hear what you say, Francisco. I don't think anyone around this table has any doubts about our ownership of the islands. But I think that what Luis Miguel was trying to say is that world sentiment has evolved in this kind of situation."

With a thankful glance at Leandro, Luis Miguel continued.

"When we first took the subject of the islands to the UN, we were able to do so in the context of decolonisation. But now that decolonisation is virtually complete all around the world, it no longer represents the same rallying cry. Add to that the fact that governments everywhere are having to listen far more closely to what their citizens are saying, to what their voters are putting in blogs and on twitter. The views of the kelpers might not be relevant. But we could be taking a risk in simply ignoring them. So it's to find the balance, as you so rightly say, Francisco, that we have to work."

Francisco nodded, clearly less than convinced, but equally reluctant to upset the atmosphere any further.

"Shall I move to safer waters, the United States perhaps?" Luis Miguel asked.

They nodded. The waiter brought Luis Miguel's steak and salad and he was allowed to eat some of it before embarking on a brief examination of the ambivalence of current Argentine policy towards the United States. To his relief, their interest soon gave way at one end of the table to a discussion of the Copa de Libertadores prospects for Fluminense, the Brazilian football club which had 'so unfairly' defeated Boca earlier in the month, whilst the stand-off with the farmers was generating a heated discussion at the other end. All in all, safer ground. Leandro's attempt to deflect the first conversation towards rugby proved a signal failure.

"A game for barbarians," one of the doctors protested. "You don't have to pick up the pieces after those matches, like I do."

By the time he and Leandro came to leave, any initial tensions had entirely disappeared and Luis Miguel was warmly invited to return the following week.

"They are quite a gang, your friends. Good guys. And frankly, at that price, the lunch is unbeatable," Luis Miguel said as they stood on the pavement.

"You're right. I always say that with people like that, Argentina can't go very wrong. The problem is, you don't find that kind of person in government. Or very rarely."

"Thank you for inviting me. It's usually every Thursday?"

"Yes, but don't worry, I sometimes don't go for months."

"I'd like to come again sometime. Can I give you a ring?"

Luis Miguel picked up a taxi to take him back to the Ministry.

It was eight thirty in the evening by the time he was able to clear his desk of the unanswered telegrams and emails ready for a new start on the following Monday. He was looking forward to a quiet weekend of reading. And to the intimate attentions of Hassan.

His apartment block in Calle Peña was usually almost empty over the weekend, as most of his fellow tenants and owners disappeared off to their country houses out in the provinces or *quintas* in the fashionable northern suburbs. In these days of growing insecurity, the latest meeting of the owners' management committee had discussed the idea of increasing member contributions, in order to be able to afford some kind of security over the weekends as well as during the week. But no decision had yet been taken.

Taking the lift up to the third floor, he stepped out onto the small landing which gave access to the two flats on his side of the building. The ceiling light must have blown, instead of coming on in the usual fashion when movement was detected. Unclipping his key ring from his belt, he opened the two locks of his front door.

He stepped into his small hall, looking for the light switch. Again it failed to come on. A fuse must have gone on his floor.

"Hassan? What happened to the lights?"

He sensed rather than heard something behind him. Then everything went black.

Saturday, 21 June 2008 (AM) - EXUMAS, BAHAMAS

Sam stepped lightly down the companionway and slipped the key into her cabin door. A small FedEx box was lying on her bed. From Carla. Peeling off the sealing strips, a couple of carefully packed parcels slid out. A small white envelope as well. A note, in Carla's hand:

"Darling Sam. Trust you arrived safely. The enclosed respond to instructions received from the Prince. Make good use of them. Love you. C."

The first parcel contained a one-piece bathing suit in metallic black spandex, the lower part cut to show a maximum thigh and butt, whilst a second box revealed a crimson bikini in wafer thin latex. Finally, in two small cases, like jewels, a couple of minute vibrators. Standing in front of the full-length mirror, she tried on the red bikini. Its Brazilian thong disappearing between the cheeks of her arse, the globes of her breasts perfectly encased, her nipples clearly showing through its gleaming skin, it was incredibly sexy. As a tits and arse man, Leandro would have been uncontrollable. Yet, however much she would have loved to keep it on, caution dictated otherwise.

"Careful, Sam. No need to be too provocative in front of Farida. Let's wait and see if the Prince really has any plans that I should use these," she muttered to herself.

After a moment's reflection, she pulled on a deep burgundy classic one-piece bathing suit with a single shoulderstrap, which she had bought on her way through Paris at Eres on the Place de la Madeleine, one of her favourite suppliers. Not too revealing, although there were inevitably some things she could not hide.

A simple white cotton pareo and a pair of matching leather sandals. A final glance in the mirror to see that everything was in order. Perhaps a little extra rouge on her lips, setting off the warm bronze sunburn she had already begun to acquire on White Lady. A wide brimmed hat, faintly reminiscent of Grace Kelly's in 'To Catch a Thief'. One of her favourite actresses. So elegant in those days.

At the appointed time, she was standing by the ladder leading down to White Lady's tender, riding alongside in the slight swell. The royal couple emerged from their quarters, the Princess wearing a pareo of off-white Thai silk, the Prince a T-shirt clearly bought in New York, judging by the big red apple on black.

"Good, well done, trust all is in order," the Prince asked, catching sight of Sam. If he was disappointed that she had not worn something sent by Carla, he didn't betray it. "Let's get on with it, I'm feeling hungry."

The look of admiration on the face of the Princess was undisguised.

"I love your hat, Samira."

The Prince turned to Malcolm by the companionway.

"A good lunch arranged on the beach? With the appropriate ration of champagne?"

"Of course, Your Highness, though they do say that too much alcohol is not wise before diving."

"They say a lot of things!"

Looking across to the beach, Sam could see that the children were already there.

"Lead the way," the Prince instructed his wife.

At the point at which the palm trees and the yellow sand met, a series of canopies had been set up and a rustic bar installed alongside a large portable barbecue. An array of fish was already simmering on the grill, one of the sailors occasionally dousing them in white wine and a mixture of garlic and olive oil, the crust of large grain sea salt beginning to turn a golden brown.

"That smells good," the Prince said. "I'm starving. But first, a quick plunge to cool ourselves off."

A number of small white tents acted as simple changing rooms for men, women and children.

"This one's ours," the Princess said to Sam, pointing to the nearest. "Let's get changed."

Sam had expected to have to wait her turn, but the Princess waved her in first, following close behind. Sam slipped out of the pareo.

"That's a beautiful swimsuit," the Princess said. Sam detected that her gaze lingered on the form-hugging one-piece she had chosen. Probably the right choice. The Princess was wearing a small Brazilian bikini of almost fluorescent orange. For a woman of her age, with two children she could hear shrieking outside, the Princess still had a remarkable figure.

Sam wasn't quite sure whether it was appropriate for her to make some comment in return, so let it pass. The two women emerged to find the Prince waiting for them.

"Spectacular! I'm a very lucky man!"

So saying, he set off in the direction of the sea, the two ladies dutifully following.

Saturday, 21 June 2008 (PM) – CALLE PEÑA, BUENOS AIRES

Only a dim glow illuminated the room. His head was throbbing dully. He tried to lift his hand. Wrists tied! Moving his legs, so were his ankles. What had happened? He shook his head, sending spasms of pain to his temples. This was no nightmare. This was reality. Carefully, he tried to shift himself into a sitting position. Slowly the room came into focus, his drawing room. Those last seconds before he had been struck from behind suddenly came back. He remembered coming up in the lift, opening the door of his flat...

"He's coming round."

A voice on the other side of the room. Looking in the direction of the speaker, Luis Miguel could just make out the silhouette of someone sitting in his armchair, backlit by the green shaded writing-table lamp. A souvenir from the Paris flea markets. Nothing could seem more incongruous now.

Behind him, he heard footsteps coming from the kitchen, the sound fading as the stone floor of the kitchen gave way to the deep pile carpet of the drawing room.

The newcomer grabbed him under the armpits and, dragging him a short distance, propped him against the bookcase. Half sitting, he had a better view of the room.

"Who are you? What do you want?"

At least he was not gagged.

As more of the room came into focus, in a corner, close to the television set, he could make out the crumpled form of Hassan, staring at him, also bound. In his case, the lower part of his face covered with duct tape, shining faintly in the half light. A look of pure terror in his eyes.

Still no one had replied to his question.

"If it's money you're after, there's a couple of thousand dollars in the top drawer of the desk. Take it and leave us alone."

The man who had come in from the kitchen moved over to the Empire *escritoire* and, flipping open the drawers, rapidly found the envelope containing the money.

"Thanks, we will, while we're about it."

About what? If robbery wasn't the prime purpose, then what? Luis Miguel tried to clear his thoughts, the pain from his head making it difficult to concentrate. He wondered how long he'd been unconscious. He swivelled his head, slowly, looking for the French 19th-century *pendule* clock on the bookshelf to his right. Ten thirty! He'd been out for about two hours. Why were these men just sitting there? It seemed to suggest that robbery wasn't the main reason for their presence.

Hassan began to moan softly. The first man got up from the armchair and delivered a brutal kick in the region of his manservant's crotch. The howl of pain was in no way diminished by the duct tape.

Luis Miguel felt the kick almost as if he had received it.

"Stop that, that's enough! Tell me why you're here. Then go. Please."

"*Callate, maricón!* Shut up, I tell you."

The tone was vicious, the allusion to his homosexuality expressed with a mixture of hate and violence he had heard once before. Many years ago. On leaving a gay bar in Paris not far from Pigalle, he had been spat upon and manhandled by three skinheads, only being saved from worse damage by a cruising police car. But the tone, the aggression, were the same.

If it wasn't robbery, then homophobia? President Kirchner might have announced his intention to legalise gay marriage and Buenos Aires was beginning to gain a reputation as a safe haven for gays of both sexes, but it had brought a backlash.

The man who had delivered the kick to Hassan came and stood over Luis Miguel.

"Listen to me, *maricón*. You and your little boyfriend are going to stay very quiet. There's no point in shouting or screaming. We've checked. Practically all the flats are empty. Next door are out. We're going to get some rest while we wait. Suggest you do the same. And tell your little friend to stop whining. Or it's going to get a lot more painful. For both of you."

The man turned and stretched himself out on the sofa. His companion sat watching Luis Miguel and Hassan for a while, before getting up and switching on the TV. Football, of course.

Luis Miguel tried to find a comfortable position, but with wrists and ankles tied, his only option was finally to lie on his side, resting his shoulders against the bookcase. Wait, the man had said. For what? For whom? Ignoring the dull ache in his skull, which had now begun to fade slightly, he tried to work out what was going on. Robbery? Apparently not. A homophobic attack? Possibly. Though why should they bother to wait for anything? They could just get it over with and leave. He looked at the two men more closely, as best he could in the poor light. There was something faintly military in their bearing, in the haircut, in the way they moved. Police? The infamous *Bonaerense*, the Province of Buenos Aires police force? Well known for being behind a large part of the crime and drug trafficking in and around the capital.

He struggled to think of a possible motive. As a lawyer, he had no recollection of being implicated in any investigation or trial around that force, which might have provoked a revenge. As a diplomat, more by luck than calculation, he'd not been involved in any of the crooked deals with third countries of which every Argentine government could boast its share. The one area which stood out, he realised, was the whole business of the terrorist bombings of the Israeli embassy and AMIA. Given his responsibility for the Iranian desk, could these be connected? The last fourteen years had seen every permutation of miscarriage of justice, of threat and counter-threat between the government, Iran and its surrogate, Hezbollah. There had, in the early days of the manipulated investigation, been a move to pin the whole AMIA bombing on people in the local military and the *Bonaerense*. Could this be a belated settling of scores? Why him? At worst, he'd only been the messenger to Tehran. And that only in recent years.

The monotonous sound of the football commentary, on low volume, finally got the better of him and he slipped off into a fitful doze. He woke briefly a number of times and saw that although the television was still flickering, both men were now asleep. Hassan also seemed to be snoring, made louder by the tape over his lower face. Poor Hassan! No one could have foreseen so horrific an adventure.

As he lay there, Luis Miguel remembered that first evening in Marrakech when Hassan, a slim boy in his late teens, had approached him at the pavement cafe beside Jemaa el-Fna square, with its water vendors, food stalls, snake charmers, all manner of tourist traps. Luis Miguel had gone upstairs to the men's toilet and Hassan had followed him. Seven years had passed, but Luis Miguel could still remember the beauty of the young boy's face and, as he discovered later in the bedroom of the ornate *riad* in which he was staying, the perfection of his body. For the rest of the days that Luis Miguel had spent in Marrakech, before returning to the embassy in Rabat, the boy had been his guide. With nightfall, the roles had been reversed. Luis Miguel had paid off the old maidservant who had been looking after his flat in the Moroccan capital and taken Hassan as his manservant. And lover in residence. On returning to Argentina in 2002, he had been able to get Hassan a work permit and identity document. Hassan had matured, but his love for Luis Miguel had remained constant. Now Luis Miguel was repaying him in this way.

He dropped off to sleep again.

Saturday, 21 June 2008 (PM) - EXUMAS, BAHAMAS

They had dined quietly on the rear deck off lobster collected from the seabed by the Prince, beautifully *sautéd*, along with fresh grilled vegetables and *linguine* perfectly *al dente*. A rich Valpolicella in attendance. The royal children had been allowed to dine under the strict gaze of their English nannies at a nearby table, before finally receiving a good night embrace from their parents and going below to play in their nursery.

Sam couldn't control her curiosity about their departed guests.

"One of the American wives," she said, "told me that her husband worked for some large defence company, Ray... something. She practically swore me to secrecy on the subject. Not that I know anything about these things anyway. But she was very proud of her husband. The lead negotiator, or something like that."

"If they weren't good for business, I'd have thrown them overboard to the sharks within an hour of their arrival."

The Prince laughed.

"Raytheon. It's a huge defence contractor. They've supplied lots of hardware to the Kingdom. Particularly in air defence, missile systems, that kind of thing. I've been involved in a couple of their deals. Also outside the Kingdom."

Sam was surprised that the Prince had responded, although nothing he'd said was in the least confidential. But it suggested that, in the informal atmosphere of his yacht riding at anchor in the Caribbean, he might prove more communicative. So as not to appear too interested, she switched focus.

"I haven't had a chance to tell you how beautiful this yacht is. I feel so honoured to have been invited on board. I've seen a few yachts in the past, but, as I flew in yesterday, I was struck by the beauty of its lines. And as for the interior. So elegant, not to mention wonderfully comfortable. My room is divine."

Turning to Her Highness, she continued.

"I detect the hand of a woman in so much of the furnishing and decoration. You must have had a wonderful time planning it all."

"It was a lot of fun, and you're right, she's very beautiful. And very comfortable. The whole family is always delighted when Kemal suggests that we get together here. You see, he spends so much time travelling, the children don't see enough of him. So it's wonderful to meet up like this. And with the two yachts, we're entirely self-sufficient. Much of the backup is handled on the other one. Laundry, bakery, that kind of thing. And luckily we can also park some of our guests over there."

"I suspect the Americans were a little disappointed not to be on board White Lady."

"Their rooms were very comfortable, of that I'm sure. I'm glad you like yours. I've tried to have one stateroom more for women in its decoration, the other more masculine. Kemal does quite a lot of business entertainment here. White Lady travels around the world, acting as a base for him when he needs it, where he needs it. Often in the Mediterranean, but also in the Red Sea or the Gulf."

Sam could see that the Prince's thoughts were wandering, as he let his wife take over the conversation.

"Samira – I think your friends call you Sam, but Samira is so much more beautiful, especially amongst members of our race. Tell me a little about yourself."

The Princess was discreetly studying her as she spoke.

"Oh, I don't know, Your Highness, I'm sure it's not very interesting for you."

"Not at all. From the little I've heard, you get around a great deal. I believe you're Argentine. That's correct, isn't it? I've only been to Buenos Aires once. Good fun, lots of atmosphere. And the women good-looking, though perhaps a little unsophisticated. That was a few years ago. Where did we stay?" she asked, turning to her husband.

"One of the big hotels, used to belong to a friend of ours, Gaith Pharaon," he said.

"That would be the Four Seasons," Sam said.

"Quite right. Though I hear there are better hotels, particularly the new Park Hyatt."

"I can't say I'm an expert. Though I do have a particular affection for the Alvear Palace. The service is impeccable," Sam added. "It's much more old-fashioned. The Argentines like it that way."

A fleeting image of the afternoon and night there with Leandro nearly a year ago.

"I'd noticed. That's a large part of the charm of the place. While the rest of the world's racing towards the next century, Buenos Aires – like Paris - reminds one there was a time of more elegance, more...."-the Princess searched for the word-"...more sophistication, more civilisation. Perhaps at your age you don't see things that way."

She smiled at Sam, who smiled back.

"I'm afraid, if I may be so bold, Your Royal Highness is wrong. One of my favourite periods in history is the last decade of the nineteenth century. *La belle époque.* Such beautiful fashions. Such elegance. And I may surprise you with my favourite writer. Oscar Wilde."

"Wilde? Really? That's most interesting. I'm afraid my education is more French than English. I went to the Sorbonne, you see."

The tone sounded genuinely interested.

"I would love to introduce you to him. He's an amazing personality. A genius, although a tragic one. And a lover of Paris."

"The little that I recall - and correct me if I'm wrong - is that he was homosexual and died there."

"In a little hotel in the Rue des Beaux Arts, L'Hôtel."

"Oh, I know it. I've stayed there. The rooms are minute, but wonderful turn-of-the-century charm. Didn't it at one time belong to someone who was gay as well?"

"Yes, I believe so. I always try and stay there. I love it."

The Princess turned to her husband.

"I don't think it's quite your scene, Kemal. Not sure where you'd park the limos in that street."

"That's what we have chauffeurs for, my darling." He smiled. "Glad to see you two girls are getting on so well."

Sam detected a tone of voice, which suggested something more than just idle conversation.

"I love Paris," the Princess said to Sam "I spent some wonderful years studying there. Do you know it well?"

"It's one of my favourite cities. I was there nearly a year, perfecting my French."

"Donc tu parles français, Samira?"

Her accent was perfect.

"Certainement, Altesse."

"En plus, un accent impeccable."

The Princess allowed a slight smile to reach her lips.

"It must have been very difficult, being homosexual in those days," she continued. "The prejudice, the bigotry."

"Wilde went to jail for it. Two years of hard labour. I think it killed him and his genius. When one thinks of the marvellous things he wrote. Tragic. But in French literature, one my favorite writers is Simone de Beauvoir."

"Oh, wonderful. Mine too. You've read *Le Deuxième Sexe*, I'm sure?"

"Of course, Your Highness."

"Wonderful. We will talk about that together. But now, Sam, tell me some more about yourself. In some ways, you're very mysterious. Isn't she?" she said, looking once again over to her husband. "You had a long chat with her, Kemal, at that dinner in London, as I recall. So, what did you find out?"

The Prince said nothing, waving his hand as if it had all been of no importance.

"I believe you were there, Your Highness. Did I not see you across the room?"

"Probably, though I was with a group of girl-friends. We dined in another salon. You know, among girls."

Again Sam thought she detected a slight emphasis. Where were these two leading her? Either way, it didn't matter to her. She thought she had come for the Prince. That's what Aziz had said. But now she was here, might the agenda be different? Maybe she should prepare to shift gears.

Her Royal Highness rose from the table.

"It's getting a little chilly, I think. Let's go inside."

"As you wish, my dear. Lead the way. Let's go in, Samira."

The Princess was wearing a light white silken toga, which fell down to her ankles, with golden sandals and a matching narrow belt gathering in the folds at the waist. No jewellery. Her hair, the kind of jet-black luxuriance characteristic of Arab women, piled up on her head, held in place by a small golden brooch. As she watched her step over the lip of the doorway into the saloon, the light coming from the room and shining through the diaphanous material revealed her as apparently naked.

The two women settled themselves on one of the large settees, while the Prince moved behind the bar.

"Thank you, Malcolm. I'll take it from here. Just bring me the usual."

Malcolm gave a small bow and, as he raised his head, shot a glance at Sam, as if to wish her luck. She gave the slightest hint of a smile in return.

"So, *Mesdames*, what can your barman offer you?"

"Your best Napoleon," the Princess replied.

"Coming up! And you, Samira?"

Sam wasn't quite sure how much she needed to stay sober.

"Perhaps a small one."

"Don't spoil what's coming. I'll pour you a big one, just the same."

The Prince poured two generous goblets of the golden brown liquid, which he placed on the small tables beside them at either end of the sofa. Refilling his whisky glass, he sat down in one of the large armchairs, surveying the two women.

Malcolm reappeared with a silver tray on which three lines of white powder were neatly laid out, along with three silver tubes. With no hesitation, the royal couple scored their lines, after which Malcolm presented the silver tray to Samira, who saw no alternative but to follow suit.

No stranger to lighter drugs, Sam had nevertheless, when given the choice, avoided them. Somewhere deep inside her, a reluctance to lose total control. The same with alcohol. She couldn't remember the last time she had even come close to being drunk. But tonight, to have refused would have been the wrong tactic.

The conversation turned to the children, a subject which brought the Prince back into the discussion. It was clear he was concerned about the directions in which the youth of Saudi Arabia was turning.

"Too many young men with nothing to do and too much money. A dangerous cocktail. And artificially separated from the one thing that interests them most. Girls. Though at least now they can communicate more on their cell phones. Motorola sex. My generation didn't even have that."

The Princess had got up from her end of the settee and, having opened the door out onto the rear deck, stepped outside, apparently to admire the night sky.

"Samira, you must come and see this. The moon is hanging low, silhouetted against the palm trees on the island. It's a wonderful night. You really shouldn't miss it," she called out.

Samira looked over at the Prince, who, with a lazy wave of the hand, gestured that she should comply.

"Go on, my dear, I'm sure it's beautiful. Don't keep Farida waiting, she's not the patient kind."

Sam stepped across the door coaming onto the deck. As her eyes grew accustomed to the darkness, she caught sight of the Princess standing with her back to the railing, the moon rising behind the black silhouette of the palm trees in the distance. Moving closer, she realised that the silk toga now hung open, revealing the beginnings of her breasts on either side and a minute triangle of white covering her pubis, into which the Princess had inserted the fingers of one hand, quietly caressing her genitals. Sam flashed a glance over her shoulder, half expecting to see the Prince standing behind her. He was nowhere to be seen. The Princess was gazing steadily at her and at nothing else.

"*Viens, approches-toi, Samira.* Come closer, so that we can see each other better. Aziz really shows good taste. You're beautiful and very sexy. Come, don't be shy, that's rather the last thing I would have expected of you."

Sam walked slowly towards her. The Princess might not have been her first choice of companion, but she was undeniably good-looking and clearly determined to take advantage of Sam being there to order.

"*J'adore ton parfum.* I've been enjoying it all evening," the Princess continued. "L'Artisan Parfumeur? In Paris?"

"*Exacte, Altesse.*"

The Princess' free hand reached for the clasp at the throat of Sam's dress and deftly flicked it open.

Sunday, 22 June 2008 (AM) – CALLE PEÑA, BUENOS AIRES

The early morning light was streaming in under the roller blinds when, on being kicked in the back, he was woken by the larger of the two men who had been sleeping on the sofa.

"Time to be awake!"

"Awake," Luis Miguel said, gasping. "For what?"

This time the kick to the kidneys came brutally fast and hard. He doubled up with pain.

"I told you to shut up, *maricón*!"

A couple of hours passed. The two men busied themselves in the kitchen, making coffee and finding something to eat. Out of the corner of his eye, Luis Miguel could see that it was nearing ten o'clock in the morning, when the kitchen buzzer sounded. Someone was ringing from the downstairs entrance. He heard a brief and muffled exchange followed by the electric release of the street door latch. A few minutes later, one of the two men opened the front door. The newcomer hardly looked at the two prisoners lying on the floor.

"Everything all right?"

"No problem."

The three went into the kitchen and closed the door. Luis Miguel could hear their voices, but not enough to make out what they were saying. After about ten minutes, they returned to the drawing room.

"We're going to have a little fun. You two are going to put on a show for us. But first, just a few questions."

The Director pulled up a chair and sat down in front of Luis Miguel. One of the other two came over and pulled Luis Miguel upright, so that he was once again leaning against the bookshelf. He saw that the third man had gone over to Hassan and was cutting him free, though the duct tape remained firmly in place.

"So, Dr Morales, I trust you are well this morning."

So they knew who he was. It was the first time his name had been used. Wary of saying the wrong thing, he merely nodded.

"We have little time, so you'll forgive me if I spare you the usual diplomatic protocol and get straight to the point. I only have one or two questions for you. Is Argentina helping those dogs in Tehran with its nuclear technology, or not? If so, who is leading the negotiation? And how far has it got?"

Luis Miguel was taken completely by surprise. For some reason, although he had spent part of the night thinking about the history of relations between Buenos Aires and Tehran, he hadn't given much thought to the nuclear angle. Was this beginning to make some kind of sense?

He shook his head, more out of perplexity than stubbornness. His uncertainty earned him a further kick in the side near his kidneys, which sent him sprawling. The pain was terrible.

"Let us not prolong this unnecessarily, Dr Morales. My friends here are in a hurry to get to the play. Do I need to repeat my question?"

Luis Miguel shook his head.

"Well?"

"It's very complicated. Our relations with Iran are far from easy. After all, they have killed more than a hundred people here in Buenos Aires."

The visitor looked impatient.

"I'm not interested in a history lesson. I know all that. But in spite of everything that your government is doing on the legal front, I suspect there is another part prepared to help these dogs to acquire nuclear weapons. Your government and perhaps that of your Venezuelan friends. Am I not right?"

There was something familiar about the way the third man spoke Spanish. It had the guttural overtone which he had heard on occasion in Morocco. The visitor must be an Arab. His features, the colour of his skin and hair, reminded Luis Miguel of so many faces that he had seen daily during his four years of posting there. Hassan also seemed to have detected it and was staring at the visitor.

"I mainly deal with official bilateral relations. Matters relating to the terrorist actions. Trade. If anything is happening on the nuclear side, I may well not see it. And all the more if it is passing through Venezuela. Our government has a number of lines of communication in parallel. My ministry is only one of them."

"You're beginning to bore me, Dr Morales. Considering your predicament, I would have expected you to be rather more interesting. If only as a way possibly to earn your freedom. I've deliberately tried to be as polite as possible. Try harder."

Luis Miguel felt the terror growing inside him. He knew what this man was looking for, and yet he would never be able to satisfy him. Very little on the subject of nuclear collaboration ever came anywhere near his desk. He shook his head.

"I promise you. That subject is dealt with elsewhere. However much I might want to tell you, I simply can't."

The Director was inclined to believe him. At this stage, he had nothing to gain by continuing to lie. No matter. Information, however welcome, was not the main objective.

"I regret that you have not taken advantage of this. Perhaps my friends can get you to focus."

The larger of the two men came over to Luis Miguel and, cutting the zip-tie at his ankles, forced him to his feet.

"Stay still."

With the razor cutter, the man proceeded to slash through the belt holding up Luis Miguel's trousers, which fell to the floor. Then he sliced through his briefs and tore them off. Going back to Hassan, he lifted the young man bodily and dragged him to a kneeling position in front of Luis Miguel. The duct tape was brutally torn off his face. Hassan could not control a cry of pain.

"There, now serve your master, you filthy little *maricón hijo de puta*."

Hassan looked up into Luis Miguel's eyes, pleading. After a moment, Luis Miguel nodded.

Hassan moved his face towards Luis Miguel's genitals. Slowly, he began to lick his master's penis and testicles, his tongue delicately swirling round. Luis Miguel could not completely banish the thought that Hassan had always been particularly good at this form of arousal.

Slowly, above the pain, Hassan's efforts began to bear fruit, Luis Miguel's member growing slowly firm and erect. Hassan took it between his lips. Luis Miguel knew of fellow gays who could only achieve arousal through a combination of pain with sex. With his hands strapped behind his back, he might as well be participating in one of these rituals. Even the fascinated audience of the three men standing around them seemed appropriate. Yet the overwhelming feeling was one of horror and disgust. And fear for what was still to come.

In the absence of any new instructions, Hassan continued the fellation, his own breath coming more rapidly as his master's arousal transmitted itself to him. Luis Miguel had always been able to contain himself, able to stretch out his sessions with Hassan for many hours without coming.

"Good work, *puto*. We should be filming you."

It was the smaller of the two Argentines who had spoken. The other laughed. The Arab had moved away and was standing in the corner, observing the scene, smoking.

Luis Miguel was getting tired, standing.

"How much longer? How much longer do we have to put on this act for you?"

"Until we get bored, *maricón*! Don't waste your breath. You may need it."

After another five minutes, one of the two Argentines stepped forward and dragged Hassan back onto his heels, kneeling.

"Here, into the middle of the room."

Hassan crawled to the point indicated in the middle of the carpet.

The man who had spoken cut through the zip-tie around Hassan's wrists. Luis Miguel could see deep bruising.

"Kneel here and put your hands on the ground in front of you."

Again Hassan looked back at Luis Miguel, as if seeking reassurance. Luis Miguel inclined his head once more and the young man placed his hands on the carpet, his position now that of a dog. The first man dragged Hassan's briefs down to his knees.

With the cutter, it was Luis Miguel's turn to have his wrists freed. He rubbed them to get the blood circulating again.

"Over here," the first Argentine ordered him, pointing at the carpet behind Hassan. "Down on your knees behind your boyfriend!"

"Go to the devil!" Luis Miguel protested, but was rewarded with a kick in the back of the knees from the man standing behind him, sending him crashing to the carpet.

"I don't understand. What purpose does this serve?"

The Director looked at him, an expression of pure contempt in his eyes.

"What purpose? No purpose. Except to entertain your Argentine friends here."

"But what is it you want to know?"

"Me? Actually, there's nothing you can tell me that I don't already know. As far as I'm concerned, you've nearly fulfilled your purpose."

The taller of the two Argentines interrupted.

"*Callate, puto*! Now mount your boyfriend. Be quick about it!"

Seeing that Luis Miguel wasn't moving, the speaker stepped forward and dragged Luis Miguel by the armpits so that he was now on all fours resting on top of Hassan. Given the fact that Luis Miguel was much taller than Hassan, he fitted closely on top of the young Moroccan, crushing him with his weight.

One of the Argentines strapped Luis Miguel's wrists to those of Hassan with the duct tape, locking them together. Duct tape was placed over both their mouths.

To his horror, he felt a hand grasp his waning erection and begin to force it into Hassan's anus.

"Go on, make love."

He could hear Hassan begin to groan in pain and despair. All that Luis Miguel could think of doing was to nuzzle the back of his lover's head, whispering through the duct tape.

"Forgive me, Hassan, forgive me."

He heard the click of a camera shutter. Turning his head, he saw that the newcomer was photographing them.

Then suddenly, it was all over.

A single bullet from a Browning 9mm, placed at an angle against the base of Luis Miguel's skull, sliced through the soft tissue and exited into the skull of the young man below. The lovers, strapped together, collapsed onto the carpet without a sound.

The Director stepped forward from the corner where he'd been standing and looked down at the two victims. With his foot, he idly prodded the head of the Moroccan. In Spanish, he spoke in the direction of the lifeless Hassan.

"Allah has passed judgement on you. Not only for an act forbidden by the Koran, but worse, committed with an unbeliever."

He was mildly surprised by his own words. Words which might have been uttered by an ardent Muslim. Something he wasn't. He couldn't have cared less about the religious principles governing sex between believers and unbelievers.

Turning to the two Argentines, he smiled. They seemed to have been impressed by his words.

"Most of your job is now done and payment will be made when everything is finished. I want these bodies found just as they are, locked together in their disgusting act. I leave it to you how and where they are found, but they must be found and identified. Within the next day or two. Do you understand?"

The two Argentines nodded, though the look on their faces betrayed that they were less than pleased by the idea of delayed payment.

"So how will we get our money?"

"You will ring the same number again once I know that the bodies have been found. You will receive instructions as to how and when to pick up the balance."

From the back pocket of his trousers, he withdrew another wedge of dollars, which he handed to them.

"Here is another five thousand. So now you have twenty. But since you've done a good job and, assuming that nothing goes wrong now, I will pay you another ten. A five thousand bonus!"

The two Argentines looked at each other. One of them shrugged his shoulders as if to indicate that they didn't have much choice.

"You have a car here?" the Director asked.

"Yes, we brought it into the underground car park yesterday."

"Since no one is here, you can no doubt put these"--kicking Luis Miguel's back--"into your car and find the best way to dispose of them. I will leave you now, after I've had a look at his papers."

For the next half-hour, the Director systematically went through Luis Miguel's desk, library and anywhere that might have concealed his papers. Finally he placed a bundle of files and notes into a briefcase, for later review.

Then, without a word or a second glance at the two inert bodies, where a pool of blood had now formed beneath their heads, he signalled his intention to leave. The taller of the two Argentines let him out onto the landing.

Sunday, 22 June 2008 (AM) – CARIBBEAN

When Sam woke late next morning, she felt White Lady vibrating softly. Looking out of the porthole, she saw that the island had disappeared and that they were now moving across the shimmering waters of the Caribbean. She wondered how long they had been on the move.

Making her way to the dining area, she found breakfast still being served to Her Highness.

"*Bonjour, Sam,*" the Princess greeted her warmly, her eyes searching for Sam's. "*Tu as bien dormi?*"

"*Bonjour, Altesse.*"

Sam thought she was looking particularly radiant.

Last night, the Princess had initially contented herself with exploring Sam's body as they stood together by the railing, her hands alternately caressing Sam's breasts, stroking their contours, and softly entering her vagina.

"*Viens, Samira,*" she had finally murmured, taking her by the hand and leading her down the companionway to her cabin. But for a dull glow on the ceiling, the suite was unlit. The Princess had propelled her towards the huge bed and delicately stripped her. The toga fell to the floor. Taking control, the Princess pushed Sam lightly onto the bed and then slipped alongside her, her fingers travelling up Sam's legs, past her sex to her breasts, which she began to kiss. Sam's initial hesitation rapidly gave way to pleasure as this woman closed with her.

The Princess revealed herself to be both a creative and experienced lover. Though not on a par with Carla. That was always going to be a hard act to follow.

Nearly an hour later, as the Princess lay on her back, Sam's tongue working hard between Farida's labia, she had suddenly felt a hand on her shoulder.

"Thank you, Samira, I'll take over now. It's been beautiful watching the two of you. Please stay if you like."

She realised the Prince had been sitting in a dark corner of the cabin since their arrival. Slipping off the bed, she made way for the Prince, whose impressive erection was clearly visible. Without missing a beat, the Princess rose up towards her husband and took his penis deep into her throat.

Picking up her dress and sandals, Sam quietly left the cabin. Making love to a man might on occasion be as good as to another woman. But watching it had never been her thing. Women making love were so much more sensuous, so much more aesthetic, than a man fucking a woman! She knew not all women would agree with her.

"I hope you enjoyed last night," the Princess asked. "I certainly did. And Kemal did as well. You're very good," adding by way of afterthought, "and very imaginative."

Sam pulled up a chair on the other side of the breakfast table from the Princess. Malcolm appeared by her side, offering orange juice and coffee. The smell of the croissants, freshly baked, was irresistible.

"I must thank you, *Altesse*, for doing me the honour. In terms of pleasure, I can only return the compliment. I'm glad you are satisfied," Sam replied, tearing apart the soft croissant to reveal its butter-coloured heart.

As she had lain in her bed on returning to her cabin, she had tried to make sense of what was happening. Nothing that either Aziz or anyone else had said could have led Sam to believe that she had been intended for Farida and not for the Prince. As they had sat together at the dinner party in London, Sam had known that she was being screen-tested, but she had always assumed it was for him. It was true that, since her arrival on White Lady, the Prince's solicitousness had, now that she thought back upon it, been rather formal, always flattering, yet hardly ever suggestive or intrusive. She had assumed that this was out of respect to the Princess. Now, it was clear that Sam's skills were to be deployed on her, not on him. She began mentally to shift her aim. But sleep had overwhelmed her within minutes.

On waking, she had given further thought to the implications of last night as she lay naked between the satin sheets. She loved satin sheets, although something told her it wasn't a sign of very good taste. A suggestion to Leandro that they might invest in some for his flat had elicited a snort of disgust and a firm negative.

The aim of her mission had originally been to find ways to insert herself on the most regular basis possible into the life of the Prince. Men like him took their pleasures as and when they found them, so to become a more regular partner was always going to be a challenge. If nothing else, the fact that some three months had passed between the dinner in London and the first invitation to join him suggested that, in the interval, the Prince must have sought entertainment elsewhere. With the Princess, things might be different. Women were often less fickle than men when it came to parallel relationships. If the invitation had taken three months to come in the case of the Princess, this might suggest that the impression she had made that evening in London had lasted longer. Although the couple was unlikely to be inseparable - the Princess had hinted as much at the dinner table - becoming a more regular partner to Her Royal Highness might provide more frequent access to the Prince than she had imagined. The first signs were good. She was sure she had opened new vistas of arousal in the Princess.

What was more, fate seemed to have come down on her side. She was not in the slightest doubt that Leandro found it easier to accommodate her lesbian bisexuality than heterosexual promiscuity, even in the name of her missions for Mossad.

"You certainly pleased me, Samira, most definitely. I feel very fortunate that Kemal has invited you. You see, it was my birthday last week. He said that he had a special present lined up. Now I know what it was."

"It seems, *Altesse*, that we are to be together for a few more days," Sam said. "May I ask where we're headed?"

"Kemal is keeping that a secret from us, so let's enjoy the uncertainty. I'm sure it will be a pleasant surprise when we get there. And you call me Farida when we're alone. Remember. Farida."

Somewhere, Sam needed a bit more precision. If they were on the move, and she was part of it, it would be better to try and find a way to pass a message to Ruth. Maybe a visit to the bridge and a bit of charm with the Captain might prove more productive. There might be a chart open on the map table she had seen.

The Princess got up and walked round to Sam's side of the table. They were alone, Malcolm having been sent to the galley to get some more coffee. Sam sensed her standing behind her and turned to look up at her. The Princess was close, her hands resting on the back of Sam's chair, looking down into Sam's eyes. Idly, her fingers strayed toward Sam's neck. Sam could feel them touch the gold chain of the Druze star she always wore.

"Yes, Samira, we have a few days without visitors… praise be to Allah. Let's enjoy them together."

The Princess stepped away, with a slight air of reluctance, and walked slowly towards the entrance to the saloon. On reaching the door, she turned.

"I have some affairs to attend to. My foundation in Saudi Arabia, you know. No doubt other emails. Come and see me after lunch. We can talk then."

Sam lowered her head. "*Avec plaisir, Altesse.*"

"*Farida! Souviens-toi.*"

She disappeared into the saloon as Malcolm returned with the coffee.

"On our own, are we? No doubt Her Royal Highness gone to deal with her correspondence. Always does, every morning. Very conscientious. So, Miss, what can I get you?"

"Just a bit more of that coffee, that'll be fine, Malcolm, thank you. Oh, and one more of those delicious *croissants*." She paused. "What time did we leave this morning? I didn't feel anything."

"About six am," Malcolm said. "She's so smooth, you hardly feel a thing."

"Where are we headed?"

"Now, that would be telling. It's always like that. The Prince, the Captain and the navigator know where we're going. But that's where it stops. I don't know whether the Prince wants to surprise us, or, for some reason, he doesn't trust us. Of course, I shouldn't be saying that. But it's always the same. As far as I'm concerned, it doesn't change anything anyway. But," and here Malcolm's voice dropped to a whisper, "what with the business His Royal Highness is in, I suspect a little discretion as to his movements is a minimal precaution. It's the same with his planes. Only the pilots seem to know from one moment to the next where he's headed."

Having returned with another basket of warm *croissants*, Malcolm began quietly to clear the other end of the table.

"Sure there's nothing else you'll be wanting? If not, I need to clear this. Lunch will be in a couple of hours."

"No, thank you, Malcolm, you go right ahead. I'll probably go back to my cabin and do some reading. Or maybe a walk up on deck first, to clear away some of the effects of last night's champagne."

"I can bring you some Fernet Branca, if you like. Very good for that sort of thing."

Sam shook her head and smiled.

"Don't worry, it's not that bad."

She made her way along the side of White Lady towards the narrow walkway in front of the bridge. She deliberately kept her gaze towards the horizon and was rewarded by the sound of tapping on the glass behind her. She turned. As she had hoped, the Captain was smiling at her, gesturing to indicate that she should come round and visit him.

"Are women allowed up here," she said as he opened the door.

"Only beautiful ones," he threw back with a smile.

These British seafarers hadn't earned their piratical reputation for nothing down the centuries! In these very same seas.

"You must enjoy this," Sam said, casting her gaze around the bridge. "You seem to require very few people to make all this work."

"With all this technology, who needs people?" he said, laughing.

"So, basically, White Lady sails herself."

"Not quite. We have to tell her where she's going."

"But with all these islands, here in the Bahamas, it presumably takes more than just setting a course."

"You're right."

Sam moved towards the map table. She could see that, in spite of all the state-of-the-art gadgetry, the Captain still believed in double-checking.

"My experience of using GPS has been that it's usually safer to have looked at the map beforehand. Not to trust oneself to a machine. Don't you agree?"

"Absolutely, Miss Samira. I never do. That's why I have the maps out over here."

She stopped beside the table. The only visible chart appeared to be a large-scale of the whole Caribbean area. On closer examination, she thought she could just detect the faint trace of a pencil line through the islands, passing between the Dominican Republic and Puerto Rico before heading on down in a south-easterly direction towards Trinidad.

"Are we going to Jamaica?" she asked, deliberately trying to dispel any idea that she might have seen something.

"No, not this time. Somewhere a bit farther south. His Royal Highness likes to keep these things a surprise. But I'm sure you won't be disappointed. It's very beautiful."

Sam adopted an expression that said she loved surprises.

"Sounds wonderful. How long do we have to wait?"

The Captain paused.

"I think we'll be there by Tuesday, maybe even Monday night," he said quietly.

Two days away. It only remained to find out the speed at which White Lady was gliding over the calm sea. Perhaps somebody else would give her the answer. Perhaps Malcolm.

Sam appeared to lose interest in the map table. For another ten minutes, she asked the Captain about the various instruments and their technology, making it plain she hardly understood a word.

"I suppose, if I end up somewhere else, I'll have to do something about my air ticket," she finally said as he escorted her to the door.

"Oh, I wouldn't worry about that, Miss Samira. Faisal in Admin will handle all that kind of thing for you. I'll mention it to him. But anyway, who says you'll be leaving us at that point?"

A good question, to which she would also welcome the answer.

On her way back to the cabin, she met Malcolm.

"Had a wonderful time on the bridge with the Captain. It's like a racing car," she enthused.

"Not quite as fast, though," he said. "Twenty miles per hour at best."

"Somehow it feels different. Anyway, what time is lunch?"

Malcolm looked at his watch.

"You've got another hour and a half, so take it easy. Do you want me to knock on the door, just in case you fall asleep?"

"That'll be nice, thank you."

She closed her cabin door behind her.

So, if her research and calculations were correct, they appeared to be headed for Trinidad and Tobago. Was this just a part of the holidays, or did something lurk behind it? Was there any way to find out? Should she even alert Ruth to this change in the itinerary? It was always possible that Mossad would have other information with which to link the new destination. A missing piece to a puzzle only they were assembling.

Now that they were on the move, she would almost certainly have to rely on whatever communication system she was allowed to use. It was unlikely to be anything very much more than some kind of satellite telephone. Not only would the number she called become known to the

Prince's staff, but a record of all outgoing calls might well be kept. Whatever call she made, it would have to be very innocent in all respects. Not easy.

She lay down on her bed and scrolled through the photographs of Leandro in her cell phone.

"Don't worry, *mi amor*. Everything's okay," she whispered, kissing the little screen.

Monday, 23 June 2008 (AM) – PASAJE DE LA PIEDAD, BUENOS AIRES

Perhaps not quite.

Sometime after midnight, several thousand kilometres farther south, Leandro was woken by someone slipping under the sheets next to him, a hand softly finding its way to his crotch. It took him only a few seconds to clear his thoughts. Sam was in the Caribbean! He spun away from the intruder and switched on the bedside light.

"Hello, Leandro. I didn't mean to scare you."

Tatyana, that mountain of red hair falling about her face, the sheet pulled up under her chin, smiled back at him. The tone voluptuous.

What the fuck was going on?

"Tatyana! What in God's name...? And how did you get in? What time is it, anyway?"

However attractive the prospect of having Tatyana in his bed might have been in the days before he had met Sam, it certainly wasn't attractive now.

She continued to smile and then leaned forward, her hand seeking him once again under the sheets.

He was momentarily torn between responding and rejecting. It wasn't as if Tatyana wasn't beautiful and incredibly sexy with her massive, perfectly shaped breasts, which he could clearly see below the sheet pulled tight against her body. But the eyes of Sam and her words of warning about this Russian girl immediately got the upper hand.

For a moment, he didn't move, but to his consternation, Tatyana did. In a single, swift motion, she dropped the sheet to reveal not only her breasts, but also a portable phone, which she carefully held at arm's length in such a way as to capture the two of them. He just caught the faint click of its camera!

"You bitch! What the hell do you think you're doing?"

It was his turn to drag the sheets away from her and, stepping off the bed, pull them round his waist. Tatyana, now fully uncovered, lay back voluptuously, resting her head on the pillows. Having first taken another photograph of him standing in front of her, she slipped the phone out of reach under her buttocks. Arching her back, with one hand she began to stroke her cunt, her breasts with the other, pressing them up towards her darting tongue.

"Come on, Leo, *amor*, don't be boring. Enjoy. How can you resist what Mother Russia is offering you for free? Hasn't Sam abandoned you? Betrayed you? And am I not *muy, muy sexy*?"

He suddenly realized she was speaking to him in Spanish. And they had thought she couldn't speak it! Just another of her hidden talents.

The temptation to fall in with her provocation had not completely disappeared. But now, with the photo, it would be suicide.

Leandro moved over to a chair by the window and sat down facing her. He was beginning to think more clearly.

"Frankly, I don't know what game you're playing, Tatyana. Is this some kind of rivalry with Sam? Trying to wreck our relationship? Seems a very crude way to do it. And why? I'm not sure what you gain."

Tatyana was in no hurry to stop what she was doing, although he had little doubt that the soft moaning and twisting of her body with which she was now accompanying her masturbation were part of the act.

"Come on, Tatyana! Don't waste your time. You may be beautiful, but you're not stupid. You must know I'm not going to fall for it."

After a moment, Tatyana rose from the bed and came to stand in front of him, hands on her hips, cunt thrust towards his face. With those breasts and hips, separated by a tiny waist, she had an amazing body. In getting up, she had forgotten the phone lying on top of the bed. She caught his sideways glance and spun round, getting to it before he did. Somehow, it broke the spell. She sat on the side of the bed, holding the phone firmly in one hand, the fingers of the other again between her legs. This time, Leandro wondered whether it was for his benefit or for hers. The scene was becoming grotesque.

Tatyana had lost the initiative.

He watched her in silence, suspecting that she would be the first to try and get back on track.

"So, Leo, *солнышко моёю*. Do you know what that means, my little sun? I cannot tempt you? How can you resist? I've heard so much about your desires."

The tone of voice softly cajoling.

Leandro shook his head in disbelief. "I wonder who from. I don't think from Sam, somehow."

"We girls talk amongst ourselves."

This conversation was going nowhere.

"Well, Tatyana, no doubt everything you've heard is true, but I don't propose to demonstrate it to you tonight. So what's it to be? I can let you sleep in my bed while I go to the drawing room. Or you can leave. Either way, it's all the same to me."

Tatyana adopted a look of abject disappointment. Again she walked over to him and this time pressed her breasts into his face.

It took all his willpower to stand up.

"I don't seem to be making myself clear. What do you propose to do with the photograph?"

Tatyana took the cell phone in both hands and began to tap out something on the keyboard.

"I think Sam might like to find it on waking, up there on her yacht. What do you think, Leo?"

For an instant, Leandro thought of snatching it away from her, but realised that in so doing he would be betraying vulnerability, leaving him exposed to worse. He could imagine that Sam wouldn't enjoy this surprise on waking, but felt confident he could handle it. And at the back of his mind, there was just a glimmer of somehow taking a minor revenge on Sam!

But how come Tatyana knew where Sam had gone?

"Go ahead, doesn't worry me."

He detected a look of disappointment in Tatyana's eyes.

Turning his back on her, he left the room, closing the door behind him. He had not got an answer to how Tatyana had got into his flat in the first place, nor, more importantly, what she was hoping to gain from this intrusion. Maybe he could coax the answers out of her whenever she chose to leave. It made him uncomfortable to think that people could walk into his flat quite so easily.

Having pulled on a tracksuit from a cupboard in the corridor, where he also found a large blanket, he stretched out on the sofa. Less than ten minutes later, he heard the bedroom door open.

Tatyana emerged, now fully dressed. An elegant dark blue overcoat with an astrakhan collar, her red hair concealed in a huge Russian fox fur *shapka* pulled down over her ears against the cold. He got up and made to bar her way into the hall.

"You seem to have wasted a night, Tatyana. What for? And how did you get in?"

In his brief minutes on the couch, he had worked out that he had not mislaid his keys. He had seen them still on the small table in the hall. The fact that she had been able to gain access to his flat indicated the ability not only to lay hands on his keys, but also to produce a copy. Neither appeared to belong to the standard skills of a Russian hooker, though he was beginning to suspect that these should not be underestimated.

There must be something more sinister behind her. He remembered leaving his keys in his overcoat at the Russian ambassador's flat on arriving for dinner that evening with Sam. That's when the imprint must have been taken. Additional proof of the fact that the dinner party had been more than just social.

"Perhaps I could have my keys back, now that you're leaving."

She put her hand in her purse and silently gave him a ring with three keys. He was under no illusion that this would be the only set. Handing them back was a formality.

"Thank you, Tatyana, very kind. I must remember not to leave them lying around in future. But you still haven't told me why you came."

She had clearly regained her composure.

"I felt we needed to know each other better, Leandro. That makes sense, surely, зайчик мой¡?"

Her eyes narrowed to convey her undying passion.

Leandro shook his head.

"Not really, Tatyana. With what you know about me and Sam, this looks like a childish revenge on her. Why would you do that? After all, you both work for Carla. Would she approve of something like this?"

He detected a flash of anger in her eyes.

"Carla!" She seemed to spit out the name. "Carla and Sam!"

But she provided no more.

"Now let me leave!" she ordered.

However unlikely it seemed that the events of the last hour might be nothing more than an act of jealousy, Leandro suspected he wasn't going to get more out of this girl.

He stepped up to the front door to open it for her. She came up close and pressed her full mouth on his. He felt her tongue dart out, seeking a way in. He pulled his head back, laughing. Not that he felt it was at all funny, but this attitude seemed more disconcerting to her.

"Here, you'll need these keys to get through the downstairs door and the gates at the end of the alleyway."

He handed her back the key ring. The gesture clearly surprised her, but since they almost certainly had another set, he had little to lose. She took the keys and without a backward glance, stepped out onto the landing and down the first flight of stairs.

He closed the front door slowly and going back to his bedroom, sat down on the edge of his bed. What to make of the visit? Rivalry between the two girls? The copying of the keys suggested the involvement of others, more than likely with a clandestine or criminal connection. Pretty girls didn't usually go around with equipment to take an imprint of other people's keys in their handbags, even if it didn't require much more than a bar of soap or some child's plasticine. But from there to the final keys, that required something extra. Perhaps the young diplomat Kuznetsov? A little too smooth all round. And yet... It was hardly good diplomatic practice to invite people to dinner and then break into their flats a couple of weeks later. At least not using a burglar as distinctive as Tatyana.

Or was Viktor Alexievich relying on something less official? Leandro remembered hearing somewhere that ex-members of the KGB, having – like their counterparts in Frobisher – turned their hands to private sector intelligence work, had opened an office in Buenos Aires. Viktor Alexievich would certainly have use for people of that kind.

For the time being, there was little to be gained by such speculation. More important was to minimize the damage of her visit. Had Tatyana sent the photographs to Sam? He had little way of knowing, but, to be on the safe side, he texted a message warning Sam to ignore whatever might reach her from the Russian girl. He could and would explain.

Monday, 23 June 2008 (AM) – CAMINO DEL BUEN AYRE

A few hours after Tatyana and Leandro parted company, the early morning shift at one of the discharging bays of the huge CEAMSE waste disposal complex arrived. The sky was still dark, the cry of seagulls the only sound other than the incoming lorries of the various concessionaires covering the six zones of the city. They had spent the night scouring the streets and were now arriving through the weighbridge entrance of this major garbage site which every day absorbed some five thousand tonnes of refuse from the Argentine capital. It was a desolate place, the surrounding shanty towns assailed by a noxious stench depending on the direction of the wind.

A blue and white CLIBA rear-load lorry, belonging to the concessionaire responsible for waste collection in the central downtown area of the city, reversed up to the end of the conveyor belt.

Looking in his rear-view mirror, the driver could see José waving him on and then signalling to stop. He pulled the levers, which would start the process of tipping the rear of the lorry to disgorge its contents onto the belt. He climbed down from the cab and lit up a cigarette. José, armed with a large rake, was making sure that nothing got stuck in the process.

He watched him idly as he drew in the first lungful, then turned towards the east where the pale light of the winter sun was beginning to stretch across the horizon.

"*Che*, Negro, what's this? *Qué carajo?*"

José was calling him urgently.

It wouldn't be the first time José had got excited about something emerging from the truck. No need to rush. His cigarette hanging from the corner of his mouth, hands in his pockets against the cold, the driver made his way in a leisurely fashion to the rear.

"What is it?"

"*Mierda!*"

Already more than halfway onto the conveyor belt, a black plastic object, wrapped tight and closed off with duct tape, unmistakably a human form. Although misshapen and almost twice the size of a normal body.

José had already switched off the conveyor. The package now rested half in, half out of the back of the truck.

"Where did that come from? When could we've picked it up? Surely you'd have noticed, *che*. It couldn't just have been lying on the pavement along with the all the rest."

José nodded.

"We didn't collect it. Too big and heavy. I'd have remembered. Somehow it got into the back of the truck. It must have been put there. *Carajo de mierda*, just the kind of thing we need. We'll be with the police all day. Perhaps if we just let it continue down the belt, that way they might not know it came from us."

Negro shook his head.

"It's not that easy. It's dead isn't it? Wait a minute, it looks more like two bodies."

José poked nervously at the inert mass with the end of his rake.

"What do you think? If your head was wrapped in that amount of plastic, you'd be dead. It's dead alright. Definitely looks like two."

At that point they were joined by one of the sorters from farther down the conveyor to discover why it had been switched off.

"*Jesus María*, what's that?"

"What do you think?"

Tuesday, 24 June 2008 (AM) – TOBAGO

On waking, Sam looked towards the curtains covering her cabin window. From below the window came the sound of voices and an outboard motor somewhere. Stretching luxuriously, as always reluctant to leave the softness of the silken sheets, her natural curiosity finally pulled her out of bed. Wearing nothing but a White Lady T-shirt with its discrete green star as only ornament, she walked over to the window and pulled the curtains.

About five hundred metres away, in the bright glare of the early morning, a spectacular beach surrounded by palm trees, behind which on higher ground rose a long pink and white building on three floors. On one of the masts, a large red flag crossed by a black and white diagonal. Was this Trinidad? Or Tobago? She complimented herself on her detective work, only regretting that she had not found a way to pass a message to Ruth in Miami.

Nor to Leandro.

Now that her cell phone might be back in range, she flicked it on. In the long list of messages, her eye was caught by one from Tatyana. Attaching a photograph! What the fuck? Just after it, one from Leandro. It had better be a good one.

"Ignore anything from Tatyana. I can explain. I love YOU! Only YOU! L."

Leo was not a liar and, knowing that girl, anything was possible. Explanations could wait.

"Make sure there is no more love from Russia! M."

She lay down on the carpet and did her fifty morning abdominals, before slipping into the shower. She found the reply as she stepped out.

"Don't worry, just a little shaken. Not stirred. JB."

She emerged onto the after deck where the Prince and his wife were having breakfast.

"Welcome to Tobago, Samira," the Prince called out.

"So that's where you've been taking us, Your Highness. How exciting, I've never been here before. It looks beautiful."

"It's a shame we've missed the carnival by about three months. I'm told it gets wild. Anyway, we may spend a couple of nights ashore or stay on board. I haven't decided yet."

Sam noted that there was still no hint of when she would leave. They seemed to be assuming she could stay as long as they liked.

"We'll need your passport to take to immigration at Charlotteville. Give it to Malcolm after breakfast."

Just before noon, White Lady's tender was alongside, the companionway lowered. Looking over the rail, Sam could see a number of small Vuitton suitcases, alongside her Italian travel bag. She had never been a fan of Vuitton. It sent the wrong signals.

"Right, let's go," the Prince instructed Sam as he emerged from the saloon, leading Farida by the hand. The Princess was wearing a man's long white linen shirt, over pale apple green slacks, her dark hair falling loose over her shoulders. Vibrations of their sessions together stirred inside Sam. Sessions which had, on yesterday's run south, been marked by several hours of sensuous, dildo-enhanced proximity in the sauna beside Farida's suite in the late afternoon. From which the Prince had been conspicuously absent.

A few minutes later, the tender bumped alongside a rustic wooden jetty at one end of the beach in front of the Blue Haven Hotel. A couple of bell boys were on hand to help the crew of the tender with the luggage.

"Welcome to Blue Haven, Your Highness. And you, Madam."

The hotel manager and the social secretary greeted them as they made their way towards the steps leading up to the various terraces and into the air-conditioned lobby. All white with a glistening wooden floor, large bouquets of tropical flowers.

The royal couple had been allocated a top floor suite and nearby suites had been taken for Sam, as well as for Mohammed, one of the Prince's business managers, and for the Princess' social secretary.

"Suggest we have lunch brought for the three of us," Her Royal Highness had called Sam on the internal phone. "In an hour. *A tout de suite, Samira.*"

Sam stood in the window looking out across the palm trees towards the sea below. The sleek lines of White Lady anchored offshore were even more beautiful at long range. What had brought the Prince here? The answer came over lunch.

"Samira, how good is your Arabic?"

"I spoke it as a child, Your Highness, and spent nearly a year between Syria, Jordan and the Occupied Territories, when I was about twenty-five. So it's pretty good, although I doubt that any native speaker would be fooled."

"I think that's going to be good enough. I have some Spanish-speaking visitors to deal with tomorrow. I would like you to sit in on the meetings, as if you were one of my secretaries, alongside Mohammed, who, as you know, is one of my business managers. None of us speak Spanish, so it might be useful if you could conceal the fact that you do. That way, maybe we'll hear something interesting."

"Of course, Your Highness. Is there anything I need to do to prepare myself?"

"Perhaps dress a bit more demurely and try and conceal some of that beauty of yours - as far as that's possible. Which I rather doubt," the Prince said, laughing. "When we speak amongst ourselves, in front of them, we'll use Arabic."

As he was leaving, the Prince turned to Sam.

"And by the way, Samira, I would only remind you that your contract contains a very strict confidentiality clause. It applies to everything you learn on this assignment for Madame Carla. Everything."

Back in her room, Sam pulled out her cell phones and made her way to the lobby, where she found a small table near the bar. She ordered a small coffee from the waiter who approached. First, a call to Leandro.

"Where are you? Why haven't I heard from you for nearly a week?" Leandro reproached her.

"I'm in Tobago, the Blue Haven Hotel. We arrived this morning. Communications from the ship were complicated and probably recorded. Now I'm on my cell. How are you, my love? I miss you."

"In shock."

"Why? What happened? Another visit from Tatyana?"

"Certainly not. An old rugby friend of mine, Luis Miguel Morales, a diplomat with whom I used to play rugby ten years ago. Found yesterday out at CEAMSE, horribly murdered, probably tortured. It's in the newspapers this morning. He had a Moroccan manservant. They were both murdered. I had lunch with him the day before he disappeared."

"I'm so sorry, Leo. That's terrible. Any idea who did it? Or why?"

"All kinds of stories flying round in the newspapers, though some, predictably, focusing on his homosexuality. Somehow, that doesn't seem to make a lot of sense. He was on the Iran desk at Palacio San Martín. And had been posted to Morocco a few years ago."

Sam was silent for a moment. Iran? Could this be more than just a simple coincidence?

"Iran. Perhaps an angle to pursue," she whispered.

"Interesting you should say that. I'll take your advice."

The way he said it had not fooled Sam. He was clearly already pursuing this avenue.

"Any other news?" she asked.

"Only that I miss you and hate every minute of your being where you are, doing what you're doing. Can you blame me?"

"When I get back, I'll tell you about it. For reasons I'll explain, your worst fears have not been realised."

"What the hell does that mean?"

"You'll just have to wait and see."

"Bitch, I hate you."

"Me too, *amor*!"

She ended the call.

Now for Ruth in Miami. She switched to the US-registered phone.

After the third ring, the call was answered.

"Hello, aunt Ruth, this is Rachel. Your niece."

"Hello, Rachel. How are you? Where are you? We were getting a little worried by the silence."

"I'm in Tobago. At the Blue Haven. We arrived this morning. It's so beautiful. May be here for a day or two. We're having a wonderful time. Great party planned for tomorrow. I'm told there may be some interesting guests. Only heard this an hour ago."

"Wonderful, Rachel. I'm sure you'll have a great time. Goodbye and take care. And don't forget to give your aunt a ring again soon."

The phone call had lasted less than a minute. Ruth wasn't taking any chances. Sam finished her coffee and went back upstairs, passing the hotel guest shop on the way to pick up a magazine. As she stepped out of the lift on the top floor, Mohammed was coming out of his suite.

"Samira, where have you been?"

She didn't think the question really betrayed suspicion.

"Just having a coffee in the lobby. And picking up a magazine. They don't seem to have many books down there. Lots of Carnival T-shirts. Not really my thing. Are there any plans for this afternoon?"

"I have a meeting with His Highness to prepare for tomorrow. I understand you may be joining us. As a listener."

Mohammed laughed.

"With you there, our guests may find it a little difficult to concentrate. Which may play to our advantage."

"I've been told to dress very demurely."

"Not something you're often asked to do often, I would guess."

Again, Sam could not detect any malice. She closed the door of her suite behind her. The house phone was ringing.

"Her Royal Highness asks you to come and see her," the social secretary said.

An hour later, Sam and the Princess were sharing her suite's spacious shower, Sam gently lubricating Farida's back with a perfumed oil.

"I have it specially sent from Morocco. If you like it, I'll give you a bottle afterwards, Samira."

The Princess arched her back, pulling the mass of her black hair to one side, thrusting her opulent butt provocatively towards Sam.

"Please, Samira, continue. You have such a soothing touch."

The Princess turned and pressed her breasts against Sam's, her hand travelling slowly down between Sam's thighs.

"And I love the fact that you're shaved."

Sam recalled that this was one of the transformations Carla had insisted upon at their very first lovemaking. Much to Leandro's subsequent delight.

Farida knelt down in front of Sam, tongue searching between her labia, hands stretched up to caress Sam's breasts, eyes seeking hers.

She caught Sam's glance towards the entrance to the sauna.

"I told you yesterday. He won't be joining us. Anyway, he's busy preparing for tomorrow. Forget about him, Samira. It's me you're here for. For my pleasure. Exclusively. *Baises-moi.*"

Wednesday, 25 June 2008 (AM) - TOBAGO

Sam had been down to the beach for an early swim, virtually deserted before breakfast. The exertions of the previous evening needed to be washed away. She had then returned to her room and taken breakfast on the small terrace. Towards noon, detecting a flurry of activity in the corridor in front of her suite, she poked her head out.

"The cocktails have started," Mohammed announced as he rushed past, files in one hand. "We'll call you."

The call to join the party in the dining room came just before one.

As she came in, the Prince threw her a glance, indicating his approval of her choice of a dark grey pencil skirt, high necked white silk blouse with long sleeves, and low heeled shoes, black. Her make up minimal, only her hair in its usual bobcut. She had not resisted offsetting the paleness of her eyes with a line of kohl, emphasizing her strong Semitic features.

"May I present Miss Harari, one of my secretaries. A little female company is always good for business, I'm sure you'll agree."

The Prince had remembered to stress the false name on which they had agreed.

Mohammed concealed a smile from the other side of the table.

"Samra, this is Señor Zumbado. And Señor Cabrera. From Venezuela. And this is Señor Villanueva and Señor Perez, from Argentina." He turned to his guests. "Samra is from Syria. Shall we sit down to lunch? Please, Señor Zumbado, on my right and you, Señor Perez, my left. We've already had cocktails, which, needless to say, would not interest you, Samira."

Sam thought she detected just the slightest hint of teasing in his voice. She could have done with a drink, but her temporary Muslim pedigree clearly ruled it out. She bowed her head to her employer's tact.

She found herself sitting between Zumbado and Villanueva, Mohammed opposite her.

"I propose that we enjoy the food and leave the rest of our discussions until after the coffee," the Prince said.

Conversation round the lunch table ranged in English from the ongoing financial crisis, through the wonders of President Chavez's Bolivarian revolution, to a clearly hostile discussion of the role of the United States and its ongoing support for Israel. At one point, her Venezuelan neighbour proudly announced to her that he had visited Damascus on a number of occasions. Sam thanked her stars for the two weeks she'd spent there, albeit nearly five years earlier. The four visitors, it turned out, were not staying at the Blue Haven but, as Señor Cabrera explained, they had come to Tobago with their wives and had divided themselves between two other luxury hotels on the island.

"Two Argentine tourist couples in one hotel, two Venezuelan couples in another. What could be more innocent?"

"We'll take coffee on board. Thank you for your services," the Prince told one of the waiters as they rose.

"Please, gentlemen, this way."

The Prince led them down the steps to the jetty, where White Lady's tender was waiting.

Ten minutes later, they entered a conference room on one of the lower decks, where a large table had been set up with an armchair at the head for the Prince and two armchairs on either side for his guests. The table was wide enough to accommodate two chairs side-by-side at the far end for Mohammed and Sam.

"Thank you for putting up with this minor inconvenience," the Prince said, as coffee was poured out. "But I believe that, given the subjects we are to discuss, the added security is desirable. No one can eavesdrop here."

To Malcolm, who had just appeared in the door, he asked that liqueurs should be served.

"I will recapitulate where we had got to at our last contact, if you agree."

The four Latin Americans nodded their agreement. Turning to the two Argentines, the Prince began.

"Your client in Tehran wishes to import certain items of high technology equipment required for uranium enrichment to the twenty percent level. I understand this represents a significant step towards the ninety percent for uranium-235 required for military use. Plans to supply such technology from Argentina were shelved nearly fifteen years ago, as a result of pressure from the United States. We are agreed, I believe, given the international context, not least the embargo, that this is by no means a normal sale. It is also my understanding that this shipment is only a part of a wider contract. Such a contract covers the supply of technical know-how and certain other items sought by your client, which may include a supply of yellow cake."

The Prince turned to the Venezuelans.

"The involvement of your company, based in Caracas, reflects a number of factors, not least the desire of your President to support the efforts of his friends and allies in the Iranian and Argentine governments. It is my understanding that Iran has undertaken very significant investments in Venezuela in a number of sectors, including energy and agriculture. There has also been talk in the past of arms sales to Tehran. Part of the logic of this triangular transaction rests on the fact that the principal parties, Argentina and Iran, have good cause to wish to hide the connection. In the case of Iran, to prevent the shipment being discovered at all. In the case of Argentina, not to be seen fraternising with the government which may have inspired the terrorist attacks in its capital fifteen years ago. Whilst President Kirchner might not worry too much about being found too close to the Iranian regime, as part of her anti-US posture, the bombings and the subsequent accusations of Iranian involvement leave her vulnerable to the views of a significant and influential Jewish community."

The Prince now addressed all four.

"For all these reasons, you have approached me with a view to seeing whether my company can act as an intermediary in such a manner as to make the trail of the contract harder to detect and also to provide the necessary transport."

He paused.

"Would this appear to sum up the situation so far?"

The Venezuelan, Zumbado, looked across the table at the Argentines, and seeing no immediate reaction, was the first to reply.

"As you have said, Your Highness, President Chavez is very keen to be as helpful as possible, both to his friends in Tehran, but also to Cristina Fernandez de Kirchner of Argentina. Relations between Iran and Argentina have been difficult at times, but thanks to his intermediation, they have come together on the all-important question of nuclear collaboration."

"Inevitably a delicate subject," said the Prince.

"Well, with our friends from Buenos Aires, we are now at a point at which we need to find a safe manner to ship certain items to Iran. My company in Caracas has been chosen to provide a possible commercial cover and to assist our Argentine friends in transportation. Your Highness, when we approached you a few months ago and had our very preliminary exchange of information, we were most encouraged. And we are most grateful to you for having made the effort to meet us here today."

He gestured to Perez that he should take it from there.

Perez downed his coffee.

"My country is interested in establishing a secure and reliable means of transport as soon as possible. We've been trying to do this for the last six months. Had a few setbacks. One of our officials, who appeared to be making progress with a contact in the Middle East, sadly died."

There was no reaction to this oblique reference to the murder of Sanchez, although Perez knew the Venezuelans had been informed at the time.

"We have been holding discussions for nearly a year, at meetings which have taken place discreetly in certain capitals. In arranging these, we're also grateful to our friends from Caracas," and here Perez made a friendly gesture towards the two Venezuelans. "Through our embassy in Caracas, using non-diplomatic personnel, we have held discussions with our Iranian friends and have finalised a preliminary shopping list, covering the supply of centrifuge equipment, as well as technology relating to Argentine scientific processes for uranium enrichment. In addition, we would be supplying a certain volume of yellow cake, having sold some to Iran some twenty years ago. At this stage, I do not believe there is any need for me to provide much more information than that. However, once we have finally agreed on the items to be supplied, we would be in a position to provide Your Highness with full details as to the volume of the shipment. Obviously, the technology software would not be included, but we expect a certain number of containers, probably of the 20-foot variety, to be required."

The Prince had been making notes, as had Mohammed and Sam.

"And where would you expect to be able to deliver the shipment for me to assure its onward passage?"

"We have not yet been able to decide that," Perez replied, before turning to Villanueva and continuing in Spanish, whilst also looking across at the Venezuelans.

"Probably at this moment, we don't need to tell them. It might be somewhere like Comodoro Rivadavia down south. If we ship through Venezuela, then the question is whether we only get him involved from that point onwards. We can expect the Americans to have far greater surveillance capacity up in the Caribbean, what with their activities related to drug trafficking up to the States. And if it's from Venezuela, how do we transport it up there in the first place?"

"You're right, let's not go firm now," Zumbado said from across the table.

Turning to the Prince, he continued in English.

"As Señor Perez said, Your Highness, we will let you know as soon as we have taken a decision. We would need to be conscious of the fact that American anti-drug surveillance is much more intense in our part of the world."

The Prince nodded.

"It would be useful to know firstly whether air transportation could be used, obviously depending upon the size and weight of the shipment. The larger the aircraft, the more likely it is to attract attention from the Americans. Alternatively, I could ship it by sea using a much less visible vessel, but this would impact on the time taken to deliver to wherever you wish it to be sent. Perhaps, until we know the size of your shipment, all I will do is provide you with alternatives, namely by air or by sea, the cost and the time involved, also whether from Venezuela or from Argentina. Although, you might perhaps wish to give thought to using a third country. I suspect, but please correct me if I'm wrong, that the Americans follow the dialogue between your two countries quite closely. Perhaps a third country from which to ship might be worth contemplating."

The Latin Americans nodded and Perez made a note in a little booklet.

"The time factor is not negligible, since our friends in Tehran seem to be in something of a hurry. But I have noted your suggestion, for which I thank you."

If Sam had hoped that more detail would emerge on exactly what was being shipped, she was to be disappointed. For another half hour or so, the conversation focused on the logistics of the deal and how this three-way discussion would be prolonged in the coming months. She was intrigued to see that the Prince made little secret of the fact he suspected his own movements would be closely monitored by the Americans and, very probably, the Israelis.

"I have little doubt that I have few friends in Tel Aviv," he said, smiling.

Sam moved not a muscle.

"However, to some extent I use my image as a playboy, as a *bon viveur*, to camouflage some of my business activities. What could be more natural than for a Saudi Prince to spend a few days in Tobago? So, to some extent, the more visible I am, hopefully, the more innocent I appear. I shall spend a few more days here. Since you are not staying at this hotel, our contact today will very probably go unnoticed, or at least unrecorded." Turning to Perez, he added, "One possibility. We use a similar approach for our next meeting. Maybe an out of season visit to some resort down south."

"It's not exactly the season, as you say, Your Highness, but a place like Punta del Este attracts the megarich - if you'll forgive the expression - in our summer. January and February mainly. That might be a possibility. A visit in winter might require some additional explanation."

"I'll bear it in mind. Thank you for the suggestion. I've never been there, though a number of my friends have. Indeed, I had one of my advisers looking at real estate down there around New Year. I understand there are some beautiful properties. Perhaps the time has come to take another look. And now, gentlemen, if you feel we have completed our business for the day, let me have you taken back to the hotel. Your wives have been too patient, though this place does have a beautiful beach."

Everyone rose from the table and, having made their way to the upper deck, the four Latin Americans said goodbye. The tender carried them back to the jetty. A final wave as they made their way up the steps towards the hotel.

The Prince turned to Sam.

"Did we learn anything from that?"

Sam shook her head.

"Sadly, not very much, Your Highness. They did mention the possibility of shipping from Patagonia as opposed to Venezuela. But they may be more attracted by your idea of a third country."

"Time will tell. Thank you, my dear. I trust it was not too boring."

The Prince turned away.

"Come, Mohammed, we need to see what we can prepare in advance of their taking a decision."

She might not have learned very much of interest for the Prince, but Sam was fascinated by the scene she had witnessed. A Prince, albeit of the lower royal echelons of the leading Sunni nation, apparently in cahoots with the most aggressive manifestation of the Shia faith in the form of Iran. Helping to provide weapons of mass destruction for which Saudi Arabia must, by any calculation, be one of the targets. How had this amazing triangle be assembled? Whose idea? And what kind of risks was the Prince taking? From the point of view of the Iranians and the Latin Americans, the benefits were obvious. A Wahhabi intermediary was as improbable as it could get. Who would suspect it?

That his friends in Tel Aviv, as the Prince had referred to them, should be interested in the picture she would be able to report was an understatement.

But not the kind of thing that could be done by cell phone. If only she knew how much longer her presence was required by Farida. The lady was showing every sign of turning pleasure with Sam into an addiction. Not for too long, she had to pray.

Wednesday, 25 June 2008 (PM) – RIACHUELO

The sun was going down as the old man picked his way through the jumble of worn-out tyres, empty oil drums and broken bicycles, all thrown down from the raised track which passed close to the fetid waters of the Riachuelo. The journey was always tiring between the point on Osvaldo Cruz at which the bus had dropped him and the shaky structure of bare bricks, boards and sheets of corrugated iron that constituted home for him, as for so many others in this *villa miseria* beside the river on the eastern edge of Buenos Aires.

He was getting too old for scavenging in the streets of Barracas, something he had been doing for much of the last ten years since losing his job as a sweeper in the Hospital Aeronautico Central about a mile away. He had set off that morning, wrapped up against the cold in a threadbare blanket which his daughter, living a few narrow streets away in the same shanty town, had brought to him a couple of nights earlier when the temperature dropped close to zero. But the cold wind and light rain had put an end to his intention to search for anything of value along the back streets he normally roamed. He had spent most of the day shivering under his blanket in the entrance to a small grocery store whose kindly owner could be relied upon to pass him a bowl of soup.

As he slipped painfully through a gap in the fence which gave access to a shortcut along the riverbank, his attention was attracted by two dogs barking on the edge of a large pile of discarded rubbish, some fifty metres farther along. On getting closer, he saw that a part of the fence which separated the track from this slope to the river had been destroyed by a car now come to rest some ten metres from the water. An ageing Ford Falcon, a model made infamous in the days of the military dictatorship, 'car of the year' for the anonymous snatch groups deployed by all three armed services to pick up suspects. For subsequent 'final disposal' in one of their innumerable interrogation centres. As a sergeant in the army in those dark days, he had belonged to one of these teams. The memories were mercifully fading, but something as unmistakable as the shape of a 1970s Ford Falcon could bring them flooding back.

Few cars ever used this track. Perhaps a stolen vehicle become too hot to keep. But dogs didn't usually bark at cars.

Painfully propping himself up on a broken fence post to steady his descent of the slope, he approached. The dogs, seeing him arrive pole in hand, thought better of it and slunk away. Steadying himself on the side of the car, he looked through the rear window. The bodies of two men, incongruously lying on top of each other on the rear bench seat. Even in the failing light, he could see a large dark stain on the white shirt of the man nearest to him. Again, the images of those 1970s operations were all too vivid.

Thursday, 26 June 2008 (PM) – TOBAGO

Though never totally averse to sitting on a beach and bombarding herself with a diet of champagne, Dagueneau Pouilly Fumé and freshly grilled lobster, by the time a further three days had passed since the visit of the Argentines and Venezuelans, Sam was getting distinctly restless. She was also beginning to run out of ideas as to how to cater to Farida's insatiable appetite. Whether or not the Prince was aware of it, or indeed cared, the late-night after-dinner overtures, at which he switched from the role of observer to lead actor with his wife, were only a part - and a minor one at that - of Sam's attentions which Farida commandeered on a daily basis. Back from the beach or the hotel's iridescent swimming pool following a late lunch, the phone in Sam's suite would herald an invitation to make herself available to Her Highness.

"Maybe Kemal should sign you up on an exclusive long-term contract with Madame Carla," the Princess murmured as they lay on the balcony of Farida's private drawing room, wearing nothing more than a layer of one of La Prairie's most expensive moisturising concoctions, appropriately going by the name of Skin Caviar. It had emerged that Farida knew all about the contents of the FedEx Sam had received and had insisted this afternoon that Sam present herself in the crimson bikini. Which, having passionately caressed Sam's breasts with her tongue, the Princess had then taken a languid pleasure in delicately peeling away.

"*Quelle bonne idée,* Farida," Sam whispered, wondering quite how exclusive and long-term it might turn out to be. One thing was giving Mossad a helping hand now and again, quite another finding herself the full-time love companion of a Saudi princess. She preferred not even to think about Leandro's reaction.

The Princess' cell phone rang.

Sam listened as she exchanged some brief words with her husband. Finally, with a look of ill-concealed disappointment, she turned back to Sam.

"We're leaving tomorrow. And, sadly, *ma chère Samira*, we have to part company. Just for now. You're booked on the early afternoon flight to Miami out of Port-of-Spain. That leaves us about twelve hours. Twelve hours to get the full value of Kemal's little birthday present to me. All of you," she added, somewhat redundantly.

Sam would sacrifice herself with good grace. Not that it was such a sacrifice, if she was being totally honest with herself.

With the late evening flight out of Miami to Buenos Aires, she should be back by Saturday morning. With just enough time in Miami between flights to report to Ruth.

Friday, 27 June 2008 (AM) – CASA ROSADA, BUENOS AIRES

"Do we know what this is about?"

The man from SIDE looked at the Foreign Minister's adviser, the man from the Ministry of Justice, and the officer from the Federal Police. They shook their heads. They were assembled in one of the more formal meeting rooms in the presidential palace, a decor which would not have been out of place in any one of the older European ministries, had it not been for the large photograph of Che Guevara, looking slightly incongruous in this setting of heavy damask curtains, flocked velvet covered walls and glistening parquet floor.

The meeting had been called by one of the advisers to the Secretary-General of the Presidency. The young man had not yet put in an appearance. Nothing strange about that. Punctuality had ceased to mean very much since the arrival of the Kirchner couple in the Casa Rosada.

"It must be fairly serious, given the fact that we all seem to be represented at a high level," the man from the Ministry of Justice murmured.

At that moment, the door opened and the Secretary-General's adviser strode in, slapping a large bundle of papers down on the table, whilst at the same time passing a series of staccato instructions to someone at the other end of the call he was taking on one of two Blackberrys in his hands. Hair unkempt, shirt open, the new youthful and informal dress code eagerly adopted by anyone who regarded themselves as bathing in the aura of presidential approval. A fashion favoured by many of the 'young Turks' of La Cámpora, the Kirchner's own youth movement, headed by their son, Máximo.

"Just make sure that this doesn't get into the press. Or else someone, I need hardly mention who, is going to be very angry. Did you get that?"

The person at the other end having apparently got it, the adviser flicked off his phone and sat down at the head of the table. Keeping them waiting for nearly half an hour seemed not to trouble him in the least.

"Señores, let's start. The Secretary-General makes his apologies, but as you can imagine, is currently much occupied by our agriculture problems. To begin with, I need hardly add that what we are about to discuss remains amongst us."

The men around the table nodded. Only to be expected.

The adviser turned to the representative of the Ministry of Foreign Relations.

"This concerns your service, but also yours," he said, looking across at the representative of SIDE. Both men shifted in their chairs.

"In simple terms, how to interpret the death in suspicious circumstances of two of our diplomats within about six weeks of each other, one in Brussels and the other here in Buenos Aires, both connected with the Iranian question? One assassination gives grounds for concern. A second takes it to another level. The circumstances of both deaths suggest a contract killing and, to my mind, cannot be regarded as coincidental. You may also recall the recent attack on one of our attachés at the embassy in Caracas, which may or may not be related. All three of your services," and here he also looked at the representative of the Federal Police, "have been involved in the investigations. What I need to hear now is how these deaths are to be interpreted. I assume that we are no nearer discovering the killer - or killers? That, and now reports coming in that the reactionary press may soon be making unfounded allegations about some kind of secret nuclear collaboration with Iran. I need hardly add that these are entirely without foundation, but it is still not in our interest for them to be given any credence."

He needed to be careful about just how much he could reveal about the existence of the nuclear discussions with Tehran. For various reasons, the less said the better. The young adviser had already had one meeting with the representative from SIDE a few days earlier. Given the fact that Sanchez and Hernandez belonged to that service, it had been agreed that questions relating to what Sanchez had really been up to would if possible not be aired in any larger gathering. The issue of Argentina's negotiations with Iran on possible nuclear collaboration were far too delicate a topic for wider dissemination. Who could tell where the loyalties of someone in the Ministry of Foreign Relations or the Ministry of Justice really lay?

"Is it possible that these deaths may in some way be linked to such allegations? Sanchez, murdered in Brussels, was one of our trade negotiators with Tehran. And Morales was head of the Iranian desk. Señores, your thoughts please."

He looked around the table to see who would begin. The representative of SIDE cleared his throat.

"Certainly, these were not accidental deaths. The torturing of Consejero Morales makes that quite obvious. Nor is there any reason to believe that Sanchez, the man in Brussels, was contemplating suicide. So these are clearly murders. The investigation in Brussels is being handled by the Belgian police and they appear to see a connection with certain Middle Eastern activists. But they have not been able so far to put a name of any organisation to their suspicions. As regards Morales, again, as far as I know," and here he looked over at the representative of the Federal Police, "we do not have any suspects to date. Finally, the case of Hernandez in Caracas may, or may not, be relevant."

The man from the Policía Federal Argentina made as if to speak, but the Secretary-General's adviser gestured to him that he would get his turn. He was used to the fact that, given a chance, these two services would have differing views on almost any subject. Little love was lost between them, the hostility having been exacerbated by the power which the Kirchners had progressively shifted in favour of the intelligence agency. A power to look at anything and everything, particularly regarding activities which the PFA had historically seen as its special preserve. There was now virtually no area in which SIDE could not operate.

The young man's attention was constantly drawn to the vibrations from one or other of his Blackberrys, but the look on his face suggested he derived as much pleasure from being unavailable as being able to show these men that he had more important matters to attend to.

"As you have indicated," the SIDE representative continued, "the common thread is Iran. But, and I do not think we can entirely ignore it, there is also the fact that both men may have been homosexual."

The presidential adviser looked sharply up from a Blackberry.

"I mention this to show that the Iranian connection, whilst most probably the principal factor, is not necessarily the only one. As to Hernandez, it is my understanding that he is a happily married man with children."

The look on the adviser's face suggested that he for one wasn't going to give the homosexual dimension much credence.

"So, to sum up, we think we may know why, but we don't know who. Would that be a reasonable assessment?"

The man from SIDE nodded.

"I'm afraid so. We're working closely with our comrades at the Federal Police," he said, glancing at the PFA representative across the table, "but so far, the leads are few."

The looks they exchanged suggested that the level of collaboration might be more fictitious than anything else.

The adviser turned to the representative of the Federal Police and gestured to him to speak. A gesture designed to convey only polite interest in what he expected to hear.

"We have only been involved on the very periphery of the Brussels investigation, for obvious reasons. But, as regards the killing of Morales, there is an additional piece of information, which we have so far kept out of the press, namely that two members of the *Bonaerense* were found shot in the back on waste ground near the Riachuelo some two days ago."

"Not unusual," the adviser yawned.

"No, sadly. But coming within forty-eight hours of the discovery of the bodies of Morales and his manservant, we are at least exploring the possibility of a connection. Add to that the fact that the bullet which killed Morales was of a calibre used by that police force. In fact, ballistics believe that it may even have come from a 9mm associated with one of the two dead men. If that is the connection, it seems to confirm a contract killing, but one for which we still cannot identify a source."

"Any thoughts on that?" the adviser turned once again to the man from SIDE.

"To be frank, not really. Obviously, it strengthens the political rather than the homosexual angle. Whilst in the circles in which he moved, there might be someone who could have had it in for Morales at a personal level, it seems unlikely that they would have had recourse to people in the *Bonaerense*."

Finally, the adviser turned to the representative from the Ministry of Foreign Relations. Although the nuclear discussions with Iran were being conducted on parallel channels, this Ministry, like SIDE, was aware of their existence. But, in front of the Ministry of Justice and the Federal Police, detailed reference to these should be avoided.

"If we assume that the political interpretation is the correct one, and I tend to share the views of our colleague from SIDE, what is the explanation? Who, or what, stands to gain from assassinating two of the people working for us on Iranian questions?"

Since no one showed any sign of answering his question, he continued.

"I presume we can rule out the Iranians themselves. There would be no purpose in that. After that? The Americans? The Israelis? Who else? And how do we assess any connection with the business of AMIA and the Israeli embassy bombing? If there is a connection, then the most likely candidates would appear to be the Israelis."

He was momentarily distracted by the buzzing of one of the Blackberrys, but a glance at the caller sufficed for him to switch it off.

"As I was saying. The Israelis. Not only because they have most to fear from any help they may erroneously suspect we might be giving to the Iranians on the nuclear front - which I must again emphasise is not the case - but also because, as we know, they are less than pleased with the way in which, over the years, we have handled the investigations into the bombings here in Buenos Aires. That Morales was running the Iranian desk would obviously be known to them. Are there any grounds for them taking an interest in Sanchez in Brussels? Or Hernandez in Venezuela?"

He surveyed the group. Their continued silence suggested either they hadn't given it much thought, or more likely, they had no answers. He frowned.

"You will need to provide me your assessment in the shortest possible time. And, please don't overlook the possibility that this may go farther. At its simplest level, do we have reason to believe that the attacks may continue? What is disturbing about both cases, and forgive me if I appear to be trespassing on your territory as investigators, is the fact that both murders were committed in the private residence of the victims. That is surely an angle that requires detailed analysis. Somehow, the killer or killers appear to have been able to get access to the homes of both victims."

He turned to the representative of the Ministry of Foreign Relations.

"Have we informed the Belgian police of the murder of Morales? We need to think about that one. The last thing we want is for third countries - and particularly countries close to the United States and the Western powers - to be alerted to some kind of systematic interference in our relations with Iran. That being said, knowing those spies down the road at the American embassy, I'd be surprised if they haven't already made some connection. Even their stupidest diplomats may try and draw a link between us, Venezuela and Iran."

The man from the Ministry of Foreign Relations raised his hand.

"If I may add our thoughts," he offered.

"Go on."

"First of all, whilst the homosexual angle is of course new to me"—he ignored a disbelieving smile which appeared on the faces of those around the table to whom the sexual inclinations of some Argentine diplomats were common knowledge - "we still have a relatively open mind on the reasons for the killings. We are also concerned that if we are to try and maintain the secrecy of our discussions with Iran, we should avoid taking any steps to confirm the delicacy of their nature," and added hastily, "however erroneous. So, I share your concern about alerting the Belgian police to the death of Morales. In fact - and here I am to a certain extent reacting on the spot - it might be wiser to play up the homosexual element, which would have the effect of apparently separating the two events."

The Secretary-General's adviser was nodding as he listened.

"I think that's a good point. Whilst we do not want to relaunch press coverage of the two murders, I will let you know the Secretary-General's views on slanting our briefing in that direction, should the stories be revived. In the meantime, Señores, please do not comment on anything we have discussed here except with your immediate superiors. And please report anything which you believe is relevant directly to me in the future."

Turning to the representative of the Federal Police, he added, "Please send me a brief report regarding the two men of the *Bonaerense*. Any evidence pointing firmly in that direction is of interest. We need to know as a matter of urgency who may have given them their instructions."

He pulled his papers together and switched on the ringer on his other Blackberry, which had hardly ceased vibrating throughout the meeting.

"If no one has anything else to add, I thank you for your presence."

The adviser rose from the table and, without affording them the courtesy of a handshake, swept out of the room, already selecting a number on his Blackberry.

The four men picked up their papers and, having shaken hands, filed out.

Friday, 27 June 2008 (AM) – AVENIDA DE MAYO Y PERÚ, BUENOS AIRES

At about the same time the meeting was coming to an end at the Casa Rosada, Leandro was sharing a coffee with Eduardo at London City. Repeating a habit he had acquired for their meetings during the pursuit of the killer of Janet Williams, Leandro had got there first in order to observe Eduardo's arrival. In the days when Dávila's 'heavies' had been tailing them, he had on more than one occasion been able to spot the follower. With the end of the Dávila affair, he had stopped worrying about these things. Now, with the murder of Luis Miguel, things appeared to have moved back into the danger zone in which minimal precautions might be warranted.

Looking through the window of the cafe, he watched Eduardo emerge from the Metro entrance next to the cafe on Avenida de Mayo. Eduardo spotted his godfather and waved to him.

"If you don't mind, I'll keep my overcoat on, it's so fucking cold."

Attracting the attention of Leandro's regular waiter, Eduardo indicated a small coffee with thumb and index finger.

"What do you know about this?" Leandro asked, pushing a three day-old copy of La Nación across the table, open at the page taken up with details of Luis Miguel's murder.

"Nasty business," Eduardo replied. "From what I've seen, his death can't have been pretty."

"He was a friend of mine. We used to play rugby together. Hadn't seen much of him for years, but we got together again a few weeks ago."

It should suffice to dress up his curiosity as an understandable concern with the death of a friend.

"I'm sorry," Eduardo said. "Can you think of any reason why he might have been killed?"

"Frankly, no. He was a diplomat. Not necessarily the kind of person to get involved with people who might do this kind of thing. But it's worrying."

Eduardo discreetly studied his godfather. Might there be another reason for this meeting? The waiter placed his coffee on the table beside him.

"Worrying? In what way do you mean? You know this happens every day. I should know. Half of it lands on my desk."

"And this one? Has this one landed on your desk?"

"Why? What's the interest to you?"

"As I said, he was a friend. Isn't that reason enough?"

"I suppose so. Though I bet he's not the first friend to meet an untimely end."

"Probably, but it's more often someone getting killed in the course of a robbery. Not accompanied by this level of sadistic brutality."

"I give you that. I've heard a little about the case because his main residence here in the city was in the area of our *Comisaría*. I don't know what part of the Ministry he worked in. Do you?"

"To my knowledge, he was working on the Middle East. He didn't tell me much about it. We mainly chatted about rugby. A very good scrum-half in his day. We drank a lot of beer together. But when I stopped playing after that problem with my disc, we drifted apart and only took up again about a month ago. A good man. Certainly didn't deserve to go that way."

"If you like, Uncle, I'll try and find out a bit more. But if SIDE are involved, it may be tricky."

"I'd be interested, but I certainly wouldn't want you to stick your neck out."

Leandro added the last confident that his son would almost invariably do the opposite.

"Don't worry, you know me, not one to take risks unnecessarily," Eduardo said, ill-disguising a smile. "What my godfather wants, he usually gets."

Eduardo stood up.

"I've got to get back, but I'll let you know if I find anything. Take care of yourself. Perhaps life is getting more dangerous for rugby players."

"Sick humour," Leandro retorted, a tinge of bitterness in his voice.

They embraced.

Leandro lingered on, ordering another *ristretto* and a small toasted sandwich. How was the story being handled in today's papers? Leaving aside the natural predilection for gory details, speculation as to the motives had not died down. Reference was made to the fact that he had never married, journalistic shorthand for suggesting that he might have been gay, reinforced by mention of his manservant and his posting to Morocco, with all that this implied for a certain Catholic and conservative readership in terms of 'unnatural' tastes. A colleague was quoted as saying he'd appeared slightly depressed of late. His involvement in Middle Eastern affairs was given only passing mention, noting that he had been responsible for relations with Iran, with implications in the context of the AMIA terrorist attack.

Quite how all this might justify the fact that Luis Miguel had been tortured before being killed was far from clear.

Leandro had not heard back from Charles Colson since sending him a secure mail about the murder the day after. Although Leandro had not up to then considered that he had anything concrete to report, the murder of the head of the Iranian desk at the Argentine Ministry of Foreign Relations would be of interest to Frobisher in its own right.

Back at his flat, Leandro flicked on his computer and plugged in the encryption software, which he carried on a memory stick. Within seconds, it told him that a mail had come in using its circuits. It was from Charles.

"Murder of Morales is worrying. Appears to be second assassination of Argentine official connected with the Iranian question, following death of one of their diplomats in Brussels, of which you will be aware. Grateful your thoughts and ideas on who might be behind this. C."

That's what I'd also like to know, Leandro thought to himself.

An incoming email announced that Sam was on her way back. About time too.

Saturday, 28 JUNE 2008 (PM) – PASAJE DE LA PIEDAD, BUENOS AIRES

Around six thirty the following afternoon, Leandro heard the key turn in the front door. Sam, on her way back from a session at the gym, judging by the dark red tracksuit she revealed on taking off her coat. Her face was flushed.

"When did you get back? Why didn't you ring me?"

He took her in his arms.

"My, Mr Grant, with a kiss like that you make me feel like Ingrid Bergman!" she whispered, pulling her lips back from his, a faintly ironic expression in her eyes.

"This is a very strange love affair," she went on, quoting the Swedish actress.

One rainy afternoon, they had played Hitchcock's longest kiss in 'Notorious' over and over. Leandro knew his lines.

"Why?"

"Maybe the fact that you don't love me."

"When I don't love you, I'll let you know."

He pulled her closer. She made no effort to escape. Bridges might need rebuilding.

"*Dios*, it's getting colder out there," she finally said, shaking her hair into place as she removed her scarf. "I need a drink."

"What would you like? Whisky? Some wine? A brandy?"

"Brandy," she said." Why isn't your fire on? On a day like this. Cold-blooded Scot!"

"You deal with the brandy, I'll do the fire," Leandro said, going out to the rear storeroom where he kept the logs.

Some ten minutes later, each armed with a brandy, the two of them stood with their backs to the fireplace where the flames were gaining ground. Looking over at his computer screen, he detected that whilst he'd been collecting wood, Sam might have played her usual trick of skimming through his open files and recent Internet searches. He hoped she hadn't learned too much.

"When did you arrive?"

"This morning, on American Airlines. Horrible flight, bumpy."

He studied her. She was very brown.

"Put on a little weight?" he teased.

"Not a gram! I checked this morning."

"Good trip?"

Inwardly dreading what he might learn.

"Very good, thank you."

She seemed determined to make him suffer a bit longer.

"And you, Leandro, any more adventures during my absence?"

The reference to Tatyana was predictable. He shook his head. Smiling, she clinked her glass against his.

"Don't worry, you needn't explain. Not now, anyway. When I need a pressure point some day."

He waited, warming the brandy between his fingers. Silence might work better than interrogation. He sat down in one of the armchairs, carefully avoiding her eyes.

After a couple of minutes, during which neither looked at the other, she finally relented, moving across to sit on the armrest. She took his glass from between his fingers and placed it next to hers on the bookcase behind him. Then she bent forward and, holding his face between her hands, kissed him long and hard.

"I can't make you suffer any longer, *mi amor*. Remember what I said over the phone? About your worst fears not being realised?"

"Yes, can't say it made much sense at the time. What did you mean?"

She paused. Perhaps she could extract just a few more seconds of delicious anxiety from the man she loved. The look on his face was so irresistible when she played this game.

"Fuck you, Sam. You're killing me. Deep down, you're a sadist. I should have spotted it much earlier."

"Sadist? Maybe. Particularly with you. You bring it out in me."

"Thanks."

He made as if to get up, but she pinned him down in the chair.

"Poor man, you do love me. Probably too much for your own good."

"Stop playing with me. It's called bullying. You're bigger than me."

In some ways, he was right. Though he was by no means above adroitly playing the role of the victim when it suited him.

For an instant, she was distracted by a thought which had occurred to her in the past. Were her sadistic tendencies pathological? Sadism was commonly regarded as a male prerogative. But was that right? Couldn't a woman also be sadistic? Could she? Hadn't she felt something like that, however briefly, when Dávila's two bodyguards, hogtied, had lain at her mercy, out on the farm at Chacabuco? After what they had done to her, it would have been fully justified.

She looked down at him. She couldn't prolong it any longer.

"Okay. In a nutshell. My client turned out to be the Princess, not the Prince. There! As I said, better than your worst fears. Am I right?"

Leandro stared at her in amazement.

"The Princess? Explain. You lost me somewhere."

"I was hired to look after Farida. And only Farida. The Prince never touched me."

She detected the expression in his eyes changing. A feeling of relief?

"Give me back my brandy," he said.

He drank half his glass.

"Well, I can't say that I'm not slightly happier about that," he murmured, looking up at her.

"I thought so. That's what I meant over the phone."

Leandro, having little of the voyeur in him, decided to leave it at that. For the time being at least. Maybe he would seek more detail some other time.

Sam got up from the arm of his chair and walked over to the fireplace. She turned.

"So what's the latest on your friend the murdered diplomat?" she asked.

"Luis Miguel? I saw Eduardo yesterday."

"So you *are* interested in his death, you see. Not just because he was a friend. You told me he was dealing with Iran. That's it, isn't it?"

Bullseye as usual!

"Actually, he really was a friend of mine," Leandro said, evading. "Tragic."

"Only tragic? Surely, more than that, Leandro? There's obviously something going on here. And with what you've been looking at, I know you're interested."

So she had been at his computer. No getting away from this girl. During her days away in the Caribbean, his review of the pros and cons of bringing her into his confidence had finally led him to the conclusion that, whatever he might say to mislead her, she would almost certainly work it out. An orderly retreat might now be in order.

"Okay. You're right. I am directly interested. In fact, that's the reason for my meeting with Eduardo, to see if he can throw any light on it."

"Just like the old days! The Three Musketeers!"

"Except that, this time, I won't be telling Eduardo anything about why I'm really interested. I've already told him that Luis Miguel was an old friend, but no more. Luis Miguel's flat was in a part of town covered by his *Comisaría*, so he may be involved in some way in the investigation."

"Good. Let's hope he finds something. That makes two of them now. Perhaps even three."

Leandro shot her a glance. "Two of what?"

"Dead Argentine diplomats dealing with Iran, as if you didn't know. And nearly three, after what happened in Caracas."

How much more did this girl know? She seemed to be one step ahead even of Frobisher. Neither he nor the people in London had spotted anything in Caracas.

"What's this about Caracas?"

"One of our diplomats got shot. He survived."

"How come you're so well-informed?"

"Do you really have to ask?"

Her friends in Mossad, clearly. But his suspicions had gone no farther.

At that moment, Sam's cell phone rang.

"Good evening, Carla. Sweet of you to ring. Yes, arrived safely. No, it all went fine. Yes. He was delighted. Very pleased. And so, more importantly, was *she*."

Again Leandro could hear Carla, though by the tone of voice, he suspected that she might be as surprised as he had been.

Sam laughed.

"I know. Anyway, I'll give you a ring later."

Again the voice at the other end.

"You're right. I'll pass it on to him."

She made a gesture towards Leandro as if to convey a kiss from Carla.

"I'll tell him. Take care. Love."

She hung up and sat down once again beside Leandro, and ran her fingers through his hair.

"Carla sends her love. And thinks you must be feeling better now that we know who the client was."

Leandro shook his head in disbelief. What had his emotional life come to when the lesbian lover of his girlfriend was apparently sufficiently sensitive to share his relief at what had happened in the Caribbean? Where were the old black and white demarcation lines?

"She's some woman, that Carla of yours," he said.

"And, don't underestimate it, a bit of yours too."

Leandro sought refuge back in the subject of Mossad. That at least was something that could be deciphered along more predictable lines.

"So, how often are you in touch with your masters in Tel Aviv?"

"Often enough," came the reply.

Leandro refilled his glass. He needed it. This conversation was clearly about to become all about Sam climbing on board. Keeping her at arm's length would in no way serve to control her.

"Do you want to tell me some more about it?" he said. "There's no point running circles around each other. Pooling our ideas should benefit both of us."

"Exactly," Sam replied. "Let me go and have a shower and get into something warmer."

About a quarter of an hour later she was back. Keeping a supply of clothes in one of his cupboards, she had changed into another, warmer tracksuit. Black. Her hair was wet. No makeup. A Sam without façade.

"I suggest we order some food. Haven't had any sushi in a while. Got a good white wine on ice somewhere?"

Leandro picked up the phone and, after consultation with her, placed an order.

"Three quarters of an hour. I'll open the wine."

Sam pulled a chair up to the worktable next to Leandro's usual place. The girl meant business. He sat down opposite her.

"You spend a lot of money on make-up and everything. But you're really so beautiful just like you are now. It's a waste!"

Sam shrugged her shoulders and sidestepped the compliment.

"Let me start," she said. "I'll tell you what I think I know about what you're doing. You can correct me or fill me in with more, as you wish. I don't need to know the most intimate details of whatever assignment Frobisher has given you. But it's my bet that we overlap in certain areas, which is wasteful. To begin with, Frobisher has given you a new assignment. That we know."

"What makes you think that?"

"Oh, come on. Don't play games! You said as much that night after dinner with the Russians. Not to mention the web searching you've been doing over recent months. Iran and Israel don't usually figure so often on your flagged websites. Add to that the briefing you asked me to give you over lunch at New Brighton. And last month at the Cuspide bookshop, what were you doing in the Middle Eastern history section? And your Amazon order. Not just trying to read up on my Druze ancestry, I bet. So stop denying the undeniable."

"Jesus. I must be more careful next time."

Leandro was kicking himself. He'd been careless not changing his password. Certainly not up to the standard Frobisher would expect of him. If Sam could deduce this kind of thing, who else might do the same? Could his flat keys have given access to someone other than Tatyana?

At the same time, however underhand, he enjoyed the fact that she took this level of interest.

"Not spying, just watching. I always watch the men I live with. Don't worry, not as many as you might think," she added, noting his frown. "Most other girls would probably spend their time trawling through your mobile phone. I sense that kind of thing differently. If you were being unfaithful, you'd have heard from me long ago. Or else I'd have disappeared."

"You've already done that once," he said softly.

Sam ignored the remark. For an instant, she was tempted to atone for her snooping by revealing the true identity of cmholland9T6. Yet better say nothing for now. She might need to send him some more anonymous clues.

"No, I watch closely. Because I love you." She smiled. "Come on, Leo, we're agreed it's Iran's nuclear ambitions."

Leandro shook his head. In disbelief, not in denial.

Sam smiled. "You see, painless!"

Not for the first time, Leandro was filled with a mixture of fascination and unease. Was he really so transparent to women?

"Obviously to do with their nuclear programme," she continued. "That makes sense, doesn't it? There's not much else to be interested in, where that godforsaken country's concerned. Iran, nuclear, Argentina. There's an obvious linkage. Almost certainly with Chavez in the middle. After all, he's one of the few to cosy up to the mullahs. That's probably as much to irritate the Americans as anything else, since he doesn't need their oil. What with Petroleos de Venezuela churning the stuff out. Admittedly with a high sulphur content which requires a lot of refining."

"For heaven's sake, Sam, why can't you be like other girls? Talk about fashion or summer holidays? What do you know about Venezuelan oil? High sulphur content indeed. You're right of course, damn you."

"Probably more than you think, but that's not what we're talking about here. Argentina has a nuclear research capacity. Been in the business for years. For a long time they hesitated about joining the Latin American nuclear free zone treaty. It had some Mexican name, as I recall."

"Tlatelolco," Leandro murmured.

"That's it, Tlatelolco. One of these unpronounceable Mexican towns! You see, if you know an impossible name like that, it's a sure sign that you're interested in the subject. So, let's drop the facade. Who knows, maybe we can even work together. Like in the good old days against Dávila last...."

Sam's trailed off, her gaze clouding over.

"Let's not go there," Leandro stretched out his hand toward Sam. She shook her head, making no attempt to take it.

"It's okay. I'm practically over it. Thanks to you and..." she hesitated,, "Carla."

Now it was Sam's turn to see Leandro's gaze waver. He took another mouthful of the brandy and cleared his throat.

"Anyway, Mata Hari, continue your interrogation. I´d prefer to keep on that subject."

"So, Argentina and its nuclear industry. We all know that Iran is desperately looking for suppliers, not only of the technology they need for their enrichment plants, centrifuges and so on, but also trying to get their hands on supplies of uranium. Argentina has both and, given the current complexion of this government, with its links to Chavez, Fidel Castro and others, there's probably good reason to believe they're in touch. In fact, I know they are."

She wasn't going to tell him why, just yet. A minor smokescreen might be in order.

"You can probably imagine who told me."

Leandro nodded. "The boys from Tel Aviv."

"Inter alia. As you can imagine, they devote massive resources to keeping track of where Iran stands on its nuclear programme. Argentina, for various reasons, is good hunting ground for them."

She paused.

"How am I doing so far?"

Leandro smiled.

"Typically, too fucking well!"

"Good. You lucky man. Not only beautiful and sexy, but brilliant as well."

"Conceited bitch!"

"Modesty never got anyone anywhere, except possibly into a convent. And you know what I think about that."

"So," she continued, "Frobisher has asked you to try and find out what's going on between Argentina and Iran on the nuclear front. That's it, isn't it?"

He smiled again.

"How much of this deduction is yours, and how much might you have been briefed by your handler? In fact, to put it more bluntly, how much have you told them about me and Frobisher?"

Sam hesitated. She wasn't going to lie to him. Or at least, not more than necessary.

"They know you have a relationship with Frobisher. In fact, when I mentioned it, they were quite complimentary about the Brits. I suspect they met professionally."

"Possibly, who knows, in that world? Now that you've told me what I'm doing, perhaps you'd like to tell me what you're doing?"

"I have to be careful. The rules that bind me are probably more constraining than those which bind you. Governments have more power than private companies when it comes to betrayal or breach of confidentiality. It's also a world in which traitors don't survive very long."

"That's exactly what worries me," Leandro interrupted.

She laid her hand on his.

"Don't worry, I can look after myself. As you know, risk turns me on. In many ways."

Leandro could only guess at how many ways she had in mind. Riding her recently acquired Harley-Davidson through the lethal traffic of Buenos Aires, working for the Israelis, her relationship with Carla, a definite edginess in the ways she made love. These he knew about. What others?

Sam watched him. She could guess what was going through his mind. There were risks of which she was confident he remained unaware. A fleeting image of Carla, latex gloved hand closing off the air on her gas mask, the rasp of breath half blocked, her lungs screaming for oxygen. The intensity of total helplessness meshed with total trust. A recent addiction Leandro knew nothing about. Yet…

She shook her head as if to clear her thoughts.

"As I once told you, Mossad gives me the occasional assignment. Also what you might call a general watching brief. Because I'm Argentine and live in Buenos Aires, a broad agenda relating to our relations with Israel. They're interested in anything about the terrorist attacks on their embassy and AMIA. They've also mentioned the nuclear question. As you know, some see the two as linked."

"Closely. Luis Miguel, when I lunched with him a few weeks ago, certainly said as much. And my friend Grunwald, the journalist, also hinted at something to that effect."

Sam smiled.

"So you see, Leo, we *are* looking at the same things."

"But that doesn't mean that what I discover is passed to you for you to pass to Mossad. We've got to be pretty clear about that. We need rules."

"Of course, that's understood. Otherwise, you would be breaking your trust. But at the same time, I suspect that if we work as a team, each can help the other without necessarily infringing trust."

"I don't disagree, but it won't be easy to handle. I know you. Never one to recognise a boundary when you reach it."

"That's not fair. I'm very respectful."

"The fuck you are! Boundaries don't mean a thing to you. Occasionally, a crash barrier does. But only occasionally."

Sam looked hurt. "Only that?"

"Don't give me that shit," Leandro said. "You know full well what I'm talking about. And as you know, it's one of the reasons I love you," he ended rather lamely.

"I know. I suspect you wouldn't have it any other way." She paused a moment "So what about these rules? Can we draw them up? You've mentioned one, sharing some but not all the fruits of our labours on behalf of our clients. That makes sense, although it doesn't mean we can't implicitly use things we learn to help the other. It's also a matter of access. The kind of people you see are never going to talk to a girl like me."

"Not about that, anyway!"

"You know perfectly well what I mean. I couldn't get to a man like Luis Miguel, poor guy. By the way, if they went for him - whoever they are - might they not go for you?"

"I thought of that, but I really don't think there's any connection. After all, I only had lunch with him a couple of times. And they - whoever they are - can't start assassinating everybody he had lunch with."

"When's the funeral? If you go, you might see who else is there. They say that murderers often return at that point."

"You see too many movies. I don't know whether they've set a date yet. But, you may be right. Whenever it takes place, perhaps you want to come along." He paused. "On second thoughts, probably better not. With you around, it's hard to remain unobtrusive."

"Complaining?"

"Just occasionally it may be a bit of a liability."

Sam toyed with the remains of her brandy.

"Do you want some more?"

She shook her head.

"Now it's my turn. You never did tell me what else you did in the Caribbean. Apart from attending to the Princess."

She appeared reluctant to reply.

"That's not fair. I answered your questions," Leandro complained. "Were you expecting your client to be the Princess?"

"Frankly, no. The bottom line is it turns him on to see his wife making love with another woman. Not that she doesn't enjoy it as well. So after I had played my part, like some kind of warm-up number, I was discreetly bidden to withdraw."

"Gives a new meaning to the words *acto vivo*," Leandro mused.

"What's that?"

"Before your time. Under Perón, cinema performances were preceded by a little amateur show. A couple of old guys with a guitar, singing out of tune. Lasted into the late 60s or early 70s. They used to come round with a hat. The audience happy to pay anything just to get rid of them."

"In my case they'd pay to keep me there."

"Not the slightest doubt."

"Feel better?"

"A bit."

She saw no reason to expand on the full extent of her sessions with Farida.

"And from Mossad's point of view?"

"Interesting and useful."

Should she tell him a little more?

"Just to say that the Prince, apart from having a role in defence, seems to have clients on the other side of the fence."

"You mean...Iran?"

Sam nodded.

Leandro whistled.

"Forget I told you that. But that's certainly what it looks like."

Deep down, she felt bad about not telling him more. There were rules that still needed defining. For the time being, the limits of discretion was one of them. Had she betrayed her trust with Mossad?

"I'm sure your friends in Tel Aviv were fascinated."

Again she nodded.

"Enough to pay for the sushi?" Leandro said, as the buzzer at the end of the Pasaje began to sound.

Monday, 30 June 2008 (AM) – AVENIDA DE MAYO Y PERÚ, BUENOS AIRES

"So, you found something?"

Eduardo was not going to be rushed. There were times when Leandro wondered whether he didn't do it to irritate him.

Leandro waited, sipping his *cortado*, and looked around the tables in London City.

"It's looking very messy and complex. Probably bound to be, given the identity of the victim. But I must say, there are a lot of strange fingers in this pie. I'm pretty sure I shouldn't be telling you all this, but then, that's nothing new."

"As you say, nothing new. Habit-forming," Leandro commented with a smile.

"As we know, your friend Luis Miguel was dealing with the Middle East. With Iran. Not an easy subject for us in Argentina, what with the AMIA and Israeli embassy attacks, for which most of the fingers point to Hezbollah. It's reckoned that Hezbollah is supported and controlled by Iran."

Leandro was tempted to say that he knew all this, but to do so might confirm the true nature of his interest.

"So the victim was obviously following the question of whether our governments have done anything to try and resolve the AMIA bombing. Which meant that he would have had the Jewish community on his back. I've got a friend - perhaps a flattering description – in SIDE. He gave me a ring the other day and we had lunch. It turns out that he was also interested in this case. Wanted to pick my brains, given the fact that the victim lived in our precinct."

"A dialogue between the police and SIDE? Unusually cosy."

"He wanted to do this more on the basis of friendship than anything else. As it turned out, I was able to learn far more from him than he from me."

"Go on."

"It seems the case has been taken away from the *Comisaría* where the bodies were found and is now being run by a special team here, of which SIDE is a part. The Casa Rosada is also taking a direct interest. My friend had seen the autopsy. Very unpleasant. The marks on wrists and ankles of both of them suggest they'd been tied for some time. And then – here's where it gets rough – they were strapped in such a way that your friend was fucking his manservant."

"And then shot?"

"In that position, a single bullet through both heads."

Leandro stared out of the window at the passers-by. Gone were the days devoted only to central bank reserves and currency fluctuations.

"Poor Luis Miguel. What can he have done to deserve that?"

"You know more about these international things than I do, Uncle."

"And the killer?"

"They've come across a lead to some of the nastier parts of the *Bonaerense*."

"All manner of mercenaries in their ranks."

"What has not appeared in the press so far is the discovery of two dead *canas* in the back of an old Ford Falcon on waste ground by the Riachuelo last Tuesday. They now think they're connected."

"I'd always assumed they were behind about fifty percent of organised crime, particularly in the province and here in Capital."

"That might be a conservative estimate. Security, as we know, practically tops the list of public concerns. But, like inflation, this government doesn't seem to want to deal with it. Occasionally, they try and grab a headline with a drug haul, but far too many of the killings in and around the city simply go unresolved."

"Get back to Luis Miguel, please."

"One theory they are working on – one of a number – is that it was a contract killing carried out by someone in the *Bonaerense*. The bodies were found at CEAMSE, strapped together, wrapped in plastic sheeting. It's not clear how or why anybody would dump something that large in the back of a garbage truck in the middle of town, late in the evening on a weekend."

Eduardo drained his coffee cup before continuing.

"One theory has it that the killers might have followed the truck in another car to where it stopped for a beer, and done the swap then. On the other hand, they do know that the torturing and killing took place in Luis Miguel's flat. There's every sign of that at his place, including blood all over the carpet in his sitting room. They must have followed him home a day or so before they were found and taken him as he was going in. It's pretty common these days, though it doesn't usually end up this way."

Eduardo paused to eat his *medialuna*.

"They spent most of the weekend with him and his manservant. Alive. The block was virtually empty. It's the kind of place where most of the residents have a place in the country and would have been away. Also doesn't have a *portero* on duty all the time, certainly not at the weekends."

Leandro wondered whether to mention that Luis Miguel had been lunching with him on the Friday. He thought better of it.

"What I don't understand," he said, "is what they were after. I mean, Luis Miguel was a regular diplomat, as far as I know."

"Dealing with a delicate area in our foreign policy. We know that some of that passes through Chavez, as part of the Kirchner love affair with the Venezuelan and with others of the same persuasion. Even Cuba."

"But something as horrific as this? Doesn't seem to make a lot of sense."

"There are clearly things going on which explain the involvement of bodies such as SIDE, not to mention the Presidency. I suppose one has to try and work out what the purpose might be in torturing and then killing your friend, and work back from there to who might be interested."

"And? Have you done any of that?"

Eduardo was silent for a moment.

"I have, but, not being an expert in Middle Eastern questions, I can't tell whether any of it adds up. I suspect we would have to try it out on someone like Sam. She knows about these things, doesn't she?"

"Yes, but, frankly, given what she's been through, I'm not sure that dragging her into yet another gruesome killing is necessarily going to do her any good."

Inwardly, Leandro had little doubt that Sam was perfectly capable of confronting something as horrific as the murder of Luis Miguel. It would probably fascinate her. But for now, he preferred to try and make up his own mind before bringing her together with Eduardo again.

"She strikes me as a pretty resilient girl, but I'm sure you're right. I rather thought she was recovering."

"She is, she's about ninety-eight percent."

"Hasn't she just been off on a trip or something?"

"Got back a couple of days ago. The Caribbean. It probably did her a lot of good."

That was certainly as far as Leandro was going to go. The Saudi royal could wait.

"Well, in simple terms, I reckon there may have been two possible motives for the murders. The first, to try and discover what our government's policy is over Iran. The second could be simply to send the government a message. They seem to have wanted the bodies found. The fact that he was tortured suggests the first interpretation might be the right one. Of course, it could be both. I don't know what you think?"

Leandro had been doodling on a paper napkin as he listened to Eduardo. He needed to be careful not to show a level of interest that might unnecessarily alert his son.

"The best I can give you is the view of someone who reads the newspapers. And with a girlfriend like Sam, the Middle East has certainly become a subject of interest. But it's no better than any reasonably informed observer of the international scene."

Over the next few minutes, Leandro's analysis, had he but known it, was strikingly similar to that presented by the presidential adviser a few days earlier. The Iranians, dismissed as illogical. The Israelis, sufficient motive, but reluctant to take such direct action. The Americans, unlikely.

"They're paranoid about a nuclear Iran. And they distrust our government. But if they could read Soviet communications during the Cold War, I would imagine ours are child's play. So, I wouldn't rate the American threat very high."

Leandro suddenly remembered the dinner at the Russian ambassador's.

"A real outsider might be the Russians. They're tied up in the whole non-proliferation issue, as one of the superpowers. But also because they've been negotiating with Iran over a nuclear reactor, as I recall. Although there again, this kind of direct action is probably reserved for KGB traitors. Like that poor guy in London, poisoned with something radioactive."

Eduardo had been jotting down the names of the countries as Leandro listed them. He looked up.

"Polonium. So on the basis of your analysis, the prime candidate would appear to be Israel."

"Yes, I suppose so." He thought a moment. "Or Iraq. They hate the Iranians. They fought for years. Sunnis against Shias. But that is more Sam's area."

Eduardo added Iraq to his first list.

"But given what they've got on their plate back home, I wonder whether they would bother."

Leandro thought for a few moments before continuing.

"As we know, Iran's the prime suspect in the AMIA explosion. Could this in some way just be a continuation of that? Though I'm not sure with what purpose. If Hezbollah flies a Shia flag, who might fly a Sunni? I don't know enough about these movements. Though, as I recall, a number of them have sprung up in and around Baghdad since the Americans invaded. Al Qaeda has been there for some time. You'd probably have to talk to a specialist."

"Which brings us back to the question of the *Bonaerense*. Why might they be involved?"

"Can't think. Though worth remembering that the original AMIA bombing produced a list of ex-military and policemen who might have been mixed up in the affair."

"And SIDE fished in that pond."

"So I suppose, you can't even rule out the possibility that this is somehow a purely domestic affair. Kirchner must have put a few noses out of joint when he lifted SIDE's immunity in the AMIA case. Not to mention sacking a whole lot of them."

Eduardo drew a deep breath.

"Jesus, why is everything so messy in this country?"

"In this kind of business, I suspect we're no worse than anyone else. It just feels that way because it's our country. How about another coffee?"

Eduardo nodded. Leandro made a sign to the waiter to bring two more.

"A lot to think about."

"Well, I'll see how much I can keep track of this. But if it's up at the level of the Casa Rosada, that may be a lot harder," Eduardo added.

Although the last thing that Leandro wanted was to get swept up in the investigation into Luis Miguel's death, it was obvious that it must be connected with Frobisher's assignment on the nuclear front. If the *Bonaerense* really had been involved, any professional intelligence organisation would have steered well clear. Not only were they criminal, they were also totally unreliable. Unless it had been some kind of 'false flag' operation, with an intelligence organisation pretending to be a terrorist movement. Terrorist organisations were always deniable. Yasir Arafat had survived for decades on that myth.

"Well, I'm not sure how much I can help you."

"Oh, but you can, Uncle Leandro. I simply don't have your kind of experience on the international front. Nor do I have an Arab girlfriend," he added, teasing.

"And probably all the better for it," Leandro rejoined with a grin. "Not recommended for anyone with high blood pressure."

Eduardo's expression had changed to one of concern.

"At your age, you need to be careful."

"Fuck off! How dare you?"

"No, seriously, Elena was expressing concern just the other day."

"Was she indeed? I'll have to have a word with that lady. Which reminds me. I owe her a phone call."

As Eduardo was leaving, he called after him.

"If you hear anything about the funeral, let me know, will you?"

Eduardo acknowledged with a wave of the hand.

Leandro signalled to the waiter to bring another coffee. He had read somewhere that coffee was quite good for the heart. It had better be the case, given his consumption.

He stared at the coffee in front of him, then dialed Elena.

"I'm told you're worrying about my health. Suggesting that my girlfriend is bad for my heart. Nice of you to express your concern."

"I won't bother to ask who might be spreading these rumours. I couldn't care less."

"I prefer to think that you do care. What news?"

"Not great. Have you heard anything from Alex recently?"

"Not for a few days. Mind you, nothing strange about that. Why?"

"She was supposed to come to dinner last night, but never turned up. I'm worried. It's not like her. At least she should have called."

Leandro could hear that Elena was worried. It was true, Alex was usually considerate enough to cancel, even if at the last minute.

"Did she mention other plans? It was the weekend."

"Nothing in particular."

"When did you last speak to her?"

"Middle of the week. She dropped off some washing as usual."

"As usual. Any more news on the Nouria front?"

"No. And I didn't press for it. I usually let her take the lead."

"So it's not over?"

"They're still sharing the flat. That's about all I know."

"Well, give her a day to make contact. Maybe you can do some discreet checking, without her knowing. You know what she's like. Doesn't like to be watched."

"No. Wonder where she gets that from."

"I wonder."

Elena laughed.

"Well, if you hear anything… She often comes to you first."

"Of course, I'll let you know. Don't worry too much."

He turned back to his newspaper.

July 2008

Tuesday, 1 July 2008 (AM) – AVENIDA DE MAYO Y PERÚ, BUENOS AIRES

Next morning, Leandro was back having breakfast at his usual table. The cold of the morning had prompted him to take a taxi, as opposed to his usual habit of walking there as part of the process of waking up. Mornings were not his best hour and only a combination of a boiling hot shower, followed by a freezing cold one, stood any chance of restoring him to a semblance of normality. From the depths of the blankets, Sam had watched him emerge from the bathroom, scrubbing himself vigorously with a large towel.

"You're *loco*, Leo! You'll catch pneumonia one day. That and your mania for keeping a window open at night! *Por Dios,* it's winter!"

She had rolled over in the bed and buried herself more deeply in the blankets.

The cafe was emptier than usual, its air a bit more breathable. He ordered a *café doble*, cold milk on the side. And a couple of *tostados de jamon crudo y queso*. The saltiness of raw ham.

Alongside steak, the sandwich was Argentina's supreme contribution to world gastronomy. He could remember early morning scenes of the bakers unloading huge loaves on their shoulders outside cafes and restaurants. He wondered whether they still did. He hadn't seen it for some time.

As he flipped the pages La Nación, his eye was caught by the signature under a quarter page article opposite the editorial column. Carlos Grunwald had finally gone into print!

Tehran the instigator of the bombings. Argentine manipulation. Dialogue between Buenos Aires and Tehran moving into deeper waters. Nuclear collaboration back on the bilateral agenda. Carlos wasn't pulling his punches.

So this was the topic Carlos had been reluctant to discuss over their lunch. He had suspected as much. He could imagine that an article of this kind was going to raise a storm at the level of the Foreign Ministry. Not to mention the Casa Rosada. Carlos had guts!

Leandro looked up, his unfocused gaze hovering in the middle distance of the cafe, wondering what the repercussions might be. He considered giving Carlos a ring on his cell phone, but then thought better of it. Carlos' phones would now certainly be tapped. He finished his coffee and, having left money on the table, caught a taxi back to his flat. Switching on the television, he skimmed through the channels to see whether anyone else had picked up the story. So far, it was only on La Nación's website. He would probably have to wait for the evening political programmes.

"TV at this hour of the morning?"

Sam, enveloped in one of his large bath robes, her wet hair under a large turban of yellow towelling, was observing him from the door of the bedroom.

He handed her a copy of La Nación, open at the article.

"Interesting," was her laconic remark.

"Carlos better look out for himself. The government is unlikely to be pleased about the lid coming off."

"And the stronger they protest, the more we can assume that the smoke hides a real fire."

"True."

"You know this guy Grunwald?"

"I had lunch with him some weeks ago. He hinted he'd soon be putting something out. He works as a freelance."

Rubbing her hair with the turban, Sam turned back into the bedroom, allowing the robe to slip to the floor. The silhouette of a violin? Man Ray?

He remembered Alex. He rang her cell phone. It was taking messages.

Although he had tried to ignore the possibility over the last twenty-four hours, and had certainly not wanted to mention it to Elena, in today's Argentina, a kidnap could never be ruled out. Shades of Sam, of Dávila.

He rang Elena again.

"Her cell phone is only taking messages. I don't like this."

"Oh, sorry, I was about to ring you. She's sent a text message saying not to worry and that she'll be in touch."

Leandro drew a deep breath of relief.

"Thanks for letting me know," he said, a little reproachful.

"It literally came in five minutes ago. I promise."

"Have you replied?"

"Yes. Asking her to ring as soon as she has a moment."

"Okay. Keep me posted."

"I will."

Wednesday, 2 July 2008 (AM) – PASAJE DE LA PIEDAD, BUENOS AIRES

In a message to Charles in London, Leandro reported the publication of Grunwald's article and the sensationalist coverage of the evening TV news commentators. Admittedly only on the one or two channels not renowned for their loyalty to the Kirchner regime. The rest of the channels had simply ignored the story. A sure sign that the Casa Rosada was hoping to stifle it. There'd been no reference to the murders, but a coherent argument could be made that these events together pointed to a dialogue between Argentina and Tehran. The challenge was to go from a reasonable deduction to concrete evidence.

Charles had come back immediately. The killings were no coincidence. From a Frobisher contact in the Belgian capital, the investigation into the murder of Sanchez had established that the killer was most probably of Middle Eastern origin.

The homosexual trappings?

Most likely a blind. The Argentine embassy were not giving much away, but the Belgian police were now convinced that Sanchez, far from being an agricultural attaché, had been involved in secret negotiations with Iran.

Frobisher clearly had good sources. The espionage 'old boy' network, no doubt.

Friday, 4 July 2008 (AM) - RECOLETA, BUENOS AIRES

He'd caught a taxi to Recoleta cemetery.

Buenos Aires' monument to the turn-of-the-century aesthetic of death, to his mind a sinister place. Hidden behind high walls, a city of the dead in miniature, narrow 'streets' of family mausoleums, packed like terraced housing on both sides, black and grey marble, weeping angels, rusting wrought iron grilles barring entrance to an inner world of caskets and coffins. On a day like today, everything was darker, the grey blocks and statuary reflecting on the wet alleyways.

The Argentine ritual surrounding death was, in Leandro's view, wholly unseemly in its urgency to get rid of the body. In the overwhelming majority of cases, people were buried or cremated the following day, giving family and friends no time to do much more than arrange the transport, chose the priest and at best get one or two members of the family to read some hurriedly drafted words beside the coffin. Ill-suited to a world of globally dispersed families, a practice no doubt carried over from the days when a semi-tropical climate could be expected to accelerate the deterioration of the corpse. So, the process tended to be perfunctory, with no one having made their peace. During his time in London, he had had occasion to attend one or two funerals and had come away with the conviction that the English way of death was much more civilised.

As he had stood waiting by the gates, a large black Mercedes hearse drew up silently on the cobbles. Two men in dark suits had appeared through the cemetery gates pulling a four-wheeled trolley, an ugly utilitarian platform with a guard rail along each side. With two men from the Mercedes, they had extracted the coffin from the back of the hearse and placed it carefully on the trolley. Four men of about Luis Miguel's age had stepped out of the group and taken their place on either side. The trolley set off down the main avenue, lined with dark green cypresses and monkeypuzzle trees, the mourners, family and friends, by now numbering about thirty, falling in behind.

Slowly, the procession moved down the central avenue, before turning right into a narrower alley, crowded with mausoleums of different styles, all sinister. A forest of crosses in every shape and size silhouetted against the grey sky. As they passed, he could read off a 'Who's Who?' of Argentine history, generation after generation of the land's richest and mightiest laid to rest in this, the nation's most prestigious cemetery. Even Evita Perón lay buried in the Duarte family vault. Her corpse had wandered the globe as the military tried to prevent it becoming an icon for the Peronista party. Spirited out of Argentina with the help of the Vatican, after stopovers which allegedly included a spell hidden behind a cinema screen in Buenos Aires, she had been buried in a Milan cemetery under a false name. In the early 70s, her husband had been able to recover the body and have it brought to Madrid where he was living in exile. Only after his return to Argentina in 1973 and death a year later, did her body return to its homeland. Wasn't there even some story about her hands cut off to prevent identification...? He tried to remember.

Another turn, this time to the left and, after a few more metres, the party had come to a halt in front of a black marble edifice, mock-classical temple in style, surmounted by a dome. The elaborate iron grille was already open and two cemetery workmen in overalls stood ready to assist with lowering the coffin through the narrow door, no doubt to be placed on some internal shelf alongside Luis Miguel's forebears.

As they stood there, the priest, who Leandro only now noticed had been leading the procession, began to speak. It was apparent that the old man had known Luis Miguel personally as well as other members of the family, judging from the intimacy of some of his remarks. An elderly couple, no doubt the parents, stood close by. As the priest was speaking, briefly rehearsing Luis Miguel's youth and diplomatic career, Leandro studied the faces of the mourners. None were known to him. Looking beyond them, he caught sight of two men in raincoats watching the proceedings from a distance. Something about them suggested police. He would check with Eduardo.

The rain had started again. Finally, the priest, accompanied by low murmuring, had given a Pater Noster, after which he had blessed the coffin. Two or three women, as well as a couple of the young men who had accompanied the coffin, stepped forward from the group and placed small bouquets of flowers on the lid. No one else spoke. The four pallbearers, assisted by the two men from the Mercedes, raised the coffin and, positioning it in the narrow space of the alleyway, lined it up with the low door, where the two workmen took the front handles and slowly pulled it in. The manoeuvre was not smooth enough to prevent one of the bouquets of flowers falling into a puddle formed by the lip of the door. The priest had moved over to the parents. With a lot of shuffling, the coffin finally disappeared into the darkness.

The group of mourners, ignoring the rain, remained in front of the mausoleum for a few more minutes before finally breaking up and slowly making their way back towards the main gates. Leandro watched as some headed into town across the square and down Avenida Quintana, others towards the underground car park.

"I need something to get back some warmth, I don't know about you? How about a coffee at La Biela?" Leandro suggested to the elderly gentleman with whom he had followed the coffin. "Funerals always give me an appetite."

"Good idea."

They walked across the square towards La Biela, passing under the majestic rubber trees, their immense branches spreading twenty to thirty metres out from the trunk, dark green leaves dripping with the remains of the rain.

Having ordered toasted ham and cheese sandwiches and coffee, the retired diplomat, who had given his name as Nelson Paz, started to talk about his friend's death. Luis Miguel had started his career working under him and they had spent a couple of years at their embassy in Moscow in the early years of Gorbachev.

"Bad affair. I don't think we've heard the end of this one."

"What makes you say that?"

The older man hesitated before continuing.

"I have reason to believe we have only seen half the story in the newspapers."

"Gruesome enough."

"But on top of that, his death has attracted the attention of some of the darker corners of our political system. Do I need to name them?"

"Are we talking about the police? Or SIDE?"

"Certainly the latter. And it appears that certain members of the *Bonaerense* were also involved. Although I am now retired, I still have a number of friends in the Ministry. Morale under the Kirchners is terrible, so people talk."

Leandro let him continue.

"As you know, the current government is much more interested in making friends with people like Chavez in Venezuela or Correa in Ecuador. The so-called Bolivarians. This new generation of Latin American leaders for whom Uncle Sam is the devil and who are prepared to make friends with the enemies of the devil."

Here Nelson Paz lowered his voice.

"And what part are we playing? A similar game certainly, but with the added complication of Iran. AMIA and its connection with Argentina's role as a supplier of nuclear technology."

"And SIDE, and even the *Bonaerense*, also possibly involved? Where do they fit in?"

"This was no simple case of criminal violence," and here Nelson Paz was practically whispering. "It's believed that two policemen who were found murdered in the same week of Luis Miguel's killing may somehow have played a part, and we all know that SIDE and the *Bonaerense* played very obscure roles in the AMIA bombing and subsequent investigations. Until someone has a clear idea of who killed Luis Miguel and why, there's a complete press blackout."

"I don't think I follow you," Leandro said, in the hope of drawing out Nelson Paz further. "Why should SIDE or the *Bonaerense* be involved in the murder of Luis Miguel? Are you really suggesting that this is some kind of internal battle inside government, even a revenge by SIDE for having been forced by President Kirchner to come clean on their role in the AMIA investigation?"

Nelson Paz brushed a crumb from his suit and looked around La Biela.

"In this country, sadly everything is possible. If the two murdered *Bonaerense* policemen had something to do with Luis Miguel's death, someone else was keen to get rid of them fast."

Having finished their sandwiches, Nelson Paz took his leave.

"Never forget that there are people in this country who will go to any lengths. Here is my card, Dr Flemming. Maybe we will meet again someday, perhaps when we know more about what has happened. Whatever it is, or whoever it is, they've taken away a good friend. Certainly mine, and I detect yours as well."

They had shaken hands and left the cafe by separate doors.

On his way home, Leandro remembered it was Perón whose hands had been cut off. In 1987. Not Evita's.

Sam was standing by the door as he came in.

"How was the funeral?"

"Bleak. Wet."

"Anyone interesting?"

"No, not really."

Would Sam take this as the whole truth? Out of respect for their new ground rules, she let it pass.

"I've tracked down Tatyana. Got to keep an eye on what that bitch is up to. And I need to thank her for taking care of you in my absence."

Leandro ignored the remark.

"I've fixed dinner at my place tomorrow evening. I've told them to bring along any men they may have in tow. Don't be late."

She pulled on her coat and covered her face with a scarf.

"See you."

"*Ciao!*"

The front door closed behind her.

He switched on his computer, wondering what to report about the funeral of Luis Miguel and the conversation he'd had afterwards.

Monday, 7 July 2008 (PM) – LARREA Y ARENALES, BUENOS AIRES

Carlos Grunwald wondered who could be ringing his doorbell at this hour. It was past ten o'clock and he was watching one of the leading political analysts on the TN channel debating the running battle between the *campo* and the Kirchners. The examination of contentious Decree 125 was now taking place in the Senate, where pro-government and pro-farm lobbies were thought to be evenly matched.

He turned down the volume and, from its wall bracket in the kitchen, picked up the intercom to the main door.

"*Hola*, who's there?" he asked, his tone not concealing a certain irritation, given the hour.

"My name is Ahmed Aboukir, I left a message for you with one of your assistants this afternoon at the newspaper."

He had been in the middle of drafting a response to various reactions to his article about the Iranian situation, when he vaguely remembered one of the girls coming up to him and saying that there was a journalist from Al Jazeera wanting to speak with him. In the middle of the stress of the deadline, he had told her to give the man his cell phone and that he should ring back tomorrow. Why was the man now standing downstairs outside his front door?

"Oh yes, Mr Aboukir, I did get your message, but I don't recall that we arranged anything. And, to be frank, it is rather late now."

Grunwald wondered how the man had discovered where he lived. Had the secretary been foolish enough to give the Arab journalist his address? He would have a word with her tomorrow.

"Yes, I appreciate that, but I believe that your recent article deserves proper attention in the region we cover. Can we not fix a time when we might meet tomorrow? You see, I fly out of Buenos Aires the day after."

Grunwald toyed for a minute with the idea of getting it over with there and then. But dealing with a Middle Eastern journalist and particularly one from Al Jazeera needed both preparation and a clear head.

"All right, let it be tomorrow then. Could you ring me in the morning and we'll fix a place to meet. I'll see if we can have lunch. Perhaps a sandwich in a bar nearby."

"That is most appreciated. Please, give me your cell phone number and I will ring you. Perhaps around ten?"

Grunwald gave him his number and thanked him for being so understanding. He sat down again in front of the television and switched up the sound. Didn't the man have his cell phone number already?

Tuesday, 8 July 2008 (PM) – LARREA Y ARENALES, BUENOS AIRES

On the following evening, as he stepped off the bus at the corner of his street, Grunwald suddenly remembered the journalist from Al Jazeera. The man had never telephoned. He'd said he was leaving tomorrow. Maybe his interest in the article hadn't been all that urgent. As he made his way towards his apartment block, he stopped to buy some vegetables from the little old Bolivian *cholita* by the wall of his building.

As she dropped the kilo of carrots into his open satchel, the traditional little black bowler hat perched at a perilous angle on her jet black hair pulled into a tight bun, her wrinkled little face smiled up at him.

"*Gracias, Señor. Que le vaya bien.*"

He smiled back.

"*Hasta mañana, Señora.*"

Pulling out his keys, he opened the main door of his block. It being past six o'clock, the *portero* would have gone off duty.

He caught the lift up to his third floor. With three different keys, he opened the dead bolts on his front door and stepped inside. Passing the kitchen, he poured the carrots from his bag into a bowl next to the sink.

At that moment, the telephone rang. He picked up the receiver of the extension hanging on the kitchen wall.

"Is that Señor Grunwald?"

The tone was not particularly friendly.

"It is," he replied cautiously.

"This is Inspector Suarez. From the AFIP."

AFIP, Argentina's internal revenue service, had in recent years been increasingly used by the Kirchners as the local equivalent of the KGB, an efficient instrument of pressure and fear.

It didn't take Grunwald more than a second to work out that the call reflected a level of displeasure in high places with his recent article. He'd been expecting it. Not that he minded particularly. His nose was clean.

"Good evening, Inspector."

A golden rule. Say as little as possible.

"Yes, Señor Grunwald. Just to say that I will be calling on you tomorrow morning with one of my colleagues. At your home address. I'd be grateful if you could prepare whatever documents you think are appropriate for us to examine."

"I see. What time?"

"I would say around nine. I look forward to seeing you tomorrow. Good night, Señor Grunwald."

There was a click at the other end of the line as Inspector Suarez hung up.

Grunwald sighed. Par for the course. Most of all, a huge waste of time.

He went into the dark drawing room. Placing his laptop carefully on the long table against one wall, with its pile of papers and books, he felt in the darkness for the light switch of the table lamp. Its dim glow lit up half the room. Pulling off his jacket, he turned towards his bedroom.

"Good evening, Señor Grunwald. I've been expecting you."

Grunwald's eyesight had never been good. He squinted towards the corner of the room from which the voice was coming. The light from the lamp only fell on the knees and feet of someone sitting in the armchair near the window.

For reasons he couldn't explain, curiosity, not fear, was his first reaction. Almost as if the softness of the voice was soothing, reassuring, even familiar.

"Who are you? And how did you get in?"

"Aboukir, Ahmed Aboukir. We spoke last night. Forgive me, if I did not ring you this morning as agreed. However, as you know, I leave tomorrow. It's really important that we speak."

Grunwald was struggling to reconcile the apparently polite manner in which his visitor was apologising for not having rung him at the office with the fact that somehow this same person appeared to have broken into his flat.

"But, Mr Aboukir, how did you get in? We never agreed to meet here. I find your behaviour very strange."

"Oh dear, Señor Grunwald, I fear you are about to discover just how strange."

The tone hadn't changed, but the man had risen slowly from the armchair and moved into the pool of light. Grunwald could see that he was holding an automatic in his right hand. Grunwald stepped back, but was blocked by the worktable. He rested his hands behind him on the surface, trying to find the long scissors which usually lay there for his newspaper cutting.

"I wouldn't bother, Señor Grunwald. I put them away as I was going through your papers. Fascinating, what you have been able to find out. And so much that was not in your article."

Grunwald toyed with the idea of using his laptop as some kind of weapon. Against a gun?

"Who are you? What do you want?"

The man smiled and sat down on the arm of a chair at the end of the worktable. Grunwald turned to face him, keeping a hand on the worktable.

"I must apologise for having led you astray. You see, I'm not a journalist like yourself. But we do share one thing in common. We both disagree with what your government is doing to help those people in Tehran. I can see that from your article. Perhaps you would like to tell me a bit more."

Grunwald could sense panic gaining ground inside him. If not a journalist, then what? As his eyes had grown accustomed to the gloom, he could see that his visitor was about thirty years old, his Spanish clearly Iberian, his physique however North African. Not someone living in Argentina. What could be so important to warrant a break in? The signs were not good.

"Can I sit down?" he asked.

The man gestured with the automatic towards a chair facing the worktable.

"Please, on that chair. And put your hands behind the back."

If he was going to do anything to resist, it had to be now. But what? He'd never make it to the kitchen for a knife. He felt helpless. At the back of his mind, a looming premonition of that sense of futility, of that resignation to their fate, which, so many agreed, seemed to have allowed eight million members of his race to walk unprotesting to their deaths. Struggling to understand what this stranger wanted, he found his concentration shifting. Was he no more courageous than those grandparents in Poland, whose blurred black-and-white photo stood on the shelf by his books?

The Director appeared to sense that Grunwald might be on the point of trying something. He stood up and walked over, placing the barrel of the gun against Grunwald's forehead.

"Please, Señor Grunwald, don't make this more difficult."

The tone remained calm, reassuring. Was this the kind of reassurance he sought?

Slowly, Grunwald placed his hands behind the back of the chair. The Director, keeping the muzzle against the side of Grunwald's head, moved round behind him. He felt the cold steel handcuffs close around each wrist. He shook his head, the feeling of nausea stronger. The opportunity had passed.

"Now, Señor Grunwald, let's review what you can tell me. Remember, I've had time to look at your files, so do not try to mislead me too much. To make it easy, let me first tell you what I'm *not* interested in. I'm not interested in the politics of the relationship between your country and those apostates in Tehran. I'm not interested in the bombings and the legal charade mounted by your government. Nor am I interested in the corruption which almost certainly lies at the heart of all of this. Those are your problems, Argentina's problems, which one day you will have to sort out. It's very simple. I want to know anything which will confirm that your government is supplying or planning to supply technology or equipment to Iran to help them to build a nuclear weapon. That is my sole focus of interest. Do you understand?"

Grunwald's brain was racing. Whose interests could he possibly represent? The Americans? The CIA? More likely Israel. And if it was Israel, that meant Mossad. Yet, if it was Mossad, then why should he, a Jew, be treated in this fashion?

"I don't understand, who are you? Why do you want this?"

The questions seemed natural and innocuous enough, but from the look on his face, he could see that Aboukir had no intention of answering.

"It just might help, to know," he added.

The Director waved the question aside.

"Do not trouble yourself with that, Señor Grunwald. It will be of no interest to you, where you're going."

Aboukir sat down on the edge of the worktable, the automatic now placed beside his thigh.

"Let me make myself clear. The information I seek, you *will* give me. Of that there is no doubt. The only variation relates to the amount of pain that *you* are prepared to accept as part of the process. That is the *only* variation. You *do* understand, don't you?"

The Director waited for the message to sink in. As so often in this kind of situation, he could detect that they were moving towards that point at which the victim would finally begin to grasp that they were not going to get out of this alive.

"How much time have we got, Señor Grunwald? Did you have other plans for this evening? When will you first be missed?"

"I'm supposed to be going to dinner in half an hour," Grunwald blurted out, grasping the faint hope that this might somehow deflect the inevitable.

"That came a little too fast, if you don't mind my saying so, Señor Grunwald. Why would you have bothered to buy carrots?"

The Director smiled.

"So, we have the evening to ourselves. How long it lasts is your call."

Grunwald's head sank onto his chest. He had often been admired for his courage as a journalist and, in the context of one investigation or another, subjected to harassment and even threatening phone calls, whenever he had strayed too close to people or affairs of the government. Not only this government, but all its predecessors. But it had never come to this. For no apparent reason, he remembered falling off his bicycle aged about ten and opening up the side of his leg. His mother had not been far away.

He raised his head, trying to decipher from the look on Aboukir's face how this would play out. Nothing to be learned there. Aboukir was clearly getting bored with the silence.

"Remember, I'm interested in facts, names and places, not in theory."

The Director got down from the table and, standing next to Grunwald, opened one of the files.

"From what I have been able to gather, the government has set up a shell company through which any transaction will pass. Does it have a name?"

Grunwald shook his head. "I haven't been able to discover it."

"But it's not registered in Argentina?"

"Not as far as I can tell. Possibly a place like Panama. Although, that would be straying rather close to the United States. So they may have gone elsewhere. All I know is that something exists."

"Fine, it's not that important. People. That's what I'm really interested in. Names?"

Grunwald hesitated.

"Señor Grunwald, please understand. This can be easy or difficult. For you. For me, it's all the same."

Grunwald had a nasty feeling that anyone whose name he passed on was soon likely to make the acquaintance of the man standing beside him. If he could no longer protect himself, perhaps he could protect others. He shook his head again.

The Director bent forward and placed his face close to Grunwald's.

"I know what you're thinking. But it's not going to help you. At the end of the day, I'll get the names. Never fear. But the price *you* pay will vary."

The trade-off couldn't have been simpler. In some ways, it became a matter of self-respect. If he was going to die, would any last-minute heroism change much?

Once more he shook his head.

"Oh dear. Bad decision."

The Director exploded into action. Spinning Grunwald round on his chair, he forced him to his feet by the simple expedient of dragging his manacled wrists up as high as they would go behind his back. Grunwald stumbled, but just about managed to keep upright. The Director pushed Grunwald towards his bedroom, where he was propelled face down on the bed, before being rolled over and completely stripped. Pulling off Grunwald's loafers, the Director dragged down his trousers and his underpants. The shirt he tore off in strips to overcome the obstacle of the handcuffs. Grunwald was now shaking violently, though not from cold. His body was bathed in sweat.

Turning his head sideways, Grunwald watched Aboukir walk over to his wall cupboard, the sliding doors of which he could see were open, the inner light sending a pale glow over his sparse clothes rack. Aboukir appeared to study the two or three belts which hung over the rail, before selecting the broadest, rawhide with decorative stitching. Grunwald remembered having picked it up one Sunday at San Antonio de Areco, a centre of gaucho handicrafts. The Director threaded the end of the belt through the buckle turning it into a slipknot. Passing it over the journalist's head, he pulled the belt tight around his neck. Grabbing the end, he dragged Grunwald to his feet and walked him towards the cupboard. In front of the door, he made Grunwald turn round to face into the room. Grunwald began to scream, until Aboukir slapped him violently into silence.

"I need your mouth to talk, not to scream," he whispered into his face. "If you do that again, I will give you plenty of cause."

Grunwald was choking. He felt rather than saw Aboukir fastening the other end of the belt to a coat hook at the back of the cupboard. Leaning forward slightly, he realised that the belt was now at full stretch.

The Director was standing in front of him, studying him. Then, almost as an afterthought, he slipped another belt behind the short chain of the handcuffs and pulled it back towards the same coat hook. As a final detail, the Director took each bare foot and placed it on the metal rail of the cupboard's sliding doors. Grunwald was now suspended by his neck and arms, pulled agonisingly back, leaning out towards the middle of the room. The weight of his body was pulling the belt around his neck ever tighter, his arms ever higher.

Aboukir sat down on the side of the bed and looked up at him expectantly.

"So, Señor Grunwald, can we make this quick, or do I have to think of more variations? You get the picture, don't you? 'Leading investigative journalist found dead in bedroom, asphyxiated in the course of obscene sexual ritual. Foul play not suspected.' Of course, if the body also shows signs of torture and mutilation, that story may not hold up. But by that time, you'll be dead anyway, so what do you care? As I said before, you're now the master of ceremonies. You dictate the pace."

Grunwald was whimpering, desperately trying to relieve the pressure on his neck. He wondered whether Grunwald was even thinking rationally any more.

"Please, Señor Grunwald, speak up. I can't hear you very well."

The Director got to his feet and stood close to Grunwald. A Jew. In his estimation, Jews came a close second to the Shia as vermin to be exterminated. Though the overall purpose of his mission was to deal a blow to the ambitions of the apostates in Tehran, a few well-placed side-swipes against Israel were perfectly acceptable. A nuclear Iran was the ultimate nightmare, to be prevented above all. But, at some point in the future, Israel must also go.

"Your files are short on names. Names, Señor Grunwald! Will I find them in your computer? Just nod your head."

Grunwald did not respond. He might be slipping away.

The Director slapped him hard in the genitals, causing the terrified journalist to rear up, screaming in agony, inevitably pulling the belt tighter round his neck in the process. His eyes were wide, pupils fully dilated, as he dragged in his breath.

"You don't seem to understand. This should bring you pleasure. Sexual pleasure."

Looking down, the Director could see that Grunwald's penis was swelling. Strangulation's effect.

"I told you so. But concentrate. Will I find them in your laptop?"

Grunwald remained stubbornly silent. The Director stood beside him and slowly tightened the belt around his neck, beginning to crush his windpipe. Grunwald's face was turning a pale purple.

"How much more can you take? Your laptop?"

Even though it would only tighten the belt even further, Grunwald finally shook his head.

"Not your laptop? Wise precaution. Laptops get stolen and hacked. So, something else? A notebook?"

Grunwald seemed to weaken. He nodded.

"Here, in this flat?"

Grunwald could just about nod his head, though a low rasping sound was beginning to accompany the froth emerging from between his lips.

The Director hesitated. After all this effort, was it worth unstrapping Grunwald to find the notebook? He had time. But perhaps with just a few more questions he could make the task easier. He sat on the edge of the bed, watching Grunwald. From his pocket, he took out his small digital camera and snapped a couple of shots of the dying journalist.

"In this room?"

Grunwald appeared to have fainted, his body limp. The Director slapped him hard across the face and once more he began to come round.

He repeated his question. Grunwald's eyes were closed. He was hardly breathing any more. The Director thought he detected something like a nod of the head. This was getting boring. He got up and stood next to Grunwald. Then he pulled the belt as tight as it would go. Grunwald's body responded feebly, but in less than two minutes, his life had drained away.

The Director sat back on the bed and surveyed his handiwork. Some minor adjustments were still necessary. With a sigh, he got up and released the belt which had almost pulled Grunwald's arms out of their sockets. The body was now only suspended by the belt around the neck. Carefully undoing one handcuff, he brought Grunwald's hands round to the front of his body and, replacing the handcuff, inserted the penis between the fingers. Sexual self-asphyxiation and masturbation gone tragically wrong. Another couple of photographs of the final *mise en scène*.

Without a second glance, the Director beganto search the room, pulling out all the drawers of the dressers, the bedside table, the medicine cabinet in the bathroom. Finally, having lifted the lid of the toilet cistern, he found what he was looking for. A tiny notebook wrapped in plastic film, weighed down to the bottom by a piece of white tiling, so that it was virtually invisible if only the top was lifted. A predictable hiding place, nevertheless.

Stripping away the cling film, he began to flip through the pages. The names in the booklet seemed to match codes in one of the files.

He returned to Grunwald's worktable and, with the booklet in one hand and turning the pages of the files with the other, quickly identified some ten names of Argentine officials and businessmen apparently forming part of the chain which stretched from Buenos Aires, through Caracas, via Brussels and other European diplomatic missions to the Iranian capital. In the notebook, he made a note of the role which each played and any indication of where they were based. Confirmation that they were genuine came with the discovery of Luis María Sanchez, based in Brussels. Also Hernandez in Caracas and Luis Miguel Morales at the Ministry of Foreign Relations. How many more of these actors would he get to know?

He got up and stretched. His neck needed massaging. Another visit to Sonia.

He took a last look round and carefully folded some of the clothes he had dragged off Grunwald. From a drawer, he produced another shirt, which, having wiped it against Grunwald's motionless body to capture some of his sweat, he crumpled as if it had been worn all day, and tossed onto the floor alongside the underpants. A man in a hurry to get his sexual kicks.

Quietly the Director let himself out of the flat. He met no one in the lift and the street was almost empty. He peeled off the skin-like latex gloves and dropped them, along with the torn shirt, into a pile of cartons waiting for the *cartoneros*. Buenos Aires' informal army of waste pickers would remove the last traces.

Tuesday, 8 July 2008 (PM) – PUERTO MADERO, BUENOS AIRES

At about the same time that the Director was making his way back to his hotel in Once, Leandro was pressing the bell of Sam's apartment punctually at ten as instructed, dressed, on her instructions, rather more formally than might normally have been the case.

"Don't forget the dinner tonight. And mind you come properly dressed."

Later that afternoon, a parcel had arrived from Ralph Lauren containing an elegant blue pinstripe shirt, a pair of grey flannels, a Ferragamo tie and a set of small gold cufflinks.

"What the hell's going through this girl's mind?" Leandro muttered as he unpacked the parcel.

He rang her.

"What's all this that's just been delivered? Are we celebrating something? Other than the two Russians, and whatever boyfriends they may have, is anybody else going to be there that I don't know. For whom I have to be dressed up like this? And by the way, I'm not sure I want to end up as a walking advertisement for Ralph Lauren…"

Sam giggled.

"No, only one person."

She hung up.

He shook his head as he surveyed the clothes. A sense of nostalgia for the days when he could just pull on an old pair of jeans and a loose sweater – and no one minded! Yet another occasion when he felt that he was losing control of his life to this slip of a girl, who seemingly could not understand how a man's cupboards should not be overflowing with cashmere sweaters, shirts from London or ties from Rome.

"Did nobody ever teach you to dress properly?" she had asked him, one morning back in May as she surveyed the meagre contents of his cupboards. "No self-respecting man can really survive on so little. Two suits, two blazers, and a couple of pairs of shoes. At least, they're from a decent shoe shop. But it's a pretty miserable display. It's almost as if you didn't care what you look like."

"Actually, I don't very much," Leandro had replied.

"Well, if you're going to be seen in public with a girl like me, you're going to have to do better than that. I can see that you won't do it of your own accord, so I suppose I'll have to do it for you."

In horror, he had watched as one of his favourite ties – admittedly frayed at both ends - was unceremoniously consigned to the garbage can, along with an old – but very comfortable – pair of mocassins.

"In my line of business, I really don't have to put on a suit very often. I only wear ties when I absolutely have to. The advantage of having rather few things is that they end up being far more comfortable."

"Well, now there are even fewer, so you should be happy. Anyway, Dr Flemming, the time has come to change. In a number of ways. We've been going out now for well over a year. How many times have we been to a decent restaurant? My figure really can't take any more of these pizzas on which you seem to thrive. And, irritatingly, not get fat! Whilst they do terrible things to my figure. Pretty soon, I'm going to ask you to pay for my membership at the gym."

He had looked at her. Frankly, hard to spot a gram of excess flesh anywhere on her curves.

"I've always told you that going out with me was going to be bad for your image," he had thrown at her.

"I said it was bad for my figure, not for my image."

Leandro pressed the bell again and this time heard the sound of steps approaching the door.

Sam occupied a large, very modern flat overlooking the interior dock of Puerto Madero, lined with moored sailing boats and motor yachts, opposite the row of fashionable restaurants, which had established themselves in the old renovated warehouses. Modern skyscrapers had proliferated over the last thirty years, a mixture of corporate headquarters and lavish apartment blocks, some catering only to speculative investments by owners deterred by the area's isolation from the city's heart. As a result, many of the flats stood empty. Others had been snapped up by a new political and business elite riding on the crest of the Kirchner success.

Sam paused on the other side of the door. Then it opened and he found himself looking at the diminutive figure of Lamai, dressed elegantly in the black and white uniform of a maid.

She bowed.

"Good evening, Lamai, how are you? How nice to see you."

"Good evening, Don Leandro, please come in. Your hostess expecting you."

That soft Thai accent…

Leandro had first met Lamai back in November. Since the revelation of that morning, Leandro had learned as best he could to accommodate Sam's bisexuality. Her relationship with Carla had, or so he thought, had the effect of causing Lamai to move out. Perhaps not.

Somewhat mystified, Leandro walked over to the large window looking out over the dock. The apartment in tones of black, grey and red, a massive dark grey sofa and two matching armchairs in the softest leather surrounding a low black lacquer coffee table. The floor of glistening black laminated parquet. An abstract painting, all reds, ochres and blacks in the style of Rothko on one wall. A huge black and white blow-up by Helmut Newton dominating the opposite wall. A woman, short slicked-back hair, dressed in a man's jacket and pinstripe trousers, smoking a cigarette, set in what might be a Parisian street at night. An example of the kind of strong woman attractive to Sam? On balance, he might have preferred this photograph to the one Sam had inflicted on his flat.

He turned to survey the drawing room. Towards one end, a dinner table had been laid for two, candles burning, silver and glass catching the sparkle of their flames. The lights in the room had been dimmed. But only for two? There should have been at least four, even six, places.

"Madame won't be minute. Please. Sit down. May I offer you champagne?" Lamai walked towards him, a bottle of Baron B in one hand, a goblet in the other.

"Thank you, I'd love that."

Madame? The maid's dress? What was going on?

He walked back to the window and, sipping his champagne, looked out towards the flickering lights of the city. A faint winter mist was hanging over the port area, the silhouette of the city mysteriously out of focus.

Lamai disappeared into the kitchen.

A few minutes passed, before he caught the sound of the frosted glass bedroom door sliding open.

The girl that entered the room was a total stranger. The same height and proportions as Sam, but there the similarity ended. A mass of glistening wavy jet black hair, parted in the middle, cascading over her breasts and down her back, framed a face more angular than Sam's. Huge eyes, massive dark red lips, the nose small and fine. The body tightly encased in a shimmering silver grey dress, high ruched collar and long sleeves puffed above the elbow, tapering tightly to the wrists, shiny black gloves. A hemline of small pleats just above the knee. The overall look faintly Victorian, but for the tightness of the body. Legs sheathed in glistening stockings the colour of bronze glass. Stiletto heels close to twelve centimetres. Around the neck, a narrow silver band like a collar, with a small silver ring at the front.

He had never seen anything quite like it before.

Overcoming his initial surprise, Leandro recovered his manners.

"Good evening," he addressed the newcomer hesitantly. "I'm Leandro."

"So, *amor*, how do you like my new look?"

The voice, trembling with suppressed laughter, was unmistakably Sam's.

Leandro drew a deep breath before replying.

"Not again! Fuck! It never ends! You're always beautiful. So why this! Not to say that you're not also handsome like that. If a bit strange.... But is it really you, Sam? What's going on? What about the others? The Russian girls?"

She sashayed towards him, one hand resting on her hip, the candles gleaming on the surface of her dress. With the fingers of her other hand, she lightly brushed the mass of hair out of her face.

She came up close.

He touched her face with the tips of his fingers.

"Jesus! What is this?"

She was wearing a skin-tight latex mask, a highly exotic look, the unblemished surface unnaturally smooth, massive dark red lips part of the mask. Only the pale green eyes, laughing, framed behind massive lashes, were Sam's. She moved her face close to his and, cupping it in her gloved hands, kissed him. He felt the smoothness of the outer lips, but rapidly pushed through them with his tongue and found hers darting in and out. The taste of the mouth behind the lips unquestionably Sam.

"Another Sam. Ring the changes. How did Leonard Cohen put it? 'And if you want another kind of love, I'll wear a mask for you.'"

She paused to observe the effect of her words.

"But I'm still Sam. Your Sam. Maybe just another kind of love."

This girl's fascination with switching identities had already destabilised him once before. In Zürich, where she had taken on the persona of Dalal, a courtesan member of Carla's team of high class escorts. Now this!

She savoured the look of confusion in his eyes.

Instinctively, his hands caressed the curve of her waist and hips, smooth, polished. She was dressed in the thinnest latex, a subtle light pewter colour. She pressed against him, rubbing the smoothness of her belly against him.

One of her hands slipped away from his face and down towards his crotch, stroking softly. Her other hand buried itself in the hair on the back of his head and pulled it down into her upturned face, her large mouth crushing his once more.

Another unknown corner of his psyche being unwrapped, challenged. The corner to be found in males brought up on a diet of Marvel comics. The events of the last twelve months had demonstrated that, when it came to Sam's sexuality, constant innovation and surprise were an integral part of her performance. Here she was again, pushing the boundaries. Testing his. He shouldn't be surprised. Sam was the first girlfriend he had known for whom the act of sex seemed virtually inseparable from the most provocative lingerie, contact with the most sensual materials, the longest of thigh boots. Call it street fetishism?

He had wondered on occasion whether her passion for Oscar Wilde might not also be connected in some way. She had once told him that Wilde was fascinated with masks, with alternative personalities, with ambiguity, often of an aesthetic nature. From what he had read about the Irishman in the biography Sam had given him, he detected that a taste for looking like a high-class courtesan often lurked just below the surface of Wilde's personality. A taste of which Sam appeared an avid disciple.

With a final deep throated kiss, Sam stepped back to admire the results of her appearance.

"In the words of Mae West, I can see that you're visibly - and tangibly - pleased to see me."

She laughed.

"I'm in no position to deny it," he admitted reluctantly.

"We've got all night. Now let's have our romantic little dinner *à deux*. Lamai has prepared a delicious Thai menu."

"But what about the others? Weren't Larissa and Tatyana supposed to come tonight? I thought that's what was agreed."

"Tatyana rang me earlier. Something had come up. Typical of the bitch! Cancel at the last moment! Perhaps afraid to confront you again. So I thought I'd surprise you."

"You've certainly done that."

Sam walked over to the dining table and began to fill her glass with champagne. Her silvery dress shone in the candlelight, the mound of hair cascading over her shoulders. Surreptitiously arching her back, she allowed the tips of her fingers to brush the slippery surface of her breasts. Their caress like an electric current passing all over her. She caught sight of her reflection in the large bay window giving onto the balcony. She had to admit that she looked like a very high-class hooker. She loved it! She'd shown herself to Leandro in that guise once before, that evening in Zürich which had nearly killed their affair. Yet here she was doing it again. Why did playing with fire give her such a kick?

She turned and studied him discreetly. That hint of confusion in his eyes, so utterly irresistible, made her want to clasp him in her arms and restore his confidence in her, in her love for him. Tell him that it didn't matter. That it was all a game. But for a little while longer, she would secretly enjoy his discomfort.

Having walked over and filled his glass, she raised hers.

"To us. To new identities, to whoever we may become."

At a loss for any form of appropriate response to such a mysterious toast, Leandro could only lift his glass. His eyes slid away from hers.

A somewhat banal question came to mind.

"Are you planning to stay like that all evening?"

She laughed.

"Why not, Leo? You might be surprised, but it's amazingly comfortable. And, very, very sensual. For a sensualist like me, it's about as sensual as it gets. Perhaps slightly warm at times, hence the air conditioning, even if we are in winter. But I adore the feel of it."

She pirouetted in front of him, before continuing.

"I was introduced to all this by Carla. I told you about her masks when we were in Punta del Este. These clothes arrived in a parcel a week ago. We shopped for them together in Zürich. This sexy dress comes from a boutique in England."

Sam caressed the sleeves with her gloved hand.

"I love the design. There's something so Victorian about it with these puffed sleeves. The kind of thing that Constance Wilde used to wear. Though nothing underneath tonight. I've been dying to surprise you ever since the parcel arrived."

Seeing the perplexity still lingering in his eyes, she added.

"Or maybe I'm shocking you...."

Silently he shook his head. Shock was not the right word. Rather a struggle to come to terms with yet another Sam, mixed with uncertainty as to what it presaged.

Placing his hand on her sleeve, she led him to the dining table.

Sitting opposite her, he suddenly detected a trace of the overwhelming pain he had felt when he thought he had lost her, first after their night in Zürich, then at the time of the kidnap. And now? The face on the other side of the table wasn't Sam, not the Sam with whom he was in love. Only the eyes. The real Sam behind the mask was beautiful. It hit him every time he looked at her. Yet in a strange way, this new Sam was also beautiful.

The girl never missed an opportunity to sow confusion in what he felt for her. The untroubled way she had allowed him to discover her bisexuality – in this very flat - the episode in Zürich in which she had assumed the role of a high-class hooker. And now this.

"I'm a bit confused," he said cautiously. "You say all that is sexy for you to wear. And you – whoever that you may be – are in some strange way beautiful, if totally unreal. It's not you. I'm looking for the Sam I know. And having trouble finding her."

With only her eyes by which to judge, it was hard to detect her reaction to his words. So far, they were still laughing.

"But why this performance? Is our sex beginning to bore you? Do you feel the need for something so different? Are there other reasons behind this disguise, this new persona? However physical you may be, you're also cerebral. Is this more than just a whim?"

He stretched across the table and took her black latex-gloved hand in his. The sensation was strange.

"Now who's being cerebral? Don't take it too seriously, Leo. All this is just for fun. You know me. Always in pursuit of new sensations, new adventures. The idea of masks fascinates me. The ability to hide behind another personality, to change the rules of engagement. And the feel of all this does turn me on, I won't deny it. Look at me as you might a new girlfriend. Maybe you want to give her another name?"

She paused. What had de Beauvoir written? Make your person? Even your gender?

"How about your old friend Dalal?"

She deliberately threw that name at him. A name that could only bring back painful memories of their night in Zürich. However passionate their sex in the elegance of the Hotel Baur au Lac, it had ended on a very bad note, when he thought he had lost her for good.

"Dalal was never my friend," he replied bitterly. "I'm not even sure that I want to give you another name. Maybe I'll just take this as one of your alter egos."

"Please yourself. I thought it might have been fun. I'll see if I can find another instead. A way of sending signals."

Lamai emerged silently from the kitchen and began to lay out a delicate selection of Thai dishes. Nothing in her behaviour betrayed any surprise at Sam's new image. Leandro noted that Sam allowed her fingers to rest fleetingly on Lamai's hand as she placed a dish on the table next to her. Everything seemed totally normal, as if this alien Sam was already part of the established scene.

However, as the dinner progressed, Leandro could not entirely dispel the feeling of disorientation. The eyes, the brain, the sound of the voice, all were Sam's. And yet, like an old picture placed in a new frame, the effect seemed very different. Sam could see this. And she was visibly enjoying it.

"So," she said, pushing aside the remains of a mint and lemon sorbet, "which of the two of me do you prefer? We're like twins, aren't we, except that we're not identical? You're going to have to make a choice. At least for tonight."

Leandro thought for a minute.

"I don't agree. To put it crudely, unless this new girl kisses and fucks very differently, when I unwrap that rubber doll, I should be on familiar territory. I've never denied that I find fashion, the clothes you wear an important part of your sensuality. So perhaps I shouldn't complain, even if this is more Avengers than Christian Dior. Very different. Needs getting used to…"

Sam got up from the table and walked round to stand beside him. She took his hand and pressed it into the elastic surface between her thighs. Her labia unmistakeable through the skin-tight material.

"As you so elegantly put it, you're going to have to unwrap this love doll to find out. But only when I say so."

She moved away and stood looking out across the marina. He watched her. The cascade of the wig falling over the shimmering silver-grey dress. For a moment, again the feeling of being with another woman. Even a faint sense of guilt. Sam's little experiment was distinctly unnerving, as if she was somehow forcing him to be unfaithful to her.

"Let's go for a drink," she announced, turning back to look at him. She seemed determined to test the experiment to its limits.

"That might just about work in a place like Zürich or London. But do you think Buenos Aires is ready for you?" Leandro asked. "I'm not sure they've ever seen anything quite like you tonight."

"Great! Let's go round the corner to the Faena. It's in such bad taste! I want to shake them up. I'll get my coat."

She stepped into her bathroom. Having taken a small jewel box out of a drawer, she rolled up the tight hem of her dress and carefully inserted a small silver plug into her anus, the rear end adorned with a Swarovski crystal. A present from Carla. Such bad taste! So vulgar! The trappings of a whore. Secret stimulation assured for the next few hours.

From the hall cupboard, she selected the floor-length red leather coat she had worn as Dalal. Lined with black fur, she revelled in the feeling of it gliding over the latex as she slipped into it. She knew it'd link up in Leandro's mind with that night in Zürich. Yet another twist of the blade. There were times when her emotional sadism troubled her. Had she been like that with all the men she had loved? Or was it Leandro's irresistible, delicious vulnerability, which provoked it so easily?

As if she owned the place, Sam swept through the lobby of Hotel Faena, heading for the bar. Leandro was beginning to learn that, in such situations, he must follow, while adopting - much against his natural inclinations - a similar air of unlimited resources and visceral distaste for all present. Inwardly, he cringed.

With its decor by Philippe Starck, including El Bistro, its walls displaying a row of brilliant white unicorns looking down on the diners, nobody could accuse this fashionable jet set hotel of understatement. In the flamboyantly decorated bar, glowing in the light of crystal chandeliers, the red and brown buttoned leather chesterfields and armchairs were packed. On the eve of the public holiday, Argentine Independence Day was already being copiously celebrated.

Sam's appearance seemed to provoke only a mild level of curiosity, as if artificiality and sartorial overkill were the norm. Having dropped onto a large dark brown chesterfield, with its low coffee table and two armchairs on either side, she imperiously patted it to indicate that Leandro should sit beside her. The long leather coat she spread wide, lightly caressing the dress shimmering beneath the candelabra and spotlights of the bar. Another pulse. She pressed down with her hips. And another from deep inside her.

"A bottle of Pommery," she commanded the waiter who appeared at their table. Turning to Leandro, she murmured, "Hope it has a better effect than back in Zürich. Though I'll grant you, the Baur au Lac is subtler. Never mind, this place goes better with my new look."

"I doubt they'd have let you in in Zürich."

He was discreetly studying the exotic fauna on display. The kind of people who liked to be seen in jet set magazines, ideally in the company of the celebrity owner of the hotel.

"Not quite your usual crowd, I detect, Leo?"

"No, not quite."

"Well, Dr Flemming, you might just have to start getting used to it."

"God help me, why?"

She looked at him. Just as much as there were times when she revelled in such a setting, his evident dislike for such society endeared him all the more to her.

"If you think that the kind of secret deals you're looking for are hatched in dark little rooms, in back streets, you might be wrong. It's in places like these that the action takes place. Trust me. I saw it in Tobago."

"Here?"

"There's an example just sitting over there. You must have spotted him as well. The guitar-playing biker who runs the state pension funds. In the flesh! And no doubt spending the money of the old and infirm as if it were his own. Whatever happened to the image of the public servant?"

"Yes, I had seen him. I'm told he's a favourite of our lady President, destined for better things. He lives somewhere nearby, doesn't he?"

The waiter brought the Pommery and filled their glasses.

"To the business in hand. To *our* business in hand."

"If you say so. To *our* business," he repeated. What business?

Looking around, Leandro could see that Sam's appearance was not going entirely unnoticed. Even in the subdued lighting, she stood out. More than one man seated at the bar had turned round on his high chair and was quite blatantly studying her.

All of a sudden, she squeezed his hand.

"Don't move, stay here. There's someone I've got to talk to."

She rose from the sofa and pulling the long coat close to her body, walked over to an empty seat by the bar, next to a man of about forty, one of those who had been staring at her. As she sat down beside him, he swivelled on his chair to look at her. They were too far away for Leandro to catch what was being said, but he detected that the man was offering Sam a drink. Leandro could hardly blame him, however much he would have liked to smash in his teeth! Nothing could have been more provocative than Sam's approach! Sam appeared to indicate that she would have the same as he was drinking. The man signalled to the barman, who began to concoct something in a shaker. Leandro wondered what her companion would make of Sam's appearance. The look on his face betrayed both fascination and perplexity. Sam's drink served, they toasted each other. Judging by the way she was throwing her head back, he was clearly making Sam laugh. Shit! Though trying to console himself with the thought that Sam was in her escort role, imagining and watching it were two different things. Leandro poured himself another glass of champagne. If he was going to have to sit out this performance, he needed some moral courage.

Just as he was beginning to wonder whether he should not make some move - either go up and hit the man, or, perhaps more in character, leave discreetly - Sam suddenly slipped off her chair. From an inside pocket of her coat, she produced a card, which she handed to the man, before walking back to their sofa, her glass held delicately between the fingers of her gloved hand.

"Mission accomplished," she muttered triumphantly.

Leandro attempted to look as though all of this was quite normal, greeting her with a deliberately controlled level of enthusiasm.

"Mission?"

"Certainly. That's one of the two Argentines who visited the Prince in Tobago. I was at the meetings. But of course, the way I am tonight, he'd never recognise me. I guessed that he was using a false name in Tobago. He called himself Perez. We've had some difficulty pinning him down, given the fact that it's one of the commonest names in Argentina.

But now I've got everything I need. Not only his name – Martín - which he was quick to give me, but even his fingerprints. Now all I need is his surname."

"You seemed very close."

"I swapped glasses at one point," Sam giggled. "He'll never notice as I asked for the same he was drinking. But what with my gloves, only his prints will be on this glass, and none of mine on his. So there, Dr Flemming, how many points do I get for initiative?"

The daring of this girl, able to seize opportunities long before he could even see them.

"Full marks for initiative. But you failed the fidelity test. Anyway, what card are you giving people like that guy," Leandro asked.

"*Que boludo que sos*, Leo. What are you talking about? I spend five minutes with a creep like that and you begin to think the world's falling apart! Don't worry. The card connects to Carla's organisation. Obviously not to Señorita Haidar! Only emails."

She paused and then added, almost as an afterthought, "He told me he has a room permanently rented in the hotel. Invited me up, there and then."

The effect on Leandro was to be expected.

"Jesus, you should see the look on your face! Come here, I need to kiss you. Anyway, he'll probably think you're another one of my clients."

Laughing, she rested her face on his shoulder, looking up into his eyes. He bent his head and kissed her. Again, that strange sensation, unreal, inhuman.

Perched on the bar chair and now, as she settled more deeply into the sofa, the soft stimulation provoked by the plug inside her had grown almost unbearable.

"Remember what I said about unwrapping you," he murmured.

She would enjoy the torture a little longer.

"All in good time. There's still a lot of that champagne left and I don't intend to lose a minute of enjoying the impact I'm making on the assembled company. And just think how jealous of you they all are."

She picked up her small handbag into which, having poured the remains of the cocktail into the ice bucket, she slipped the empty glass.

"We'll have to get Eduardo to take a look at it."

"And how am I going to explain that one?"

"You'll think of something. Now stop fussing and as soon as the bottle's finished, let's get out of here."

But it wasn't to be quite so simple.

Leandro sensed Sam tense beside him, leaning back in such a way as to move farther into the shadow around the table.

"Look," she whispered. "No wonder she cancelled dinner."

Leandro scanned the room and immediately spotted the mass of red hair. Tatyana, standing in the doorway, clearly looking for someone.

"Better if she weren't to recognise us. She won't recognise me, but you... All the more after your little nocturnal chat," she added. "Quick, turn away as if you're making a phone call."

Leandro swivelled round on the sofa so as to present his back to the room and put his hand to his ear as if taking a call. In her disguise, Sam continued to sip her champagne, relaxed in the knowledge that Tatyana could never recognise her.

He need not have worried. Tatyana had found who she was looking for. Swathed in a floor length mink coat, under which her patent leather boots flashed with every step, she made straight for the bar. Her target turned out to be the same man that Sam had just left. Tatyana tapped him on the shoulder. On turning, he clearly recognised her immediately and pulled her towards him. With a toss of the head, she accepted his passionate kiss, before sliding onto the high chair which Sam had so recently vacated. The conversation between them was immediately animated.

"They know each other," Leandro murmured.

"And in the biblical sense of the verb, I'd say," Sam said out of the corner of her mouth. "So, my little arms dealer is also in bed with the Russians. Literally."

"You think she's acting on orders from Viktor Alexievich?"

"Who else?"

As they watched, Tatyana and the Argentine concentrated fully on one another until, having finished her glass of champagne, Tatyana took the man by the hand and began to lead him out of the bar. Sam and Leandro had not been spotted.

"Looks as though she knows the way," Sam commented, acidly. "Presumably going to spend all tomorrow's public holiday with him."

"So, whatever else she may be up to, Tatyana also seems to be part of the Russian marketing effort."

"They may have changed some of their politics, but not their methods," Sam commented. "It also suggests that this Argentine really is a key player on the nuclear front, whether for their more clandestine dealings with Iran or in their negotiations on future power stations."

Sam watched them leave, quietly drinking her champagne.

"Well, let's play a little game. And while we're waiting, give me some more."

She allowed a couple of minutes to go past and then, taking her cell phone from her handbag, proceeded to dial back a number.

"So, Tatyana, I wish you luck with your friend."

She paused, a broad grin almost visible through her mask. Leandro could hear an explosion at the other end of the line. "No. Don't worry. I'm not going to come upstairs and spoil your party. You can tell me all about it in the morning. *Potselui*. Good night!"

She turned to Leandro.

"That should shake her. She'll be dying to find out how I know. What do you say? On balance, my little disguise isn't just sexy. It's proved extremely useful. Come on. I want to go back to the flat and find out just *how* sexy. *El chico* has permission to unwrap his parcel."

She couldn't hold out much longer.

Leandro called over the waiter for the bill. Never cheap, these excursions with Sam in her escort role.

They got up from the sofa and, not without attracting the attention of others in the bar, made their way to the long entrance hall and out onto the street. As they walked slowly back to her flat, Sam took Leandro's hand.

"I don't want to get you even more jealous, but did you see my Russian beau Kuznetsov? In the bar? Watching the proceedings?"

"No. Where?"

"Over in the far corner. I'm pretty sure he saw you. He'll no doubt report to his boss Mikhail that his favourite economic analyst has a taste for very exotic hookers. Just think what they'll lay on when you get invited to that conference in St Petersburg. Or was it Moscow?"

She laughed out loud.

Once back in Sam's flat, she spread the long leather coat round Leandro and pulled him into her arms. Ripping off his tie, he slipped the narrow end through the small ring on the front of the silver collar round Sam's neck and brutally pulled her in the direction of the bedroom.

"Been dying to do that all evening," he chuckled. "Put that piece of mediaeval jewellery to good use."

Sam followed, submissively. Sliding shut the frosted glass door of her bedroom, he dimmed the lights.

"I always loved unwrapping presents," he whispered, turning her round and beginning to pull the long back zip of the skintight dress down towards her waist. She bent forward to press her glistening arse into his crotch.

As he unpeeled the dress, his eye was caught by a jewel flashing between the cheeks of her butt.

Wednesday, 9 July 2008 (AM) – BARRIO ONCE, BUENOS AIRES

In a far less elegant part of town, a similar conclusion as to the role of Tatyana's escort was being reached. Sitting in his sparsely furnished hotel bedroom in Once, the Director was studying the little notebook he had found in Grunwald's toilet alongside the notes he'd made whilst waiting.

He pushed his papers aside and drained the last cold drops of the coffee he'd brought up from the self-service machine in the lobby. The pizza he had eaten round the corner on the way back from Grunwald's flat was lying heavy on his stomach. Inflicting pain always gave him an appetite.

"Disgusting," he muttered.

So far, he had every reason to feel satisfied with the mission. Well paid indeed, as the third large transfer into his account had shown a week previously. Every victim generated a payment under his contract. A payment for which the invoice was simply a photograph of his victim, backed up with another of any newspaper article reporting the crime.

Sanchez had been the first, a key link man to the ayatollahs, positioned far forward in a European country. His name, like that of Morales, had been supplied to him before he had left Baghdad. The group commander had shown no inclination to explain how they had come by the names, and he had not pressed the point. It was none of his business. The Sons of Ibn Taymiyyah had their sources. He could imagine that the death of these two men, following so closely one on the other, would have set alarm bells ringing in the Casa Rosada or wherever Argentina's conspiracy with Tehran was being coordinated. Given its reputation for violence, the attack in Caracas might or might not have been factored in. The publication of Grunwald's article had been a stroke of good luck, coming less than a week after the murder of Morales. As he had lain low after disposing of the bodies of the two *sicarios* from the *Bonaerense*, he had cast around in Morales' papers to come up with his next target. Then Grunwald's article had appeared, opening up a new lead to pursue.

He hadn't bothered to charge for the two men from the *Bonaerense*. Strictly speaking, they didn't qualify as bona fide targets, more a case of precautionary housekeeping. They had most unprofessionally allowed him to climb into the back seat of their Ford Falcon on a street corner in Avellaneda to hand over their final payment. Unwise also to choose an ill-lit side street. A silenced shot in the back from his SIG Sauer had taken less than five seconds. From there, he had driven the old car to a deserted piece of waste ground near the stinking Riachuelo and allowed it to roll down the bank. No mention so far in the press.

He flattered himself that, one way or another, the police investigation was not even getting close. Press coverage of the two first murders had ceased, and as far as he had been able to detect, none of it had made the connection between them. That was not to say that, inside the government machine, the thread of Iran's nuclear interests running through what would soon be seen as three assassinations and a knee-capping would not be interpreted differently. But, almost certainly, the government would not wish to see any hint of this in public. The emphasis, in what coverage there was, had been mainly on the sexual perversion. To that extent, his trademark was proving useful.

He got up from his chair and lay down on the bed, studying the shortlist he had made from Grunwald's notebook. Many were senior figures in the government, ministers or state secretaries, probably identified by Grunwald as being involved at the decision-making level. Below that, references to the embassies in Caracas and Brussels, alongside the names of Morales and Hernandez. The diplomatic bridge-builders to Tehran. Finally, three names of what appeared to be business contacts involved in the negotiation. Not always associated with any company or enterprise. Consultants or intermediaries perhaps. On balance, he suspected that these might prove easier targets than moving up to the ministerial level.

He went back to his worktable and googled the three names. Disappointingly, two of them produced no result. The third, Martín Caballero, came up on a number of social pages and there was even a photo or two, usually in the company of a cheap blonde. The man obviously enjoyed the good life, perhaps keen to live up to his surname. This should make him an easier target. Trawling through the Buenos Aires telephone directory however produced no likely address under that name, although there were several Caballeros. Further research would be required.

He went back to Grunwald's notebook in the hope of finding something more. Tucked away on a back page, a list of what appeared to be

Buenos Aires telephone numbers. But how to link them with the names?

Idly he turned the last page. Two more names, by themselves. Each with a phone number.

Leandro Flemming (***?). Next to the name, in brackets, three stars and a question mark, followed by a phone number. Next to that a date. 13 May. Some time ago. Did the question mark indicate that Grunwald had not known how to categorize Flemming?

Lucio Gonzales Madero. In his case, only a phone number.

The Director was pretty sure all the names in this notebook were connected in some way. Caballero's name had also carried a code in brackets: (KK$$$$). K presumably stood for Kirchner, the dollar signs perhaps for some kind of financial involvement. Some of the earlier names of officials had carried one or two 'Ks', but not all had been accompanied by dollar signs. Morales, for instance, had had neither. Perhaps the number of Ks indicated the level of fidelity or proximity to the Presidential family.

Why were Flemming and Madero on a separate page?

The research into Flemming proved more promising. There were only one or two in the phone book and, as far as any Leandro was concerned, a search on Google suggested he might be some kind of economic consultant, having participated in a seminar on the Argentine economy a few years earlier. The link to his name produced an economic bulletin entitled 'Centro de Investigación Económica', which had been quoted on a couple of occasions in the financial press. How would an economic analyst fit into the scheme of things? On the face of it, he didn't appear to be a key player, although the mere fact that his name appeared in Grunwald's little notebook was suggestive.

An economist? The Director's banking identity might need resurrecting.

He could thank one of Wall Street's richer operators for his first steps into the world of finance.

In the United States in the summer of 2001 on a tourist visa to find ways to get enrolled at a minor business college, he had run out of money. 9/11 striking a couple of months after his arrival had only made matters worse. Prostitution had seemed a relatively easy way to solve the problem and his dark skin, slim body and soft but handsome features had rapidly found takers. Living in the underworld of New York's bars had enabled him to pass unnoticed at a time when every Arab in the street might be stopped and questioned. In those cellars, he had become a specialist in pain, administered in all the complicated ways these strange people sought. Somewhere, deep inside him, he had detected not only an inclination to enjoy such practices, but also a desire for revenge. Little interested in politics until that day, watching the collapse of the towers had unlocked inside him a latent sense that the time had come to pay back these Christian infidels.

At a certain point, becoming the lover of a Wall Street trader had taken him off the streets and into a world of unlimited cashflow.

A year after 9/11, the multi-millionaire had fallen in love with the lurid torture sessions he had received in the underground cells of the gay bar on the East Side at the hands of this handsome young Moroccan. He had hired the Director on the spot as his personal manservant. As time passed, the hedge fund specialist had rapidly discovered that this young man's talents extended far beyond fellation, anal sex and the inflicting of exquisite pain. A facility with numbers seemingly a gift from his Jewish maternal grandmother. Along with a computer in his 5th Avenue apartment overlooking Central Park, his master had given him oversight of a million dollar portfolio, to see what he could do.

His young lover proved to be a natural margin man. With his master's full knowledge and the seed capital of a hundred thousand dollar bonus paid after a particularly stimulating long weekend on the slopes and in his master's private sauna at Vail, he had been granted permission to make money for his own account. A year later, having emptied his personal account, as well as the banker's now much larger portfolio, and deposited its owner's naked and manacled corpse in a builder's waste container in a small alleyway in Queens, the Director had made his way south to enter Mexico along one of the wetback routes. Practically the only person heading in that direction, apart from returning drug mules.

Back in Morocco, his career had taken a more conventional direction for a couple of years, joining the bond market trading team of Banque Populaire. At weekends, he had specialized in alternative services to one or two millionaires in their extravagant villas in the Palmeraie outside Marrakech. When a particularly extreme bondage session with one of these had gone horribly wrong, his anonymity on this occasion leaving something to be desired, the next morning had him boarding a Royal Air Maroc flight for Marseilles and from there, some months later, to Beirut.

That had been over three years ago. He had been thirty, handsome, socially proficient, and speaking three languages. Just what was needed to carve a niche in that Mediterranean playground, recovering from years of civil war.

In the highly politicised tension which passed for the norm in the Lebanese capital, the arrival of this young Moroccan, whose unusual tastes and skills progressively found a wealthy clientele to supplement his bank account, did not pass unnoticed. As a Sunni, he finally came to the attention of one of the underground groups attempting to maintain some kind of resistance to the dominant position which Hezbollah had established over the years. His language and social skills, not to mention his unusual facility for inflicting pain, found him one day blindfolded and handcuffed in the back of a Mercedes, on the way to a meeting with this group's leader. Unlike some of these figures, often an ageing mullah commanding spiritual respect and ideological recognition, this one, younger than the average, had appeared more interested in the Director's homicidal tendencies than the future of his soul.

In exchange for being allowed to pursue his special tastes unmolested, he had accepted a first mission to dispose of an American businessman, suspected of being interested in something more than the sale of petrochemical products on behalf of an obscure corporation in the middle of Idaho. An imaginative scenario, involving an Egyptian prostitute and a liberal cocktail of drugs and alcohol, had played out in the American's Radisson Hotel room. The hotel management had finally broken down the door at around ten in the morning, to find the American with a small bullet hole in his left temple, face down in the bathroom. Of the Egyptian girl, no trace, other than her fingerprints. Only hers and the American's. The company in Idaho had covered the bills and, with the assistance of the American embassy, shipped the dead man back to his family.

"Well done, Ahmed. I like your style. We'll have more work for you, well paid work. Our cousins in Baghdad may also have need of your services at times."

And the Director had gone back to the playboy lifestyle which fed both his address book and his bank account. He sometimes wondered whether he had missed a career in the film business, given the pleasure he derived in stage-managing his assignments.

Dawn was breaking when he got up from the table and stretched. This enforced isolation in his hotel bedroom wasn't doing his body any good, not to mention the fact that it seemed almost impossible to maintain a healthy diet at any of the restaurants and cafes in the vicinity. How could a nation run only on pizzas or steak and *papas fritas*?

After a couple of hours' sleep on the worn-out mattress, he resolved to go back to the fitness centre at the Hilton in Puerto Madero. In the meantime, there were other remedies closer to hand. He picked up his cell phone and dialled Sonia's number.

After Sonia, he would devote time to Caballero and Flemming, as well as the gym. He also needed to draw cash on one of his cards. Not only cash. Before leaving Baghdad, he had agreed a simple communication formula with the Sons of Ibn Taymiyyah, whereby, if they deposited one hundred dollars in his account, it meant he must make contact via the email they'd set up. Five thousand meant he should break off the mission.

Wednesday, 9 July 2008 (AM) – AVENIDA DE MAYO Y PERÚ, BUENOS AIRES

"Listen, I know it's highly irregular and I really shouldn't be asking you this. You'll just have to trust me. You're perfectly at liberty to refuse. I can't give you an explanation. If you can do it, and in such a fashion that it doesn't get back to whoever's fingerprints they are, I would be very grateful. One day, I'll explain it to you."

Eduardo remained silent, thinking through the implications. Finally, he shrugged his shoulders and took the small plastic bag containing the glass.

"I must be crazy. But, never mind. I'll see how far I can get by myself. I did a course on this last year and a large part of the fingerprint record which goes with the issue of every identity document is accessible to us. I presume it's an Argentine? If I have to go to anybody else, I'll ask you first. That'll be an extra crate of champagne at our wedding."

Eduardo paused, studying his godfather.

"Might there just be some connection with the death of your friend? The rugby player?"

Leandro didn't reply, which, to Eduardo, was as good as a confirmation.

"Got to be going. I've a meeting at 9.30 with Fonseca."

Wednesday, 9 July 2008 (AM) – LARREA Y ARENALES, BUENOS AIRES

María Rosa, Grunwald's cleaner, fumbled her keys. The light on the landing was bad and her eyesight not much better. Finally getting the door open, she was surprised to find the light in the hall still on, even though it was past nine o'clock in the morning. Not like the Señor to waste electricity in this fashion. She bustled into the kitchen and put her bag down on the sideboard. And why had the Señor left all those carrots out in the kitchen, for the flies to find? She placed them in a bowl in the refrigerator. Pulling on the apron hanging on the back of the door, she made her way to the drawing room, taking the antiquated hoover from its wall cupboard on the way. More lights on and, although she could not hear a sound, Señor's laptop open on the table. By this time of the morning, if he was not at home, he was usually at work.

After about ten minutes' hoovering and, with a duster, sweeping the surfaces of the tables - always too many books and papers lying around - she was making for the bedroom when the entrance buzzer sounded in the kitchen.

"*Hola, si. Quien es?*"

"This is Inspector Suarez. Señor Grunwald is expecting me. Please open."

She pressed the button to open the main door downstairs. If he had visitors, hoovering would have to wait.

About a minute later, the front doorbell rang. On opening, she was confronted with two men, whose dark blue windbreakers sported the white initials of the AFIP.

"Señor Grunwald is expecting us," the taller of the two announced, walking confidently into the drawing room. His companion, immediately spotting Grunwald's open laptop, walked over to his worktable.

"Who should I announce?"

"Inspector Suarez. Of the AFIP."

She tapped lightly on the bedroom door, but there was no reply. She tapped again. She looked back at Suarez, who indicated with some impatience that he did not propose to stand around for long.

Shrugging her shoulders, María Rosa pushed open the door.

Friday, 11 July 2008 (AM) – BARRIO ONCE, BUENOS AIRES

Thanks to the combined attentions of Sonia and a two-hour work-out at the Hilton, the Director was feeling much better. Yesterday's newspapers had carried headlines about the murder of one of Argentina's bolder investigative journalists. Out of respect for one of their own, however, most newspapers had not dwelt too much on the details. He had scanned a number of the dailies and watched the evening TV coverage, in which genuine respect for this journalist's courage had been mixed with veiled allusions to the fact that the government was unlikely to mourn the passing of someone not afraid to lift the lid on some of their less palatable activities.

The newspapers had also carried a story that, in the wake of Iran test-firing its Shahab-3 missiles a couple of days previously, the US Secretary of State had warned its government that the US would retaliate in the event of Israel being attacked. Although that kind of threat was unlikely to deter those fanatics in Tehran, hopefully his own efforts might slow down their progress.

As he sat over a cup of coffee in the café next to the hotel, the Director took another look at Grunwald's notes. Caballero appeared to occupy a central position in the government's lines of communication, judging by the group in which he'd been included. To that extent, the choice of Caballero as a target could have a bigger impact.

But in the case of Flemming, at least there was an address and a phone number to work with. With a little specialist persuasion, he might even find that Flemming was a key player. He toyed with the idea of making an approach as an investment specialist on the lookout for opportunities in Argentine real estate, but decided against the waste of time briefing himself. The journalist cover was still unblown. Grunwald had so far been the first to make its acquaintance.

There was also the opportunity provided by Grunwald's funeral. Who could tell who might be there? He studied the death announcements in La Nación and a couple of other newspapers. Following the death of Morales, he had discovered that Argentine social traditions fostered a plethora of brief messages of condolences, not only from the family, but also from the person's workplace and from friends. Everyone seemed to want to get in on the act. He scanned the list in the faint hope of finding one of the names in Grunwald's notebook, but without success.

In the identity of Mario Azoulay, he made discreet enquiries as to when the funeral service would take place. No one seemed to know until a small item appeared in one of the newspapers announcing that the burial would take place on the following Monday at one of the main Jewish cemeteries in the Buenos Aires suburb of La Matanza, following a brief service at the Libertad synagogue.

Housekeeping first. Loose ends to be cleared up. To the old man in La Plata, he had already paid a return visit. There was also Hamid. He was still in two minds what to do about that young man. A Playboy magazine was perhaps insufficient evidence on which to terminate someone's life. But he was a weak link, probably too weak to resist any sustained enquiries. He should be advised to leave the country until further notice. He'd give him a call and get him to take a holiday fast.

Friday, 11 July 2008 (PM) – PASAJE DE LA PIEDAD, BUENOS AIRES

"Come in. I'm Leandro."

"Albert. Pleased to meet you."

On returning from his meeting with Eduardo, Leandro had found a mail from Charles, indicating that someone by the name of Albert would be calling on him in the afternoon of the following Friday. Could he confirm that he would be in? Leandro sent back a reply to say that he would expect him.

He had then forgotten about it, his attention fully taken by the news of Grunwald's murder, which he had also immediately reported to Frobisher.

Leandro found himself looking into the piercing blue eyes of a small, wiry man, aged about fifty-five, a short stubble of grey hair, his face weather-beaten. He was dressed in jeans, with an ageing tweed jacket over a dark blue roll neck sweater. No overcoat, in spite of the weather.

The strong trace of an English accent. Stronger than any Anglo-Argentine. He switched into English.

"Please, sit down, make yourself at home. I got a mail a couple of days ago from a mutual friend telling me to expect you. That's all, so I'm afraid I don't know what it's about."

Albert seemed relieved by the prospect of talking in English.

"Not a problem. I can explain."

"Can I offer you something to drink? I've got some wine, some beer, or whisky. What would you prefer?"

"Whisky will be great. Nice place you have here." Albert was looking appreciatively round Leandro's sitting room. His eyes rested on the photographs of the Malvinas campaign.

"You fought in Malvinas?"

"Yes, I flew a Pucará. Got shot down. Were you there?"

"Yes, with 3 Para."

"Same as Charles?"

"Exactly."

"Is that where you knew him?"

"Yes, although I'd actually met him a couple of years earlier."

"Here's your whisky," Leandro placed a glass on the small table beside the sofa. "Ice?"

"No thanks."

Leandro settled himself into an armchair, while Albert placed himself in the corner of the sofa.

"So, what can I do for you?"

Albert hesitated a minute. Then he made a sweeping motion of his hand, followed by a gesture as if he was listening to something. Leandro shook his head.

"It's alright, I've checked. Our friend passed me a little electronic toy. Anyway, those who were interested in me before are no longer with us, if you see what I mean."

Albert gave a thumbs up.

"Charles told me that you might need some help on something you're doing for him."

He saw a glimmer of surprise on Leandro's face.

"Let me give you a little of my background. I first came to Argentina in the mid-70s."

"Rough times."

"Indeed. The British ambassador had been given a small detail to guard him, drawn from ex-members of the SAS. I was one of those. I had three years in Buenos Aires. We spent about as much time keeping an eye on the Argentine bodyguards attached to the embassy as anybody else."

Leandro nodded.

"To be frank, we never fired a shot in anger. We had a great time though, accompanying the ambassador. Official engagements, weekend stays in somebody's estancia. We did a lot of shooting then. Mainly red partridge and duck."

Albert chuckled, before continuing.

"Good times. Amongst other things, on one of those weekends, I met a girl. From the other side of Saladillo in the Province of Buenos Aires. She was very good for my Spanish, although, as you spotted, it's still not good enough. She was also very good for me in other ways."

Albert paused, sipping the whisky.

"Very nice. What is it?"

"Balvenie. One of my favourites. I pick it up at the duty-free when I can. Can I fill it up?"

"No, still got plenty. Anyway, as I was saying, in '79 I was called back to England. The girl came with me and we were married. In Edinburgh as it happens. We had a daughter. Or to be more precise, we have a daughter. And a son."

"Then came the war," Leandro interjected.

"That's right. As you can imagine, it wasn't easy, but somehow, our marriage survived the test. And then, in 1987, I could see she was finding life in England hard. So we came back here. We now live out in the Province, beyond Lobos. I run a farm and a small business. It pays the bills."

Leandro was still at something of a loss. Why had Charles sent this man to see him?

"I'm glad. But, I'm not sure I quite understand how I can help you."

"I think Charles rather saw it the other way round. Me perhaps being able to help you."

"Oh, I see. Well, that's always welcome."

Luis Miguel's killing, and now Grunwald's, had clearly set the alarm bells ringing in London.

Albert cleared his throat.

"As I mentioned, I'm SAS trained. You've heard of them?"

"Anybody who's fought against the British in the last fifty years knows about the SAS. You're the best!"

"Who knows. However, we're trained to be useful in difficult circumstances."

"Typical British understatement," Leandro laughed.

"Charles didn't tell me anything, except that you've apparently accepted a new assignment, which just might get a bit complicated. I'm not asking to know anything more about it. But if things get rough, basically I know how to look after myself and anyone with me. They taught us a lot of fairly nasty ways of dealing with someone whose intentions might be less than honourable."

Albert grinned.

"That's the phrase used by my martial arts trainer. Not a thug from the back streets of London. More like Eton and Oxford. Upper-class accent as he breaks your leg. Fantastic guy. Can't imitate his accent, sorry. Anyway, small arms. Easy. Heavier calibres. Also, if necessary."

He looked over at Leandro.

"Have you got any kind of gun?"

Leandro got up and, opening a small drawer in his desk, produced the Bersa Thunder 9mm he'd bought after the assassination of Sosa back in September last year. The compact handgun was still in its case, which made Albert smile. Albert sniffed the barrel.

"You don't seem to have used it yet."

"No. And, frankly, hope I won't have to."

"We all do, but sometimes, we don't have a choice. How good are you with it?"

Leandro dug around at the back of the drawer and produced the target he'd used as part of the formalities to get his registration.

"Pretty good. Twenty metres?"

Leandro nodded.

"Accuracy is only part of it. Readiness and speed count too. We'll see about that later. Unless of course you feel quite comfortable about these things."

"Not really. Most of my life has been spent either on the rugby pitch, under the bonnet of my car or in front of a computer screen. I never thought I'd have any need for this kind of thing. But last year all that changed."

"Argentina used to be a safe country to walk around in," Albert smiled.

""It's nowhere near Mexico or Honduras or Brazil, but yes, things are no longer the same. It's sad, but perhaps all the world is moving in that direction."

"You're right. It is sad. Do you think this assignment is going to involve any kind of surveillance? By that I mean, not only are you likely to be followed, but also are you going to be doing any following? And eavesdropping? Is someone likely to be going after you? Or you after them? These are also areas in which I can help. I think Charles put it as me watching your back."

Leandro thought for a minute. At this stage, it was hard to tell how the Frobisher assignment was going to evolve. He had, perhaps for reasons of self-preservation - or was it self-delusion? - assumed that it was going to be largely a matter of research. But recent events suggested the research might come with its share of violence. If Charles had sent Albert to him, it must be that Frobisher also saw things that way.

"Perhaps I haven't given this enough thought. Who knows how it'll play out. But, on reflection, Charles was probably right to send you. How's your whisky?"

"A little more would be good."

Leandro refilled their glasses. He had been studying Albert discreetly. From his accent, he detected what in England might have been called a working class background, possibly from somewhere in the North. In his time in London, Leandro had learned that the English, in spite of regular doses of post-war socialism, still categorised people by the way they spoke. On the trading floors of Citibank in the City, he had found traces of a certain class-based segregation, between middle management and the boys who really made the money. The trading instinct of the East End 'barrow boys' had shifted from the fish and meat stalls of Billingsgate and Smithfields to the computerised trading floors of the glass fronted high-rise City institutions. A taste for risk, the ability to spot a margin between one price and another, backed up by all the computer power of the day, had turned many of these young traders into overnight millionaires, flashing round town in their Ferraris and Porsches. Leandro had usually found their company far more stimulating and entertaining than that of their bosses.

"You look fit, Albert. Spend a lot of time out of doors?"

"Yes, on the farm. A lot of horses. We're close to a polo area. We do a little breeding. And inevitably, too much soya. Bad for the soil, better for the purse! Do you know the area?"

"A bit. I've driven through there on a number of occasions, usually heading a bit farther south. It's a pretty area."

"Well, if you're ever passing through some day, let me know, come and have something to eat."

"With pleasure."

At that moment, Sam appeared in the doorway.

Saturday, 12 July 2008 (PM) - DELTA

"So, what did you make of Albert?"

The glowing embers of the *quebracho* in the fireplace threw a flickering light across the room. Outside, the temperature had dropped to around five centigrade and a soft wind was sighing through the *casuarinas* along the riverbank. Sam was lying on her back in front of the fire, her head resting on a rolled up horsehair blanket, balancing an almost empty glass of rum between her breasts. Winter had arrived with a vengeance this year, but this had not deterred them from coming out to Leandro's house in the Paraná Delta. After a boiling shower, Sam was wearing a soft tracksuit - and nothing much else.

The small building, bought by Leandro on impulse many years earlier and gradually restored to a level of basic comfort, stood nearly two metres above ground to cope with any sudden rise in the water level. A combination of tide and south-easterly winds blowing in across the Rio de la Plata would flood the islands up to a metre or more above ground level, transforming the landscape into a boundless lake. This silent drama never failed to fascinate Sam, standing even on the coldest nights on the verandah wrapped in a blanket to watch the waters rise and fall.

Hidden away up a narrow channel running into the main artery of the Urión, the shack was sheltered from the heavy weekend traffic of motor cruisers, jetskis and assorted yachts, which, since the prosperous days of President Menem's 1990s, had turned the usually deserted rivers and streams of the Delta into a watery reflection of Buenos Aires traffic on a weekday. It was here that Sam had first recovered after the horrors of her kidnapping some three months earlier. The sound of lapping water, the wind in the trees, were now irrevocably associated in her mind with that first morning of freedom regained, waking to find Leandro sitting beside her bed, silhouetted against the window, watching her as she slowly convinced herself that the nightmare was over.

She rolled onto her side, her back to the fire, placing the glass carefully on the floor. Leandro was sprawled in one of the two old armchairs, relics of some men's club, the leather worn and cracked.

"I liked him. On the one hand, it's clear he can look after himself, from the little you've told me. Matches his physical appearance. On the other, there's a kind of vulnerability, a bit like a little boy. Brings out the protective instinct in me."

"Good grief! I wonder how he'd react if he heard you. But I know what you mean. Perhaps your sudden appearance caught him off guard."

Sam had slipped silently into the flat while Leandro and Albert were talking. The burble of the Harley-Davidson's exhaust in the yard below had not escaped Leandro, so he wasn't surprised when she suddenly appeared. As usual, dressed as if she were on her way to a meeting of some Hells Angels coven, albeit one which bought its kit on Madison Avenue. Skin-tight black leather jeans, ankle boots with stiletto heels, a fleece-lined USAF leather jacket, suitably distressed, a full helmet, jet black with darkened visor. Albert had betrayed a momentary anxiety, but the welcoming smile on Leandro's face had put him at ease.

"He liked the look of my Harley from the window."

"You brought out the old biker in him. Him and his 'ton-up' boys. And he liked your comment, what was it—?"

"I like to ride something good-looking?"

Sam had helped herself to a tumbler of whisky.

"I'm interrupting something? I can always go and watch something next door."

The look on her face had told Leandro that he would have to find a very good reason indeed to get her to do that. Not worth the effort.

"No, join us. Albert, Sam has over the last twelve months begun to control an unacceptable proportion of my life. It's probably my fault. Weak willed. But there it is!"

"You do talk crap sometimes," Sam snorted, straddling the arm of Leandro's chair. "Anyway, Albert, tell me about yourself."

Albert had thrown a glance towards Leandro, seeking some guidance as to how much Sam might or might not know. He was clearly still somewhat disconcerted by her appearance.

"It's okay, Albert. Sam knows about Frobisher. At least, in principle."

Since Albert, at this stage, seemed not to have any idea of the assignment given by Frobisher, Leandro hadn't been too worried that the little Englishman might say too much. Other than of course possibly to convey to Sam the impression that the risk factor had moved up a couple of notches, if the services of someone like Albert had suddenly become necessary. But knowing Sam, this was more likely to whet her appetite than anything else.

"Frobisher? Oh, now I understand. I want to hear it all."

Sam had turned the full force of her charm on Albert. A glance at Albert suggested that he might well be receptive.

Albert had gone on to provide Sam with a shortened version of his life history, dwelling only briefly on his SAS credentials. Living in Argentina had probably taught him over the years that, like the Gurkhas, the SAS were not always *persona grata* in certain circles after the war. At the time of the conflict, the Gurkhas had been portrayed by the Argentine press as something little short of diabolical. Leandro could remember the horrific tales circulating among the troops, of throats being silently slit with the dreaded kukri in forward trenches in the wind-swept blackness of the Malvinas night.

"And now? What happens next?"

"Oh, I guess we just get to know each other. Maybe something'll come up we can work on together."

"All three of us?"

As usual, Sam hadn't been taking any detours.

"I mean, I'm sure there must be some reason for this get together," she continued, turning to Leandro.

Again he ducked it.

"No, nothing in particular."

She shot him a glance which made it plain that she didn't believe him. Given their conversation about the Iranian assignment, it was obvious that Albert's visit was in some way connected. But she quickly realised that Leandro might not wish Albert to get the impression that she was fully in the know.

"I need another whisky."

Leandro had detected that she was angry that they hadn't taken her more into their confidence. She might drop the subject now, but she would certainly return to it later.

They had continued talking a little while longer about life in Argentina until, finally, Albert had asked to see her motorbike. Delighted, she had led them down into the courtyard where the gleaming pearl grey and chrome Softail Night Train, with its black engine and drag bars, contrasted sharply with the *fin de siècle* pale yellow elegance of the narrow private street.

Albert whistled.

"1600 cc, twin cam in V, air cooled, six speed. Perhaps not the fastest bike on the road, one hundred and fifty kilometres an hour. But one of the best looking. It's my first serious bike. When I get better at it, I'll get something faster."

Leandro had been struck by what could be considered unusual prudence for Sam. Only a hundred and fifty kilometres an hour! It could only get more dangerous!

"Put another log on the fire will you? And some of the eucalyptus bark and pine cones as well for a bit of perfume. I'm glad you liked him. I did too."

Sam rolled in the other direction and stacked the fireplace.

"That should keep us going well into the night. Let's have a bit more of that rum. It really is delicious."

She stretched out her glass which he dutifully replenished.

"I thought that in some ways he was rather touching. Did you notice, Leo, when he suggested that we might drop by some day and have an *asado* on his *campo*? There was almost a note of apology, as if he felt it wasn't going to be good enough. If you're going to work with him, we should make a point of going."

"That'll give you an excuse to get out your Harley, I know."

Albert, having suggested that they visit his farm, had turned to Sam.

"It's after the Laguna de Lobos. If you're a biker, you'll know what I'm talking about."

"I haven't been a biker for that long. Tell me."

"Oh, every weekend, the 'ton-up boys'..... that's the way they used to be referred to in England in the 1950s and 1960s. Ton means one hundred miles an hour. That was a lot in those days. About the same speed as that machine of yours. Anyway, the bikers from Buenos Aires take advantage of the *autopista* from Ezeiza to Cañuelas to go way beyond the speed limit. With usually a couple of fatalities every weekend. I'm sure you'd be a great success."

"And probably either get raped or killed into the bargain," Leandro had interrupted. "Albert, stop giving this lady ideas. She's quite dangerous enough without help from people like you."

"Thank you, Albert, I take note."

Sam had looked defiantly at Leandro.

Albert had finally left after they had promised to take him up on his invitation to visit him on his farm. Having clearly overcome any initial doubts about Sam, he had shown little resistance to the warm kiss Sam had given him.

"Come and join me, here, by the fire." Sam almost purred the words. "Now that we both know what you're doing for Frobisher, I need to know where Albert fits in. That's what teamwork is all about. Why have they sent him to you? I want answers, Flemming. You've evaded too many of my questions already."

She would never give up. As usual, was it Sam - or Mossad - talking?

"In that case, I think I'll stick where I am, in case you try any of your third-degree on me."

"Do I scare you that much?"

"Frankly, yes. The onslaught of your hands and your questions is more than the average man should be asked to withstand. So if you don't mind, I'll just take the questions."

Sam positioned herself cross-legged with her back to the fire. Carelessly, she unzipped the top of her tracksuit, revealing the shadowy cleavage he found so irresistible.

"That's cheating. No long-range weapons allowed either."

"I haven't even declared war yet," Sam protested. "Not to mention the fact that you're also looking very romantic in this light."

There were moments when she felt that the combination of his pale grey eyes and dark Mediterranean features made him the handsomest lover she had ever had. And a brain as well! It seemed too good to be true.

Leandro sighed and poured himself another inch of rum.

"Fire away."

"It's obvious they've sent Albert to look after you. As if I wasn't already doing that."

"Perhaps they had a slightly different kind of protection in mind," Leandro said. "You look after my spiritual well-being. I was going to say my moral, but that would be a lie. Albert's here for the physical."

"And what I give you every night, wouldn't you describe that as physical?"

He smiled and sipped his rum.

"So, if you need someone from the SAS, it's obvious things are getting more exciting."

Just what he dreaded most. The lure of the chase.

"I don't think you..."

"Come on. Two men you've had lunch with in the last six weeks have been murdered in very nasty circumstances. No wonder they sent you Albert. In fact, thank God. If they hadn't, I'd have picked up the phone to London."

"I'd rather you didn't."

"Not this time. But what interests me even more is, where do you go from here? Now that you've got Albert. Not to mention the resources I could mobilize if things get rough."

Leandro shook his head. The respite was over. Sam was now fully on board. Somehow, he needed to erect a crash barrier.

"Who said I had any intention of allowing you to get involved? Let alone those masters of yours in Tel Aviv."

Sam smiled. Little did Leo know how much they might already be involved.

Sunday, 13 July 2008 (AM) – CASA ROSADA, BUENOS AIRES

The presidential adviser glanced at the two new faces. He had asked for the police *Comisarías* in which the murders had taken place to be represented in an expanded group. Calling the meeting on a Sunday morning was an extra touch of power.

"Señores, things are not improving. Whatever the press may be trying to imply, we all know around this table that the murder of the journalist Grunwald has nothing to do with us. But, when they drag their noses out of his sex life, some of the press, particularly those under the control of corporate groups hostile to our government, are not above insinuating that he was murdered as a reprisal for his article about Iran."

He ignored an exchange of glances between the representatives of the Policía Federal and the Ministry of Foreign Relations.

"It's my view, and that of the Secretary General, that this murder is connected with the two we discussed last time. The common thread is obviously Iran. Whoever, or whatever, is behind these killings, our relations with Iran are the target. A number of candidates appear obvious. First and foremost, Israel."

"Surely," said the policeman, clearing his throat, "the assassination of one of their own race would be excessive."

"If the intention in murdering Grunwald was to muddy the waters, we should not allow ourselves to be fooled. Obviously the calculation will have been that the assassination would be seen as our work. A reprisal. Then there's the United States, who have every reason to be keen to stop any possible collaboration with Iran. After that, the field is relatively open. If anyone has any other suggestions, I'd be interested to hear them."

He detected hesitation, the company unused to having their views sought in the presidential entourage. The outgoing president, Nestor Kirchner, and to an even greater extent his wife who had now replaced him, had always seen the exercise of power as a one-way street. There had never been a full Cabinet meeting since their arrival in 2003. No wonder his invitation to contribute their thoughts had left them somewhat confused.

He waited, ostentatiously consulting his BlackBerrys.

The representative of the Foreign Ministry caught his eye.

"Perhaps, if I may be permitted to suggest it, we should throw the net a little wider. By that I mean, contemplate the possibility that this is not a campaign instigated by a state, but rather by some terrorist organisation. After all, the two attacks here in Buenos Aires in the 90s were the work of Hezbollah, although we are all agreed that Tehran was probably behind them."

Although his thumb continued to hover over his Blackberry, the adviser looked expectantly at him, an invitation to proceed.

"I recently asked our Middle Eastern Department to draw up what you might call an order of battle, to identify not only nations, but also organisations, which might be expected to take direct action against our interests. The result of that analysis is almost ready, and when it is, I would of course be pleased to share it with you all."

The adviser looked around to see how the suggestion had been received. He detected a nodding of heads. In spite of the low esteem in which he held the diplomatic profession, it might be tactically prudent to accept the offer. One never knew. If it turned out to be a load of diplomatic half-truths and elegant turns of phrase, it would be another stick with which to beat the Ministry.

"I thank you for that suggestion. Please ensure that the study comes out as soon as possible."

Gesturing towards the two new additions to the group, he continued.

"We have decided to bring in representatives of the two *Comisarías* in which the murders were committed, in order to speed up the exchange of relevant information. We would be reluctant to see crucial evidence lost somewhere in the machine."

With which he cast a rapid glance in the direction of the senior representative of the Policía Federal. Although it was answerable to the Presidency, each body would almost certainly have its own agenda. By going down a few echelons, he hoped to involve people with more modest political ambitions, perhaps keen to advance their careers through good detective work directly on behalf of the Casa Rosada.

"Please introduce yourselves," he added, pointing in their direction with his BlackBerry.

"Inspector Raul Fonseca, from *Comisaría 17a.*," the first man replied. "The murder of Consejero Morales took place in our precinct."

"Inspector Juan Domingo Jimenez, from *Comisaría 19a.*, responsible for the precinct in which Carlos Grunwald died."

Though noting that the man had the same first names as the illustrious Perón, which probably said more about the political inclinations of his parents than anything else, the adviser reacted swiftly to the implication.

"Died? Are you in any doubt that he was murdered?"

"So far," Inspector Jimenez began, "we have not been able to rule out completely the possibility that Grunwald strangled himself by mistake. Our forensic teams have failed to discover any trace of another person in the flat at the time of his death. No fingerprints, door closed on the inside, no sign of a break-in. Very different, as I understand it, from the circumstances of the other death, of Morales."

The adviser couldn't conceal his distaste for this apparent deviation from the line he had taken right at the start. There was some discreet shuffling of papers around the table.

"Well, we will rely on you to do your job. As soon as you find evidence to support the view I have carefully presented, I would be grateful if you would make it available to all present."

He turned to the representative of the Ministry of Justice.

"What progress have we made on immigration records? Suspects?"

The man from the Ministry shifted in his chair.

"I regret, nothing so far."

"I've been looking at the records from the time of the AMIA and Israeli embassy bombings. Back then, your Ministry was unable to provide a single lead. Apparently the immigration system wasn't up to it. Has nothing changed in fifteen years?"

"We are working on it. And very soon we'll have the new system, which we're buying from the Cubans, with digital fingerprint and photographic information on every traveller."

"I personally vetted the contract with the Cuban Ministry of the Interior. Good technology at a good price. But too late, I fear."

He looked around to see if anybody else had any ideas. Everyone appeared content to leave it at that, perhaps relieved to have avoided the trap into which their colleagues from the *Comisaría 19a.* and the Justice Ministry had fallen.

"With three murders and a possible fourth attempted in Caracas, we must act. Whoever has launched this attack on our system must be found and neutralised. For that, I rely on your efforts. "

He looked at the representatives of the Policía Federal and handed a small sheet of paper to the representative of SIDE.

"For the rest, we must take measures to protect anyone who might constitute the next target. I have prepared a list of names, and I would wish you to formulate whatever measures you consider necessary to protect these people. Once you have decided on your course of action, please show it to me first for final approval. As you will see, some of these people may prove reluctant to be subjected to too much attention."

What he wasn't saying was that some of the names on the list, and in particular people like Martín Caballero, were involved in affairs close to the Presidency, the existence of which not even SIDE should uncover. If possible. More parallel agendas. The Kirchner family relationship with SIDE did not always run smooth.

Turning to the representative of the Policía Federal and the two *Comisarías*, he went on.

"What has been done as regards the telephone records or emails of Morales and Grunwald? We need to review those, if we haven't already, to see whether anyone appears on both lists. Or indeed how much communication there was between them. Do I really need to tell you this?"

"We'll have an analysis within a couple of days," the Policía Federal representative said.

"No more than that."

He looked around the table once more.

"If that is all clear, we meet again as a group in a week, unless of course something else happens in the meantime."

The adviser pulled together his papers and, glancing at his two Blackberrys, swept from the room.

"If you can't find any trace, you might just have to fabricate something," Fonseca whispered to his colleague. The latter shrugged his shoulders.

"Wouldn't be the first time, nor the last," he grunted. "Take care, *che*."

"You too."

The senior representative from the Policía Federal joined them.

"I presume you got the message, Jimenez!"

"Certainly, Señor Director."

As they made their way from the meeting room towards the main exit, their route took them along a first floor balcony giving onto an inner courtyard of the Presidential palace. The hubbub below, which had only faintly penetrated as far the meeting, was deafening. Leaning over the balustrade, they were confronted with the sight of a seething throng of teenagers, rhythmically chanting the name of the President.

"Cris – ti – na! Cris – ti – na!"

"New recruits to the Cámpora," the Foreign Ministry official muttered, a note of sarcasm ill-concealed. "They'll be sending them round to the Ministry next. Tell us all what to do."

"All good things come to an end," his colleague from the Justice Ministry murmured.

The two men separated, sensing that the representative of SIDE was not yet out of earshot.

Monday, 14 July 2008 (AM) – AVENIDA DE MAYO Y PERÚ, BUENOS AIRES

"Well, Uncle. Sure you can't tell me more?"

Leandro looked at Eduardo, wondering whether he had any choice.

"Any chance that I might do that at a later date?" he asked.

Eduardo shook his head, but rather to convey the fact that he knew that there was little point in taking the issue any farther.

"Actually, given the identity of the person, it doesn't really matter. I can work out most of it for myself."

Eduardo signalled to the waiter to bring over a couple of coffees.

"You seem to be in touch with an interesting person. At least, I assume you're in touch. I was a bit surprised not to find your fingerprints on the glass. Not sure how you did that. There are two sets. One, we can dismiss straightaway as it turns out to be a barman at the Faena hotel. The other one, on the other hand, well…"

"Go on, Eduardo, spit it out!"

"Well, as I was saying…. The owner of the fingerprints is someone called Martín Caballero. Strange fellow. Quite a reputation on the jetset circuit. He's had some pretty lurid girlfriends in his time. A regular feature in ¡Hola! and Gente. But, under the surface, there's more to him than just that."

"What does he do?"

"Turns out he belongs to a certain fauna which has flourished under the Kirchners. Businessmen and financiers, operating on the margins. Intermediaries, facades. Real estate, government contracts, casinos, that kind of thing. Which explains his lavish lifestyle. You seem to have met him at the Faena. It appears he has a room reserved full-time there. Travels a lot as well. Most recently to Venezuela, accompanied by one of his blondes."

Eduardo sat back to observe the impact of his news. Slightly to his disappointment, Leandro was nodding his head in a way that suggested he already knew.

"You don't seem very surprised, Uncle. Perhaps you already had the answer."

Leandro stretched across the table and grasped Eduardo's arm.

"I won't deny it, but I needed the confirmation. Thank you."

He knew that to be too effusive in his gratitude would only embarrass Eduardo. He could see from the look on his son's face that the gesture was all he needed.

Eduardo dug in his pocket and produced a piece of paper, on which he had jotted down Caballero's details, his business address and a few other items.

"Here, this may be of some use as well," as he passed the paper across the table.

Leandro picked it up and after a quick glance put it away in his pocket.

"And the lady Samira in all this?" Eduardo asked, teasing.

"Oh, a simple accessory," Leandro replied.

Perhaps not the most generous description of the part she had played. He got up from the table, having placed twenty-five pesos under the napkin holder.

"I've got to run, and you're in a hurry too, I think."

Eduardo didn't move.

"I've got a little bit of extra news. No doubt unconnected," he added.

Leandro sat down again.

"Since about two weeks, they've set up some kind of task force on these murders in the Casa Rosada. Fonseca has been asked to join it. He told me this morning. He's such a conceited bastard, he simply couldn't resist bragging about moving in presidential circles. Anyway, what's interesting is that not only is our *Comisaría* represented, but also the *19a.*, where Grunwald was murdered. Which means they see a connection. Fonseca swore me to secrecy. If you're interested, I'll keep you posted."

He could see from the look on Leandro's face that he was certainly interested.

"So, not just a rugby playing buddy, after all."

Leandro blushed slightly.

"Don't worry, Uncle, your secret is safe with me. However, that's not quite all."

Eduardo again adopted his air of mystery.

"You remember I mentioned the two dead guys from the *Bonaerense*? Well, according Fonseca, that lead has got a bit farther as well. A look at the cell phone log of one of them took them to a house in La Plata, where they found another body. A former member of the *Bonaerense*, an old man well known to the police. Ran a number of shady businesses in the 90s, one of which had blown up in his face at the time of the 2001 crisis. Hadn't been seen for a number of days, but when they broke down the door, they found him strangled in his sitting room. His cats had started to feed on him. Research also revealed a contact with a young Syrian in Boedo. That *Comisaría* was a bit slow in following up, and by the time they got there last Saturday, whoever it was had left. All bits of a jigsaw puzzle, but certainly pointing to the fact that there's an assassin - or more than one - on the loose."

"That's very interesting. I'm grateful."

This time, Eduardo was the first to stand.

They hugged each other. Picking up the first taxi coming down the street, Leandro made his way back to his flat, where he found Sam installed in front of his computer.

"Curiosity killed the cat," he muttered, as he kissed the nape of her neck.

"Judging from what I find in your search history, it's your curiosity that's deadly. What's this?" she asked, flicking to a website of one of Carla's rivals.

"Got the result from Eduardo," Leandro evaded.

Sam turned her chair. "And? Confirmation?"

"I would think so. Seems to be a wheeler-dealer in the secret business empire of our president's family. Also has a taste in cheap women. No wonder he fell for you."

"*Andate a la mierda,* Leandro Flemming. But that's brilliant. Just what I needed. Any more detail?"

Leandro handed her the piece of paper from Eduardo.

"So his name's Caballero. Martín Caballero. Great!"

The note of triumph in her voice was unmistakable.

"Got to rush. See you later."

"I may have to go to another funeral. This afternoon. Grunwald."

She shot a quizzical look at him as she made for the hall, where she pulled on her overcoat. Opening the front door, she turned.

"And try and spend a little less time on those websites. You'll become brain-dead."

Laughing, she pulled the door closed behind her.

Monday, 14 July 2008 (PM) – BARRIO ONCE, BUENOS AIRES

"Welcome, Señorita Haidar, come in. Your dress is ready. It didn't need much in the way of alteration," the young man greeted her.

Within minutes of Leandro passing her Eduardo's list, she had alerted her Mossad contact via a dedicated chat room. A return message had come through to her cell phone, ostensibly from a tailor and dressmaker whose services she occasionally used in the Once district.

Like so many of his modern orthodox fellows in the area, he was dressed in traditional black trousers and white shirt, the small black velvet *kippot* perched on the back of his head. He pulled aside a heavy carpet on the wall of the small work room, revealing a door into which he disappeared, gesturing to her to follow. Once inside, it was safe to speak. The young man had once explained that the room was surrounded on all sides by other rooms of the same flat and that the apartments above and below were also controlled. The walls were lined with geometrically porous material, like a recording studio.

"You have news?"

Without going into any detail, Sam explained that she had been able to establish the identity of one of the Argentines she'd met in Tobago.

"Perez's real name is Martín Caballero. These are his telephone numbers and address," she added.

"Useful confirmation. We had already suspected Caballero had some role in all of this, but we're most grateful to you. Most of the time, he leads the life of a playboy, a lifestyle not always easy to follow. We'll have to take a closer interest now."

Sam was tempted to pass on the news that the Russians appeared to have found a way to penetrate Caballero's lifestyle, but - without being entirely sure why - thought better of it. Although the fingerprints had provided the final confirmation, she decided not to reveal the fact that both Leandro and Eduardo had been involved in confirming it. Mossad would no doubt be less than pleased at the thought that her role and interests had become known to anyone else.

Perhaps, one day, they would find out. She would face that when the time came.

Monday, 14 July 2008 (PM) – LA TABLADA

Later that afternoon, at the time indicated in the small press announcement, the Director in the guise of Mario Azoulay, a small black *kippot* held in place on the back of his head with a hairpin, stood to one side of the steps leading up to the ornate entrance of the Libertad synagogue. Over the weekend, a couple of days of stubble had been allowed to accumulate on his face, and his sideburns dyed a darker brown. Sun glasses completed the transformation.

Family and close friends were distinguished by the small black ribbon they wore on the left or right hand side, according to their proximity to the deceased. Perhaps predictably, the groups of Jews and non-Jews mingled little as they waited for the service to begin. Given that his targets were more likely to be Gentile than Jewish – judging by names such as Caballero and Flemming - he tried as unobtrusively as possible to remain closer to the former group. All around him, conversations were speculating on the causes of Grunwald's death, one side advancing the political argument that his investigations had taken him too close to sensitive areas of government policy, others – apparently less numerous - talking discreetly about the strange sexual scenario in which his body had been found.

Finally, he decided to join in the conversation of a small group of Jewish men of about Grunwald's age, close to where he was standing.

"Azoulay," he introduced himself.

They shook hands.

"Azoulay? I don't think we've met," one of the men replied, a look of wary curiosity on his face.

"No, I live in Spain. I met Carlos in Madrid once, a few years ago. A good man. I was shocked to read about it a couple of days after I arrived."

"Schonmann. Samuel Schonmann," the man replied, relaxing.

"I don't quite understand what happened," Azoulay asked. "The press. There seem to be different versions. Apparently, he seems to have written an article or displeased the current government. Is that it?"

"It's a long story, but it seems he'd been investigating the government's nuclear activities. Very sensitive. That and his reporting on the AMIA case. They certainly didn't like that, when he wrote an article a week or so ago, tying the two strands together."

"You're suggesting he might have been killed as some kind of political revenge?"

"I don't know whether one can go so far as to say that, although in this country, nothing is impossible. All I know is that the circumstances in which he was found - which I got from a friend - seem out of character. Although, what a man does in the privacy of his home is something none of us are in any position to condemn."

Another man in the group asked him what had brought him to Argentina.

"Some of my relatives emigrated here from Morocco in the second half of the nineteenth century. I was trying to see whether I could track down where they might have been buried."

"You should go and see the people at AMIA about that kind of thing, though this week, they'll probably be busy with the anniversary of the bombing. But they have a number of specialists there who can probably help. And there are certainly Azoulays here in Argentina. Some very successful in finance. Good luck."

With the general move into the synagogue, the small group broke up.

Once inside, it was clear that the throng of mourners was not going to make things easy. Perhaps the group accompanying the plain coffin to the cemetery would be smaller. On the steps of the synagogue, the family and friends tore the black ribbons in the tradition of the *K'riah*, before moving towards their cars or taxis.

By the time the cortege had reached the Tablada cemetery, the numbers had dwindled to some thirty or forty, in which the Jewish component made up by far the majority. Azoulay, having checked once more which cemetery, had followed in a taxi.

"Might this be the man they found dead in his apartment in strange circumstances?" the taxi driver had thrown over his shoulder once Azoulay had given him the address.

He nodded. "Yes, bad story."

"One of my passengers was commenting on it the other day. It seems his investigations were too close to the bone. A government inside job, if you ask me."

"Really? I don't live in Argentina."

"Spanish? Your accent."

"Yes, Madrid. Just visiting. I met Grunwald there a few years ago. A good man."

"You a journalist like him?"

"No, I'm in business."

"Well, I'm sorry for your friend. But, in his line of work, you have to be prepared for the worst. Journalists have a shorter life expectancy in Argentina," the driver smirked.

The taxi dropped him at the gates. Again, the mourners had divided into two groups. The majority, members of the family, friends and representatives of the Jewish community. In another group, perhaps a dozen, the Gentiles. And standing apart, two men observing the scene. Police? He shifted slightly so as to be out of their direct line of sight. His dark glasses should go some way to protecting him.

Leandro had noticed the same division into two groups and his eye had also been caught by the two men. Neither family or friends, nor press colleagues of Grunwald, by their manner. Preferring to stand some fifty metres away from the main group, one of them appeared to be taking the occasional photograph. Police? Perhaps even SIDE. Not surprising, really.

It struck him that he was attending the second burial of someone with whom he'd had lunch in the last couple of months. He would have to start issuing a health warning. In part because of the weather, this burial struck him as less depressing than Luis Miguel's. A pale sun was breaking through the clouds, bringing a little warmth, its rays seeming to brighten the spirits of those around the grave. In contrast to the oppressive accumulation of black marble and rusting iron work at Recoleta, this cemetery was green, with trees and grass growing between the stones.

He wasn't quite sure why he had decided to come as far as the cemetery. In spite of all the innuendos in the press, Leandro gave scant credence to the suggestions of deviant sexual practices. Although one could never tell, it somehow didn't seem to fit Carlos' character. On balance, the emergence of a pattern relating to the three deaths over the last ten weeks appeared more credible. Mingling with the other journalists at the entrance to the synagogue, he had been reassured by the fact that most of them favoured the political angle as well.

"Did you ever work with Carlos?" the journalist from Clarín whispered, standing next to him near the grave. Only a couple of representatives of the press had continued as far as the cemetery.

"On and off. Occasionally helped him a little. Finance or banking. Nothing regular," Leandro muttered.

The brief laying to rest was finally complete, with a few of the mourners seeking closure, as the Jewish rite would have it, by shovelling earth onto the coffin until it was completely covered. Then came the solemn recital of the *Kaddish*, before they took their place in the *Shura*, the traditional double row through which family and close relatives would pass, to receive words of condolence or compassion. Leandro and the Clarín journalist joined on the end of the row. Once the family had gone on ahead, the rest fell in behind, talking quietly.

On reaching the street, the groups mingled more easily. The journalist from Clarín flagged down a passing taxi. As he was climbing in, he called over to Leandro.

"Hey, Leandro, want a lift?"

The roar of a passing *colectivo* having drowned his words, he called again.

"Leandro! Flemming!" he called more loudly.

Leandro turned and, seeing the door of the taxi being held open for him, quickly shook the hand of the man he was talking to before walking briskly over to the cab and sliding into the seat beside the journalist. The taxi pulled out into the stream of traffic.

The Director had been standing only a metre or so away from Leandro. Now he also had a face.

Wednesday, 16 July 2008 (PM) – BUENOS AIRES

The Director stepped out of his taxi at the entrance to the Plaza Hotel. An hour of shopping had ensured he was now smartly dressed in blazer and slacks, pulling a Samsonite suitcase behind him, which he had slightly 'distressed' in the bedroom of his little hotel in Once. He was keen to get off the streets. In a few hours the massive demonstrations against law 125 were scheduled to begin, for which large segments of Buenos Aires' middle class were already loudly mobilising. Conscious of the fact that Argentina's wealth had always come from the land, the *porteños* had shown their support for the farmers through regular *cacerolazos* and street marches. Tonight was to be a big one, given the imminent vote in the Senate. No point in getting caught up in something like that.

"I've got to go away for a few days," he'd told the manager of his little hotel, "I like your hotel and the rates are good. I'll be leaving a few things, just some of my old clothes. Perhaps you could lock the room."

"No problem, Señor Azoulay. I'll keep the room for you. Your things will be safe there. Just as long as you don't leave any money or anything valuable."

"I don't have anything valuable," Azoulay had smiled, as he pulled the suitcase out of the door onto the crowded street and hailed a cruising taxi. He made sure that the door was closed and the window up before giving the driver the name of the Plaza.

"You'll be a lot more comfortable there, as long as you've got the bank account to go with it," the driver had advised.

The streets were already beginning to fill up. Faced with opposition, in true Kirchner style, the President and her husband had simply upped the ante. Farmers leaders had been accused by compliant judges of conspiracy, incitement to violence and illegal possession of firearms. The Peronist party had even accused the farmers of being '*golpista*', of trying to bring down the government through a coup.

At the check-in desk of the old fashioned Plaza, a family affair now run by one of the major chains, his forged French passport in the name of Aboukir passed the idle scrutiny of the desk manager. Born 1980 in Valenciennes. Currently resident in Lebanon. Profession, journalist. An impeccable forgery he had picked up in Marseilles on his way to Brussels in April. Five thousand euros well spent. It had only taken a few minutes with the rubber stamp and a biro to insert the Ezeiza Immigration entry stamp provided to him by Hamid, dated mid-June. The Visa card had also gone through. Linked on an account opened in the same name by a compliant senior manager of Byblos Bank in Beirut, in exchange for discreet services rendered in his private torture chamber.

"Welcome to the Plaza, Dr Aboukir. We wish you a pleasant stay."

"As long as things don't get too rough on the streets outside...."

"Don't worry, Dr Aboukir. You'll be safe in here."

Thursday, 17 July 2008 (AM) – SENADO DE LA NACIÓN

Very early in the morning, after an eighteen hour debate, the showdown between the government and the farmers came to an end in the Senate, as cliffhanging as it was unexpected. The howls of pleasure and of protest in the streets even woke the Director in his bed.

Endless debate and posturing had produced a stalemate, which only the vote of the Senate President, none other than President Cristina Kirchner's running mate, Julio Cobos, could break. To the amazement of his compatriots – and to her hysterical disgust - he had cast his vote against the law, thereby putting an end to the Kirchner ambition to tame the farmers.

At least for now.

Friday, 18 July 2008 (AM) - SALADILLO

The large yellow grapefruit stayed resolutely in place, perched on its pole, whilst large splinters of wood could be seen flying off the wall of old *lapacho* fence posts about a metre farther back.

"It's getting better, and anyway, it's a very small target. For the kind of situation in which you'd use that," Albert said, indicating the Bersa 9mm, "the target would be much bigger. In other words, a man moving towards you at about five metres. To try and hit something like that grapefruit, you'd be using a rifle with telescopic sights. We can try that afterwards. Let's have a break and some *asado*."

"You better not serve any wine, otherwise we won't even hit the boards."

Albert laughed.

"It's up to you. The wine'll be on the table."

Sam had been observing them for the last hour or so from a deck chair behind the firing line. They made a funny couple. Tall, lithe Leandro alongside this tough little Englishman, with his close cropped hair and reddish, weather-beaten face. She returned Albert's smile, as he waved an inviting arm in the direction of the *quincho* from which the light breeze was carrying the irresistible scent of grilling meat.

"Don't the ladies ever get a chance?"

"Any time they like. In fact, Paula is very good with a handgun."

"With you as a husband, that doesn't come as a surprise. I'll have a go after lunch."

Albert collected the two guns and the box of empty cases, and led the way in the direction of the *quincho*.

Leandro helped Sam out of her deckchair and slipped his arm round her waist.

"I hope none of this becomes necessary," she whispered to him.

He squeezed her waist.

"So do I."

Paula greeted them with a large dish of steaming *empanadas* in one hand and a small tray of glasses of red wine in the other. She must have been very cute when Albert, as one of the bodyguards accompanying the British ambassador, had first met her some thirty years earlier. Probably a seventeen-year-old at the time she had caught Albert's eye, perhaps doing just what she was doing now, serving an *asado* to the guests. What might initially have started as a ploy to get away from the life of a housemaid, where the most she might expect would be to accompany the mistress of the house to Buenos Aires, had visibly become a solid marriage between them. Their children, from the little Sam had heard, had broken the mould again. The son was now working in Scotland in the oil industry, having studied engineering in Buenos Aires before heading off to his father's homeland. The daughter, studying medicine in Buenos Aires.

"Mmm, they are delicious," Sam spluttered through a mouthful of *empanada*. "The beef cut with a knife. Not ground with a mincer."

"Not in this household," Albert said. "It's the job I always get. And Paula makes them at least a day or so early. Soaks up the flavour."

One of Albert's *peones* was tending a barbecue which could have nourished a platoon. A couple of metal-sprung bed frames set at an angle over an expanse of glowing wood, fed from a small side fire of redhot embers. This in turn was replenished from a logpile of mixed *quebracho* and eucalyptus. Virtually every part of the animal had been laid out on the bed springs, timed to the traditional order. *Chorizo, morcilla, chinchulín, riñones, molleja, asado de tira, bife de chorizo* and *bife de lomo.* Two other *peones* had now joined the group. Sam was delighted to see that they all respected the traditional gaucho dress of *bombachas, alpargatas* on bare feet even in the cold of the winter, a broad plain cowhide belt from which the inseparable *facón* protruded in the small of their backs, a check shirt. Not complete without a large, floppy *boina*, the gaucho's version of the Basque beret or, in the case of one of them, a broad-brimmed rawhide hat, held on by a thin strap at the back. Probably from one of the Mesopotamian provinces, Entre Rios or Corrientes, judging by his multicoloured woven overtrousers. Bow legs betrayed a life in the saddle.

"Come and meet my guys," Albert said, following Paula, who was now serving the farm hands, having replenished the dish and tray of wine.

Albert introduced the four men, one of whom looked to be at least twenty years older than the other three.

"Cacho used to work on the same estancia where I met Paula," he explained.

"You must be delighted by last night's vote on the 125. Got guts, Cobos, to go against Madame President – considering he's her Vice President."

The four gauchos lifted their glasses. The sentiment was unmistakable.

"To the health and long life of Julio Cobos," Cacho intoned.

They all drained their glasses, which Albert was quick to replenish.

"How many hectares have you got here?" Leandro asked, looking around the horizon.

"A bit over five hundred, mainly agriculture, soya. Also about fifty for grazing. Horses and polo ponies."

"How ecological are you?" Sam said.

Albert detected from the look in her eye that it wasn't an idle question.

"Fairly," he replied cautiously. "I don't crop spray. Everything is no-till. Occasionally that means that we don't reach the production levels of some of my neighbours around here. And we rotate much more often. Soya ultimately kills the soil."

"I also noticed you had some solar panels on the roof," Leandro said.

"To be frank, I'm not sure if it's a good deal. Solar panels in this country are way too expensive. But then so are the unsubsidised electricity prices outside Buenos Aires. We pay about ten times as much as you do for your power."

"Don't get Leandro started on energy policy," Sam interrupted. "He'll never stop. That's the trouble with living with a man who's an economist."

"Let's enjoy this day," Leandro said, "by not talking politics."

"I'll drink to that," Albert echoed. "Besides, I'd rather hear about that Harley. How was the drive?"

"Fast," Leandro said. "I struggled to stay a hundred metres behind her, like some nervous bodyguard."

She was pulling on her gloves beside the machine in Pasaje de la Piedad.

"What's the point in investing in all this Italian leather," Sam said, "if I can't take it out? I had to adapt their design a little bit. Look slightly more feminine. Those garish reds and yellows. All black is so much better. Even the zips. And a bit of streamlining here and there."

Streamlining was presumably her term for the result being virtually sprayed on.

"The less feminine you look, the better, to my mind," Leandro retorted. "I don't trust you anywhere near those predatory bikers on their way to the Laguna de Lobos or wherever they hang out at the weekend. I'll be right behind you."

She straddled the large machine, adjusting her helmet. Leandro stood watching. Everything black, faintly sinister. She pressed the starter and the unmistakeable burble of a Harley echoed around the *Pasaje*.

She turned and flicked up the visor.

"Did you ever see that film, many years ago, 'Girl on a motorcycle'? Came out in the 60s, I think."

"No. Why?"

"Definitely fetishist. You'll find it on one of your websites. You'll see I'm much sexier than Maríanne Faithful. Though sadly, you're not quite as sexy as Alain Delon! And look out for the shot of the petrol pump attendant filling the tank!"

With which she slipped the clutch and purred towards the wrought iron gates leading out of the *Pasaje*, which Leandro now held open for her.

For over an hour and a half, Leandro had followed her as she roared along, the Harley's exhaust plainly audible even through the closed windows of the 1964 vintage Alfa Giulia TI Super. The third woman in Leandro's life, coming after Alejandra and Sam, "but before me", as Elena had once put it. A box-shape design by Giuseppe Scarnati, all white, with the 1600 twin cam engine, as driven by the Italian police in the early 1960s. It being a fine winter's day, the old lady deserved to be taken out to stretch her legs.

Sam had thrown a set of more normal clothes into the back of his car, which she was now wearing. A normal look, by Sam's standards, though unfailingly attracting the surreptitious attention of the three younger gauchos.

The decision to take up Albert's invitation to some weapon's training had followed a prompting from Charles in London, a few days after Albert's first visit to Pasaje de la Piedad. Over a secure VOIP line, Charles had recommended that Leandro take advantage of Albert's support.

"I pray you'll never need it, but it can't do any harm. I'll get him to ring you to fix a day."

"I hear from Albert he met your girlfriend," Charles had mentioned in the course of the conversation. "Very impressed he was, too. Something about a motorbike as well. Likes living dangerously, given the way they drive in your country. Would you take her along?"

"Try stopping her!"

Albert had begun by taking Leandro through his paces in the handling of his Bersa 9mm. After listening for a while, Sam had settled herself in a nearby deckchair to watch.

With his own Glock 17 9mm, Albert demonstrated an uncanny accuracy over the twenty metres which separated them from the grapefruit which he had plucked from one of his trees.

With his first shot, Albert blew the fruit off its pole. Nothing left for a second shot.

"What do your gauchos think of all this?" Leandro asked, observing a couple of them standing under some trees watching the proceedings.

"Oh, don't worry. Everybody has a gun out in the *campo*, even more so now, with insecurity on the rise."

"Do they know you're ex-SAS?"

"I've never breathed the word, although they know I fought in Malvinas."

"Any hostility about that?"

"Practically never. And even less from anybody who actually fought on the islands."

"Same in London, I found. But it can work both ways."

"Most of the ground troops came from the north, poor young guys doing their military service, totally unprepared for a winter in the South Atlantic. I've come across veterans down here. We swap stories and share the tab. They're a great race, the Argentines."

"Just not their politicians," Leandro muttered.

"Bastards everywhere," Albert said. "To be frank, we were caught with our pants down and, but for Maggie Thatcher, the Argentines would probably be sitting in the islands today. We were lucky. We only just made it."

"Okay guys, that's enough on that subject," Sam interrupted.

Leandro smiled at her.

"Well, I certainly can't match your skill with a handgun, Albert."

"We're getting there. You can clearly control the weapon. And you're quick to react to a threat."

"Thank you."

"Anyway, I think Charles assumes I'll be there in a sticky spot."

"Hope he's right," Sam prayed aloud.

The four of them were now sitting at a rough wooden table, a long bench on either side. The youngest of the gauchos, Manolo, brought a tray of grilled lamb from Patagonia.

"Out of the deep freeze, I'm afraid," Albert said. "It's not the season."

"This red is the perfect complement, though" Sam said.

"From Mendoza. Somehow an *asado* only tastes right if the wine is rough."

Albert had selected an old staple, Chateau Vieux from Bodegas Lopez, one of Argentina's traditional vineyards.

"Reminds me of the 70s."

They raised their glasses in a toast.

Some hours later, after a siesta by the fireplace in Albert's drawing room, followed by a strong coffee, they were back in front of the target. In response to Albert's question whether she would use Leandro's 9mm, Sam had, with a look of the utmost seriousness, expressed a preference for a Walther PPK. Albert smiled.

"Another Ian Fleming reader, I detect."

He had disappeared into the house, reappearing a few minutes later with a small case under his arm.

"Funny you should ask for that one," he said, opening the case for her.

"I don't believe it!"

Reverently Sam turned the automatic over in her hands.

"Amazing. I love you, Albert!"

Much to his evident delight, she proceeded to kiss him on the mouth.

"Lucky Paula's asleep," he muttered, blushing visibly even under his tan.

Sam's enthusiasm was perhaps not matched by her skill, only skimming the grapefruit with the automatic.

"You'll have to come back again for more practice."

"Any time. I'd love to. It's such a beautiful place."

Having finally been persuaded by the two men that she really should not contemplate the ride back to Buenos Aires after dark, Sam and Leandro had gratefully accepted Paula's suggestion that they spend the night. As they strolled near the paddocks, Leandro could see the softness and mystery, which so often accompanied twilight in the Argentine *campo*, beginning to captivate Sam.

As the sun set, wrapping a thick poncho round her shoulders, she settled herself in a large armchair under the covered veranda of the unpretentious colonial-style house, looking out over the fields, where four or five polo ponies were grazing.

She rested her head on the pillow that Paula had placed behind her head.

"This is wonderful. You're so lucky, you and Albert."

She watched the darkness creeping over the land, the grey slowly turning to black, the soft call of the doves, the occasional cry of the plovers in some far-off paddock, the mewing of the *chimangos*, all gradually dying away, leaving only the occasional faint squawk from an owl. A light breeze had sprung up and, in the darkness, she could hear rather than see the horses making their way back to the water trough nearest the house.

"It's beautiful, isn't it?" Leandro whispered.

She hadn't heard him as he silently squatted down beside her chair.

"It's wonderful. I feel I could live here forever," she murmured, resting her hand on his shoulder.

Leandro wasn't going to break the spell by casting doubt on the ability of Sam to sacrifice her adrenaline-driven lifestyle for the more bucolic tranquillity of a farm.

"Maybe we should think about it," he replied, after a moment. "Did Borges say something about this being the hour when it feels as though the *campo* is whispering to you?"

Sam made no comment.

The moon began to emerge behind the black silhouette of a *monte* in the distance, a massive golden disc.

They sat watching as it slowly rose above the horizon, losing its yellow tinge, seemingly shrinking at the same time.

"There's tea in the kitchen," Paula called to them from the door of the drawing room. "Albert's made some scones."

"England is alive and well in distant Argentina," Leandro whispered.

Tuesday, 22 July 2008 (AM) – PASAJE DE LA PIEDAD, BUENOS AIRES

Leandro had spent the days following their return from Albert's farm reading the newspapers and calling political commentators to try and assess the impact of the Vice President's 'betrayal' of the President in the Senate vote.

"Very courageous," one told him, "avoiding a major social confrontation."

"But he'll be cast even farther out into the wilderness," another had pointed out. "Not that that'll necessarily harm his prospects. As governor of Mendoza, he's still in the public eye. But it clearly went down very badly. There were rumours of resignation."

"Cobos?"

"The presidential couple."

"Seriously? After the Senate defeat?"

"They're saying the Argentine doesn't appreciate them as Presidents, so they might as well go."

Leandro wasn't minded to give this too much credence. The Kirchners were tough, perfectly capable of absorbing a setback. A measure as drastic as Law 125, sprung upon an unsuspecting agricultural sector with no prior consultation of any kind, was bound to be a high-risk game. Black and white politics. No compromise. But from there to giving up power? It sounded like a visceral reaction from Nestor Kirchner himself, one from which he would almost certainly allow himself to be dissuaded.

Leandro poured himself a whisky and stared at his computer screen. Although he was pretty sure they'd cling to power, he wondered how long the Kirchners could keep up the confrontational style. Finally the only resignation had come from Alberto Fernandez, the Kirchners long-standing Chief of Cabinet of Ministers. That took courage. Leandro was sure they would take this betrayal personally.

In the background, Julius Caesar. One of his favourite Handel operas.

The phone rang on his worktable. He turned down the volume.

"Could I please speak to Dr Flemming?"

"This is Leandro Flemming. But I'm not a doctor. Who is that?"

"My name is Ahmed Aboukir. I'm a journalist. I work with Al Jazeera in Beirut."

"The line is very good. Are you calling from Beirut?"

"No, I'm in Buenos Aires. I'm staying at the Plaza. Please forgive me for disturbing you, but I would have welcomed the opportunity for a chat about the economic situation in Argentina. It's part of a wider survey about the economic impact of Middle Eastern communities in certain Latin American countries. A *reportage* that I'm planning to sell to Al Jazeera when it's ready."

"Well, I wouldn't claim to know much about the Arab communities here in Argentina. I am more of a macro economist." Leandro paused. "By the way, how did you get my name and number?"

Somewhere at the back of his mind, all these Middle Eastern vibrations… simple coincidence?

"I was trawling the web last night, looking up economists here in Argentina. I found your name. You gave a talk at a conference a year or two ago. That also gave me the name of your consultancy. Your website came up. Someone in your office kindly gave me this number. And there aren't many Flemmings in the phone directory anyway."

"No, you're right."

"At least, not with two 'Ms'," Aboukir added.

The vibrations were fading.

"Well, shall we fix a date? Where would you like to meet?"

"I'm sure you know the restaurants far better than I do. Please suggest somewhere. You would be my guest, of course. Would tomorrow be possible?"

"We can argue about the bill later. Let me think. Depending on whether you have room for more meat since you arrived, there's a large restaurant down the hill from your hotel. A place called Las Nazarenas. What with the smell of grilling meat and the sight of the roasting spits in the window, you really can't miss it."

"Sounds good. I've still got room for more Argentine beef. It's delicious. Would tomorrow be okay?"

Leandro thought for a minute. Sam wasn't leaving for Punta del Este until the day after tomorrow. Perhaps he should push it out until after she had left.

Better get it over with.

"Yes, that would be fine. Shall we say one thirty?"

"Excellent. How should I recognise you?"

"I'll leave my name with the elderly gentleman who's always at the entrance to guide people. Smartly dressed in a dark suit. No doubt paid for by all his profits."

"Excellent. See you tomorrow."

The telephone clicked.

Leandro turned up the volume again. One of his favourite passages of Act One. Jennifer Larmore's Julius Caesar suspecting Ptolemy of duplicity. '*Va tacito e nascosto quand' avido è di preda, l'astuto cacciator.*' 'The cunning hunter moves when he is eager for prey....' The triumphant brass was best at full volume. 'And he who is disposed to evil Does not wish the deceitfulness Of his heart to be seen.'

The phone rang. Regretfully, he turned down the volume again.

It was his partner at the office.

"An Arab journalist rang about thirty minutes ago wanting to speak to you. Something about Arab business in Latin America. Hope you don't mind, I gave him your number."

"No, fine. He just rang. We're lunching tomorrow. I'll keep you posted if anything interesting comes of it. I'll be sending you some text about Cobos and Fernandez in about an hour."

"Fine. I'll send it back if I've got any thoughts or corrections. Ciao. Take care. Oh, by the way. I had a phone call from the AFIP. They're coming round. Something about an inspection."

"That's all we needed. Do we need to prepare for it?"

"My instinct is to be unprepared and wait to see what they want. Then we can see how we respond."

"You're probably right. With our reporting, there was bound to be a moment when someone in the Government raised an eyebrow. Keep me posted."

Leandro had hardly put down the receiver when the phone rang again.

"Hi, Sam. Getting ready for Punta del Este?"

"Just packing a few things. I've got to go and see my father tonight. Haven't had dinner with him for a long time. He sounded a little frail on the phone. But tomorrow I'd like to get my hands on you again. Because the day after that, I leave."

"Any idea how long you're going to be away?"

"Please don't start that, Leo. You know it's open-ended. Anyway, what are you doing tomorrow?"

"I just fixed lunch with a journalist from Beirut, doing some kind of story on the Arab business communities in South America. But I'm free after that. If you'd rung me five minutes earlier, I'd have been free all day."

"Where are you lunching? I might even join you. After all, I know far more about the Arab business community than you do."

Although she was right, Leandro felt a sudden reluctance to see Sam not only take over his private life, but his professional one as well.

"Let's just say that you pick me up. Or maybe have a coffee."

"Oh, all right."

The note of disappointment was unmistakeable. He ignored it. This girl couldn't have her way all the time.

"Why don't you come along at about two thirty? Las Nazarenas on Alem - the first block, opposite the Sheraton."

"Undiluted cholesterol. Glad I'm not joining you. See you there."

She hung up. No final term of endearment. She was clearly pissed off. A very minor revenge for her disappearing again into the Saudi harem.

Leandro turned back to his draft. Another idea had come to him. Almost the most important.

'The failure of the Kirchners to capture an even more significant share of Argentina's agricultural revenues might turn out to make all the difference between Argentina surviving in its present form or following the path set by Chavez for Venezuela. Direct access to the cash reserves of Venezuela's national oil company, Pedevesa, had provided Chavez with a treasure chest with which to buy votes. That this was the way the Kirchners intended to use public money was already apparent. With his casting vote, Cobos has stopped them getting their hands on far more!'

He picked up a copy of The Economist. Reading between the lines, it was evident the weekly was beginning to worry about the direction of the Argentine economy. Was Argentina peering into yet another crisis? He remembered the articles at the time of the 2001 melt down, when The Economist had virtually written the country off for a decade. But thanks to the incredible efficiency and dynamism of the *campo*, Argentina had bounced back far faster than expected.

Was it true there was a ten to fifteen-year cycle of crises for Argentina since independence? What was it about his nation that this so often seemed inevitable? Part of it, he felt sure, could be attributed to the lack of democratically elected parties alternating in power. The longer a President remained at the helm, the more inevitable their stubbornness and reluctance to adapt. The Kirchners thought that Argentina could sit on the side-lines of the world. Leaving them free to do with the country what they pleased. Could anyone?

Wednesday, 23 July 2008 (AM) – RECONQUISTA 1132, BUENOS AIRES

The man gazing down at him from the opposite side of the table looked to be in his early thirties, handsome, physically fit. Leandro took in the blazer, the striped tie, the pale blue shirt. In his experience, journalists tended to fall on the scruffier side of the scale. Still, one never could tell.

"Dr Flemming?"

"Mr Aboukir? As I said yesterday, I'm not a doctor. Please sit down. Presume you found the place with no trouble."

The Director stretched out his hand before sitting down. Easing himself into a more comfortable position on the wooden chair, he looked around. With its long bar down one side, shelves of wine stretching from one end to the other, the tables crowded, Las Nazarenas was popular, not only with a certain class of tourist, but also with the executive crowd from the tower blocks stretching towards Avenida Córdoba on the opposite side of the wide avenue. Engineering partners and accountants, mostly.

Leandro passed Aboukir the menu. A foldout of colour photographs of steaks and more steaks, ranging from a modest two hundred and fifty grams up to a kilo, alongside every other edible part of the animal.

"As you see, for carnivores only," Leandro smiled.

"Fine with me. Thank you, Señor Flemming, for having chosen a restaurant so close to my hotel."

"Please, call me Leandro. No problem. Haven't been here for some time and the meat is usually quite good."

"Please call me Ahmed,"

"I suggest you study the menu so that we can place the orders. Will you have some wine?"

Aboukir shrugged his shoulders. "Will you?"

"I'll probably have a glass of red. But, if you'd like more, we can order a bottle."

"No, a glass will be fine."

The two men studied the menu.

"Two *bifes de chorizo*," Leandro told the waiter. "How do you like yours done, Ahmed?"

"Medium will be fine."

"One medium, the other rare. And some *papas fritas*, as well as a tomato salad. Olive oil and balsamic vinegar. Please prepare it. And two glasses of the house red, a cabernet or merlot if possible."

The waiter provided the names of two or three vineyards.

"The Catena. Thank you. And some mineral water."

The Director had been studying Leandro. Handsome, mid-forties. Probably quite successful with women. Didn't seem to have run to fat, unlike some of his compatriots. All these steaks and pizzas!

"So, Ahmed, when did you arrive?"

Since Flemming was unlikely to catch a glimpse of his passport, he could say anything he liked.

"About a week ago. Got about another week, before I move on to Chile."

"What countries are you covering for this programme?"

"Colombia, Brazil, Uruguay, Argentina and Chile. I would have liked to do Mexico, but I'm not sure I'll have the time."

"And you're going to sell this to Al Jazeera?"

"Yes, that's the idea. As you know, it's become the most popular station in the whole of the Middle East. And in the Maghreb. Of course in the West they tend to be seen as specialising in terrorism and the ongoing wars. But since the countries in South America have seen some fairly significant migration from the Middle East, it's the kind of story which may well appeal. That is, if I get it right."

"Have you got a camera crew lined up?"

The Director hadn't been expecting that one. A brief hesitation.

"Well no, not yet. First I need to do the research, which is where people like you come in. Only after that will I need to see about what to film. Perhaps in the provinces, where there are some quite substantial Arab communities, I understand."

Leandro nodded. "Yes, many really flourished in the provinces. I wish I knew more about them, I could introduce you. As you will certainly know, with the gradual collapse of the Ottoman Empire, there were a number of waves of immigration down here. Often Christians, keen to escape from persecution in the Empire or, in the case of the Lebanese, attracted by stories of new business in Argentina."

"Quite a few came from Aleppo, I gather. Some of my family came from there. Though I'm a French citizen. Born in France."

Leandro caught sight of Sam walking into the restaurant. She came up behind Aboukir, who had not seen her arrive.

"*As-Salāmu 'Alaykum,*" she greeted him.

His physical reaction bordered on physical shock. His eyes narrowed, his body tensed, one fist clenched. But it was over in an instant. Leandro only caught it out of the corner of his eye, as he was looking at Sam.

"*Wa alaikum salam,*" Aboukir replied, standing up to face her.

"May I introduce Miss Samira Haidar," Leandro said. "She is one of my most valuable research assistants. Sam, this is Ahmed Aboukir. He works with Al Jazeera in Beirut."

Whilst Aboukir busied himself pulling up another chair from a neighbouring table, Sam flashed a look at Leandro which conveyed distinct reservations about the lowliness of her new title.

"With a name like that, and your accent, you must come from the same part of the world as I do," Aboukir began. "Lebanon?"

Sam smiled. "Not quite, my family comes from Syria. And I spent some time in the Middle East a few years ago."

She sat down at one end of the table. Leandro could see that she was carefully studying Aboukir.

"So, Dr Aboukir, how long have you been here?"

"Nearly a week. And, as I was telling Leandro, I have another week, though it's possible I may stay on longer."

"And you're doing a programme for Al Jazeera?"

"Yes, about the economic impact of Arab communities in a number of Latin American countries. It's a freelance job which I hope to sell to Al Jazeera. Leandro has been kindly giving me a lot of useful information."

"Well, as his Middle Eastern business research assistant, it's probably to me that you should be talking. Only I fear that I have to go to Uruguay tomorrow and still have a few things to get done this afternoon."

Again she sent Leandro a look which told him that he had better prepare for recriminations when they were alone.

"Perhaps we could arrange for another meeting when you come back," Aboukir suggested.

"With pleasure."

Aboukir signalled to the waiter to bring the bill, but Leandro stopped him.

"You're a guest in our town."

"But you've been giving me such useful information," Aboukir protested.

"No arguments, please."

"Well, Leandro, that has been most useful. I'm most grateful to you and would welcome an opportunity to return the hospitality. Are you going to Uruguay as well?"

Now it was Leandro's turn to send a look to Sam.

"No, I'll be staying here. Give me a ring. You have my number."

"Can I still have a coffee?" Sam asked Leandro.

"Of course."

Aboukir got up and shook hands with both of them, before turning on his heel and leaving the restaurant. He was hardly out of the door before Sam placed her finger against her lips, as if to silence Leandro.

"Something wrong there."

"What do you mean? Seemed a nice enough fellow." Leandro replied, .

"Well, for one thing, he didn't arrive just a week ago."

"How do you know?"

"Because I first saw him more than two weeks ago."

"Are you sure?"

"Positive. Good-looking guy like that, I don't make mistakes."

"Now you're just trying to provoke me."

"No I'm not. I definitely saw him. At the gym in the Hilton. It's round the corner from my flat. He was definitely there."

Leandro was silent for a moment, turning over the implications.

"And do you think he knows that you may have recognised him?"

"I don't think so. Although, when I greeted him in Arabic, he did look slightly startled. No, I'm pretty sure that I was wearing my hooded tracksuit, and even possibly dark glasses. Hotel gyms can be lecherous places. Add to that, I probably had on my big white earphones. Not quite the same profile as today."

"So what do we make of that?"

"Well, as a first step, I could try and check him out through my friends. That name, the Al Jazeera connection. See if they match."

"I can try it out on Frobisher as well. See what their database throws up."

"Right, I really do have to be running. Some packing to do before my flight to Punta tomorrow."

Seeing a look of unhappiness flit over Leandro's face, she added.

"And when I've finished packing, I'll expect you to take me out to dinner. That's if you got any room left after all the garbage you've just been ramming down your throat."

"You never did have your coffee," Leandro muttered.

"That was my reason to stay behind. Got to run."

Along with a significant number of the male customers of Las Nazarenas, Leandro watched her leave. He was increasingly getting the impression that he would find it very difficult to operate in the murky world of espionage by himself. Not for the first time, Sam appeared to be fully justifying her involvement.

Thanking the *maître d'* as he left, he caught a taxi cruising along Leandro Alem.

"Take a right on Marcelo T. Up to the Plaza. I've just got to drop something off. I'll only be a minute."

Parking some twenty metres short of the main entrance to Aboukir's hotel, Leandro made his way to reception.

"Excuse me, do you have a Mr Aboukir staying here?"

The manager behind the counter confirmed that he was. "Would you like to speak to him? The house phone is over there."

Realising that he needed some pretext, Leandro thanked him and walked over to the phones. He picked up the receiver and pretended to speak into the mouthpiece. The operator at the other end finally lost patience and hung up on him.

Twenty minutes later he was back in his flat. Slipping the Frobisher encryption device into his laptop, he sent a brief message to Charles Colson.

"Grateful for any confirmation of existence of Al Jazeera Beirut correspondent Ahmed Aboukir and news of his possible whereabouts. Appears to be in Buenos Aires. L."

Within minutes, a reply had come from London.

"Will check and revert. C."

Sam passed a message via her chat room asking for a trace on Aboukir. Whilst she was about it, she confirmed she'd be leaving for Punta del Este next morning, at the request of the Prince.

All three of them had been going over their meeting.

Wednesday, 23 July 2008 (PM) – HOTEL PLAZA, BUENOS AIRES

As he walked up the hill back to the hotel, the Director analysed the results of his lunch. On the one hand, he had uncovered nothing that might confirm Flemming was in any way involved with the Iranian question. At least, not until the arrival of that Middle Eastern girlfriend. Leaving aside the fact she was very attractive, something about her had rung a very faint alarm bell. Nothing she had said could explain this. But, for a man in his profession, however soft the ringing, such things could not be ignored. Where had he seen her before?

"No messages, Mr Aboukir," the desk manager confirmed as he passed.

He made his way down to the elegant wood panelled bar in the basement of the hotel and ordered another coffee. The restaurant next door was disgorging some of the late lunch guests, including a noisy American family, their two little children beginning a game of hide and seek between the bar tables. He detected a look of disapproval on the face of the older barman, no doubt nostalgically remembering the days when his clientele would never have included such people.

Where had he seen her? He prided himself on having something approaching a photographic memory for faces. Yet, in the case of the Arab girl, it was a blur. Something about her profile. Something about the way she looked at him. If he couldn't resolve it, should he just ignore it? Unwise.

She had said that she was going to Uruguay tomorrow. So, if she was a threat, any action she took was likely to be today or else at some point following her return.

As he stirred the remains of his espresso, he needed to make up his mind. In his experience, the decision must first and foremost be one of prudent evasive action. He would check out. Between allowing them to confirm that he was in the hotel or forestalling their attempt to take advantage of that knowledge, the latter was the safer course.

He signed the chit and left a tip for the barman, before walking upstairs into the lobby. As he emerged from the narrow passageway, he caught a glimpse of the back of Flemming going out through the main entrance doors.

Seeing the desk manager trying to attract his attention, he walked over.

"A gentleman was looking for you, Dr Aboukir. I believe he tried to get you in your room. He's just walked out. Perhaps you can catch him."

That was the last thing he was going to do.

"Thank you. Did he leave a name?"

"No, sir. But perhaps he left a message for you on your voicemail. Would you like me to check?"

"Don't worry. If he did, I'll no doubt find it upstairs. Thank you."

If the lunch had not provided any leads, the aftermath appeared to have done so.

Going up to his room, he could find no message. He quickly packed his suitcase and checked out.

"Sorry to see you leave so soon, Dr Aboukir," the front desk manager said.

"Is there an ATM in the hotel?"

The manager pointed him in the direction of one of the corridors.

Checking the balance on his account, he found that a credit of one hundred dollars had been made the day before. He needed to make email contact.

The disappointment of the Plaza manager was balanced by the warm welcome he received back in his little hotel in Once.

"Welcome back, Señor Azoulay. Successful trip?"

He nodded.

Up in his room, he checked the dedicated email. The message was cryptic, but surprising.

Investigate Martin Caballero, aka Perez. Priority target. Interested in transport.

Were they reading his mind? How, thirteen thousand kilometres away, had they come up with the same name?

The Director stared at the computer.

Although he now knew more about Flemming, this message meant he must set the economist aside for the time being. Concentrate on Caballero. In some ways, irritating. His contact with Flemming, with the Arab girl, had the makings of an interesting little scenario. After all, Flemming was in Grunwald's little book. Still, clear instructions had to be respected. He'd find time to get back to the others.

For the next hour, the Director crisscrossed the web and social pages trying to build up a picture of Caballero. Finally, in a website dedicated to corporate information and credit analysis, he found a small company registered in the province of Santa Cruz, which boasted Señor Martín Caballero as a board member. Tecnologías del Sur srl claimed to have an office in the Puerto Madero district of the Argentine capital. Convenient. He would combine a visit there with another session in the Hilton gym. Tomorrow morning. He only needed a plausible cover story by then.

Thursday, 24 July 2008 (AM) – PASAJE DE LA PIEDAD, BUENOS AIRES

"Re. yesterday's enquiry. Person exists, but appears to be travelling. Cannot confirm current whereabouts. Has not been seen in his usual haunts for a month. Personal details as follows. Age approximately 45. Born Aleppo. Medium build. Has done freelance work for Al Jazeera. Can you confirm current presence in Argentina? C."

Leandro was only partly reassured by this information. If nothing else, the age did not seem to fit. And if he'd been born in Aleppo, that would mean he was Syrian. Could Sam confirm that from the way he spoke Arabic? Not that they had spoken very much. But hadn't he said he'd been born in France?

"I'll have to ask you to control your legitimate curiosity," he told Eduardo, in a café near his godson's *Comisaría*. "As you've no doubt worked out, I'm investigating something on behalf of one of my clients."

"Tell me something I don't know."

"Sorry, but for now I can't tell you any more. But what I'm about to tell you may connect in some way with the murders."

Eduardo was watching Leandro closely, his face expressionless. He knew better than to press for more, trusting his godfather to tell him as much as he needed to know.. All the same, he wondered to what extent the old man wasn't being dragged into murky waters by that Syrian girlfriend of his. However much he admired her for the courage and initiative she had shown in the pursuit of Dávila, there was no doubt she was involved in a lot of strange activities, to which his godfather seemed at times irresistibly drawn. The association of the murdered diplomats with Iran was hardly reassuring. To what extent was the she leading him even farther out of his depth?

"Go ahead," he said. "What do you want me to do *this* time?"

But the tone was not intended to be negative.

"I've come across a rather strange individual. A certain Ahmed Aboukir. Currently staying at the Plaza. Says he's from Beirut, putting together a story for Al Jazeera on Middle Eastern business in Latin American countries. He and I had lunch yesterday. For various reasons, I suspect he's not everything he seems to be. I don't know if there's any way you can check out his story."

Eduardo toyed with his empty coffee cup.

"The Plaza's not actually my territory. Retiro is the area covered by *Comisaría 15a*. So I would have to be careful. The desk managers probably know people from that *Comisaría*. Let me think about it. How urgent is it?"

"Yesterday? He seems to be taking some interest in me. He rang me in the first place, suggesting lunch."

Eduardo looked up sharply. "He rang you? Why would he do that?"

"Claimed to have heard of me as an economic consultant. Asked me general questions about the economy, claiming that he needed to get some kind of perspective on how these businesses have evolved. I had to admit that I couldn't tell him much."

"Perhaps your reputation as an expert on Middle Eastern affairs is spreading," Eduardo teased. "But, more seriously, what's made you suspicious?"

Leandro thought for a minute. Did he want to reveal that Sam had also been at the lunch? On balance, probably not yet.

"Well, as you've spotted, I was a little surprised when he rang me. Seemed very insistent to meet. I suppose there must be other journalists or contacts with whom he's been in touch. Perhaps I should try ringing around to see if anyone else has come across him. He claims to have arrived about a week ago."

Leandro studied his son. Eduardo's curiosity had been sparked.

"I know there are territorial jealousies in your line of work. I don't want you getting into difficulties. Perhaps you'd better forget it."

"Leave it with me. I've got a fairly quiet afternoon. Are you in this evening? If so, I'll drop by for some of that Glenmorangie. Unless you've got something better?"

Leandro smiled. He sometimes wondered whether his guardianship also extended to ensuring that his godson had good taste in whisky.

"I'll see what I've got. I've been hiding a bottle of Oban single malt from you since my trip to Europe in February. About time you two got acquainted."

Thursday. 24 July 2008 (AM) – PUERTO MADERO, BUENOS AIRES

Soon after ten that same morning, the Director was standing in front of the glass doors of a modern office tower in Puerto Madero, pressing the buzzer beside a small label bearing the words 'Tecnologías del Sur srl'. After a few moments, a husky female voice asked who was there.

"My name is Aboukir. From Lebanon. I have a shipping business. I have been given the name of Señor Caballero to speak to urgently."

So far, aside from the front desk manager of the Plaza, only three people knew the name Aboukir. And one of those was dead.

After a momentary hesitation, the voice replied.

"Señor Caballero is travelling. He won't be back for a few days. Perhaps...if you came back then."

"Most inconvenient. Perhaps if I could come up and give you my card, you could transmit my details to him."

Again a hesitation, followed by a buzzing sound with the main door clicking open.

"Which floor?"

"Please give your details at the reception and they will indicate the floor."

Having taken the precaution of dark glasses to mislead any CCTV, he presented himself at reception, where a pretty girl took down his details. He was relieved to see that security had not got as far as taking a photograph of visitors. Judging by the looks of the receptionist and the uniform she was wearing, this office building prided itself on the quality of its clients.

Handing him a printed pass in a transparent plastic holder and keeping his passport, she indicated the lifts.

"Third floor."

Beside the opaque glass entrance door to Tecnologías del Sur, another intercom.

"Aboukir," he announced. The door swung open.

Tecnologías del Sur appeared to consist of a small reception area, the walls adorned with colour photographs of industrial plants or laboratory experiments, giving onto two or three small offices or meeting rooms. Other than the girl behind the desk, there was no one to be seen. Remembering the class of girl to be found with Caballero in some of the photographs he had dug up on the net, the all too visible talents of this blonde came as no surprise.

"I regret, but Señor Caballero is out of Buenos Aires. He left this morning. Perhaps, if you were to tell me what it is about, I might be able to help."

The huskiness of her voice made it sound like an improper invitation.

Concealing his conviction that the areas in which this girl might conceivably be of assistance bore little relationship to the business he wished to propose to Caballero, he feigned an expression of disappointment.

"This is most unfortunate. I came to Buenos Aires specially to meet him. Would you have any way of communicating with him?"

The girl hesitated. "I could pass him a message. He's not very far away. In Uruguay, in fact."

This girl was better looking than she was discreet. Perhaps, with a little help, she might be coaxed into revealing where in Uruguay.

He stood there, looking down at her, toying with the options. He had little doubt that he could extract anything he wanted from her in less than five minutes. However, it would almost certainly serve to alert Caballero if his sexy secretary suddenly went missing or claimed to have been raped by a client.

Rushing things might be tempting, but the price would be the loss of surprise. It being Uruguay, the chances were that there were only two places - at most three - in that tiny country that would warrant a visit from the playboy Caballero. Montevideo, Punta del Este or perhaps Colonia. He preferred to take his time.

"Perhaps, if you could pass him a message. I can leave you my number."

The girl leaned forward with a small block of paper for him to note it down, momentarily distracting him with the cleavage she revealed in the process. He resisted the temptation to get a respite from the affluent contours of Sonia.

"Please explain to him that I have specialised shipping services to the Middle East which might be of interest to him."

The blank expression on her face as she made a note suggested she had little idea of what line of business Caballero was really in.

"I will pass on your message, Señor."

Thanking her, he left, recovering his passport at the reception desk on the way out. He would skip his session at the Hilton.

Back in his hotel room, he knew he had to get to Uruguay. He had sent a message to Caballero, which would hopefully soon provoke a response. As in all such situations, he needed to be ahead of the game. If he was actually in Uruguay when the call came through, the ability of Argentine security to pin down his exact location would most likely be greatly reduced, even though they could probably work out that he was on the other side of the Rio de la Plata. On top of that, getting to Caballero outside Argentina should hopefully be less risky than in Buenos Aires itself, where Caballero, if he was as important a player as things suggested, might now have been accorded some form of close protection.

Just as long as, when Caballero called, he could be persuaded to give away his precise whereabouts. If he could, then the shorter the distance that separated them, the better.

Thursday, 24 July 2008 (AM) – JOSÉ IGNACIO, URUGUAY

After her night with Leandro, Sam flew into Punta del Este's Carlos Curbelo international airport on the late morning flight. Any plans to make her arrival unobtrusive were shattered by the noise of a red helicopter parked nearby, its blades feathering in the winter sun, the flight attendant Joslyn waving to her as she stepped down.

"A little chillier than the last time we met," Sam said as, ducking below the blades, she slipped into the rear seat. Joslyn had traded the short skirt of the Bahamas for a shiny black jumpsuit, tighter fitting than any normal flight attendant might wear. Playboy centrefold smile and silhouette. She really must check with Carla whether she wasn't subcontracting these services to the Prince.

"And not enough room, nor time, to offer you a coffee," Joslyn replied. "We had to rent this one. Our's stayed with White Lady in Bermuda."

Sam was under no illusion that her arrival could pass unnoticed. Although Punta del Este saw its fair share of millionaires, particularly in high season, and most of Argentina's business barons came and went by private jet, the arrival out of season of the Prince and his retinue could not have gone unnoticed. His all-white Bombardier stood out on the empty airport. At least the two yachts had been left behind.

The Prince had rented a large, ultramodern villa just north of José Ignacio, one of the fashionable villages in the nexus of resorts running northeast from Punta del Este towards the Brazilian border. To facilitate their movements, a simple helipad had been arranged within a hundred yards of the house. This being low season on the Uruguayan coast, few neighbours were likely to be disturbed by the helicopter's comings and goings. To forestall any speculation, a story about the Prince contemplating a real estate investment in the area had been handed to the local press.

Sam had found confirmation of the arrival date of the Saudi Royal party in a mail from Aziz on her return from Albert's farm, followed up by another one from the Princess' private secretary. The news had not gone down well with Leandro.

"You know what I think of that," he had responded bitterly, as Sam read out the contents of the mail on his computer. "Even if you are there just for the benefit of Madame. And who's going to look after the husband? Or, come to think of it, of me?"

Sam shook her head.

"Frankly, I don't know. But somewhere in all of this there's a hint that there will be others present. You see what Aziz says. 'You'll meet some old friends'. As for you, I could give Tatyana a ring before I leave."

"Bitch!"

That the Prince had moved so far south appeared open to only one interpretation. As foreseen at the Tobago meetings, the negotiation with the Argentines was being pursued closer to their base, presumably a positive sign. Sam had passed the news back to her Mossad contact in the usual way.

It was only a matter of ten minutes before the helicopter was back on the ground beside the large villa. Sam was glad to recognise Malcolm standing ready to receive her.

"Welcome back, Miss," he greeted her, the warmth clearly genuine.

"Everybody's here, I see," Sam replied. "Perhaps a few extra?"

She pointed in the direction of a couple of young men in dark grey jogging suits, earpieces visible, watching from the line of trees bordering the large lawn on which they had landed.

"The usual, Miss. Plus a few extra. Just in case. Let me show you to your room."

Sam had been allocated a room at the end of the north wing of the long, low villa.

"How many rooms are there?" she asked Malcolm.

"About twenty-five, I would say. I haven't counted."

He placed her two suitcases on their stands.

"I'll send someone along to unpack for you."

"No, don't bother."

She wasn't keen to have someone else going through them. She lay down on the bed and looked out through the vast plate-glass at the waters of an artificial lake at the end of the lawn, a strong wind now ruffling its surface. She was glad it had risen after the helicopter ride.

There was a knock on the door. "Come in."

The door opened to reveal a smiling Carla.

"I don't believe it," Sam cried, leaping up from the bed and embracing her.

"The Prince felt we could all have a good time together. I flew in yesterday, via São Paulo."

"You might have told me."

"Much better to surprise you this way. I'm staying at my place. It's only a few kilometres west. Maybe you'll be able to slip away and we can be alone."

"You're looking fantastic."

Carla was wearing a two-piece trouser suit of the finest red leather, the waisted jacket opening onto a black silk blouse with a ruffle collar in a matching red. Ankle-length stiletto heeled boots in the same colour.

"And to think that, in the old days, people thought redheads couldn't wear red!"

"Special instruction via Aziz, from the Prince. He must have been planning this for some time, but it was still a rush job. I had to pay Amadeo double."

"As usual, impeccable. How is he, your personal couturier?"

"Sends you his regards and wants to know when you'll be back. Claims to have some great idea for you. Wouldn't tell me what it was."

"That's just to make you jealous. Good for Amadeo!"

The phone on Sam's bedside table rang. The Princess' private secretary.

"Her Highness would like you to come and see her in the study. Second door after the large living room on the lake side."

"Of course. I'll be there at once."

She turned toward Carla.

"My client wants to see me," she said, laughing.

"I'm beginning to feel just a tiny bit jealous," a hint of seriousness not entirely absent from Carla's voice.

"That, my love, you need never be."

Sam pulled Carla towards her and kissed her. Carla prolonged the kiss.

Sam slipped out of the dress she had worn to fly over from Buenos Aires and quickly pulled on a pair of dark grey flannel trousers, topped off with a pale cream Ralph Lauren shirt under an alpaca wool cardigan with small, pearl grey buttons. Having stepped into the bathroom to refresh her makeup and check her hair, she swept past Carla, planting a kiss on her cheek as she went.

"See you later."

Her fingers lingered fleetingly on the soft leather moulding Carla's breasts.

"Beautiful."

Checking with one of the bodyguards in the main hall, she found her way to the door of the Princess' study and tapped lightly.

"Come in."

Farida was standing with her back to the large picture window, which gave out onto the neat lawn behind the house.

"*Quel plaisir de te revoir, Samira.* I trust you are well?"

Since the Princess remained where she was, Sam walked towards her and stretched out her hand.

"Thank you, Your Highness, I'm quite well. And it's a great pleasure to be with you again."

"*Quand on est seul, tu m'appeles Farida*. Or had you forgotten?"

"*Pardon*…Farida."

The Princess turned and looked out of the window.

"A rather boring garden, wouldn't you say? They may charge a lot, but little goes into the fixtures and furnishings, to my mind."

"I don't know who the owners are, though presumably Argentine," Sam replied. "Unfortunately, most of the investments in this part of the world are just a way to make money. And no doubt, if they can get a client like yourselves out of season, they take full advantage. I apologise on behalf of my countrymen."

"No need. We Saudis are used to it. It's probably our fault anyway. Now, tell me, how have you been keeping? I retain some very special memories of our days together in the Caribbean. I can see, from your *bronzage*, that you haven't had much sun recently. Though, with that lovely skin , that's of no consequence."

The Princess had stepped closer and lightly stroked the contour of Sam's face. As she withdrew her hand, Sam caught it and placed a kiss in the palm.

The telephone beside the large sofa rang.

"We'll be along in a minute," the Princess answered. "Thank you." She turned to Sam. "They're calling us to lunch. We can talk later."

Leading the way, Farida walked through the vast, coldly furnished drawing room towards a glass-enclosed outer conservatory where a small round table had been laid. The Prince was already there, talking to Carla, looking out towards the lake.

Hearing the sound of their steps on the marble floor, he turned.

"Ah, there you are, my dear. And Samira as well. The party is complete!"

He greeted Sam with a warm embrace, then turning to Carla, made as if to introduce the two women.

"But, I believe you know each other."

"Indeed, Your Highness. We are both most honoured to have been invited."

Carla's voice was deep and resonant, slightly husky. The voice Sam had heard her adopt in the company of certain men. Not the softer tone she used with Sam.

"And the children?" Sam asked.

"Oh, we left them in London. It's the summer holidays and they'll join us once we go north again," the Princess replied.

"Let's sit down," the Prince said. "With three women like this as company, I must be the most fortunate man on the planet," he added as they took their places. "So, ladies, whilst I'm away negotiating with these impossible people, what will you be up to? I need some light entertainment."

Carla was sitting to his right, Sam his left, Her Royal Highness opposite the Prince at the small table. He extended a hand towards each of his neighbours and placed it over theirs in a gesture of what Sam took as surprising intimacy in front of his wife. She stole a glance towards Farida. No reaction. The smile on the Princess' face appeared genuine.

Having adjourned briefly to her bedroom after the coffee, Sam quizzed Carla.

"There are times when our foursome leaves me a bit mystified. That the Prince should've had me along as some kind of birthday present for Farida, just about makes sense. But that she should appear so relaxed about your sitting with us, that's pushing things, isn't it?"

"It's because you haven't understood my relationship with the Prince," Carla smiled. "You're assuming I'm there for his personal benefit."

"Aren't you?"

"Not in the way you think. You see, the Prince has a contract with my company. To provide him with girls and other services, whichever he may need, wherever he may need them. To some extent, your serving Farida is one of those contracts. Like Joslyn, the flight attendant. What did you think of her?"

"I suspected as much. Serves a nice coffee."

"And a bit more, don't worry. So, if I'm here, it's as a business partner and nothing else."

"Though the way you're dressed might suggest otherwise."

Carla laughed.

"That's not to say he doesn't like to take a look at my marketing style."

"He's got good taste."

"So, does it make sense now? Because he was coming to Punta del Este and since he knows I have a house here, he suggested I come along. All expenses paid, of course, including my time."

"And you spend it all on him?"

"Depends on who he's targeting. Without going into detail, you'll probably discover that things are not always what they seem. Remember that night back in January, one of our early evenings together?"

Sam paused, caught in the memory of their first moments of intimacy.

"I'm not likely to forget."

"When I went to see that client at the Conrad, all dressed up, with a mask? I can't remember if I told you at the time, but he was running guns in and out of Lebanon. The Prince wanted me to find out as much as possible. After he'd won a lot of money at the tables, he became much more expansive - not to mention passionate."

"I see," Sam murmured.

"Don't worry, my love. By now you should know that I draw an impenetrable line between pleasure and business, between you and me and all the rest."

"By the way, when you sent me to London with Aziz to meet Kemal, did you know I was going for Farida?"

Carla paused before replying.

"I suspected it more than anything else."

"And you still let me go?"

"I trusted you. I felt what we had would survive anything Farida might throw at you. And it has, hasn't it?"

Sam blew her a kiss. "What do you think?"

Carla got up from her armchair to look out of the window towards the lake. She turned.

"When are you going to come and see me? Presumably, they'll give you an afternoon off."

"I haven't seen the contract. In fact, probably only you have. So, boss, what are my hours?"

"Fully in line with Swiss workplace regulations. Eight hours on, three full meals a day, appropriate clothes provided."

Sam burst out laughing.

"That particular item can't be too heavy."

"Probably not, when you're actually on the job."

"Now you're getting vulgar, Carla."

"You should have seen the bill Amadeo sent me for your first little visit to him back in February. Nothing light about that. Still, it was my present to you. All that pale grey leather. And that corset - stunning. Wearing it to see the Prince in London no doubt one of the reasons you're here now."

The house phone rang.

"Business calls," Sam muttered, heading for the bathroom. She poked her head round the door. "The Prince reminded me of the confidentiality clause in my contract again after lunch. What does it actually say?"

"It's very firm on that score. How could it be otherwise? Governed by Swiss law. And as you know, they're pretty tough on confidentiality. Why?"

"He may want me to sit in on one of his business meetings. Very secret stuff."

"Probably no more secret than half the stuff he gets up to. Strangely enough, what you're up to with the Princess might be even more damaging for him. But the clause covers everything."

"I'll bear it in mind. Maybe you really should give me a copy of my contract some day."

"Run along now. And remember, I'll be waiting for you. Perhaps after dinner?"

"After dinner tends to get a little hectic. But perhaps after that."

As she was leaving, Carla held her back momentarily by the door.

"I love you, Sam. Never forget that."

Sam kissed her fingers tips and pressed them onto Carla's lips.

"I know."

She prayed that her evening overture with Farida would not end too late. Time with Carla was becoming an urgent necessity.

Thursday, 24 July 2008 (PM) – LA BARRA, URUGUAY

At about the same time that Sam had been touching down at the Prince's villa, Martín Caballero had arrived at his hotel north of Punta del Este. Travelling once again on his Perez identity documents, courtesy of SIDE, he had come via Montevideo, where he had hired a car. Tatyana had been on the same flight, but they had agreed not to be seen together until they got to the hotel.

He checked in at the Mantra, a large modern hotel complex complete with casino, tucked away in the woods behind La Barra, the next village east of Punta del Este on the coast. Tatyana had arrived almost at the same time in her taxi. Here too she had recommended that, at least for their arrival, they should conceal their relationship. After that, well... strangers often made acquaintances at the bar – or in the sauna. Given the fact that it was very low season, getting to know one another publicly should be relatively easy. They could hardly miss.

"Miss Kalyagin, welcome to the Mantra. I hope you enjoy your stay, though it may be a little quiet at this time of the year."

"Thank you. I need a rest and a change. I'll probably spend most of the time in your spa. I need to get fit."

The look on the manager's face betrayed his doubts as to her need for body toning. Still, the years had taught him that Russian super tourists were unpredictable in their habits.

"I will ask the spa's supervisor, Maya, to call your room, to tell you what's on offer and perhaps work out a programme for you."

"Don't worry, just give me her extension. I'll ring her."

A queue of bell boys stood eager to help with her single suitcase - albeit enormous. Having finally seen off the competition, the tallest was already by the lift, her case on his trolley.

"Your first visit, Señorita?" he asked, as he pressed the button for her floor.

She shook her head. He was handsome and would no doubt, given the flush on his face, have required no prompting, but for the time being she'd better keep things simple. Caballero was her prime concern.

Once in the large corner suite, all skygreys and whites, looking out into the woods beyond which she thought she could catch a glimpse of the sea, she waited by the door for him to deposit her case on a folding rack, a ten dollar bill between her fingers. Detecting he seemed bent on prolonging the usual litany about the suite's air-conditioning, minibar, TV set, view and guest services, she cut him short.

"I'll work it out for myself. That'll be all, thank you."

She held the door wide open. The look on his face was painful, the ten dollars only partial consolation.

A few doors down, Caballero rang back his secretary in Buenos Aires. Her message about some Arab visitor had been confused and the line had been bad. There were times he regretted his recruitment criteria for secretaries. Just occasionally, a bit more brain and a little less bosom might be more useful.

"So, tell me again, *linda*. What's this about a visitor?"

"Martín, don't be cross with me. Please. I told you. This man came looking for you this morning. His name is Ahmed Aboukir. He said he came specially to see you about a shipping question to the Middle East. That's all he said. He left a number. A cell phone."

Caballero was silent. Another unsolicited shipping proposal. Wasn't that what had led to the murder of Sanchez?

"Okay, it's all right, Valentina. I'm not angry. Give me his number and I'll ring him back."

She blew him a kiss down the line.

Thursday, 24 July 2008 (PM) – PASAJE DE LA PIEDAD, BUENOS AIRES

It was near a quarter to eight that evening when Leandro's doorbell rang. He had just texted Sam to find out whether she'd arrived safely. No reply.

"So, the lure of a good single malt."

"Yes, that and some news," Eduardo said.

Throwing off his coat, he stood in front of the fireplace, rubbing his hands before the glow.

Leandro produced the promised bottle of 14-year old whisky. Removing the cork, he gently waved the neck of the bottle within an inch of his son's nose.

"What d'you think of that?"

"Wonderful."

Each with a glass in their hand, father and son stood silently staring into the fire.

"So?"

"Incredible. Faint taste of orange. How many bottles did you bring back?"

"Only two. And that's the second."

"Hardly fair. Concealing it from me all these months."

Leandro relented.

"Okay, that's the first. There's another in the cupboard. You can take it with you."

Eduardo was visibly relieved. He took another sip.

"Well, I tried to find your Arab journalist friend. Little success. He seems to have checked out of the hotel yesterday afternoon.

Presumably soon after your lunch. And the manager let drop that he'd checked in about a week ago."

Leandro remained silent, uneasy. A week at the Plaza seemed to tally with what Aboukir had said, but it didn't explain where he might have been before that.

"I decided not to use my official credentials. Less efficient anyway than a fifty dollar bill, which the assistant was happy to accept for a photocopy of his passport when he checked in. So you owe me fifty dollars. Probably should have warned you about my expenses policy."

"Don't worry, I signed up for that a long time ago. Carry on."

"Armed with the photocopy, I did a little research on the immigration side. When did you say he'd arrived?"

"About a week ago."

"Well, officially, he's never arrived at all. No trace. Which, to be frank, is a little worrying, wouldn't you say?"

Leandro nodded. Sam's suspicions had been well-founded.

"And you say he's checked out?"

"Yes."

"And, presumably, he's now disappeared."

"I would guess so. Leaving us with little more than a rather poor photocopy of his passport photo."

He dug into his pocket and produced a sheet of paper, which he handed to Leandro.

"As you say, a poor likeness. Though it's certainly Aboukir."

Leandro sat thinking.

The broadening of the Middle Eastern dimension was disturbing. The diplomat in Brussels, Luis Miguel, Grunwald, three deaths coming on top of his acceptance of the Frobisher assignment, Sam suddenly getting swept up on the fringes – assuming they were they only the fringes - of some highly suspicious deals involving Iran, and now this mysterious journalist making contact. And not the person he claimed to be. Born in Valenciennes in France. Not the same as Aleppo!

So many pieces of a puzzle of which he had only the faintest outline. How much to share of all of this with Eduardo?

"Not sure what to make of all this. What do you think?"

It was Eduardo's turn to remain silent. He stared into the embers and took another sip of the Oban.

"Well, at the very least, we've got an illegal French or Arab tourist behaving strangely."

"And that at a time when the temperature on Argentina's involvement in the Middle East seems to be rising."

"Is Aboukir in some way directly connected with the murders of Morales and Grunwald? We can't rule it out. How did he seem to you?"

Leandro chose his words carefully.

"Thirty to thirty-five. Handsome, probably something of a ladies man. Fit. Strong handshake. Intelligent. Not your typical journalist. Not at all. Too well-dressed and clean living. Certainly confident. Sure of himself. Asked a lot of intelligent questions which seemed to fit his brief."

"No obvious distinguishing features?" Eduardo asked.

"No, not really."

"So where do we go from here? I can hardly turn up in Fonseca's office tomorrow and tell him I think I have a suspect for the murders. He'll want to know how I came by it. Which, unless I mention you, is going to be a little difficult to explain."

"At the same time, we can't allow someone like this, assuming he has something to do with the murders, to prowl around this city on the loose."

"And he seems to be interested in you. Hardly reassuring."

"I need a drop more," Leandro said, uncorking the bottle. "How's your glass?"

"Just a little. Far too precious."

Having served both of them, Leandro sat down and crossed his legs, to relieve the pressure on his back, that dull ache from his old rugby injury always awakened in times of stress.

"We do have one possible avenue, though hardly an attractive one."

"And that would be?" Leandro said.

"We wait and see why Señor Aboukir is interested in you."

"As you say, not reassuring. Explain yourself."

"Well, I can't think why, but he seems to have invented a pretext to contact you. If we look on the dark side, perhaps he's sizing you up as his next victim. I know, hold on, let me finish," Eduardo added, seeing Leandro about to interrupt. "If we assume he's the assassin, then presumably, to make the list complete we need to add in the man in Brussels. No one seems to think that that was suicide. So what do we have? Two diplomats - or apparent diplomats - both involved with Iran. And then a journalist writes a story about Iran and our government. So he gets killed. The thin red line therefore appears to be the nuclear question. Now, how do you fit into that pattern, if that's what it is?"

The same analysis had of course already been worked out by Frobisher. Not that that was something he could pass on to Eduardo.

"To be frank, I don't know. I've had lunch with two of the victims in the past four or five weeks. But beyond that? It doesn't seem enough."

"You're probably right. We know that Luis Miguel was tortured. Any reason he might have given your name? And whatever the official version may be, the presidential committee is convinced that Grunwald was murdered, not that he strangled himself. Given the way he was killed, there must have been an element of torture in that one as well."

Leandro was shocked by this analysis, though he couldn't fault it.

"Jesus Christ, I hadn't thought of that."

"Sorry, afraid I'm paid to think that way."

Leandro tried to think through the implications. Their lunch together had enabled Aboukir to size him up. He now knew much more about Leandro. Not to mention Sam. If he really was a professional killer, hired by someone to cut down the Argentine-Iran negotiation team, then Sam was also at risk.

"If I understand you, what you're saying is that we should sit and wait for Aboukir to make a move against me. You'll forgive me for not viewing that strategy with enormous enthusiasm."

"Worst-case scenario. Although there may be other options."

"Such as?"

"I'll have to think about it."

"Also not reassuring."

Leandro downed the rest of his glass.

"At this rate, I'm going to be opening that second bottle," he muttered, pouring himself another half glass. He waved the bottle in Eduardo's direction, but his son shook his head, and stood up.

"I need a clear head. I'll go home and give all this some thought. Let's meet tomorrow at about eight at London City."

He pulled on his coat and bent over his godfather, who had remained sitting, twirling his glass between his fingers, a depressed look on his face. Eduardo placed a kiss on his forehead.

"Don't worry, Uncle. You've seen worse. I'll have a solution by tomorrow."

Leandro watched him leave. Eduardo turned in the doorway and gave him a thumbs up, before disappearing.

Within a minute, he was back.

"You promised me the other bottle."

"Shit! Thought I'd got away with it."

He sat there thinking until the whisky had vanished. Then he got up and plugged the encryption software into his laptop.

> "Re. yesterday's enquiry. Not the same person. My version born in France. Has now disappeared again. Will keep you advised. L."

Any more detail would prompt Frobisher to ask where it was coming from. The role of Eduardo was better hidden for the time being. He also hesitated about sharing any more of their analysis with London. And yet, wasn't this exactly the kind of situation for which Frobisher had put him in touch with Albert? If he called on Albert's protection directly, Frobisher would find out? How would they react? Pull him off the case? Or let it run?

Confused, slightly tipsy, he felt an overwhelming desire to share all this with Sam. But she was busy with her own mission. Not to mention the fact that she might see it as weakness. He was supposed to be able to look after himself without running to his girlfriend for help.

"Time for bed, Leandro," he muttered aloud. "Things will look better in the morning."

He had just switched off the light when his phone rang.

"Hi. Hope I haven't woken you. Or upset any other activity."

Elena, clearly in a better mood.

Leandro grunted.

"No, I'm in bed alone and just about to go to sleep."

"Well, I've got some news. Alex just rang me. She and Nouria have gone off together to Punta del Este. She seemed to imply that this was a good sign. The main thing is that she's okay. I knew you'd want to know."

"So what do we make of that? You say Alex sounded optimistic. Is that actually what we want?"

Elena paused.

"You're right. Though, in today's world, it's hard to tell what one does want. Twenty or thirty years ago we might have been delighted if her relationship with Nouria was over. Now I'm not so sure, even if it reduces my chances of ever becoming a grandmother. I used to look forward to that."

"I know what you mean. Nowadays we seem to focus more on whether a person is happy, whatever the relationship."

"All I know is that being against it would almost certainly be counter-productive. And who knows? She may change. Suddenly find herself a nice guy. It's hard to tell."

"I agree. She has to find her own way and all we can do is to ensure that the damage is limited. If damage there is. Anyway, I've got to make some phone calls. Keep me posted. Do you think I should try and give her a ring?"

"I don't see why not. But be careful not to give the impression that we're putting her under pressure."

"Good advice. Take care."

Thursday, 24 July 2008 (PM) – COLONIA, URUGUAY

He was sitting in a cafe in the centre of Colonia, looking out onto a statue of José Artigas, Uruguay's heroic 'father of its nationhood' in the central square. It was getting on for 9 o'clock. The call from Caballero had still not come. He hoped the day's efforts had not been wasted.

"Off once more, Señor Azoulay?" the hotel manager had asked.

"Just for a day or two. Keep my room as usual, please."

He had slipped the man another hundred dollars.

"*Muchas gracias, Señor. Muy amable.* Have a safe journey."

First port of call, the little car rental found online. The problems he needed to overcome had been several. To get to Uruguay as soon as possible transporting his SIG Sauer, which ruled out airlines or ferries where passengers were inevitably scanned. If he could take a car across, this would not only enable him to conceal the automatic, but also give him mobility in Uruguay. Given the fact there was no trace of his arrival in Argentine immigration, he could not travel on his Aboukir passport, but only on his identity document in the name of Azoulay, sufficient under the Mercosur agreements to travel to Uruguay. Hertz or Avis would insist on a credit card, which meant the rental agency had had to be informal enough to take a large cash deposit and not ask questions.

At around noon, he was driving up the ramp onto the car ferry. The sales representative at the offices of Buquebus in the port area had initially been reluctant to take cash, but a well-placed hundred dollar bill had demonstrated significant powers of persuasion over the hirsute young man behind the counter. An hour-long crossing during which he had been able catch up on some sleep.

On landing, with the pretext of using the toilet, he'd done a quick reconnaissance of the ferry terminal, before driving towards the gates where the Uruguayan customs officials were posted. They had asked him to open the boot of the Peugeot and looked through the side windows of the car, but from their questions he detected they were more interested in agricultural imports than anything so banal as a 9mm.

Friday, 25 July 2008 (AM) – PASAJE DE LA PIEDAD, BUENOS AIRES

Leandro woke on the sofa still dressed, his empty glass in his hand, no texts from Sam on the phone by his side, and a realisation. Frobisher needed to know more about Aboukir.

"Given Aboukir interest in me, would Albert be available? L."

Within ten minutes, his laptop was ringing - Frobisher wanted a secure conversation. He went through the change of software and heard Charles' voice at the far end.

"No names, as usual. How are you? Your message is troubling."

Leandro wondered whether it had been a wise move after all. He didn't want to appear to have panicked. But it was too late.

"I've been analysing the implications. There may of course be some perfectly innocent explanation for--"

"We don't think so. Something came to light overnight. It's very probable that the real journalist was murdered about two months ago. It seems to have been hushed up locally. Maybe he was on to a story that someone didn't want to see in print. Anyway, the fact that part of his identity is being used down in Buenos Aires certainly indicates that his death has ramifications beyond his home country. So you're right to take it seriously."

This wasn't getting any better. Leandro paused, wondering which way to go. Charles helped him.

"Your suggestion that our mutual friend get involved appears quite right. I've sent him a message. He should be contacting you soon. Obviously I leave the details to the two of you."

"Fine. I think it's just a precaution. Until things become clearer."

"Anything more you can tell me about this gentleman?"

Leandro gave Charles a quick summary of his conversation with Aboukir. Nothing about Eduardo. Frobisher would be sensitive to the involvement of an Argentine policeman, whatever the relationship.

"No doubt a forged passport. We need to find out whether he used it anywhere else. Strictly speaking, he's the Argentines' problem. But since he's taken an interest in you, we have to set up countermeasures. You think he's disappeared?"

"I fear so."

"I'm sorry to say this, but the next time you hear from him may be face to face."

Cast by everyone in the role of the goat tied to a tree as bait for the lion, Leandro was beginning to get irritated.

"I see. At which point our mutual friend will no doubt come in useful."

"Well, whether by design or by chance, you seem to find yourself closer to the heart of our investigation than any of us could have dreamt possible. When I gave you the assignment, it was to know *if* something was going on. The answer to that is clearly yes. Now, perhaps, we need to know *why* and *how*. That being said, let there be no doubt in your mind that you are in control. If things get nasty, you must be the judge of when to pull out. And I need hardly add that no one wants all this to end up with any suggestion of British fingers in the pie. That's got to be the golden rule, particularly given the anti-British sentiment of the present leadership."

Fingers in the pie indeed! Corpses in the gutter more likely!

"No, of course. But I don't think we're anywhere near that yet."

Leandro hoped that the tone of his voice, even over the scrambler, would not betray a lack of conviction.

"Well, take care of yourself. Try and let me know whatever you arrange with our mutual friend. Been good talking to you."

"And to you. Thank you."

With a strange buzzing sound, the line went dead.

Leandro leaned back in his chair, stretching his legs under the table and clasping his hands behind his neck.

This was getting more complicated by the minute. There were times when he wondered whether he shouldn't have his head examined.

To his surprise, Albert appeared on a similar secure VOIP network less than an hour later.

"Charles asked me to call you. What's the latest?"

Leandro filled him in with as much detail as he was prepared to see passed on to Charles. He told him about the murders of Sanchez, Luis Miguel and Grunwald, what he knew about the way they had been killed, the possible involvement of the *Bonaerense* – "nasty lot, they are" - and the formation of a 'task force' at the level of the Presidency. Albert listened carefully, occasionally asking a question on a point of detail.

"Assuming Aboukir is the killer of Morales and Grunwald, we can make a few deductions about his MO. All the more, if we add in this guy Sanchez in Brussels. In all three cases, the killer seems to have preferred to carry out the job in their flats."

"Hardly reassuring," Leandro muttered.

"Secondly, he seems to go for a strong sexual trademark. At least, from what you know about the two murders here. Do we know if there was anything like that in the case of Brussels?"

"I can try and find out."

"Then there's the question of how he gets in."

"We only know for sure in the case of Luis Miguel. He may have used the two men from the *Bonaerense*. In my case, presumably, he would just ring me up and arrange a meeting here at my flat. After all, he has the address and the telephone number."

"Or he might break in. If he's a professional assassin, he knows how to pick a lock."

"I'm not sure I'm very happy about just sitting here, waiting for him to choose his moment to come and torture me to death."

"Oh, I think you're overdoing it. We're not going to let that happen."

"So what do you suggest? How are we going to play this?"

"Well, part of the trouble is that we don't actually know if he wants you or not. And you can hardly sit holed up in your flat for the next few weeks. So we have to be sure about his interest. Any ideas?"

Much against his better judgement, Leandro came up with a proposal.

"I could contact him. He did leave me a cell phone, after all. My ringing him may also serve to get some idea where he's gone."

Albert was silent for a moment.

"At the first sign of trouble, I can be up there in under two hours."

Friday, 25 July 2008 (AM) – LA BARRA, URUGUAY

As he sat over breakfast in Tatyana's suite, Caballero remembered he hadn't yet rung the Lebanese who'd made contact the day before. Tatyana's dominatrix performance had blown everything from his mind. The combination of her explosive Slavic obscenities, as she ground the stiletto heel of her boot into his groin or caressed him with a small black riding whip, had completely turned him on. Her blow jobs might have been administered by an alien from another planet.

He got up from the table by the window to look for his cell phone, catching a glimpse of himself in her dressing table mirror. He looked terrible. He'd have to do something about that before his meeting with the Saudis.

The girl was spread out, fast asleep in the middle of the huge bed, her virulent red hair like a pool of blood against the white sheets. A surge of lust gripped him. He could always postpone the meeting until after lunch.

He rang the number given to him by Valentina, but after three unanswered rings, thought better of it. He was being foolish. Going out onto the balcony, he dialled another number.

"Caballero here. Is that you, Muñoz?"

One of the deputy directors of SIDE. There was a brief silence, before the voice at the other end replied.

"Where are you? I thought you were in Uruguay."

"I am. Got here yesterday. The meeting is later today."

"Oh, okay. Go ahead. What's the problem?"

"Just wanted to pass on something."

With so little information, it didn't take Caballero more than a minute to pass on the news of Aboukir's visit to his office. When he'd finished, Muñoz was silent, clearly thinking.

"I agree. Something isn't quite right. Almost a repeat performance of what happened in Brussels. You say the name's Aboukir? I'll do a trace.

Presume he'll show up somewhere in immigration. Give me an hour or two."

Muñoz hung up.

Caballero leant against the balcony, looking at the phone. A couple of hours. Tatyana would have ways of making that pass quickly enough. He went back into the bedroom and sat down on the edge of the bed. Gently, he inserted his hand between her thighs, the tips of his fingers finding the warm softness of her cunt. She stirred. As his fingers worked on her, she purred almost inaudibly, the tip of her tongue flicking between her lips, her eyelids quivering.

Suddenly, uncoiling like an enormous cobra, she threw herself on top of him, sending both of them to the floor. The volley of Russian insults resumed.

It was about eleven in the morning when Muñoz called back.

"Bad news. We can't find any trace of that name in immigration. We've been back three months, nothing. Another interesting detail. Someone from one of the *Comisarías* has been looking for the same name in the last twenty-four hours."

"Who?"

"We don't know, but we'll find out and why. I've called a meeting with my team in about twenty minutes. We have to decide how to react. If he's involved with these murders, it would be good to smoke him out fast."

"Won't that push him to me?"

"One possibility is that you set up a meeting and we have it staked out. We could get a couple of guys over to you by the end of the day. We're not keen to ask our Uruguayan friends to help out. Not sure they'd be very helpful anyway. I'll call you back as soon as possible. In the meantime, don't do anything."

He dropped the cell phone on the floor beside the bed and turned back to Tatyana. The look on her face suggested she could well do without these minor interruptions.

On balance, he would limit himself to a phone conversation with the Prince. No harm in giving the impression that he, Caballero, controlled the pace. Who knew how the negotiation with the Saudi would go? If it went badly, he might want to have the security of a fall-back position before taking the negotiation with the Saudis close to breaking point. The art of good negotiation.

Friday, 25 July 2008 (PM) – JOSÉ IGNACIO, URUGUAY

The sun was setting behind the trees on the other side of the lake. The Prince and Mohammed looked frustrated. It was clear to Sam that, as so often when it came to doing business with her countrymen, things were never simple.

"You Argentines really are very complicated people, Samira," the Prince began, shaking his head. "They look like Europeans but negotiate like Uzbeks. Just when you think you have something agreed, it starts all over again. Not to mention that they turn up late. Or not at all. The meeting was supposed to start in the morning. They finally cancelled at three in the afternoon!"

"I'm sorry, Your Highness."

"Maybe we should bring you back, Samira, like last time."

Turning to Mohammed, he asked, "What do you think?"

"I agree, Your Highness. We can pretend our normal secretary has fallen ill and is being replaced again by Miss Samira."

"Miss Samra, remember. Fine, we'll do that tomorrow. You'll have flown in from Beirut this evening. Now I need a drink."

The Prince rose and, with a wave of the hand, indicated that Mohammed could leave.

"And Madame Carla? Where is she?" he said, turning to Sam.

"Shall I try and find her, Your Highness? She may have gone back to her place. We can ask her to come over."

"No, if she's gone there, don't bother her. I'm going to have a shower. We meet in an hour for dinner."

Friday, 25 July 2008 (PM) – LA BARRA, URUGUAY

It was around seven thirty. Caballero was sitting at the bar of the Mantra, when his cell phone rang. Muñoz. He took it out onto the terrace.

"Sorry not to have got back to you earlier, but I know you were in meetings. How did they go, by the way?"

Caballero didn't feel like sharing the frustrations of the day with Muñoz in Buenos Aires.

"No progress. They cancelled."

A minor deviation from the truth. That he should have preferred the attentions of Tatyana was not an acceptable pretext.

"Oh dear. Well, we've been analysing this question of Aboukir. The result is complex. If the guy is genuine, then it would be interesting to see what he has to offer. If this is the killer, we have to make sure you're safe. Two of my men, Rios and Santos, will join you tomorrow midday. They'll find you. Once we've got a good idea of where and how you might meet this man, then you should make contact. But not before. Is that clear?"

Caballero was in no mood to start taking unnecessary risks. He wanted to be around to enjoy the large bonus which he could expect if he got this deal set up with Iran. Anyway, since the man Aboukir was presumably in Buenos Aires waiting for his call, they should have enough time to take the necessary precautions.

"And what about the *Comisaría* looking him up? Did you find out why?"

"No. We still haven't traced that."

"Okay. Understood. I'll look out for your guys."

The line clicked at the other end. He went back into the bar. It was now a matter of waiting. He asked the barman to pass over the menu for room service. Tatyana had made it clear that she was expecting him back very soon.

Caballero's margin of safety was smaller than he imagined.

Friday, 25 July 2008 (PM) – MONTEVIDEO, URUGUAY

The Director had moved on to Montevideo on the evening of his arrival in Colonia, finding himself a small hotel in Carrasco, an eastern residential suburb of the Uruguayan capital. Located in Montevideo, he would be sitting halfway between the two possible extremes of the three locations he suspected might be Caballero's destination. Either could be reached in about two hours driving. At around ten o'clock in the morning, his cell phone had begun to ring. The number he'd given Caballero's secretary at Tecnologías del Sur. He watched it ring a few times and then, just as he was about to pick up, the ringing stopped. He checked, but there was no trace of the caller's number. Could it have been Caballero? Why had he not waited? Second thoughts perhaps.

During the rest of the day, he waited, but no call came. He wanted Caballero to take the initiative.

He had booked himself a table for dinner at Francis, recommended by his hotel concierge as one of the best restaurants in town. Nine o'clock saw him coming through the door, where an attractive receptionist pointed him in the direction of the bar.

"Your table will be ready in about fifteen minutes. I'm sorry, Señor, as it's Friday night, we're very full. Please order a drink."

Standing with his back to the bar, the Director saw virtually every table was taken. The layout was attractive. In tones of red and ochre, the tables downstairs covered in white linen, illuminated by a single candle, the colour scheme warm and inviting. To one side, above the bar, a balustrade, painted black like the chairs, gave onto a mezzanine gallery of tables, all of them full. Hearing the barman address him, he turned.

"What can I give you, Señor?"

"A glass of chilled Chardonnay. Thank you."

As he sat on the bar stool sipping the smooth Chilean wine, he idly turned the pages of the latest edition of Caras. Underdressed blondes and socialite chatter. As he skimmed from one article to the next, his eye was caught by a full-page photo of a white private jet parked at Punta del Este airport, with archive photographs of a large yacht somewhere in the Caribbean. The article went on to report the arrival in Uruguay's prime seaside resort of a Saudi Prince and his retinue. A telephoto shot of a large villa near water north of José Ignacio completed the piece. The Prince might be contemplating real estate in the area, it said.

A Saudi Prince in Punta del Este? Out of season? And not any Prince. One he had on occasion observed at Le Gray, one of Beirut's leading hotels. Nor was his main line of business exactly a state secret. In Uruguay at the same time as Caballero? There must surely be a connection.

At all events, something inside told him that of the three possible destinations for Caballero, Punta del Este was now the most likely. He needed to get there. As long as he didn't drink too much now, there was still time to enjoy a good dinner.

The waitress came over and showed him to his table.

It was about three in the morning when, having taken the empty road which follows the line of the coast from Montevideo to Punta del Este, he was steering the small Peugeot into the silent seaside town. In the summer, this might be its busiest hour, but in the middle of winter...

The time he had spent in Colonia before setting off for Montevideo had not been wasted. One area of research had been the major hotels in Punta del Este still likely to be open at this time of year.

But where was Caballero?

Saturday, 26 July 2008 (AM) – CALLE 5, LA BARRA, URUGUAY

Only a single candle burning in one corner, the blinds of the large panoramic window drawn to reveal the pale metallic tones of the cloudless winter sky, fusing into the vast expanse of the Atlantic. In the foreground, the black outlines of the parasol pine trees at the foot of the garden, seeming to rise straight out of the horizon pool.

"You're so lucky. It's summer over there. Not to mention those days on that yacht in the Mediterranean."

"You haven't lost all of your tan from your trip to the Caribbean. You're still very brown. Must be that Semitic blood," Carla teased, the tips of her fingers following the contours of Sam's breasts and stomach, as they lay side-by-side on the enormous bed in Carla's villa.

"You never did tell me about that one. Who was the client?"

"A banker from New York. Spending a fraction of his bonus. Along with all his friends. Apparently oblivious to the havoc they're causing. It's frankly immoral!"

"Are you beginning to get a taste for morality? Might complicate business a little, don't you think?"

"Let's not go into that. You know giving pleasure has never struck me as so immoral. Perhaps a trifle amoral."

Sam kissed her softly. "I know. You're different. That's why we're together."

After a moment, Sam continued.

"On that subject, you never did tell me how you got into the escort business."

Carla remained silent, looking out towards the sea. Finally she turned back toward Sam.

"There wasn't any particular reason. And you didn't ask."

"If you don't want to reply, my love, it doesn't matter."

"In some ways, I don't know if it's important. It's quite a long story. Perhaps for another evening."

"Of course. And if you don't want to, that's also okay."

Having performed her curtain-raiser with Farida for the Prince, Sam had finally slipped away at about two in the morning, the compliant Malcolm having passed her the keys to one of the armoured Mercedes hired over from Buenos Aires. Uruguay was a more tranquil country, in which the business of armouring limousines had little future. He had also provided her the passwords for the guards at the far end of the long entrance drive.

At the first roundabout, the turning leading to José Ignacio had flashed past and once on the straight, Sam had given the five hundred cc engine its head. She loved driving. In spite of the extra weight of the armouring, the huge car had rapidly devoured the twenty kilometres down the empty moonlit road separating José Ignacio from Calle 5, which led to Carla's ultramodern villa in the pinewoods. There was something to be said for being in Punta del Este out of season. In the height of summer, this would have been one long queue of cars in both directions, particularly at this hour.

Even so, she failed to spot the SIDE tail which had picked her up on leaving the gates. Thanks to the moonlight, it was driving without lights and could follow her from a long way back.

Carla greeted her, wearing very little more than a glass of champagne.

"Come in, darling, it's cold out there. Don't worry, I've sent Naya to bed."

Taking Sam by the hand, she led the way downstairs to the huge bedroom, her bare feet making no sound on the marble floor.

"You're in much better shape tonight than the last time you were here," Carla whispered as she gently propelled Sam, now also naked, onto the bed.

An allusion to the days spent with Carla in this house following her rescue from the farm, where for two weeks she had been held hostage and tortured by Dávila. As the images of her captivity flashed before Sam's eyes, a shiver of fear.

"Please, don't remind me. That's the past. I'm here for the present."

"I'm sorry. I didn't mean to."

"I know," Sam said and pulled Carla down on top of her, her mouth seeking Carla's, her fingers searching for the soft lips of her mistress's cunt, their breasts tingling with arousal, as Carla swayed gently above her.

"So, how do I compare with the Princess?" Carla whispered.

"Don't ask silly questions. Be quiet. As I said, it's the present I want. Pure pleasure, no business."

Sam pressed herself against Carla.

"Anything else?" Carla asked after a while. Was Sam in a mood to push the limits?

"Not tonight. I have to rediscover you. You're my benchmark of pleasure. Your body, the taste and scent of your sex. You, my love."

Slowly, Sam slipped backwards down Carla's body as she lay on her back, her tongue leaving a trail between her breasts, past her navel, over the base of her stomach until finally it slid between her labia, seeking out the tiny bulb of her clitoris. With her hands, she parted Carla's thighs and then, with the tips of her fingers, pulled the labia wide apart.

Carla's fingers joined hers, whilst she placed her other hand in the small of her back, arching her body for her lover.

With Sam, Carla was a silent lover, not one to fill the darkness with contrived moans of ecstasy.

"I only do that when I'm paid," she had explained one night. "That's for whores."

Saturday, 26 July 2008 (PM) – ROCHA, URUGUAY

The story that a Saudi royal might be buying property in the area had predictably caused a minor stir in out of season Punta del Este and one or two journalists had posted themselves outside the gates. Two decoy cars left the Prince's villa around three in the afternoon, causing the journalists to set off in pursuit towards Punta del Este. Once they were out of sight, two large Mercedes, this time containing the Prince, Mohammed and Sam in one, and a couple of bodyguards in the second, set off inland from the coast.

According to Mohammed, the choice of venue for the discussions had not been an easy one. The Prince had ruled out the villa he was using, suspecting that the Argentines would have had plenty of time to bug it anyway. The Argentines had initially insisted on their hotel, the Mantra, appearing chronically concerned about the possibility of hostile eavesdropping by the Americans or the Israelis. Finally, the parties had agreed that the Argentines would place a private residence at their disposal. The location would only be made known an hour before.

"It looks as though it's being handled by the Argentine intelligence service. Presumably to ensure that neither the Israelis nor the Americans plant any microphones. Whilst, of course, busily planting their own," Mohammed had commented to Sam.

On arrival, the staff of the estancia, belonging to a close supporter of the Kirchner couple, shepherded the party towards the terrace where a tray of coffee was served. Sam badly needed it. She had finally returned from Carla's at around seven in the morning and collapsed into bed. On emerging at noon, she had met the Prince in the hallway.

"You're looking good, Samira, considering..."

She had probably been naive to assume her nocturnal movements might go undetected by her client.

True to his performance on the previous day, Caballero and his assistant negotiator, Villanueva, managed to arrive some twenty minutes after the Prince. It being an unusually warm winter's day, they found the Saudi party admiring the view of the rolling hills stretching west towards the interior of Uruguay. Sam had spotted a number of bodyguards and kept on her large designer dark glasses, assuming they would certainly be taking photographs of their group.

"Ah, Señor Perez, I'm glad you've made it."

The Prince's words contained not a hint of irony.

"You've met Mohammed and Miss Harari before, I believe. Up in Tobago. She arrived yesterday. This is a beautiful property," the Prince continued. "I see the owner breeds horses. I also have a stud, back in Saudi Arabia. And I keep horses in England. They have the best trainers."

At Perez's suggestion, the coffee finished, they moved inside to the drawing room, where a large table had been arranged for the meeting. Again Sam and Mohammed were placed at the far end, opposite the Prince.

"To begin with, Your Royal Highness, we would like to thank you for having made the effort to come down here," Perez began.

The Prince acknowledged the courtesy with a tilt of the head.

"Although the commercial transaction was originally going to involve our friends in Caracas, we agreed with them that there was no need for them to be present today. Our current thinking is that we would wish you to collect the shipment from a port in Argentina. Although one cannot underestimate the ability of Washington to monitor practically everything on this planet, it is our view that activities in Venezuela are more vulnerable to surveillance."

"Geographically closer to the US. Always a handicap."

"Indeed, Your Royal Highness. Not to mention the fact that the Americans clearly regard President Chavez's regime more unfavourably. With our enormous coastline, it should be easier to load the cargo under cover of darkness than might be the case elsewhere. We are looking at possible options on the coast of Patagonia. Would you agree with that, Your Highness?"

The Prince had apparently been expecting the Argentines to go for this option.

"I do. My research and calculations support it. But I need to know the dimensions of the shipment and the likely date of departure. On top of that, the nature of the cargo, in case any particular precautions need to be taken."

"At this particular moment, negotiations are not sufficiently advanced to be able to determine whether the shipment will consist exclusively of centrifuge equipment, or whether there may additionally be a shipment of yellow cake."

"Obviously the latter concerns me."

"Of course, Your Highness, although we will not be shipping the yellow cake like we might ship meat!"

Perez smiled.

"I presume not," the Prince replied drily.

"It's important to bear in mind that the most hazardous elements associated with raw uranium are extracted by the milling process and end up in the milling plant's disposal site. The yellow cake itself is not particularly radioactive, although it should certainly not be inhaled."

"What are the dangers?"

"Well, one breath would be the equivalent of smoking many packets a day for an entire lifetime. No, the yellow cake will be stored in the appropriate containers, with all the necessary precautions taken. In most countries in which yellow cake is processed, it is usually transported by road. Naturally, the authorities are getting concerned in the face of growing public opinion. Fortunately, we don't have to worry much about public opinion in Argentina."

Again Perez smiled.

"Since we will be transporting this by sea, we're thinking in terms of one 20-foot container of yellow cake, and two or three containers of centrifuges. The 20-foot container will hold up to about forty-eight or fifty sealed 200-litre steel drums of yellow cake. Each drum would be closed by a tight fitting lid secured to the drum with a steel locking ring and clamped by a locking ring bolt. The drums would be stowed securely using a strapping systemThe health hazard, as I said, is very low.

"And the centrifuges?"

"They are often crated in pairs. As they stand about two metres tall, we will see how many will fit into each container and decide the final number at that point. We are still in the final stages of the negotiation about the number of centrifuges, which our Iranian friends wish to purchase, and the volume of yellow cake. Once we know, we will inform Your Highness. That being said, I do not believe that the shipment will be very large in itself."

The Prince sat thinking a moment.

"Obviously, the vessel we choose should as far as possible merge unobtrusively with ships operating in the region. What sort of traffic do you have down there?"

"There is a major port at Bahia Blanca in the south of the province of Buenos Aires."

"Yes, I've seen it. A large harbour. Grain, wool, fruit coming and going. Also oil. And there appears to be a smaller port not far away, Puerto Galván, sunflower and soy oil, and chemicals such as urea from a large plant nearby. That might provide some measure of cover."

"Add to that the fact that, only last month, a major LNG unloading facility was opened at Bahia Blanca, which my government bought from a supplier in the US."

"What happens farther south?"

"Probably the largest port facility is Comodoro Rivadavia, which serves the oil industry. And right at the bottom, in Tierra del Fuego, Ushuaia, above all a tourist attraction, regularly visited by large cruise liners. In between, a number of smaller harbours such as Puerto Deseado. The fishing industry mainly uses Mar del Plata, as well as Rawson down in Chubut Province. So, not only is the coastline huge, but there would appear to be a number of options in terms of the kind of vessel or its apparent business."

"True. But the fewer observers around to see the loading, the better. I presume that we can't rule out some form of interest from the British in the Falkland Islands - apologies, the Malvinas," the Prince rapidly corrected himself.

Perez smiled.

The Prince made some notes, before continuing.

"Do you think we're in a position to hammer out some of the main headings of our agreement?"

Perez suddenly stood up and left the table. The Lebanese. Before entering into more detail, a fall-back position would be useful. He again rang the number given to him by Valentina.

Watching him, the Prince politely concealed his irritation. He had got used to the fact that good manners had largely given way to the pressing needs of constant communication, even in the middle of a delicate negotiation.

Perez walked out onto the terrace.

"Señor Aboukir, I'm sorry not to have been in touch with you sooner. I understand that we should meet. That you have a proposal which may interest me."

Aboukir briefly indicated that he was aware of the fact that the Argentines might be requiring a discreet shipment to somewhere in the Middle East, a business in which his agency specialised.

"Are you still in Buenos Aires?" Perez asked.

"No, in Montevideo, where I also have some business to attend to," Aboukir lied, knowing the phone he was using would not be registering its number.

"How soon could you get over here? I'm in Punta del Este. It's a bit late this afternoon and I am in a meeting, but perhaps we could have breakfast tomorrow morning."

"Fine. I'll make my way over there this evening and we can meet tomorrow morning. Where?"

Perez hesitated for a moment. But by tomorrow morning, in a public place, with extra bodyguards, he could handle matters.

"I'm staying at the Hotel Mantra, outside La Barra, east of Punta del Este. Perhaps we could meet at about ten?"

"Perfect, I'll be there. I'll ask for you when I arrive."

"Excellent. See you tomorrow then, Señor Aboukir."

Perez returned to the meeting. By tomorrow, he might be negotiating from a position of strength with the Saudi Prince.

"Your Highness, forgive me. I fear we will have to postpone this discussion until tomorrow."

Even the Prince had some difficulty in hiding his annoyance at this cavalier treatment by the young Argentine.

He stood up and bowed to Caballero.

"I will expect your call tomorrow morning. Before noon, Señor Perez."

The tone left no-one in any doubt that this was the deadline.

Without a further glance at the Argentine party, he left the room, followed by Mohammed and Sam.

Saturday, 26 July 2008 (PM) – LA BARRA, URUGUAY

"I can see you now, my friend," the Director muttered on hanging up his call with Caballero, as from less than a kilometre away, he had studied Caballero through his binoculars.

It had been easier to track him down than expected.

After some four hours sleep curled up in the back of his car on arriving in Punta del Este from Montevideo, the Director had made his way to one of the cafes near the harbour. Over a breakfast of coffee and croissants, in the guise of a society journalist for the Spanish edition of ¡Hola!, it hadn't taken him long to chat up the waitress using the story about the Saudi Prince.

"Nice place they're staying in," he said, pushing the Caras page in her direction as she laid out his breakfast. "Maybe you should act as my guide. Get you into the story. Or at least one of the photographs."

"Did you say you worked for ¡Hola! in Spain," she asked, a hint of repressed excitement in her voice.

"I freelance for them. They love this kind of story. A lot of Spaniards come down here in January and February. Should be able to sell it easily."

The waitress was looking at the magazine over his shoulder.

"That's up beyond José Ignacio. The place they're staying. Probably belongs to some rich Argentine. They practically own this part of the world. Though, mind you, there are more and more Brazilians now and even some Russians. So why not a Saudi Prince? Probably good for business."

"How far is that? Maybe, with my telephoto lens, I could get some shots from the beach."

"I'm not sure it's on the beach. More inland. This time of year, you'd probably be the only person there."

"Not counting you, if you come with me and help me find it."

"I don't get off until five today."

"It'll be dark by then. And tomorrow? It's Sunday isn't it?"

"Oh, I get tomorrow off."

She began to wonder whether this attractive man might have anything better to do that evening.

"Let's think about tomorrow. In the meantime, I need to find a nice hotel. Presume quite a lot of them are closed at this time of the year."

"Most of the big ones are open. The Conrad, the Mantra, places like that."

"Why don't you give me your cell phone and I'll call you later," he said.

"I'll bring it with the bill," she smiled, turning away.

When she returned, she not only provided her number, but also that morning's edition of El Este, the local paper. She opened it to one of the inner pages and placed it on the table next to him.

"This might help," she said, pointing in the direction of a half-page spread.

The Saudi royal couple had arrived. There was even a rough map of their villa and a couple of poor quality colour photos of the convoy of Mercedes leaving the airport, then entering the large gates of the property.

"It's where I thought," the girl said. "About five kilometres north of José Ignacio, in the direction of Laguna Garzón. Maybe we could get there tomorrow," she added.

"Is that your phone number?" he asked, picking up a piece of paper behind the bill.

She nodded.

"I'll give you a ring. You've been very helpful. I'll try and get you into the story somehow."

Having paid, he made his way back to the car, tearing her number in half as he went. He might not have any information about Caballero's whereabouts, but, had he been a betting man, it was more than even odds that the Prince would lead him to his target.

At the first petrol station, he filled up the car and then headed north-east out of Punta del Este towards La Barra and from there through the increasingly overbuilt coastline towards José Ignacio, some thirty kilometres away. It was mid-morning but, at this time of the year even on a Saturday, there was hardly any traffic. His journalist cover might work with a waitress but, given the absence of any photographic equipment in the car, not to mention the relative flimsiness of the Argentine identity under which he was travelling, it was unlikely he could withstand much questioning from security around the Saudi visitors.

Beyond José Ignacio, he turned inland, the newspaper sketch map in one hand. It had been careless of the Prince's security to allow the paper to find out so much. But then, in a dead-zone like this, it probably hadn't taken the journalist long to work it out.

Having arrived near the Prince's villa, he took up a position on higher ground about half a kilometre farther north. From there, through his binoculars, he had been able to observe movement around the house and detected the ploy of the decoy cars being prepared. He could see that the second pair of cars were receiving more attention, the first having driven off. Driving closer to the point at which the side road leading to the villa joined the main road, he parked out of sight and was reassured some fifteen minutes later by the appearance of the second pair of Mercedes, which, from a safe distance, he followed. Once the Prince's cars had turned into the gates of the estancia where the meeting was to take place, he drove past to the next road junction a kilometre farther on and waited.

He saw the arrival of Caballero and his party, coming from the same direction as the Prince. Caballero was almost certainly also staying somewhere on the coast. Now it was just a matter of waiting for him to re-emerge and following him back to his hotel.

As he sat waiting, a voice message came through on one of his phones. Flemming had rung during the morning, leaving a message which, owing to the vagaries of the Argentine cell phone system, had taken a good six hours to come through.

"Good morning, Ahmed. This is Leandro. I was just wondering whether you still needed any input from me for your television programme. Ring me on this number. It's the same I gave you at lunch."

The man wanted to meet. Good. He would follow up when Caballero was dealt with.

Then the call had come in from Caballero.

Detecting that the meeting with the Prince had suddenly come to an end, the Director had allowed the convoy of cars to set off before tailing Caballero from a safe distance. Caballero had mentioned the Mantra, but he wanted to be sure.

At the hotel, noting that security seemed relaxed, he made his way to the rear staircase and checked that it'd take him to all floors. Learning Caballero's room number also proved relatively easy, the product of a hundred dollars exchanged between a Spanish gossip column journalist and a well-informed chambermaid. The young girl had also thrown in the bonus that Señor Caballero was just as likely to be found in the corner suite occupied by a Russian lady, Señorita Kalyagin.

"A wild one, that girl. But tips well. Very generous. Mind you, they get up to some things in there. Quite a lot of clearing up to do in the mornings."

Saturday, 26 July 2008 (PM) – LA BARRA, URUGUAY

Caballero's driver stopped first at the Mantra. A second car, carrying the two SIDE bodyguards from Buenos Aires, pulled in behind them.

"How about a drink?" Villanueva asked as he was getting out.

The last thing Caballero wanted was his co-negotiator discovering the presence of Tatyana.

"Great idea, but perhaps tomorrow. Something seems to have upset my stomach," he replied.

"Well, you can always have a Fernet Branca, if you don't feel like anything else."

"I don't know..."

Too late. Villanueva had already joined him by the steps to the hotel. To stop him now might not be such a good idea. These SIDE people came with so many agendas. Anyway, Tatyana might well be in her room watching TV. If she wasn't, he would have to hope she would be discreet.

Caballero and Villanueva walked into the lobby, one of the bodyguards going first, the other bringing up the rear. He saw no sign of Tatyana as he walked over to the reception, where the front desk handed him a small envelope. Tatyana fixing their next rendezvous in her suite. Good.

"I need a hot bath and a good night's rest," Caballero said, leading the way towards the bar. "Perhaps we won't make it too long."

And they didn't. Having signed the chit, Villanueva left for his downtown hotel, piqued by his taciturn colleague. Signalling his intentions to his two bodyguards, Caballero disappeared in the direction of the suites.

He had no reason to pay any attention to the man sitting in one of the lobby arm chairs reading a magazine. The Director had immediately detected the two bodyguards by their earpieces. Four of them. Then one of them left. Once his target was in his hotel room, the number would presumably come down to two.

The guards seemed to be in no hurry to finish their drinks, seemingly convinced that the level of threat was low. Not that they'd done much to check out the situation, apparently taking their steer from Caballero heading for the bar on arrival. The Director toyed with the idea of taking advantage of their continued presence in the bar. On reflection, better to neutralise them once they'd taken up position.

By this time, only the bodyguards remained in the lobby, having picked up their drinks, watching tennis on a flatscreen at the other end. The hotel staff were showing all the signs of hoping they'd soon head for their rooms.

Since both Caballero and Kalyagin had their rooms on the same floor, the Director wondered whether the guards would know which room to watch. Maybe they didn't even know about Señorita Kalyagin. He needed to check whether there might be more guards in place. Getting to the top floor of the annexe wouldn't pose a problem. Service stairways were a given in this type of hotel.

He ordered a large cognac. He needed an hour or so to go by, for everyone to settle down. Come on the scene too early, they might be anywhere.

"Supposed to be meeting someone here, but it's getting late. Hope nothing has happened to them," he confided to the barman. "I'll take it with me. That way you can close up if you want to."

On re-emerging into the hall, the two guards had disappeared. He sat down with some magazines in a corner of the lobby out of sight of reception.

Having allowed about an hour to go by, he slipped into the inner stairway linking all the floors and the wings of the hotel.

Sunday, 27 July 2008 (AM) – EDIFICIO MARTINEZ DE HOZ, BUENOS AIRES

The SIDE director's cell phone buzzed furiously at his bedside. Muñoz had only gone to bed two hours earlier. The *asado* laid on by one of his colleagues at their place out in the Nordelta gated community had ended around two, after which he'd taken another half hour to drive back to his house in San Isidro, full of Malbec, untroubled by the risk of police. His SIDE ID would look after that. He had finally staggered into bed at about three, even failing to respond to the overtures of his mistress, who'd finally fallen asleep by his side. She wasn't going to be in a good mood when she woke up.

"Who the hell rings at this hour," he growled.

"Señor Director. Forgive me for ringing you so early. We've had an incident."

"Who's that? Who's speaking?"

"It's Rios. Sent to guard Caballero. In Punta del Este."

Now he remembered. He had had Rios, along with his colleague Santos, in his office on the Friday afternoon to brief them, before they caught the plane to Uruguay the following day.

"What's happened?"

"There's been an incident."

"Yes, you've just said that! Get on with it! What's happened?"

"It's the assassin. He got into Caballero's suite. There was shooting."

"Caballero? Is he all right?"

"Yes, Señor Director. He's all right. But Santos was wounded. And also a Russian woman, Señorita Kalyagin. She was with Caballero when it happened. She was hit in the arm."

"And Santos? How is he? Was he shot?"

"No, he was knocked out. He still hasn't come round. Both in the clinic in town."

Muñoz was silent. What the hell was going on? How had the assassin found them? Could this Russian woman, who ever she was, be involved in some way? Things were out of control.

"Where is Caballero now? I need to speak to him."

"He's here at the clinic. Seeing to Santos."

Not to mention Tatyana. In fact, Caballero had shown no interest at all in the bodyguard, but was now sitting beside Tatyana's bed, as she slept, having been sedated after the operation to sew up the flesh wound.

"You have the number of the clinic?"

Rios gave him the number.

"Where are you now?" Muñoz asked him.

"I'm in the lobby of the clinic."

"You're supposed to be protecting Caballero," Muñoz snapped. "Find him straightaway and don't let him out of your sight. That's what I sent you there for. Not that that seems to have done any good."

"Si, Señor Director. At once."

"Prepare a report and have it on my mail within the hour. I'll fly over there as soon as I can get on a flight. And stick with Caballero."

Muñoz hung up and lay back against the pillow. Just what he needed! He toyed with waking up the presidential adviser. That young bastard would have no qualms about waking anybody at this hour. But first he needed more information.

He picked up the phone and dialled the number of his driver, to whom he'd given a free weekend.

"Cacho, sorry to wake you! Get over here to my place. I'll need you to take me to the office and then probably to the airport. I have to get over to Punta del Este today."

Cacho had been his driver in the army. He was used to taking orders.

He got up and made his way to the bathroom. A couple of large aspirins followed by a long hot shower.

By seven o'clock, having stopped to pick up a strong coffee on the way, his driver was dropping him off at the main entrance of the SIDE building. With the sun only rising in about an hour, Plaza de Mayo was dark and still. The duty officer waved to him as he came through the door.

"Thought you were planning a quiet weekend? Was the party out at Nordelta good?"

Muñoz nodded, as he pressed the button for the lift.

"Presume everybody was there. Would have liked to have made it. It's been dead here."

Again Muñoz nodded. The duty officer was known for being chatty. He could do without getting it today.

At his desk, he fired up his computer. Rios had sent the promised report. Muñoz hoped it would bear some resemblance to the reality of what had happened.

According to Rios, once Villanueva had left for his hotel, Caballero had gone up to his room. Neither of the bodyguards had suspected the existence of the Russian woman, Tatyana Kalyagin. Rios was relatively discreet, but could not conceal the fact that Caballero, on the basis of his subsequent enquiries, appeared to have spent a lot of time with this lady since arriving two days ago. The two guards had decided to take turns watching Caballero. Rios had gone to bed, setting his alarm to five thirty, in order to take over at six in the morning. Santos had posted himself near the entrance to the suites. At about two thirty in the morning, Rios had been wakened by the sound of shouting and, rushing upstairs to the top floor of the wing, had found Santos unconscious by the entrance. He hadn't even been able to draw his gun.

From the suite belonging to the Russian, Kalyagin, Rios had heard the voice of Caballero. On entering, he had found Caballero propping up the Russian woman on the bed, which was already extensively stained with her blood. There was also blood on the floor of the bathroom, where she had sought refuge when the killer had fired two bullets at her. Apparently the first had hit her in the arm, but, as she fell, the second had missed. At this point, the hotel security had also arrived, along with the night manager.

According to the version provided by Caballero to the manager and to the police when they arrived, he had been out on the balcony of the suite when the killer had come in. Being surprised by Kalyagin emerging from the bathroom, the killer had fired twice at her. Hearing her scream, Caballero had just had time to jump across onto the terrace of the next-door room, where he had hidden. Through the net curtains, he'd caught a glimpse of the killer looking for him, then climbing over the railing and lowering himself to the ground by the intervening balconies. Taking care not to be seen, Caballero had crawled to the edge of the balcony and, in the pale moonlight, had seen a man sprinting towards the perimeter of the hotel. He had been unable to provide any description, but, on the basis of further enquiries, it appeared the man had been sitting in the lobby much of the evening. The Uruguayan police were currently trying to obtain descriptions and any other information they could from the hotel staff that had served him, including the barman. They were also waiting for the CCTV to tell more, including anything about his car. The police would be interrogating Kalyagin when she woke up.

Rios promised to be in touch again as soon as he had more information.

Sunday, 27 July 2008 (AM) - PUNTA DEL ESTE, URUGUAY

The Director was biting into one of Uruguay's ubiquitous *chorizo* steak sandwiches in the cafe of an ANCAP petrol station on the Ruta Interbalnearia beyond Piriapolis, on his way to Montevideo. He was not best pleased with the night's work. Apart from the general messiness, he had only succeeded in knocking out a bodyguard and shooting, probably only wounding, a whore. Perhaps not quite any whore - a statuesque redhead. He had just caught sight of her impressive breasts silhouetted against the backlight of the bathroom, patent red thigh-high boots, a pair of handcuffs in one hand, what looked like a pistol in the other. Caught off guard, he had loosed off two silenced rounds through the door. Of Caballero, no sign.

He'd searched for him out on the balcony. The screams from the bathroom were growing louder and were bound to bring security within seconds.

The scenario he would leave behind might not be as tailor-made as some in his career, but with a bit player like the redhead, no one could accuse him of lacking imagination. Even more so when, on replaying the scene in his mind, he realised that the gun she was holding had been no more lethal than a strap on dildo! The headlines promised to be lurid.

Once in the garden, he had easily got out of the hotel grounds and made his way to his car parked on one of the side roads.

Driving from the hotel towards Punta del Este, he had passed two police cars and an ambulance racing in the opposite direction. Driving into town, he had spotted a large car park and a block of flats rising beyond it. Leaving his own car on the street and armed with a screwdriver from the toolkit, he slipped in amongst the cars and, crouching down out of sight, carefully unscrewed the number plates on a Peugeot similar to the one he had rented. Working fast, he slipped these in the place of his Argentine plates. Any police check he might run into would spot the discrepancy with the car's papers, but it would do for now.

As he sat drinking his coffee, a newsflash brought the breaking story of a violent attack at the Mantra Hotel in La Barra. Two people wounded, a man and a woman. So far, they were only showing archive footage of the hotel, but promised on the spot coverage within the hour. He decided to spin out his breakfast a little longer to see what they'd show. He strolled over to the bar and picked up a pile of newspapers.

Half an hour later, the news was updated. The two injured, an Argentine man and a Russian woman, had been taken to a clinic in Punta del Este. Names were withheld. Apparently neither of them was in serious danger. The interview with the hotel manager gave a brief outline of events and one of the Uruguayan police officers added that they were looking for a man between thirty and forty, possibly Spanish. When asked, he could provide no reason for the attack. Nothing had been stolen. The coverage switched to the front of the clinic where, according to another reporter, the local police were providing protection to the victims. Two police cars waited in the forecourt, their blue lights flashing. They were not being allowed to film inside the clinic.

On the basis of what he'd seen, the Director felt he could remain relaxed. The police were a long way from finding him. But what had he actually achieved? Who was the Russian woman and what was the connection? Presumably just one of Caballero's many whores. From his Beirut experience, he knew that some of the most beautiful and exotic prostitutes on the international circuit these days were Russian. And some of the most expensive. But no sign of Caballero. Should he now just disappear and put the whole episode down to experience or persevere in his attempt to eliminate him? Whatever might have happened overnight, Caballero presumably still needed to attend to his business with the Saudi Prince.

He was just getting up to pay for his breakfast at the counter when the news picked up the story again. The same journalist outside the clinic was reading from a medical bulletin from the doctor on duty. The Argentine was still unconscious, having received a serious blow to the back of the head. The butt of a SIG Sauer tended to have that effect. The Russian lady, whose name was now given as Tatyana Kalyagin, was said to be comfortable, with only a flesh wound in the arm. She was currently resting, but expected to make a complete recovery and leave the clinic the next day.

Behind the journalist, a couple of large Mercedes had drawn up. They looked familiar. Out of the second car stepped a woman, the door held open by the front passenger. By his wire, a bodyguard. The woman, in a dark blue coat and headscarf only partially concealing long blonde hair, pushed her way through the group of journalists into the clinic. The Mercedes resembling one of those being used by the Prince. Now he remembered. There had been a woman in the second group of cars.

Not wanting to engrave himself too deeply in the memory of the cafe waitress, it was time to move. Having paid, he drove out of the parking place and onto the main road, heading back towards Punta del Este. Attacking a member of the Saudi royal family would not be acceptable to the people in Baghdad, but he needed to have a clearer idea of how all these pieces fitted together.

The police would now be armed with a description of his appearance from the hotel lobby. He needed to shift to something more informal. Dark glasses. Something sporting. Cruising the streets in the centre of the town, he found a store selling sports clothes. A dark green padded jacket with a hood, more suitable to the winter slopes of Patagonia but still appropriate given the winter temperatures. Some black trousers to match.

"I'll wear them home. It's getting chilly out there," he said, stopping the sales girl from opening a carrier bag. Stepping out onto the street, he pulled up the hood.

The risks of returning to the hotel or visiting the clinic were high. Caballero would be heavily guarded or would have changed hotels and anybody enquiring after him was likely to be closely interrogated. The Russian woman, Tatyana, just as much.

Were the negotiations ongoing or aborted? A clear indication would be whether or not the Prince was still in residence.

Three quarters of an hour later, he was back at the spot from which he had seen the Prince's Mercedes leave. Through his binoculars, he could see that all the cars were parked in front of the house and that the perimeter guards were still in place, patrolling the outer fence. As he watched, a silver Mercedes SLK convertible appeared from the direction of the main gate and parked alongside the larger cars. From it stepped the blonde woman he had seen arriving that morning at the clinic. The guard's friendly greeting suggested that she was known to him. Judging by her appearance, more provocatively dressed now with huge dark glasses, a mass of blonde hair over a long coat of heavy brown leather tightly belted at the waist, the flash of a patent leather boot as she walked up the steps, she hadn't come to arrange the flowers! The press had reported that the Prince had come in the company of his wife. How the hell did a woman like this fit into the picture?

Five minutes later, the same blonde emerged onto the terrace on the lake side of the house, accompanied by another woman and the Prince. They settled down at a table, where they were served coffee by a manservant. The discussion appeared intense and from the body language it looked as though all three were on familiar terms with each other. He studied the second woman. In spite of her large dark glasses, unmistakable! That hairstyle and jawline were one in a thousand. Señorita Haidar! Last seen sharing a coffee with Flemming at Las Nazarenas! She had said she'd be in Uruguay. So what was going on? What was the connection between Flemming's assistant and the Saudis? And through the blonde, with the Russian girl and therefore with Caballero? And pushing the analysis farther, what of Flemming? Maybe the economist was much closer to the process than had at first appeared. The picture had suddenly grown far more complex. And far more promising.

At one point, when the Prince had got up to answer his cell phone, he detected a gesture of intimacy between Haidar and the blonde. Who was this woman?

However tempting the idea of taking a closer look at these two, he suspected he might be allowing himself to get distracted. His client in Baghdad had given him a simple remit. Dispose of Argentina's negotiators. What they did in their spare time was of only marginal interest. And a direct assault on any member of the Prince's entourage would almost certainly be condemned in Baghdad. Biting the Sunni hand that fed their groups was unacceptable.

Except, that in this case, the Haidar girl also had a connection with another name in Grunwald's notebook. Flemming.

He might fool himself that his reasoning was purely professional, but getting closer to Haidar might also resolve the issue of Flemming. He toyed with the idea of finding a way to bump into her as if by chance. But something told him that, even if such a meeting could be engineered, she wouldn't fall for it easily. After all, he was supposed to be concentrating on his reportage for Al Jazeera, not wandering the beaches of Punta del Este. An alternative would be trying to get a better understanding of the role of the Russian woman. Or even of the blonde who'd gone to the clinic. Where to start?

Absorbed by the small group on the terrace, he failed to notice he was not the only one observing the scene. From the edge of the wood, over to the west, a couple of agents from the SIDE team escorting the Argentine negotiators were also studying the Prince's residence. And as one of them traversed towards the edge of the property with his binoculars, he picked out the silhouette of the Director, engrossed in the movements around the villa. He nudged his companion and drew his attention towards the lone figure. The companion spoke quietly into his walkie-talkie.

The Director put down his binoculars and began to walk back towards his car. As he approached through the trees, he spotted two men standing beside the Peugeot. Security, judging by the walkie-talkies. He withdrew quietly into the trees and waited. One of them was talking into his radio, probably checking out the number plate. Judging by their civilian clothes, these were not local Uruguayan police. Perhaps members of the Prince's bodyguard. Or possibly Argentine security. From what he had seen of the previous day's meeting, it was clear that a measure of collaboration existed between the Prince's bodyguards and the Argentine surveillance team. From the Argentines to the Uruguayan police was probably but a step. He stayed hidden, preferring to wait until they left rather than brazen it out with them in a direct confrontation.

The time was fast approaching for a discreet return to Buenos Aires.

The two men finally walked away from the Peugeot and set off down the road towards the main gates to the villa. Once they were out of sight, he stepped out of the trees and, having checked they'd disappeared, climbed into the car and drove in the opposite direction, reckoning he'd soon find a side road to the main highway back to Punta del Este. Once he felt confident he was out of sight of any surveillance around the Prince's villa, he pulled over and quickly replaced the Argentine number plates. If anyone was on the lookout for him, they'd be looking for the Uruguayan numbers. These he threw into the bushes, before continuing on towards the sea.

But there was a detail he had failed to notice. All Argentine cars leaving the country were obliged to have their number plates etched into each window and the windscreen. A precaution against car theft, replacement glass considered a reasonable deterrent. One of the security men had spotted the discrepancy and radioed both numbers.

Sunday, 27 July 2008 (PM) – JOSÉ IGNACIO, URUGUAY

"This is terrible, Viktor Alexievich. How did this happen?" Carla exploded. "Who would attack her? And why? Was it a robbery at the hotel?"

Viktor Alexievich had woken her with the news.

"I'm trying to find out, but it seems somebody was trying to kill the Argentine she was with. It's my fault. These Latinos are too unpredictable. I should never have used her. But you know what she's like. Foolhardy. She was never meant to accompany him."

"One of your businesses, I presume?" Carla said, her tone matter of fact.

Viktor Alexievich paused.

"Yes."

Carla detected he wasn't going to tell her any more. No matter. With Sam on the other side of the negotiation, she already knew about Caballero. She always made it her business to know who her girls were serving. A more worrying factor was that this was likely to lead to a situation in which the spotlight of SIDE would move closer to her escort business than was desirable. Some damage limitation was in order.

"How is she?"

"She was lucky. A flesh wound. The bullet passed right through her arm, missing the bone. She'll be all right soon. She's tough. There's some Tartar blood in there somewhere. You can see it in her eyes."

"What do you want me to do? I can go and see her. What's the name of the clinic?"

"Yes, please go. I've also alerted our ambassador in Montevideo. An old friend of mine. He may go and see her as well. Make sure she has everything she needs."

"Sam is over here. Shall I take her along?"

"Why not? It might reconcile Tatyana to her. You may have detected they're not the best of friends. Such foolishness."

Carla wondered how sincere Viktor Alexievich was being about this. Like Sam, she had her doubts about Tatyana's agenda where she and Sam were concerned.

She waited until just after seven before calling Sam.

"Tatyana's been shot. At the Hotel Mantra."

Sam chuckled.

"Don't be unfriendly. She may not be your best friend, but no one deserves to be shot."

"No doubt in the company of Caballero. Teach her to meddle with people like that. He's bad news."

"Why don't you come and pick me up with one of the Prince's cars and we'll go and visit her this morning."

Sam was silent for a minute, trying to work out the balance of risks of being so visibly associated with Tatyana. In the minds of Caballero and his group, Tatyana should not, after all, have any links to people in the Prince's party.

"I think I'll let you go by yourself, if you don't mind, my love. I've got to be careful not to be seen too much in public. There are bound to be reporters. This kind of thing doesn't happen often in Punta del Este. At least, not out of season. I'll get a car to you, so you have some protection. You never know."

"You're probably right. You must be the best judge of your own security. I'll give her your regards nevertheless."

Carla had found Tatyana in surprisingly good spirits and delighted to be the centre of so much attention.

"You know, Carla, I've already been interrogated twice. I don't know who they are. One appeared to be Argentine, the other definitely Uruguayan police. Obviously wanted to know if I saw the attacker. The trouble is, I only saw him for a couple of seconds and the room was in darkness." She giggled. "I was all dressed up for my little Argentine friend. He couldn't wait for me to take the hell out of him. You'd have been proud of me."

Carla had to smile. Viktor Alexievich was right. This girl was tough.

Having checked that Tatyana had everything she needed, she made to leave to report to the Prince. On her way out, she was stopped by a Uruguayan police inspector, who asked for her identity. She produced her Swiss passport.

"Are you a friend of Señorita Kalyagin?"

"She visited me in Switzerland where I live. She told me she was coming to Punta del Este. And then I saw the news broadcast this morning."

"Do you have an address here?"

Carla saw no need to conceal the fact. Thanks to her lawyer, she'd almost certainly covered any trace of her former connection with Dávila. She gave him the address of the villa.

The police inspector appeared satisfied.

Watching her leave, one of the SIDE agents made a note of the exchange.

It was about eleven thirty by the time she got back to Calle 5. The phone was ringing. The Prince.

"What the hell's been happening?"

"It appears that an attempt was made on the life of the Argentine negotiator. He seems to have got away, but a girl he was with, who happens to be one of mine, was injured."

The Prince said nothing for a moment.

"You better get over here and tell us more."

An hour later, she had joined Sam and the Prince on the terrace looking out towards the lake.

"Mohammed has been in touch with Perez. He escaped an assassination attempt in the early hours of this morning at his hotel. And you say the girl he was with is one of your team? I sincerely hope I was going to get the benefit of anything she might find out."

He looked hard at Carla. She needed to be careful.

"She wasn't working for me, but I had an idea who she was with. She's the niece of my Russian partner. It was he who put her alongside the Argentine. No doubt in pursuit of some business deal."

The Prince thought for a moment.

"The Russians have been chasing the nuclear power plant contract for some time. Presumably connected with that."

He saw no reason to share more with Carla. He looked across at Mohammed.

"What do you make of all this? Is it wise to continue? Why should someone be targeting the Argentine team?"

"Perez let drop something about this not being the first attack of its kind recently. He sounded pretty nervous. My guess is they'll call off the meeting today."

"Better we do it first. I've had enough of my movements being dictated by these people. If they can't look after themselves, I doubt they can look after us. Call back Perez and tell him we're leaving, if not today then no later than tomorrow morning. No more meetings on this trip. Ask the pilots to get us the first flight plan they can. I'll ask you to stay behind for a day or two, whatever it takes to tidy all this up."

"Of course, Your Highness. That'll be no problem."

"I'll announce our departure to Farida. She'll be delighted to get back to the children."

He stood and called the two women to join him on the lawn.

"Anything that either of you can find out about what is going on would be helpful. I'm sorry about your girl," he added, looking at Carla.

"Don't worry, Your Highness, she's very resilient."

"I suppose your girls have to be."

He turned to Sam.

"Farida may suggest your joining us in London at some point. In the meantime, thank you for all your help. I'm sure this isn't the end of our discussions with the Argentines. There are bound to be more meetings. But, as far as I'm concerned, north of the Equator."

He embraced the two women and walked away towards the house.

"Perhaps you can stay on a day or two," Carla said.

"How long are you planning to be here?"

"About another week. Now that I've come, I can sort out a few more things."

"Probably better if you stay on this side of the river. Were you questioned this morning? At the clinic?"

"A Uruguayan policeman took my details. I told him I was a friend of Tatyana's, that she'd visited me in Switzerland."

"I should be careful, if I were you. Your visit probably won't have gone unnoticed by the Argentines. SIDE are crawling all over this place at the moment. Who knows whether they've really given up on Dávila."

Sam remembered Eduardo's remark over breakfast in May.

"Don't worry. As I told you, my lawyer has been closing down everything that might've tied me to that bastard. But I'll be careful, my love."

They began to stroll back arm in arm.

At that moment Sam's cell phone began to buzz. Leandro.

As they stood there, Carla could hear him asking about what had happened and whether Sam was safe.

"It's alright, Leo. I'm fine. I'll be back tomorrow evening or Tuesday morning. Don't worry, please, *mi amor*. I'm in good hands."

She heard him ask whether Sam meant Carla.

"Yes," Sam replied, keeping her voice as neutral as possible.

She hung up and looked at Carla, shrugging her shoulders.

"What do you expect? The man loves you. Of course he's worried."

"I know."

Sam looked up towards the house. She caught a glimpse of Farida waving to her.

"My client is calling."

Sunday, 27 July 2008 (PM) – PUNTA DEL ESTE, URUGUAY

Muñoz had arrived that afternoon and called together the three men in charge of the SIDE escort team covering Caballero and the negotiation. He had settled into the bar at the Hotel Conrad, reluctant to go to the Mantra. Principally because he had little desire to confront his Uruguayan counterparts who, he suspected, must now be out in force. Embarrassing questions about what was going on and what all these SIDE operatives were doing on their side of the river were best postponed as long as possible.

Rios, the report he had emailed earlier in one hand, began to rehearse the same story. Muñoz cut him short.

"Have you got anything new?"

Rios looked embarrassed, turning to another of his colleagues for support. The man, more confident than Rios, took a step forward.

"There are a number of items which may fit into what is going on."

Muñoz nodded to let him speak.

"Whilst two of our men were observing the Saudi villa this afternoon, they spotted another man doing the same. It wasn't possible to establish his identity, but others in our team found a Peugeot parked nearby, presumably his. They checked the plates with our Uruguayan police contact. They rang up the owner who denied being in the area, then called them back to say that his plates had been stolen. So it would be logical to assume that the person watching the villa was involved in last night."

"Window engraving?"

"Didn't match. An Argentine rental car. We've been in touch with the agency. Rented last week to an Argentine by the name of Mario Azoulay. Paid cash. So far the attempts of the Uruguayan police to find the car have failed. But they will certainly be vigilant around the Mantra and the Saudi royal's villa, in case another attempt is planned."

Muñoz had been taking notes.

"I presume they also took a description of the car, in case the driver is back on his original plates."

"Yes, but it's a dark blue Peugeot. There's a million of them."

"Have you alerted everyone back in Buenos Aires? In case he goes back?"

"We've put out an all services alert. Immigration included."

"Better be ready. We'll need to decide whether to pick him up straight away or watch him. People like that don't talk. We need to know if he's acting alone."

"As soon as we hear anything, I'll let you know."

"Anything else?"

The man hesitated.

"One thing. On Friday night, a day before the attack. It may not be important. We had stationed a couple of cars in the vicinity of the Prince's villa. At around 2am, one of the Prince's Mercedes drove out and headed down towards Punta del Este, then took a side road around Calle 5 to a private residence. The driver appears to have been the woman who sat in on the negotiations on the Prince's side. We're trying to find out who owns the house."

Muñoz toyed with his drink, swilling the ice cubes around in the whisky.

"Give me the address as soon as possible. I'll have it checked out at the office."

At that moment Caballero joined the party with Villanueva in tow. Muñoz was secretly pleased to see that Caballero's customary bravura had been dimmed by the events of the night. Instead of trying immediately to dominate the conversation, he slipped into a chair, ordering a whisky from the waiter, glancing around. Muñoz decided to take advantage.

"So, Martín, I'm glad to see you're still alive."

Without concealing a tinge of malice, he added, "And how is your companion in arms?"

Martín had the good grace to blush slightly, even under his tan.

"She'll recover," he said.

"I'm glad. Should I send her some flowers?"

Caballero shook his head.

"I'm sure that won't be necessary. She's already in good hands. The Russian ambassador in Montevideo is visiting her as we speak."

Muñoz took a large slug of his whisky to conceal his surprise. That the Argentine lead negotiator should have been caught in a compromising situation with someone worthy of a personal visit from a Russian ambassador didn't sound any too healthy. Caballero's sexual antics were nothing new to him, but his choice of partners was looking decidedly erratic. For the moment, he said nothing.

At around six that evening, Argentine immigration in Colonia picked up a certain Mario Azoulay catching the ferry to Buenos Aires.

Sunday, 27 July 2008 (PM) – BUENOS AIRES

The Director disembarked in the port of Buenos Aires from the Buquebus ferry. He had left the Peugeot in a quiet side street in Punta del Este and taken a long-distance taxi back to Colonia with all the returning weekenders. The absence of body scanners at either end had allowed him to pass the SIG Sauer undetected. His arrival would be the most risky bit, given the interest shown in the car. Although he had no way of knowing who the two men worked for, and had no evidence his Azoulay identity had been compromised, precautions were in order.

His experience of Buenos Aires traffic, particularly now it was dark and the Sunday crowds were heading home, meant he'd have to take anti-surveillance precautions on foot. Although usually able to spot followers in normal light and given enough time, on this occasion he must rely principally on his ability to lose them.

Emerging from the terminal, he began to walk up Avenida Córdoba in the direction of 9 de Julio. The traffic was heavy, which, as he climbed the slope towards Calle Reconquista, allowed him to cross the wide avenue through the slowly moving cars to the far pavement. No one crossed behind him. Reaching San Martín, he walked through the swing doors of Galería Pacífico, a multi-storey shopping mall with four main exits, and sprinted up an escalator to the next level. If his surveillance were professional and in sufficient numbers, they might have foreseen this and covered the entrance. The place was packed. Not ideal. Finding a cafe near one of the far corners, he sat down, ordered an espresso and pulled out the newspaper he'd picked up on the ship. Staying still when surrounded by a constantly changing crowd sometimes served to make a follower stand out, simply because they never disappeared completely from the field of view. For fifteen minutes, he watched those around him, but no one stood out.

He paid for his coffee, picked up his bag, and left his newspaper behind on the table in full sight. A good follower would either remain in place to see if it was picked up by an accomplice, or pick it up like another customer looking for something to read with their coffee, in case it contained some form of message. As he wandered round the shops, he watched out of the corner of his eye. The waitress finally came and cleared everything away without anybody intervening. Emerging onto Florida, a major pedestrian artery overrun with cheap souvenirs for tourists, he chose the most crowded side and began to head for the centre of town. Seeing an ill-lit shopping arcade, he walked briskly through it, emerging on a quiet side street. Any follower would have had to sprint around the building to see him come out. Again no sign. The traffic was thinner here and, watching the stream of slow cars, he chose the last in a series of empty taxis, instructing the driver to head towards Avenida Corrientes.

An hour and a half later, having taken a couple more taxis and a bus, he felt safe enough to make his way back to his hotel in Once. He might have failed to spot the surveillance, but he felt confident he'd lost them. The hotel manager greeted him like a long lost friend.

"Have I have had any visitors or calls?"

"No, nothing. All quiet, Señor Azoulay."

Monday 28 July 2008 (PM) – CASA ROSADA, BUENOS AIRES

On landing at Aeroparque next morning, Muñoz was met by his two assistants with a SIDE car.

"Take me through it again. *Carajo!* It's a fucking disaster!"

"It was going very well, until it wasn't. He got off the Buquebus ferry at around 7pm. All systems on alert. The immigration official who'd spotted him was travelling with him, to point him out to our team on arrival. Then we lost him."

"How is that possible? Is he that fucking invisible?"

"The consolation is we got an up-to-date photo, as he sat drinking coffee in Galería Pacífico."

"Well, we know Caballero's wounded playmate too, and her relations with the Russian ambassador in Uruguay. The bad news is the Saudi team have decided to terminate the discussions."

"Maybe they'll continue at long range?"

"It hardly seems relevant now. Any way you look at it, it's a bloody mess. Caballero's sexual antics are of minor importance, however ill-judged. The reality is that although he got away with his life, it was a very close thing, and our failure to protect him is just another nail in our coffin. Losing Azoulay or Aboukir – or whatever we call him – is the worst of it. I'll have to report all this to the Casa Rosada adviser, who hasn't left me in peace since the story first broke. I've a meeting with him late this afternoon, so we'd better get our story straight."

He looked at them, in the hope that someone might have some positive news.

"Have you been able to find out who was trying to track Aboukir through immigration? From one of the *Comisarías*?"

They shook their heads.

"It seems to have been done through one of the secretarial terminals and we haven't yet been able to identify who was using it."

"It's more than a coincidence, to my mind. It means someone was alerted to the name Aboukir even before we were. That should never happen. We shouldn't have some idiot policeman getting ahead of us. As soon as you know who it is, we'll get him in."

As he was climbing out of the car, he turned to one of his assistants.

"You were involved in the Dávila investigation, weren't you?"

The man nodded.

"I came in on the tail end of it."

"When they found his body up in the Delta, in that strange coffin, they also found his laptop, didn't they?"

"That's right. There's a file on their findings."

Dávila had been a senior adviser to SIDE up until the time of his death. His body had been discovered enclosed in an inflatable rubber bodybag, his appearance bearing all the hallmarks of extreme fetishist sex. Clutched in his arms, his laptop. Muñoz knew its contents had revealed that Dávila, amongst other things, had been running a highly complex and lucrative blackmail operation.

"Wasn't there some connection with real estate in Uruguay?"

"There was, but I'm not sure how far we were able to take it. He used a lot of shell companies, in Panama and the Cayman Islands, to hide that sort of thing. But it certainly looked like it."

"If I were to give you an address north of La Barra, might you find a trace of it?"

His assistant looked unsure.

"We can try."

Muñoz passed him a piece of paper with Carla's address.

"Tell me if you find anything on this. OK, that's all for now. Better get myself ready for my meeting across the road."

Muñoz had occasionally worked with Dávila. He had detested the man, who had made little secret of his contacts with the current Presidential entourage, many of them drawn from the guerrilla movements of the 1970s. Muñoz wondered to what extent any of these had learned that Dávila had betrayed them at the time of the 'dirty war'.

Another source of irritation was the fact that, like the political appointees imposed on SIDE by Kirchner, Dávila had been allowed to keep his own name. No professional pseudonym like all other agents, Dr Dávila had remained Dr Dávila, as if the transparency somehow made him superior to his colleagues. An impression he had been happy to foster at every opportunity.

Muñoz had shed no tears when Dávila's body had been discovered up river. Ever since, deep down, he had nurtured a desire to find out more, to find the entrance into Dávila's secret world. He had always silently opposed the decision not to pursue the case, imposed by those in the Casa Rosada who feared collateral damage to current senior figures in government. Perhaps this address might provide another key. A backdoor key.

Not surprisingly, the meeting at the Casa Rosada did not go well.

"What am I supposed to report about all this, Inspector Muñoz? It seems to have been mishandled all the way down the line. I haven't met this man Caballero, but I know he has friends in very high places," the young man added, casting a meaningful glance towards the presidential apartments. "Someone needs to talk to him. But worse than that, your men, not content with allowing this killer to get within an inch of our lead negotiator, when handed the killer on a plate, allow him to vanish!"

The adviser took a step closer.

"Why was he not just picked up on arrival? There was always a risk you would lose him."

"We opted for surveillance. If he had accomplices, just picking him up would not have solved the problem. These people don't talk."

The adviser shot him a quizzical look.

"With all the techniques your people practised during the *dictadura*, I don't find that reply very convincing."

These Camporistas were always quick to remind people of their much vaunted human rights credentials.

Muñoz had no answer to that one.

The Presidential adviser handed him a collection of photographs from a jihadist website.

"What do we make of this?"

Poor quality, clearly taken at the murder scenes of Sanchez, Morales and Grunwald. Muñoz studied them carefully. He looked up at the adviser.

"Where do they come from?"

"The American embassy sent them round a couple of days ago. Apparently put out by a Sunni terrorist movement based in Iraq. Go by the name of Sons of Ibn Taymiyyah."

The back of the photographs carried a translation of the Arabic:. "Justice done to those who aid the Shia dogs!"

"Not that we needed it, confirmation that this is an orchestrated campaign," Muñoz muttered.

"At least we know this comes from Iraq. Not that that helps us much."

Muñoz shook his head.

"You can have those copies, for what they're worth."

"Don't suppose the *Yanquis* could be persuaded to be a bit more helpful…"

"Not a chance. Not after what your people in SIDE did a few years ago, blowing the face of the CIA station chief across the newspapers! It was good of them to go this far. Anyway, my boss would never contemplate asking them a favour. So, when is Caballero back? If he values his life, we'd better make sure we protect him properly. We can't rule out another attempt. And this man Aboukir. Put all the resources you've got into finding him. Fast. In the meantime I'll have to see how all this is presented higher up. I'll need to speak to your boss. This isn't going to look good for your service."

Muñoz was tempted to point out that part of the problem lay in the calibre of the people entrusted with such delicate international missions. The unwavering Presidential preference for a limited number of close friends and associates, with whom they trusted their affairs and who seemingly could do no wrong, was always likely to blow up in their faces at some point. They were always in such a hurry. Loose ends all over the place. But he thought better of it. That kind of remark, added to everything else that had gone wrong, could reap a rapid transfer to one of the more insalubrious outposts of the SIDE empire.

Monday 28 July 2008 (PM) – CALLE 5, LA BARRA, URUGUAY

"You should be careful, Sam. Your proximity to the Saudis could get you into trouble. Serious trouble. With your government, I mean. Have you thought about that?"

Sam looked at her. The expression on Carla's face had given way to something almost maternal. She found it slightly unnerving, hinting at a very different dimension in their relationship. Not for the first time, Sam was struck by the faint sensation that, in Carla and Leandro, she might subconsciously be looking for more than just a love partner. The physical, the cerebral... and perhaps something else.

She shook her head and looked out at the sea through Carla's huge picture window. A thought for another day.

"Don't worry," she smiled, "I'm aware of it."

But Carla was not to be deterred so easily.

"Do you think the Argentine negotiators have worked out who you are?"

"I don't think so. At least I hope not. They have me under another name. I agreed that with the Prince right at the start. They know me as Harari. As far as I know, they don't even suspect that I speak Spanish, let alone that I'm Argentine. And I've taken every precaution to avoid being photographed. Just in case."

"For the little *that's* worth," Carla laughed. "For Christ's sake, Sam, you don't exactly disappear into the crowd. What would happen if you bumped into a member of their negotiating team on Calle Florida?"

"Not a chance! I never set foot in that vulgar shopping precinct."

"You know what I mean."

It was Sam's turn to laugh.

"Their lead negotiator, Caballero, practically propositioned me the other night. Except that, thanks to one of your wonderful masks, there wasn't a hope in hell he could recognise me. Not with everything else I was wearing. That beautiful silver dress, the latex one you chose for me. Along with a massive black wig. You should have seen the look on his face. On Leandro's too, come to that."

Carla looked at her quizzically.

"And what does your man make of all that? His scene?"

Sam's expression clouded over.

"I'm not sure. Judging by his performance, he finds me sexy in that stuff. But on the other hand, he's also confused. He has trouble in adjusting to my different roles. Dalal in Zürich, a fetish doll in Buenos Aires. Somewhere, deep down, there's a streak of the conservative in him."

"I'll bet there is. Thank God. It's what you need, to control you just a little bit."

Sam nodded.

"I suppose you're right. For the time being anyway."

"I don't like that remark. He's one of the few people who can protect you from yourself. Never forget that."

"Like you, my love."

Sam got up from the table and stood behind Carla, resting her hands on her shoulders. Carla tilted her head back and looked steadily at Sam, who finally averted her eyes and looked out again towards the sea.

After a moment, she walked over to the window and sat on the ledge, pressing her cheek against the cool of the glass. These moments of calm were so precious.

"I'll be off tomorrow, back to Buenos Aires. I'll miss you. Zürich is so far away. In fact, Argentina is so far away. Far from the rest of the world."

Too far from Europe, from Carla, from Sophie. And from so many things which, in spite of her love for Argentina, not to mention Leandro, she needed. Perhaps someday…

Carla rose from the table.

"Don't worry. I'll miss you terribly as well. Come on. Let's go to my room. I've got a few new toys for you."

Tuesday, 29 July 2008 (NOON) – AEROPARQUE, BUENOS AIRES

No sooner had Tatyana passed immigration at Aeroparque in Buenos Aires and collected her suitcase, then she felt a hand on her arm and was politely led, protesting, by the SIDE agent into a small office in the main building.

"Señorita Kalyagin, we have a few questions we would like to put to you," the taller of the two men said, gesturing in the direction of a metal armchair in front of a grey steel desk. "Please sit down."

Tatyana, initially at a loss, quickly recovered her self confidence.

"I am staying with the Russian ambassador here in Buenos Aires, I would have you know."

She stood up, a full ten centimetres taller than her interrogator.

"We know that. You provided his address on your immigration form, Señorita Kalyagin. But you do not, as far as we know, have diplomatic status."

"As far as I know, I don't need it. I haven't done anything. Why are you detaining me?"

"We are not detaining you, Señorita Kalyagin. We merely want to ask you some questions."

The man's tone of voice remained steadfastly polite, unthreatening.

"Please sit down, Señorita Kalyagin. You will be more comfortable."

"Can we get you a glass of water?" said the second man, "Or perhaps a coffee?"

Tatyana began to relax. She turned and, having shrugged the long fur coat off her shoulders, revealing her arm in its sling, settled herself in the chair which the first man was now holding for her. In so doing, she couldn't resist a slight sway of her hips, tossing her hair out of her face. From the expression of the man who had offered her the drink, the effect was not completely lost.

"A coffee. Please."

"You've just come in from Punta del Este. That's correct?"

The first man sat on the side of the desk in front of her while his colleague went in search of a coffee.

She nodded.

"Where I believe you suffered an unfortunate accident," he continued, indicating her arm. "Very frightening, I'm sure."

"I'm fine."

"I'm glad. Most unfortunate. It's my understanding that you were in the company of a certain Señor Caballero at the time. Is that correct?"

Tatyana could see little reason to deny it.

"You met... here? In Buenos Aires?"

"Yes."

"I see. How long ago would that have been?"

Tatyana paused. Where was this line of questioning going? She needed to be careful to ensure that there was no blowback to Viktor Alexievich.

"Sometime in June, as I recall."

"In what circumstances?"

"At a cocktail party at the Russian embassy. I can't remember the date."

"To which you had also been invited, of course."

"Of course. As I said, I am staying with the ambassador. I'm an old friend of his daughter."

"And your trip to Punta del Este, Señorita Kalyagin. Was that your idea? Or Señor Caballero's?"

"He invited me to accompany him. I understand he had business meetings. I didn't know Punta del Este. I'd been told it was a lovely place, so I accepted."

The man nodded.

At this point, his colleague reappeared with three cups of coffee on a small tray.

"The machines weren't working. I had to go to one of the cafes."

"And now, Señorita Kalyagin? How long will you be staying in Buenos Aires?"

Tatyana looked deliberately vague as she took her coffee.

"I don't know. As long as the ambassador will have me."

She smiled. The line of questioning appeared fairly innocuous. They seemed more interested in Caballero's motives than her own. She could imagine all manner of interpretations and speculation surrounding what Argentina's lead negotiator got up to in his spare time.

"Juan, please place Señorita Kalyagin's suitcase on the desk. You don't mind if I open it?"

She shrugged her shoulders, adopting an expression of total disinterest. She only hoped he was fairly broadminded.

"Please."

"Could you pass me the key, please, Señorita Kalyagin?"

She rummaged in her handbag and passed it over.

"Thank you."

The man who had been addressed as Juan carefully unlocked the large Vuitton suitcase. Initially, he appeared only to be discreetly moving the top layers aside, but by the time his search had uncovered her favourite pair of red PVC thigh boots, as well as at least one large black rubber dildo, his search became somewhat more diligent. Delicately, he laid the items on the desktop, where they were soon joined by a whip, a leather corset, two pairs of handcuffs and a small assortment of chains. Not to mention a ballgag.

Tatyana watched, impassively.

The first man, who had been observing the growing collection of gadgets, finally turned to her.

"And all this?"

"What of it?"

"Do you always travel with such items?"

"Certainly."

He raised an eyebrow.

"To my knowledge, there is no law against it," she added.

"No," he said, drawing out the word. "Perhaps a little unusual?"

She smiled.

"The new, liberated woman," she stated evenly. "Perhaps there are fewer of them in Argentina. But in my home country…" She left the sentence unfinished. "You should come to Russia someday," she added as an afterthought.

The look in his eye suggested the possibility had not escaped him.

He turned to Juan.

"Please replace everything as you found it, Juan. We will not be detaining Señorita Kalyagin any further."

He took a step towards Tatyana.

"That'll be all, Señorita Kalyagin. For the time being."

"I can go?"

"Of course. However, after your last misadventure, you may wish to reconsider your relationship with Señor Caballero. For your own safety, of course."

She suspected that he wasn't thinking only of another attack from the unknown assassin.

Having repacked the suitcase and locked it, Juan handed her back the key.

"Please, let us find you a taxi."

Tuesday, 29 July 2008 (NOON) – PASAJE DE LA PIEDAD, BUENOS AIRES

Sam's plane from Punta del Este landed a couple of hours after Tatyana.

Having dropped her bags at her flat and changed into her black leather jeans and biker jacket, she went down to the garage under her building. Lovingly she removed the Harley's dustsheet. Pulling on her helmet, she turned the key. The Harley's throaty burble such irresistible magic.

Sam rode first to Once to report to her Mossad contact on the events of the weekend. Although the young man made careful note of what she told him, she came away with the impression that the attempt on Caballero had not come as a surprise.

From there, she went round to Leandro's flat. The look of relief on his face was instant. The Argentine press and television was still trying to make sense of the story, clearly oblivious to the identity of the real target and Caballero's activities with the Saudi Prince. *Página 12*, a daily renowned for its investigative journalism, but also for its proximity to the Kirchner line, was beginning to scratch the surface. The latest story on their website alluded to rumours that some kind of security operation had been mounted in Punta del Este over the last few days. The reasons for this were still not apparent, but the journalist was clearly trying to pull the threads together. Perhaps all would finally be made to lead to a red herring.

Sam read the story on Leandro's computer.

"They're digging hard. Wonder how long before the real story breaks."

"I suspected as much," Leandro said. "Our killer. Moved across the river? Though this time, he seems to have missed."

"Not entirely. Sadly for your nocturnal girlfriend. But she'll pull through. You should have taken up my suggestion that she come out to the island with you."

"Bitch. The poor girl didn't deserve to get shot."

"Who says? Don't worry. She'll recover quickly and be in fighting form for you."

"You talk too much."

Leandro pulled Sam towards him and kissed her hard. She sensed tension in the pressure of his embrace.

"What's wrong?" she asked.

Before he could reply, the buzzer from the entrance to the *Pasaje* sounded in the kitchen.

"It's Eduardo. Says he has some news."

Leandro let him in.

"A bit early for a drink. Coffee?"

"No, thanks. I'm in a hurry. But I just wanted to give you the latest."

"Go ahead."

Eduardo shot a glance at Sam. Why was this girl always around at these moments?

"Fonseca dropped by my office about two hours ago. He'd been to another meeting at the Casa Rosada. Couldn't resist telling me about it. Your man Aboukir is the focus of everyone's attention. Seems to be the person who attacked the Argentine at the Mantra Hotel on Sunday morning. They spotted him and the car he was driving. In spite of everything, he returned here Sunday night and got away from the surveillance SIDE had put on him when he came off Buquebus. Useless lot! Certainly seems to be a professional killer. Also goes under an Argentine identity, Mario Azoulay. Fonseca gave me a photo. Every man on the street has been given one."

He passed the photo to Leandro. Sliding her large dark glasses onto the top of her head and pressing her head against the side of his, Sam looked over Leandro's shoulder.

"Yes, that's the man I had lunch with."

"Didn't I tell you?" Sam murmured, ill-concealing a note of triumph.

"So you were there too?" Eduardo looked at her, surprised. "You didn't tell me that, Uncle."

"Sorry. But it didn't seem relevant."

Eduardo saw little purpose in saying what he thought about Sam's unflinching capacity to be in the proximity of his godfather whenever trouble loomed.

"Anyway, you'd better not accept any more lunch invitations. See you. Have a meeting."

Having closed the front door behind him, Leandro turned to Sam.

"At least you didn't mention what you knew about Tatyana."

"No point."

"You're right. Where d'you think we go from here?"

Sam thought for a moment.

"What do you think?"

"Chances are that Aboukir may have little cause to suspect us. Trouble is, I left him a voicemail last Saturday."

Sam looked at him, an anxious expression on her face.

"Was that a very good idea? Why?"

"In some ways, I wanted to smoke him out. And it makes me nervous just to sit and wait for somebody."

"Well I'm back, Leo. No more waiting."

Leandro laughed.

"Never miss a chance to turn a phrase to your advantage, do you? I wasn't actually thinking about you."

"Exactly. Can't allow that state of affairs to continue. Come here."

For once, Leandro decided to play hard to get.

"No. You can wait a bit. Anyway, you haven't told me what happened yet. How was the Princess?"

Yes, the situation must be getting to him. The look in his eye suggested she would be wise to play along.

She sat down.

"I'll have that coffee."

From the kitchen, Leandro called out to her.

"Go on. What happened? I can hear you from here."

"I saw Alejandra. And Nouria. Yesterday."

Leandro came back into the drawing room.

"How are they? Did you get any idea what they think they're doing?"

"Two girls in love. And for the time being, that's all that matters to them."

Leandro nodded.

"Any plans?"

"Not at this stage. They just want to be together. Nouria clearly needed to get away from the pressure of her parents."

"So nothing much we can do from this end. Is that it?"

"I would say so."

For the time being, Sam had decided not to tell Leandro that, to help the two girls, she had given them the keys to her father's house.

Without a word, Leo went back into the kitchen. He would pass on the news to Elena, who would not be pleased. They would have to be patient.

"And what about everything else?" he asked as he brought Sam her coffee.

"It was all pretty messy. The Argentines very frustrating. The Prince didn't appreciate their behaviour very much. In fact there was only one meeting before the attack. After that, the Saudis decided to pack it in for the time being."

"And the Princess?"

"As demanding as ever. Carla was there too."

"Yes, I saw her on TV arriving at the clinic. Presumably to see Tatyana. Is Carla sticking around?"

"Not sure. She sends you her love. You know she's a great admirer of yours."

Leandro laughed. Sam noted the tone of pleasure where, in earlier days, it would have been loaded with scepticism.

"I'm sure you sent her mine."

"Of course. She seems to think you're good for me. Save me from myself."

"I do my best, but at times, it seems more like mission impossible."

"Rather like getting you to make love to me today," Sam muttered as he brought a coffee.

"All in good time, Señorita."

She watched him deliberately choose to sit on a chair by his worktable.

"What have I got? Some contagious disease?"

"Quite a good definition of love, come to think of it," he replied, grinning. "Fortunately, I've been vaccinated. Though I'm just beginning to detect that my vaccination may be wearing off."

"I'm afraid nurse Haidar is going to have to take a look."

Finishing her coffee, she stood up and walked over to him, pulling down her glasses.

"It's my understanding that the first signs of the disease are to be found in the region of the groin. Rather like the Black Death."

"Given the way you're dressed, an appropriate image, if I may say so."

He thought for a moment, as if making some mental calculation.

"It seems to have taken exactly six hundred and sixty years to come back."

"This is a more virulent strain, you'll see."

The ensuing blowjob proved to be merely the incubation period.

Wednesday, 30 July 2008 (AM) – JUNÍN Y LAVALLE, BUENOS AIRES

Research assistant? Like hell. Not the way they looked at each other, the Director thought.

He was sitting with a coffee in his hotel lounge in Once.

But where did that put Flemming? And the Saudi Prince?

Either way, he needed to move. It wouldn't take anyone long to trace his car. From last night, they probably had his photo and were at this very moment hawking it round every hotel in the area.

Hamid's flat was an option, but since he had instructed him to leave Buenos Aires, he must conclude that it'd be watched.

He could contact the people in Baghdad or even Foz do Iguaçu to see whether there were any other members of the group he might approach. But he remained wary of them.

The sight of the young hotel waitress coming towards him to sign the chit sent his ideas off at a tangent. A woman. It was going on for a week since his last visit to Sonia. Sonia? For the right amount of money, she might accept a temporary lodger.

He went over to the phone cubicle in a corner of the lobby.

"Sonia? How are you? Good, I'm glad. I was wondering whether I might come and see you. It's fairly urgent."

He joined in her laughter at the other end.

"Yes, I know. We men are terrible. In an hour and a half? You've got a client at the moment? I'll be there."

That gave him just enough time to clear up everything in his room and check out. Other than his name, he must make sure to leave no trace when the police came to call.

Speaking loudly enough for the benefit of the hotel manager, who had solicitously carried his bags outside onto the pavement, he told the taxi driver to go to the airport. As they rounded the corner, he suddenly 'remembered' that he must first pick up something at a friend's house five blocks away. The look on the driver's face reflected the loss of the fare as far as Ezeiza.

"Sorry about that. Here, take twice the fare."

"*Muchas gracias, Señor.*"

Having watched the taxi disappear down the street, he walked the three blocks to Sonia's building.

An hour later, as Sonia began to dress again to receive a client genuinely coming for some massage, he had got what he wanted. On both fronts.

For a hundred dollars a day, Sonia was delighted to place her small spare bedroom at his disposal. She had also been happy to give him the key to the back door. No questions asked. She was a sufficiently good observer of human nature to guess that this attractive man, whose sexual tastes at times verged on the perverse, must have some good reason for wanting to go to ground. In this part of town, nothing unusual in that. On that basis alone, in answer to his questions, she had been economic with the truth when denying that any of her clients might have connections with the police. How could it be otherwise? Her legitimate physiotherapy practice had no real need of such arrangements. But the word 'massage' had connotations everywhere in the world. And, in order to be left in peace, the Deputy Comisario from around the corner could count on a weekly session. Om the house, of course. Anyway, he was a kindly man who always sent her a couple of bottles of good Argentine champagne at Christmas. Not all her clients were as thoughtful.

As she pulled on her thin white overall, her concession to professionalism, she turned to him as he lay on her bed. An amused smile on his lips, he was watching her as she struggled to close the buttons over her opulent contours. Massage was hard work and she never wore much underneath.

"So, Mario, I've got to leave you now. There goes the buzzer."

"Your next client?"

"If you're hungry, we can always make the arrangement full board. There's some food in the fridge. Help yourself. I'm booked up now until about seven this evening. See you then."

"That's kind. Thank you."

He threw her a kiss. She had a warm, likeable personality. Like so many of these Argentines. He only hoped that, by staying with her, he would not get her into trouble. Or have to dispose of her himself.

He heard the front door opening and Sonia greeting her client.

He propped himself up on the pillows. If they had photographed him, better to spend the daylight hours off the streets.

Time to think.

Score to date. Three targets down, one knee capping and one failed attempt. In financial terms, nearly a hundred and fifty thousand dollars in his bank account in Switzerland. He had checked from Uruguay. Expenses? Not much more than ten thousand dollars. A reasonable piece of business for just over three months work. The Sons of Ibn Taymiyyah had made it clear that, within reason, it was his call when to stop. If the objective had been to send a message to the Argentine government that their collaboration with the Iranians was misguided, he had arguably fulfilled his mission. Although his professional pride might have taken a knock with the Mantra failure, the client would be satisfied. Even a failed attempt had a positive impact. The Argentine negotiating team must be feeling increasingly exposed. Even the Iranians might be getting worried.

Had the time come to call a halt and get out of the country in one piece? It came down to the efficiency of Argentine intelligence and police. Leaving aside the risk of being physically identified, he would need a new persona. Only one remained.

Another fifty thousand dollars. Tempting. A couple of months of good living somewhere away from it all.

And he didn't like ending an assignment on a failure.

Spin a coin? A trick he had learned in the United States. As a Muslim, your fate depended on the will of Allah. Not on the aerodynamics of a piece of metal. Anyway, it might come down the wrong way.

Flemming. How long would it be until the security system alerted him to the danger? His window for action was probably small, particularly if this economist really did have a connection with the Argentine negotiation.

Tuesday, 29 July 2008 (PM) – PASAJE DE LA PIEDAD, BUENOS AIRES

"So, Leo, what are you going to do?"

An hour or so later, Sam and Leandro were sitting on the rug in front of the fire, the usual glass of Zacapa rum adding to the warmth of the flames.

"I'm not sure. He must have got my message last Saturday. He didn't ring back then."

"Not surprising. He was busy shooting up Tatyana. And since then, presumably trying to avoid getting caught. I mean, he must have an idea they're onto him. In fact, it wouldn't have surprised me if he had pulled out. Strange that he's come back here."

"Yes, you'd have thought it easier to escape from Uruguay."

"Which makes me think he's got another target. And I don't want to depress you by saying who."

"Don't worry. I'd worked that one out for myself."

Sam stretched out her hand and stroked his face.

"Poor Leo. Target of an assassin and only little me to protect him."

"It's no laughing matter. And anyway, luckily, there's a bit more than just you."

"Albert?"

"Yes. He's on call."

"Won't be much use if Aboukir decides just to break in unannounced."

"My guess is he won't. With Albert, we've been analysing his modus operandi. Or 'MO' as Albert likes to call it."

"And?"

"From what I've been able to pick up from Eduardo, it seems he likes to put together something of a scenario. Apparently the diplomat in Brussels, as well as poor Luis Miguel, and also Grunwald - all of them killed at the end of some kind of sexually perverted session. To make their deaths particularly lurid."

"That doesn't sound very reassuring. And what about what happened at the Mantra?"

"You tell me. Did you get anything from Tatyana?"

"She told Carla that Aboukir simply walked into their bedroom and, just as she was coming out of the bathroom, all dressed up to give Caballero a good time, he shot at her."

"Well, having seen Tatyana perform, admittedly not dressed up as you call it - in fact the exact opposite - I can imagine he might have been scared."

"According to Tatyana, she was holding a large strap-on in one hand."

"Then I'm not surprised he shot at her," Leandro said with a smile. "Come to think of it, that would have been quite a scenario for him."

"Stop daydreaming about Tatyana, Leandro."

His grin grew wider.

"Could be fun," he added. "Even a compensation for being the target."

The look on Sam's face warned him that it was her turn to be losing her sense of humour.

"By the way, did I ever tell you what she thinks of you and Carla? She clearly doesn't like you two."

"Tell me something I don't know. Anyway, I don't want to waste any more breath on her. Back to Aboukir. Let's be serious. If he rings you, what are you going to do? It's not up to you to try to catch this assassin. That's SIDE's business. Or the police."

"In theory, of course you're right. But, somehow, I do feel involved. If we're right, this man killed two of my friends, Luis Miguel and Carlos. I'd like to help catch him."

Sam was watching him closely. What was going through his mind? In spite of his rugby and the Malvinas, he couldn't really be described as a man of action. Yet she was sure that, if the cause was in his eyes worthy enough, he might stop at nothing.

"Leo. What are you thinking? Don't be foolish."

He looked at her. She saw something in his eyes that had not been there a minute earlier. His jaw set hard.

"Leo. Please."

She caught herself almost pleading.

He smiled at her.

"Don't worry, Sam. Just thinking."

"What are you thinking, *mi amor*. I tell you, this really isn't your business."

"Is Islam your business?"

"What do you mean?"

"You know what I mean. You're prepared to take risks for something you believe in."

She said nothing.

"That might have been you, Sam. In the room with Caballero. Don't deny it."

She shook her head. He was right of course. Perhaps not with Caballero, but in principle.

"If there's some way I can help catch this bastard, I'm prepared to try."

Sam sat still, staring into the fire. Her brain was clearly in overdrive. He waited.

"I can understand that. But you have to think it through. Not just the risks. The whole context."

"Go on," Leandro replied slowly.

"This isn't just a killer on the loose. This is a man with a clear agenda. Taking on something which also has a clear agenda. The Argentine government. The presence of SIDE in Punta, however useless it may have turned out to be, is evidence of that. And we can't entirely forget Tatyana and her boss."

"I see that. So?"

"Well, to begin with, half the Argentine security services must be looking for Aboukir or Azoulay or whatever his name is. Whether the Russians are involved, I don't know. But Viktor Alexievich is unlikely to take it lying down. That's not his style. The way he rescued me from Dávila proves that."

"Something like that had occurred to me."

"Whereas we might expect Viktor Alexievich, for various reasons, to be on our side, I don't think I would feel so confident about our own government. Let's suppose you can in some way deliver up Aboukir. They're not just going to thank you and buy you lunch. Inevitably, they're going to crawl all over you. At the very least, they're going to ask you how you got involved. Even if you say that Aboukir contacted you, they're going to want to know why. What is it that he saw in you that they haven't yet? Given your assignment for Frobisher, you can't afford that."

"Why are you so fucking intelligent?"

"Which means that, if you're really determined to do something, you're going to have to try and remain invisible. You can't be around when they find him. Alive or dead."

She paused.

"Who alive or dead? Me or Aboukir?"

"Are you actually thinking of killing Aboukir? Yourself?"

Leandro shook his head.

"Obviously, not if I can avoid it. I'm not trained for that."

"But Albert is. Isn't he?"

"Of course. But Frobisher have made it clear that none of this must be seen to have a British connection. In any way."

"Which suggests that we either find a way to kill Aboukir unattributably, or--"

"I see you're even getting familiar with the spy's vocabulary," Leandro interrupted.

"Or..."

"Or what?"

"Or we have to do it in such a fashion that we're not around when the Argentines finally catch up with him. Maybe even not have any direct contact with Aboukir. Just in case, when they do catch him, he drops your name or mine. If this is all about stirring up trouble, throwing names at his interrogators could have that effect."

"Which suggests that...?"

"He's better dead!"

Leandro stared at her. Was this ruthlessness yet another facet of her personality he'd yet to experience fully?

She dropped her gaze and stretched across to the bottle of Zacapa.

"Want some more?"

He shook his head.

"What would Wilde have responded to your last suggestion?"

"For once, dear Oscar has nothing to do with it. I'm serious. We have to regard that as a real option. I don't think we have any choice. And I don't think we're going to be given two chances."

Leandro thought for a minute.

"Which probably also means we have very little time to decide. Aboukir could ring at any moment."

"Precisely."

"And we have to get Albert involved. He's the professional."

Sam didn't reply at once. She toyed with her rum.

"How do you think Frobisher would react to the idea of killing Aboukir?"

"Not warmly. In fact, they'd almost certainly be dead against it. They want to slow down Iran's nuclear capability, but my instinct tells me they don't want to get their hands dirty in the process. They don't see it as their business. Not to mention the fallout if it went wrong. In fact, you might say that they'd be happy to see Aboukir carry on until the Argentines stopped dealing with Tehran."

"Even at the expense of one of their consultants? You?"

Leandro hadn't thought about that one.

"Now that you put it that way…"

"You bet I do. Of course I would do anything to decrease Tehran's chances of wiping Israel off the map. Including letting Aboukir get on with it. But - and please don't get conceited - losing you is too high a price to pay."

Leandro raised his glass.

"I'll drink to that," he said and blew her a kiss.

"There has to be a way," he muttered. "If we were to tell Albert that the aim was to kill Aboukir, it would be bound to get back to Frobisher. So perhaps, we're on our own."

"Unless..." Sam began.

"Unless what?"

"Unless he thought he was doing it to defend you. In response to a threat. After all, however much Frobisher might like to hamper the Iranian effort, at the same time they'd probably not be keen to lose you if it could be avoided. Surely?"

"Probably not," Leandro replied, though perhaps with less than total conviction.

Sam stood up, as if putting an end to the conversation.

"As far as I'm concerned, certainly not! So whatever we do, I want you alive. And Aboukir dead!"

Her conviction was impressive.

"Time we got to bed. Things will be clearer in the morning. In the meantime, and until we've got our plans sorted out, you're just going to have to stall our friend Aboukir. If he's keen to kill you, he'll wait."

Wednesday, 30 July 2008 (AM) – CASA ROSADA, BUENOS AIRES

The President's adviser was threatening to hold these meetings on a daily basis.

It was clear that serious concerns were being expressed at the highest level and that, even if no solution could be found easily, a semblance of dynamic reaction was called for.

"Señores, certain people are anxious for results. And not only because we cannot allow this kind of terrorism to flourish, but also because the President has now received a telephone call from her opposite number in Uruguay, asking embarrassing questions about what may have been happening on their territory. Naturally, she wants to assure everyone that everything is under control. That the government has nothing to do with what happened in Punta del Este, and that rumours of a SIDE operation are typical fabrication by a hostile press. I'm told that the Uruguayan President may not have been convinced."

Muñoz, representing SIDE, shifted uncomfortably in his chair. He knew there had been Presidential phone calls to his own superiors over the weekend. He faced an enquiry into the way he'd handled the security of the Caballero meetings. Not to mention the failure to capture Aboukir. His decision to opt for surveillance over a quick snatch at the harbour terminal was looking decidedly questionable.

"I presume we have no one on the ground anymore," the adviser said.

"No, everybody came back last Monday," Munoz replied.

"Good. As far as I'm concerned, there's not much we can do about what has happened except to continue to deny everything. It's how we go forward that interests me. Please outline what steps you are taking to put an end to this."

Muñoz cleared his throat. It irritated him that this young man made him so nervous.

"Since the return to Buenos Aires of Aboukir - or Azoulay - when we so unfortunately lost him, we have been concentrating all efforts on trying to find him. The man is clearly a highly trained professional, Señor

Asesor, so it may not be easy. All the police on the streets have now been given copies of this photograph."

Muñoz handed out photographs of the Director.

"My experience is they spend most of their time looking at their cell phones," the adviser muttered. "What about the hotels? And this Azoulay identity? What else do we know about it?"

"His DNI is presumably a forgery. Although the name does exist under that DNI. Or else the computer check at immigration would have thrown it up when he crossed to Uruguay last week. We'll be working on the hotels, though as you know, the list is long and we cannot rule out the possibility that he has gone to ground in some private location."

"Is that all?"

"I'm afraid so."

"Well, Señores, not a good story for our bosses. But I suspect there's nothing further we can do here today."

He turned again to Muñoz.

"I want a report on my desk every evening. of exactly what has been done during the day. Obviously, if there is any major development, get in touch with me at once. And there must be a total news blackout. He must not see what we're doing. All the more, since the Mantra story is still running on most of the agencies. We may have to call a few editors and put on the pressure."

He pulled his papers together and left the room, switching on his BlackBerrys as he left.

Wednesday, 30 July 2008 (PM) – PASAJE DE LA PIEDAD, BUENOS AIRES

Had anyone of the residents of Pasaje de la Piedad happened to look out of the window at around ten pm that evening, they would have caught sight of a man in dark grey overalls walking slowly down the cobbled street, a small grey travel bag in his hand.

The Director had finally emerged from Sonia's flat about an hour earlier and, taking his usual precautions and a particularly roundabout route, which had also enabled him to pick up two boxes of *empanadas* and a couple of Cokes from a corner kiosk, he had made his way to Flemming's address.

Taking advantage of someone leaving through the wrought iron gates at the end of the passageway, he had slipped into the private road, studying the buildings. He identified Flemming's standing on the corner and could see from the brass door plate that his flat was on the second floor. The lights were on and through the curtains he could see the shadows of movement inside. He walked back the way he had come, but had only gone some twenty metres when he spotted a 'For Sale' sign on the building on the opposite side of the passage, slightly set back behind a narrow paved patio fronted by a low wrought iron railing. Its one disadvantage was that it was not directly opposite Flemming's building, but set at an oblique angle some forty metres to its left. It appeared to be a single house, with an elegant portico over the front door. All the windows were shuttered.

As he stood there, an elderly couple emerged from one of the buildings farther down, walking in his direction. He greeted them as they passed.

"*Buenas noches.*"

"*Buenas noches, Señor.*"

He waited until they had rounded the corner. As quietly as possible, he pushed open the small gate. Judging by its stiffness and the creak it made, it didn't get much use. The streetlamps on the *Pasaje* being set fairly far apart, most of the building was in shadow. Apart from the main door, the facade had two windows on either side and on all levels.

He edged along the building, testing the shutters and the windows, until he found one which appeared to be looser than the rest. With a screwdriver from his bag, he was able to lever open the shutter on one side.

The sound of a door opening farther down the street made him duck behind the shrubbery, largely overgrown in the space between the railing and the house. A young couple walked past, both apparently more interested in their cell phones than in each other. As soon as they rounded the corner, he returned to the task.

Five minutes later, he was inside the house. No furniture, except for a broken sofa in one of the back rooms. Damp and very cold, clearly unoccupied for some time. He made his way to the top floor, which put him on a level slightly higher than Flemming's apartment. The drawn curtains still made it impossible to see what was going on inside. He would wait for day. He stretched out on the sofa. Within minutes, he was asleep.

Thursday, 31 July 2008 (AM) – PASAJE DE LA PIEDAD, BUENOS AIRES

"The saviour has arrived," Sam beamed.

Albert smiled shyly.

"Where can I put these?" he asked, turning to Leandro and holding up a heavy-looking carrier bag. Leandro was amused to see that it carried some stencilled lettering advertising the plumbing services of a shop in Villa Crespo.

"Got a new profession?" he asked.

"Trouble is they clank rather a lot."

"If they're what I think they are, probably best in the maid's bedroom. There, through the kitchen."

"We're just about to have some lunch," Leandro said when Albert re-emerged. "Takeaway, I'm afraid."

"Better get used to it, Albert. In the company of this man, it pays to have a high tolerance for pizza," Sam said.

"Ignore her," Leandro said. "She bitches if it's not caviar and champagne."

"That has to be a lie," she snapped back, with a grin. "And on the rare occasions when we do, it's usually me that pays for it."

Leandro detected from the expression on his face that this kind of banter wasn't really Albert's style. He changed the subject.

"How's Paula," he asked.

"Fine. Sends her love."

As they sat around the table, having demolished several large pizzas and a single bottle of wine, and Albert having been brought up to date with the latest on Aboukir, Leandro laid out the options.

"From one of my sources, I've heard that Aboukir has returned to Buenos Aires. Apparently all the security services are on the lookout for him. If they pick him up, we'll probably hear quite quickly. On the other hand, there appears to be a risk he's turning his attentions to me."

"What makes you say that?"

"I called him as we agreed, leaving a message last Saturday. Coming back here, even he must realise is like climbing into the lion's cage, with all of SIDE after him. So there must be a reason. And I suspect that that reason may be me."

"Do the people in London know that?"

"Up to a point. After all, they suggested I should get in touch with you."

Albert got up from the table and walked over to the window. It was one of those winter days in Buenos Aires, the air very cold, the sun blinding so that the buildings seemed to shine in the glare. He pulled out a cigarette.

Turning to Leandro, he asked "Can I smoke?"

"Go ahead. I have one a day, though I tend to open the window. But don't bother. It's too cold for that."

Albert continue to look out of the window as he smoked. He scratched the back of his head with the same hand.

"And he hasn't made contact so far?"

"No," Leandro said.

"According to our analysis of his MO, he'll presumably try and find you here. I mean, he's not going to try and take you down in public. Not unless..."

"Unless what?"

"It's not important. The fact is, whatever his intentions may be, we have to control how and when you meet. If we don't have control, we simply don't know how and when he might choose to attack.

Presumably, he may think you're not suspicious of him. How much time do you think we have?"

Leandro shrugged his shoulders.

"I've no idea. I'm told he's been back since Sunday night. Who knows what he's up to. We know that Frobisher's general interest must remain undetected by the Argentines. Which means that whatever happens, we have to do everything we can to ensure that we don't get mixed up in the fallout."

"Unless of course he succeeds," Sam interjected.

Leandro flashed an angry glance at her.

"Thank you for that suggestion. That's another thing we have to ensure. That he doesn't succeed."

"Just joking."

Sam looked suitably contrite. Her man was under stress.

He turned back to Albert, who was pretending not to pay attention. He had picked up a sheet of paper and a pencil from Leandro's worktable, and was jotting down some single words. They waited.

"If we assume that Aboukir has come back to Buenos Aires for you - which is after all why we're here - we have to draw him into a situation which he thinks he can control, but which fulfils two other purposes. The two you just mentioned. Firstly, that you come out of it alive. And secondly, if it leads to his capture, that our involvement isn't apparent to anyone investigating. That's not going to be easy."

Albert went back to jotting. From what he could see, Leandro detected that he appeared to be breaking ideas down into four or five main categories. Place. Pretext. Threat. Response. Result. After a few minutes, Albert began to throw out some conclusions.

"In terms of where such a meeting might take place, there seem to me to be a number of options to be ruled out straightaway. Any place of his choosing is obviously the first, unless for some reason he were to choose some place which also suited us. So we must listen to what he suggests and not necessarily rule it out. The second unacceptable option is any place related to you. Such as here or your offices, for instance."

Leandro agreed.

"If we think of some public place, then somehow we have to ensure that, whatever happens, there are no witnesses to identify you. Or me."

"Or me," Sam said.

Albert looked at her, but said nothing. She gave him a winning smile. His expression gave nothing away. Leandro watched, amused. It was going to be interesting to see how Albert dealt with her.

"So whatever public place we choose, probably better if it's fairly empty."

"But, coming back to his MO, is he likely to fall for that?"

"He may, if he thinks it gives him some measure of control. Not easy, I agree."

"I see you've got a column entitled 'Result'. Perhaps we should look at that one first," Leandro suggested.

"You're right," Albert replied. "What are we looking for?"

"Well, apart from not ending up dead, maximising the benefit to Frobisher and minimising the risk to London."

"That's your department. I'm here for the action. I take orders. It's people like you who are responsible for the strategy."

"You flatter me, Albert. I'm a beginner at this game," Leandro said. "You've probably seen far more situations like this."

"Are you proposing to discuss this with Charles?"

"I suspect he'll go along with whatever we suggest, as long as it meets the second criterion."

"So what would meet it?"

"That's one aspect to which I simply don't have a clear answer," Leandro replied. "Does what Aboukir is doing suit London's objectives or not? You could argue that the more he disrupts the dialogue between Buenos Aires and Tehran, the better."

Albert closed his eyes.

"But probably not if you're the target," he whispered after a moment.

"Albert, I adore you," Sam said.

He opened his eyes and smiled at her.

"You'll get my invoice in the morning, Señorita."

He turned back to Leandro.

"Except for that, I suspect you're right. But, in my book, your survival probably overrides the other. After all, they specifically asked me to get involved to protect you. So, protect you I will, if I can."

"Well, thank you for that!" Leandro said. "So the second of Frobisher's concerns must be that our involvement goes undetected as far as possible."

"That's much harder. We have to get him to show himself and we have to leave no trace. How long have we got?"

"Better assume very little time. As I said, he's been back in town since Sunday night."

"Presumably he knows where you live. As well as your phone number."

"I'm afraid so."

"He might just be standing outside at this very moment. Or at least recceing the place."

Turning to Sam, he asked.

"And he's met you as well. Does he know where you live?"

"I don't think so. I'm not in the phone book."

"Anything else he might know about you?"

Sam was not inclined to mention that she'd been in Punta del Este when Aboukir had attacked Caballero. And certainly nothing about Tatyana.

She shook her head.

"Can't think of anything."

She avoided looking at Leandro, who was picking up his coffee cup.

"As to his methods, we know that, given the right situation, he'll try and stage-manage some weird scenario. Obviously, we're not going to let him get there. What else do we know?"

"We know that he used a gun in Punta del Este. So he's armed."

Albert made a note.

"When he makes contact, assuming he does in advance of a meeting, he's going to pretend to want to discuss his TV programme."

"Presumably," Leandro said.

Sam sat back in her chair.

"It's just possible he might make contact with me first."

Leandro looked surprised.

"Remember, when he left us at lunch, we did vaguely indicate that I might be able to give him more detail on his Arab immigrants. I suppose he might use that as a pretext to get together."

"So we have to be ready to respond both to a contact with me, or else one with Sam," Leandro added.

Albert made another note on his piece of paper.

The three of them went on discussing possible scenarios until, at about four, Albert seemed to draw a line under the discussion.

"Until he makes a call, to my mind, there's really only one thing I can do. That's to be close at hand for the moment he makes contact. Whether it's with you, Leandro, or with you, Samira. Before getting here, I took a room in a small *pensione* down the street. I'm literally only five minutes away. We have to be in a position to react both if he telephones or if he turns up on your doorstep. And react fast."

"Agreed. How can we make that more effective?"

"In the case of a telephone call, there should be time for me to get round. On your doorstep, there'll be less time. He gets very rough very fast. Two things. I need keys to get into this flat and also Samira's, in case he goes for her. And we need a simple system to alert me. For that, I suggest you prepare a text message to my cell phone, something harmless. Just in case he checks your phones. Maybe ordering a pizza, since you seem to do quite a lot that."

As he was speaking, Leandro had gone over to the chest of drawers and taken out a spare set of keys.

"The big one is for the gate at either end of the street. This SAMA is for downstairs and these two are for the front door. This pair gets you in the back door."

Sam had produced her keys from the pocket of her USAF flying jacket and handed them to him.

"I'll just have to find another way to get in," she said.

"Where do you live? It might be better if you stayed here."

"In Puerto Madero."

"Apart from the time it would take me to get there, would I get access as easily as here?"

"Probably not. It's a modern block with a full-time *portero*. So staying here makes sense. Apart from anything else," she added with a faint smile.

Albert having given them his cell phone number, they each prepared a text message apparently ordering two large *quattro stagioni*.

"Just leave it in your outbox. Then you only have to press a button."

Albert went through the kitchen to the back entrance, beyond the utility room and maid's room. He tried the locks.

"Got any oil? They're noisy."

Having squirted a liberal dose of rapeseed oil into each lock, he pronounced himself satisfied.

He did the same on the front door locks.

"I hope it won't come to it, but this way, I should be able to get in more quietly."

"I'll put my gun somewhere I can find it fast," Leandro told him.

"Good. I'll be going now. Just give me a few bits and pieces I can put in that bag to make it look full again."

After his departure, Sam and Leandro looked at each other.

"Well, I suppose one consolation is that I stay here," Sam said.

"We don't need to have Aboukir after us for that to happen," Leandro replied, laughing. "Any idea how we're going to spend the time?"

"I'm sure we'll think of something."

Thursday, 31 July 2008 (PM) – PASAJE DE LA PIEDAD, BUENOS AIRES

The Director had been awake since daybreak and after eating some more of the cold *empanadas* and finishing his bottle of Coke, he had spent the next half-hour manoeuvring the sofa up the stairs to a vantage point set back from the window, from where he could observe Flemming's building.

He had seen Flemming emerge at about nine thirty, returning ten minutes later with a loaf of bread and a paper bag, presumably *medialunas*. He could have done with some of those. At around twelve thirty, he'd seen a plumber arrive, well protected against the cold.

Watching the comings and goings through his binoculars, he had been able to determine that entry at the ground floor door only seemed to require something like a Yale key. No doubt the locks would be more sophisticated at the entrance to each apartment.

For the rest of the afternoon, there appeared to be little movement across the street and at one point he had caught himself dozing off. At around five, the plumber had left.

He set aside a set of grey overalls, soft black tennis shoes, and black surgical gloves from his carrier bag. Into a holdall he placed various handcuffs, a large selection of zip ties, duct tape and a set of skeleton keys and tools. The SIG Sauer he placed beside him on the sofa.

Night fell and a light drizzle had begun. The lights had come on in Flemming's apartment and he could now see more clearly at least one side of the two rooms giving onto the street. The movement of shadows on the wall told him there were at least two people in the flat, which was soon confirmed by the sight of the girl, Haidar, pulling the curtains, whilst apparently speaking to someone else in the room. As long as they didn't leave, he might get two for the price of one. In terms of fees, if not necessarily in terms of effort, it could well prove to be a very profitable night's work.

August 2008

Friday, 1 August 2008 (AM) – PASAJE DE LA PIEDAD, BUENOS AIRES

The glare of the ceiling light woke Leandro. He sat bolt upright in the bed, his hand instinctively looking for Sam beside him. She was lying, face down, apparently fast asleep.

"Don't worry, Dr Flemming, your research assistant hasn't gone."

The unmistakable voice of Aboukir. Standing at the foot of the bed, arms crossed, an automatic pistol fitted with a long suppressor in his right hand resting in the crook of the other arm. He was smiling. The tone of voice friendly, reassuring.

Leandro sensed Sam beginning to wake up, stretching under the bed clothes.

"Mmm, are you alright, Leo," she murmured, beginning to roll over onto her side.

Her eyes fell on Aboukir. Totally naked as always, she pulled the sheet up to her throat.

"A rather early wake-up call. Perhaps not the one you had booked," Aboukir added, still smiling. He sat down sideways on the end of the bed, the automatic now pointing in their direction.

"Mr Aboukir! What the hell are you doing here?" Leandro intended to convey complete astonishment. Anything less might cause Aboukir to conclude that they'had been expecting him.

"A house call, you might say. To continue our little conversation. Now that you're back from Uruguay, Señorita Haidar. Where you also appear to keep some strange company. Perhaps... I don't know," Aboukir appeared to be searching for some appropriate phrase, "perhaps planning your *hajj*?"

He had seen her in the company of the Prince. How?

"I don't know what you're talking about," she replied firmly.

"Come, come. You and a good-looking blonde. In a dark brown leather coat...?"

So he had seen her at the Prince's villa. After the attack on Caballero. He had stayed in Punta del Este, when half the police force was out looking for him. Not content with that, he had even gone to spy on the Prince. Strong nerves. How much more had he been able to find out?

"Does your government know that you are working with the Saudis? I would guess not. That could be quite embarrassing."

Leandro stared at Sam, trying to keep up the impression of ignorance. She turned away.

"What is he talking about?"

"Nothing. Nothing you would understand, Leo."

Leandro shrugged his shoulders, but as he did so, allowed his gaze to stray for a split second in the direction of the small table on his side of the bed. Aboukir caught the look and, pointing the SIG Sauer directly at him, waved it sideways to indicate that Leandro should get out of the bed.

"Please don't touch anything."

Still gesturing silently with the automatic, he pointed Leandro to move to the other side of the room. Then, while still watching him, he stepped up to the small table and, pulling open the drawer, took out the Bersa.

"I don't think you'll be needing this, Dr Flemming."

He tossed it under the bed. Turning to Sam, he continued.

"Please, Señorita Haidar, you too. Stand beside him."

"What is all this about? Saudi Arabia? I don't understand, Ahmed."

"I rather suspect you do, Dr Flemming. But it's of no consequence, whether you do or you don't."

Sam and Leandro were standing together at the end of the bed. The Director looked at them for a minute, deep in thought. What scenario could he put together with this couple? The raw material, if that was the word for it, was perfect. A beautiful girl, an older lover. It must be spectacular, the sexual finale of this mission.

"Please, this way."

He pointed with his pistol to the drawing room. From the small bag he had placed on Leandro's worktable on his arrival, he took a pair of handcuffs.

He cuffed Leandro and Sam, her left wrist to Leandro's right as they stood facing each other. The same at the level of their ankles, the handcuffs larger.

Sam began to shiver in spite of the fact that some of the warmth from the fireplace had remained, the embers still glowing.

With the automatic, he waved them into the centre of the room.

"Stay there. Please don't make a move."

With the automatic still pointing at them, the Director backed into the kitchen, switching on the light, apparently looking round for something. Leandro watched and finally saw a smile on Aboukir's face, as if satisfied with what he had found. From the draining board, the Director removed the cutlery, including a large carving knife, and placed them with care into a drawer of the sideboard.

"Please. Into the kitchen."

He picked up his carrier bag and placed it on the kitchen sideboard.

Leandro and Sam shuffled into the kitchen.

"Over here."

He manoeuvred them in such a fashion that Sam was now standing with her back to the end of the kitchen table, a narrow rectangular combination of thick glass and chrome legs.

From his bag, the Director took two large zip ties, which he fixed tightly around their necks. A final hard pull would crush their throats and ensure slow but irreversible strangulation. Sam and Leandro now knew how they would die.

Aboukir unlocked the handcuffs from Leandro, leaving them dangling on Sam's wrist and ankle.

"Lie down on the table on your back, Samira. I can call you Samira, can't I?"

The look which Sam threw him said it all. She hesitated.

"On your back, I said." The voice had acquired a harder edge.

Sam looked at Leandro. Aboukir took a step back. Just out of range, should Leandro make a move. The automatic pointing squarely at the centre of Leandro's chest.

"Please, Dr Flemming, don't try anything. It would be a shame, if I had to kill you now. Ruin my little *mise en scène*."

Against an automatic, the slightest false move would be suicidal. Leandro had not given up, but at this point the options were zero.

Aboukir appeared to read his mind.

"Very wise. Nothing you can do."

He looked back at Sam.

"Please, don't keep me waiting. I'm not renowned for my patience. On your back. Now!"

The last word came like a pistol shot.

Sam stood on tiptoe, placing her naked butt on the edge of the table.

"Now lie back, I said."

The shock of the icy glass against her skin caused her body to arch, her breasts straining upwards. Slowly her body adapted to the cold and she relaxed a little.

"You, Dr Flemming, will help me."

From his bag, the Director produced his digital camera and four more sets of handcuffs, two larger, two smaller.

Handing the smaller pair to Leandro, he continued, "Please attach her wrists on each side to the table legs."

The narrowness of the table, chosen to fit the small kitchen, meant Sam could drop an arm towards the floor on each side. As Leandro leaned over her before crouching to attach the loose end of the first handcuff to the table, her eyes bored into him, her fury and frustration on the verge of exploding. Then suddenly a fleeting smile.

Although still without an idea of what he was going to do, he smiled back. The look in her eyes softened. He moved around to the other side of the table and attached the second pair of handcuffs.

"Now her ankles, to the other end of the table."

Leandro looked at him. The automatic didn't waver. Aboukir gestured with it towards the other end of the table and handed him the two larger pairs of handcuffs.

Leandro bent down and attached one of Sam's ankles to each leg.

She now lay spread-eagled on top of the table in the centre of the kitchen, her head dropping off the end, the tension on arms and legs causing her back to arch, her body to curve upwards.

"I'm sorry if the edge of the table is cutting into your arms, Samira. Still, only a minor inconvenience in the circumstances."

Aboukir, his head slightly tilted to one side, his eyes narrowed, was studying Sam's majestic breasts, wasp waist and curving hips, the arch of her back.

"Very beautiful. You're a very lucky man, Dr Flemming."

The provocation was obvious. It was all Leandro could do to resist the temptation to attack him, whatever the consequences.

Sam was beginning to moan, very quietly.

"Please, Samira, no noise. It spoils it."

With his left hand, the Director took the roll of duct tape out of his bag and waved it above her face where she could see it.

"If you continue, I will have to use this. A shame, for a girl as beautiful as you."

Sam fell silent.

Satisfied, the Director lent against the sideboard, surveying the beginnings of the scene. Images of performances not so different came to mind, some in the East Side gay bar, others in the large palaces in the Palmeraie of Marrakech. In one of these, a beautiful Egyptian whore had been chained to an X-shaped frame whilst their host for the evening had raped her brutally. A large wad of *dirhams* had seemed to console her at the end of the night.

His eye was caught by the small tattoo on Sam's left breast.

"The Druze star. Am I right?"

Sam held his gaze until he finally looked away.

Seeking inspiration, the Director surveyed the kitchen. On the far end of the sideboard nearest the door leading into the utility room, a large earthenware bowl containing fresh fruit and vegetables. Protruding from among the apples, an unusually long, slender aubergine.

Keeping the automatic pointing at Leandro, he moved across to the bowl and picked up the dark purple vegetable. He weighed it in his hand. Perfect. Standing just behind Sam's head, he turned and looked towards Leandro at the opposite end of the table. He leaned forward and placed the shiny aubergine in the centre of Sam's stomach. She jerked her body, trying to throw it off. He caught it with his free hand.

"Don't do that again, Samira."

His voice low. He meant it.

He placed the aubergine back on her stomach and this time she stayed quiet.

"Well done. Now, although I don't usually do this, I feel on this occasion that you both deserve an explanation. I have reason to believe, and in your case, Sam, I know, that you are both somehow involved in the discussions between Argentina and Iran on nuclear questions. I have been given the mission of disrupting these discussions. From what I have discovered, you, Dr Flemming, were known at least to the journalist Grunwald, whom I disposed of a few weeks ago. I cannot tell how much you have been directly involved, though I have no doubt that you are in some way. As to Samira, you are clearly a part of it, though rather curiously associated with the Saudi Prince. His meetings with Señor Caballero, who so unfortunately escaped my attentions, point to a high level of collaboration with the Argentine government. Though I must confess to you that I have difficulty in understanding why a member of the Royal Family, guardian of the Holy Places, should want to help the Shia state. Still, politics in our region have always been complex."

Aboukir paused to see their reaction. Flemming was clearly paying attention. Sam had tilted her head back and was staring up at him as he stood behind her.

"I cannot tell whether the Argentine side have identified you, Samira. Whether they know who you are. But when they find you here in the next few days, they will have no trouble in doing so. To discover that you have been working on the other side will only increase their confusion."

Sam's gaze did not waver.

"So far, I have disposed of at least three key people on the Argentine side. The purpose? To persuade the Argentine government that negotiating with those dogs in Tehran is a mistake. A mission initiated by my Sunni clients in Baghad, for which I am only the instrument of Allah's will. Killing you to tonight will further strengthen that message. When they find you, they will be in no doubt that you have been murdered by the same person who disposed of Sanchez in Brussels, and Morales and Grunwald here in Buenos Aires. And also attacked Caballero in Punta del Este. Why will they be in no doubt? Because you will be found in such obscene circumstances as to match the *mises en scène* of the other murders. It will require no imagination, no superlative detective work. It will be staring them in the face. Perhaps literally."

For a moment he enjoyed their visible confusion.

"Now, I suggest we get on with it."

He looked across at Leandro and pointed at the aubergine.

"Take it and insert it into Samira. I don't need to tell you where."

Sam's body jolted violently, but Aboukir had been expecting that and stopped the dark purple vegetable from falling to the ground.

Leandro stood frozen. In analysing Aboukir's so-called MO, no one could have imagined this.

Aboukir waited, watching Leandro closely.

Suddenly, the SIG Sauer twitched to one side, followed by a sharp crack. A bottle of wine, which had been standing on a shelf in the corner crashed to the floor, the red liquid spraying the worktop and wall. Sam's head jerked up in terror. Leandro ducked.

The only sound the dripping of the wine onto the floor below the shelf.

"I'm prepared to waste one shot. But no more. Take the aubergine and do as I say."

Sam began to moan again and this time, he slapped her face so hard that she cried out.

"Silence!"

Slowly, Leandro stood up.

Sensing that Leandro must realise that his room for manoeuvre was rapidly disappearing, Aboukir remained where he was, the table with Sam's outspread body between them. He pointed at the aubergine on Sam's stomach.

"I repeat. Dr Flemming, take it and do as I say."

Leandro moved slowly up to the table, standing between Sam's legs. He finally brought himself to take the aubergine in his right hand.

"Now, insert it."

Sam raised her head again. A faint red stain was spreading on her face where Aboukir had slapped her. To Leandro's amazement, she nodded faintly. Her eyes narrowed.

"It's okay," she whispered.

Leandro looked away. Then, gently, he placed the slender aubergine at the entrance to her vagina. He fleetingly registered the white triangle of skin from sunbathing with only a *cache sexe*.

"Go on," she whispered.

Slowly, he inserted the narrow end between the labia, its shiny smoothness allowing it to enter easily, almost as if lubricated. As he did so, Leandro sensed Sam thrusting towards it. He looked up at her. Her expression betrayed a terrifying determination. But also a trace of desire. With a series of small pumping rotations, he pushed it in farther until he felt it being held. He stepped back.

"More, Leo. Don't stop. More, please."

He couldn't believe his ears. How was it possible that Sam, seconds away from oblivion, should apparently be enjoying this terrifying ritual?

She looked at him. Willing him to obey.

Reluctantly, he resumed the thrusting motions. Sam's body swayed upwards and sideways in concert.

He wondered if he was going to be sick.

He could see that Aboukir was watching, fascinated. Sam had thrown her head back over the far end of the table and was staring up into Aboukir's eyes, holding his gaze. Defying him to put an end to it.

Aboukir looked away, snapping out of his dream. He must return to the script.

"Take the other pairs of handcuffs," Aboukir ordered. "Place them on the floor next to you."

Leandro still didn't move. Staring at Aboukir. Provoking him. Not that that would serve much purpose. Yet if he was going to do anything, it would have to be in the next few seconds.

Seeing Leandro hesitate, Aboukir continued.

"So that we get it right, let me explain what I have in mind. Once you have locked yourself to the table between Samira's legs, you will be on your knees with your mouth at the level of her vagina. I don't need to tell you what you do next with your end of the aubergine. And as she starts to enjoy it, I will pull the zip tighter. Her pleasure will increase, but there will be no going back. She will suffocate slowly. After that, your death will only cost me a second bullet."

He savoured the look of horrified realization on both their faces.

"Dr Flemming, time is running out for you. For you both. Please don't do anything which would make it even shorter."

As Leandro stared at Aboukir, he suddenly thought he detected a slight movement in the half open door leading into the utility room behind the Arab. Could it be the wind? With his back to the door, Aboukir could not have seen it. The door moved again, silently, more deliberately this time. Leandro briefly looked down at Sam. If something was happening, he must not give it away. Sam had raised her head and was looking towards him. Had she seen it too?

He looked at Aboukir, whose expression was beginning to betray a growing impatience.

"I repeat, Dr Flemming. Take the handcuffs and get down on your knees with your face between Samira's legs."

Leandro stepped across to where Aboukir had placed the handcuffs and picked up the last pair. As he turned back towards the table he stole another glance at the door behind Aboukir. To his amazement, a hand appeared for a few seconds, giving first a thumbs up sign, before then pointing down towards the floor as if urging him to obey Aboukir. Then it was gone. Albert!

He knelt down as instructed, his eyes on a level with the end of the black aubergine gently swaying in Sam's cunt.

"Place the handcuffs on the floor to your left. Attach the handcuff you are wearing on your right wrist to the table leg on your right."

Aboukir seemed to know the sequence by heart, his monotone suggesting this was all very familiar to him.

Once he had attached his right wrist to the table, Leandro knew his freedom of action would virtually be at an end. He bent down to place the handcuffs on the floor and in so doing, found himself looking under the table, so that he could see Aboukir's legs and the lower part of the door into the utility room behind the assassin. He saw it open halfway, the dim outline of Albert just visible close to the frame. A hand appeared holding a matt black revolver by its short barrel.

"Now attach your other handcuff to the table leg."

The voice of Aboukir broke through.

The last thing Leandro wanted was that Aboukir should move away from the far end of the table. Still keeping his head down, so that he could see behind Aboukir, he clipped the other end of the handcuff on his right wrist to the aluminium table leg. Now only his left hand was free.

Aboukir took a step to the left of the table so that he could check that Leandro was firmly attached. In so doing, he moved out of the path separating Albert from Leandro.

It all happened in seconds.

Leandro saw the revolver come spinning across the tiled kitchen floor towards him. At the same time, the utility door flew open, revealing Albert crouched against the door jam, his Glock in his right hand. At the noise, Aboukir spun round, just in time to receive two bullets, one in the neck, the other in the face. A target larger than a grapefruit! As Aboukir was falling against the dresser, still alive and visibly trying to bring his SIG Sauer to bear on his attacker, his blood spraying across Sam's naked stomach, Leandro caught the short-barrelled revolver in his left hand. Sam was screaming and he could hear her handcuffs crashing against the table legs. Another shot. A second later, firing from his kneeling position below the table, Leandro loosed off a round at the collapsing shape of Aboukir. Striking him in the chest, the 0.38

Magnum propelled Aboukir sideways. Silently, Aboukir rolled onto his side, his head coming to rest at an incongruous angle against the edge of the dresser. As his grip on the SIG Sauer relaxed, it slid to the tiled floor.

Albert, still crouching by the door, held his gun steadily trained on Aboukir. Taking no chances.

Slowly Leandro stood up as far as his cuffed right wrist would allow.

Sam had stopped screaming and, head up, was straining to see Leandro.

"Please, Leo," she whispered, indicating in the direction of her cunt with her eyes.

He placed the revolver on the table beside her and gently withdrew the aubergine. As it finally slid from her body, Sam's head fell back. She began to sob, her body jerking uncontrollably.

Albert stepped forward and kicked the SIG Sauer out of Aboukir's lifeless hand, sending it sliding across the floor towards the stove.

"Get the keys, can you, Albert?" Leandro asked, pointing in the direction of Aboukir's bag. "And cut off these things," he added, pushing his finger between his throat and the zip tie. "They're very painful."

Friday, 1 August 2008 (AM) – PASAJE DE LA PIEDAD, BUENOS AIRES

Once the first effects of the shock had worn off, Sam had taken a long, boiling hot shower. There she had been joined by Leandro and together they had made love, rediscovering their bodies, exploring them as if for the first time, washing away the horrors of the night.

"That's the second time in less than six months," she whispered. "You're a dangerous man to be with, *mi amor*."

"I could say the same of you."

"These near-death experiences give me an appetite. I'm starving. But first, just one more time. Soft and smooth."

As she wrapped her legs around his waist, he pinned her to the wall, the water streaming over her upturned face. Her beautiful eyes, ringed by the thickness of her drenched lashes, said it all.

An hour later, the three of them were sitting in front of the well-stacked fire, Leandro and Albert each in an armchair on either side, Sam wrapped up in one of her jogging suits, cross-legged on the fur rug. The remains of a delivery of *empanadas*, the bottle of Oban whisky on the floor between them, disappearing fast. Calm and strength returning.

"Albert, were you listening to what Aboukir had to say? All this business of a campaign launched by the Sunnis in Iraq?"

"Yes, I heard that bit. Not that I know very much about it. Shades of 9/11, I suppose."

"Yes and no," Sam said. "This isn't so much about attacking us, the West, the Christians. More like the latest instalment in the long battle between Shia and Sunni Islam. They hate each other. They're fighting each other all across the Middle East. Al Qaeda is Sunni. And from what Aboukir told us, he was working on behalf of another Sunni group, to try and stop Shia Iran getting its hands on a nuclear bomb. Whoever these people are, they seem to have decided that Argentina is helping Iran. So by killing Argentines involved in that, they hope to send a message to this government. To stop helping Iran."

"Does it make sense?"

Sam thought for a minute. She must tread carefully.

Leandro said nothing.

"In some incredible way, yes it does. I think we're only seeing the beginnings in Iraq. When the Americans pull out, which they will very soon, the place will probably fall apart. Don't forget that under Saddam Hussein, the Sunni minority dominated the Shia majority. Now the Americans have handed power to the Shia and the Sunni minority feel threatened. That's why we're seeing these battles between Al Qaeda on one side and Shia groups on the other. Syria will follow any time now. The reverse of Iraq under Saddam. A Shia minority controlling a Sunni majority. And in the background, Iran seeking to dominate the Middle East. The largest Shia state in the region. The Sunnis will do anything to stop Iran getting its hands on a nuclear weapon. So preventing Argentina from helping them would make perfect sense. Though the method is a bit original, I'll grant you."

No one could disagree with that.

"Any chance that there are some more Aboukirs where he came from?" Leandro finally asked.

When he had agreed to help Frobisher, the last thing he had imagined was to be part of the action.

"Probably not. He seemed to imply that he'd done it all alone."

"Still, we'll never know."

"'Fraid not."

"All a bit above my head," Albert said, shaking his head. "I wouldn't trust the Iranians with a nuclear bomb, but I don't feel bad about having got rid of this guy."

"Nor do I," Leandro added. Turning to Albert, he asked. "How did you know?"

"That lady. She sent me a message," pointing his glass toward Sam.

Leandro stared at Sam.

"For God's sake, when?"

She smiled quietly.

"In the very first seconds. I happened to be awake when he walked into the room. I'd kept my cell phone under my pillow, the text ready to send. Thank you, Albert, for being so quick."

"Not quick enough by half," he replied ruefully. "Would have liked to spare you all that."

"Forget it. I will. The main thing is that your timing seems to have been perfect."

Leandro listened to this exchange, saying nothing. Certain questions remained unanswered.

They sat for a while, saying nothing, until Leandro finally raised the question which was on all their minds.

"What do we do about him?" he asked, tossing his head in the direction of the kitchen.

"I've taken a few steps in that direction," Albert said. "You don't seem to have noticed that one of your carpets is missing. Whilst you were having your shower, and before he got stiff, I rolled him up in it. Thoughtful of him to bring that duct tape. He's out in your utility room."

"I'm not worried about the carpet. I picked it up in one of the antique stores in San Telmo. Paid nothing for it. If it helps, it will have earned its keep."

"When it's dark, I'll bring a small van and, just in case anybody's watching, we can load him in with a couple of chairs and a picture or two. Then we dump it. Let CLIBA or the waste pickers find him. Some other part of town. By the way, wear a pair of these surgical gloves whenever you're near him. Don't want our fingerprints or DNA showing up on his corpse or anything else."

"Have you got a van?" Leandro said.

Albert shook his head.

"That's an unnecessary question. Not yet."

Sam couldn't conceal a smile.

"You're wonderful, Albert. I love you. Almost as much as Leandro. Almost."

Even above the effects of the whisky, Albert blushed visibly.

"I'm also going to try and find out where he came from. My suspicion is the empty house opposite. The one for sale."

Leandro picked up the bottle and refilled their glasses.

"Well, we're alive. Thanks to you, we've solved that problem. As to the involvement of Frobisher, I think we can handle that. If we dump the body without being seen, nothing will connect it with any of us. I presume they won't be able to trace anything from the ballistics?"

"Not to my mind."

"I'd however be tempted to find a way to alert the police to the body. The sooner they and SIDE stop chasing round, the better for all of us. Aboukir was calculating that, on finding us, they would discover that Sam was working with the Saudis. With no trace of us, that loophole is closed as well."

"So all in all, your plan, Albert, has been brilliant. One hundred percent."

"Less of a plan. More a lot of luck."

Leandro shook his head. Irritating British modesty. He wondered whether it might be possible to find a way to tip off Eduardo to the whereabouts of Aboukir's body. On second thoughts, that might establish a link back to them.

"It's nearly five o'clock. We all deserve some sleep. That couch over there, Albert, is very comfortable."

As they lay in the darkness, Sam with her arm resting on Leandro's stomach, the moment had come to address what had been troubling him.

"Sam, I have to understand. You were within minutes of dying. In the most horrible way. Aboukir's *mise en scène* as he called it was horrendous. I'd rather not think about how it was supposed to end. And yet you... you were somehow... in control. Willing me to do it. Even - I can hardly bring myself to say it – apparently... enjoying it? I don't know how you could do it. I think the look in your eye will stay with me for ever."

Sam propped herself up on her elbow and passed her fingers over his lips.

"Stop it. Don't torture yourself. I knew Albert was on his way. But I couldn't know how long it would take him. Our only hope of survival rested on drawing the whole process out as long as possible. Once I'd got a clue as to what Aboukir had in mind - which was as soon as he had got me on top of the table - I had to take the initiative somehow. Obviously, I also hoped you had a plan. Though, my poor love, with a gun pointing at you, almost anything would have been suicide. And if he shot you, I would immediately be next."

"The same thought occurred to me."

"It struck me that these *mises en scène*, as he called them, weren't just for the benefit of those discovering the bodies. They were for him as well. He got a massive sexual kick out of them. In a strange way, he seemed to send me the message that he wanted to prolong it. Maximum pleasure. So instead of kicking and screaming, I wanted to go along with it, play to his phantasy, make it last longer. The longer it lasted, the more time Albert had to get to us."

She kissed him.

"There, please don't read anything else into it." She paused, and then added, laughing. "In the words of Iron Maiden, 'If you're going to die, die with your boots on!' You know me, I don't go anywhere without my boots. And it wasn't my intention to die without them."

Unbelievable. At the same time, it terrified him. If she was capable of this, what else could she do?

Had she been able to see his eyes, she might have detected that Leandro, the more he thought about it, had only been partly convinced by her explanation. There must be more to it.

He pulled her closer and she coiled herself around him.

"I never knew you listened to Iron Maiden…"

"I don't tell you everything," she whispered.

What she had also not told him was that her plan had been only one of the reasons. As the handcuffs had closed around her wrists and ankles and the rape had begun, she had dimly sensed a strange new yearning welling up inside her. A different kind of submission…

Friday, 1 August 2008 (PM) – PASAJE DE LA PIEDAD, BUENOS AIRES

At around seven in the evening, Albert had disappeared for about an hour. He came back with a soft travel bag.

"Found this opposite. Clearly belongs to our friend," he said. "Change of clothing, shoes, couple of keys. Presumably to where he was staying. An identity document in the name of Azoulay. Might add that one to the body. I also cleared up the remains of his meals. Seems to have survived on a diet of *empanadas* and Coca-Cola."

"No wonder we got the better of him," Sam said.

"That house has been for sale a while. The agents would probably have found the bag someday and handed it in. Which could have brought SIDE or the police round here. Presume you haven't left any fingerprints."

"Thanks for the vote of confidence," Albert replied, not without a hint of hurt pride.

"Sorry. I wasn't thinking.".

"Don't worry. Anyway, we'd probably better wait a couple of hours before loading the van."

"You've already got it?"

"No, but I will in about an hour."

And so it was that at around ten that evening, the owner of the second-floor flat could have been observed apparently starting the removal of some of his furniture. They left the small Renault for another hour. On arrival, Albert had muddied the number plates with earth from the shrubbery of the house opposite.

It was a little before midnight when Albert parked the van beside the perimeter wall of the railway lines bordering Avenida General Juan Domingo Perón behind Once station, seemingly a spot favoured by fly-tippers, judging by the abandoned refrigerators, broken plastic garden chairs and a large bed spring. It was the work of less than a minute to add the remains of Aboukir to the pile, along with his travel bag and ID.

To make things even easier, Albert had added the barrel section of the SIG Sauer for the benefit of the ballistic experts. Leaving the whole gun might have been too tempting to any casual passer-by. The digital camera was also included. They drove a few more blocks down the avenue before abandoning the Renault and picking up a taxi a couple of streets away on Avenida Rivadavia.

Saturday, 2 August 2008 (NOON) – PASAJE DE LA PIEDAD, BUENOS AIRES

Sam had returned to her apartment, having subjected her British hero to a passionate embrace which had left him visibly shaken.

At the door, she had added, "I need a little break from your flat. Don't get me wrong. Just a quick change of scenery."

"And no doubt of clothes," Leandro said.

Following her departure, Leandro and Albert discussed just how much they were going to tell Frobisher. In professional terms, there appeared to be little choice. As employees of the London agency, they could hardly conceal the role they had played in the death of Aboukir. They agreed they'd give it twenty-four hours to report any fallout should the body be discovered.

Albert finally left at around noon.

Leandro's phone rang in the middle of the afternoon.

"Hi, Uncle, it's Eduardo. I've got good news. You can relax. Come out from under the sofa."

He laughed.

"What's that?"

"Your friend Aboukir is dead."

"Jesus! Really? How did that happen?"

"I've only just heard. Fonseca rang me. He didn't have any detail, except to say that the body had been found. As soon as I get anything else, I'll let you know."

"Well, great news. What a relief! And yes, let me know when you have more. By the way, good game. Two nil against Independiente."

Eduardo was a San Lorenzo fan.

"And defeating River a few days ago. We're in good form."

The buzzer at the end of the *Pasaje* was sounding.

"Coming for a ride?"

"What?"

"Nothing like a Harley to make you feel alive. I've got an extra helmet for you."

He wasn't sure which was more lethal. Aboukir with a SIG Sauer or Sam navigating Buenos Aires traffic.

"Give me five minutes."

Monday. 4 August 2008 – CALLE LEVENE, BUENOS AIRES

"You say he's broken off contact," Viktor Alexievich was asking.

She nodded her head.

Tatyana wasn't enjoying the meeting. Her uncle and the Russian ambassador were sitting opposite her in the drawing room of his Recoleta apartment. She could see that Viktor Alexievich was angry. He was angry because his old friend, the Russian ambassador, had been let down. Embarrassed by the visible role she had played in the botched Mantra Hotel attack. Getting herself and her name on TV in a situation in which the Argentine government had also been caught with its pants down.

Viktor Alexievich had specifically targeted her to get alongside Caballero and see how this might be exploited to best effect in the context of his interest in the Atucha nuclear power plant. She thought she had done that pretty successfully. Not that Caballero had ever shared any details of the negotiations he was conducting. But, one way and another, her cell phone contained a lurid series of photographs of the Argentine in various compromising positions. On waking in the clinic, one of the first things she had done had been to check that the photos were still there.

"Just a text message. To say that we shouldn't see each other for a bit."

"Before or after they stopped you at the airport?"

"After. We came back together on the same day. The message was a day later."

No doubt Caballero's SIDE minders had warned him off this Russian honey trap.

Viktor Alexievich looked at the ambassador.

"What do you think, Mikhail?"

The ambassador shook his head.

"I'd be surprised if he was allowed to see her again. A shame!"

"But I do have a lot of photographs," Tatyana protested. "We can always use those."

"I'm not so sure," the ambassador said. "To be frank, with everything that's happened, it's all too public. We'd look ridiculous trying to use them."

He looked at Viktor Alexievich.

"'Fraid so. It's a pity."

Tatyana looked down at the floor, her red hair falling into her face.

Viktor Alexievich put his hand on her shoulder.

"Don't worry, none of us could have foreseen the attack. But I suspect that your Argentine holiday may be over sooner than you planned."

"I've been called to a meeting at the Ministry tomorrow afternoon," the ambassador said. "They haven't told me why. It might have something to do with this. Though, I don't think they can make much of it. Arguably, it's their negotiator who needs to be taught a lesson or two."

"You may be right. Let's see what they have to say. But I don't rule out that Tatyana may have to catch a flight back to Moscow. It's possible that the longer she stays here, the more exposed she becomes. These Argentines are an unpredictable lot. If anything went wrong, I'd have to answer to my sister. I don't want to have to do that - ever. Even less to her father!"

"So, Tatyana, let's leave it at that. In the meantime, avoid Caballero."

"I'm sorry, Mikhail," she said, standing, stretching her hand out towards the ambassador.

"Don't worry, Tatyana. Viktor Alexievich always sorts these things out. And anyway, the Argentines are going to go on needing someone to help them with their next power station. They know we can do it. A little episode like this won't get in the way for long. I'll make sure of that."

Tuesday, 5 August 2008 (AM) – CASA ROSADA, BUENOS AIRES

The presidential adviser looked down the table at the representatives of SIDE and the police and smiled. It was the first gesture of appreciation they had received to date.

"Congratulations. One way or another, our problems appear to have been solved."

He could see that his comment had left some of them confused, if not unnerved. He knew as well as they did that no one had the slightest idea how Aboukir's body had come to rest in Avenida Perón. Their reports had made little secret of the fact.

"It is important for all of us that Aboukir's death can be presented higher up as the result of a well-planned and executed anti-terrorist action. The President has shown interest in the case and forcefully expresses her belief that heads no longer need to roll."

The adviser had called together the representatives of SIDE and the police at a meeting a few hours earlier to coordinate a story which would send the required message.

"I know that you people make it your business, if not your hobby, to contradict each other, but I recommend you withdraw your reports for the time being. I give you a couple of hours to come up with a version which we can discuss at the meeting. It doesn't have to be detailed, but his death has to be attributable to something you were doing. Surveillance, house searches, tailing suspects, pulling together information from hotels. That sort of thing."

Turning to Muñoz, he had added, "You can even appear to be reluctant to go into too much detail about the methods you used. Make some reference to applying your usual tactics. Something to impress the Ministry of Justice and the Ministry of Foreign Relations. Something we can refer to as if it was too secret for the others in the room."

"So, Inspector Muñoz, can you tell us anything about how this was achieved?"

Muñoz swallowed, then began a long, rambling description of how, in close collaboration with his colleagues from the Policía Federal, and thanks to concerted and detailed research, using CC video footage and hotel records, they had finally been able to establish the whereabouts of Aboukir to within a block in the district of Once. Thanks to the diligent work of one of the Inspectors in the *Comisaría 5a.*, they had pinned Aboukir's hideout down to a flat belonging to a local physiotherapist.

"On the basis of information we received, we searched her flat and found items belonging to Aboukir, which enabled us to set up the necessary surveillance which finally led us to him."

The fact that Sonia, suspecting that her lodger's prolonged absence boded little good for her, had finally decided to hand over Aboukir's suitcase to her Policía Federal client a couple of days after the discovery of his body, was of little consequence. If pressed, they would be able to produce the suitcase and some evidence of the fact that Aboukir was the killer. Including, interestingly enough, a small notebook, the origins of which they were still trying to trace.

"Amongst the items we recovered with the body, we found a notebook which contained a number of names, including those of our diplomats who so tragically lost their lives to this assassin. Also the names of a number of other people who were clearly being targeted. The attack in Punta del Este was one of these."

Smiling, the presidential adviser asked Muñoz whether he could elaborate on how Aboukir had died.

Muñoz shifted a little on his chair, as if trying to remember.

"You will forgive me if I do not provide too much detail on the ways in which we conduct this type of operation. What is regrettable, obviously, is that it should have ended in his death. We made every effort to capture him alive, but, as is the way with these Islamic extremists, suicide is their preferred option."

"Are you saying that he shot himself?"

"At this stage, Señor Asesor, you will forgive me if I do not provide the answer to that question."

The adviser nodded. Turning to the meeting as a whole, he summed up.

"I believe that we can congratulate the representatives of SIDE and the Policía Federal on a very professionally executed operation, which has brought to a close this most disagreeable episode. In so doing, you have made it possible for us to continue our discussions with Iran, a country which, as you know, we value highly as a commercial partner. I will be pleased to report the results of your work to the Secretary General, who will no doubt make sure that it reaches the highest levels of the Presidency."

Addressing the representative of the Ministry of Foreign Relations, he added, "Could you please send me your assessment of where our discussions go from here and how we can ensure that those who we're dealing with regain their full confidence in us. And before I forget, a suitable report should be sent via our Brussels embassy for the Belgian police, to say that we have found Sanchez' assassin."

"Perhaps we could send a photo of the man," the Ministry official replied, looking at Muñoz. "And maybe some DNA, since they said that had found some, but needed a match."

Muñoz made a note of the request.

"Please do that, Inspector Muñoz. And please let me know how some of the issues surrounding our negotiating team have been dealt with, in such a fashion that they will not be repeated in the future," the adviser added.

Then, with a nod of his head in the direction of the group, he left.

There was a moment's silence until the representative of the Ministry of Foreign Relations coughed in a manner intended to attract their attention.

"We must congratulate you," speaking to Muñoz and the two police representatives. "Whatever the truth of the matter." The irony was clearly detectable, "We can presumably stop worrying about our careers. For now."

The laughter was nervous and brief.

Thursday, 7 August 2008 (AM) – AVENIDA DE MAYO Y PERÚ, BUENOS AIRES

Two days later, the news broke, half-truth, half-opportunism.

Eduardo had rung in the late morning suggesting they meet for a quick lunch.

"I've got a bit more detail. Courtesy of my boss who's just back from a meeting at the Casa Rosada. You've seen today's papers."

"Yes. Strange story. How much of it is just misinformation?"

"Why do you say that, Uncle? Do you have another version?"

Leandro shook his head.

"Not at all. It's just that with this lot, you never know. What's your version?"

Eduardo looked at his uncle. The expression on his face was a fraction too innocent. He wondered... Studying the crime scene photographs, he sensed he'd seen the carpet somewhere before.

"The body was found by waste pickers on Saturday night. Rolled up in a carpet. Dumped along with a lot of old furniture and kitchen equipment. At least four bullets in him. Interestingly enough, two weapons, different calibres. One in the head, one in the neck, and two in his chest. One straight through the heart. He was handcuffed, wrists and ankles, and blindfolded, but forensics think those were added afterwards."

"Interesting."

"They also found a small bag of clothing and other bits and pieces, including the main barrel section of a SIG Sauer pistol. And a camera with photographs of his previous murders. Also the Argentine identity document in the name of Mario Azoulay. They're going to try and get the ballistics results from Uruguay to see whether they also match the SIG. They already match those that killed the two *canas*. And most interestingly, a little notebook containing the names of your friend Luis Miguel, as well as the guy in Brussels and the other one who was shot in Caracas. So whatever they may be saying in the press, Fonseca had to admit that, whoever killed him, it wasn't either SIDE or the police. They had apparently lost his trail a couple of days earlier."

"So what you're saying is that no one has any idea who did it."

"That's right. Obviously, the investigation is ongoing. But the Casa Rosada committee has been disbanded, so it's likely that Fonseca won't hear very much more about it."

"Well, I guess our diplomats can start to sleep happily in their beds at night."

"And not just our diplomats," Eduardo added, looking at him carefully .

"What's that supposed to mean?"

"So can you. Or had you forgotten?"

"No, of course not. As you can imagine."

"By the way, before I forget. Yours was another name they found in the little notebook."

Leandro, who had been studying the bill brought by the waiter, looked up at him sharply.

"What do you mean?"

"Nobody's sure yet, but they think that the notebook may have belonged to Grunwald. More by a process of elimination, since his is the only name that doesn't appear in the book. Did you have contact with him?"

"Yes. I knew him quite well. We lunched together in May. I thought I told you."

"Well, Uncle, I wouldn't read too much into that. Anyway, I'd better be getting along. Busy afternoon."

Briefly summarizing the press coverage, Leandro sent a report to Charles in London. The account provided by Eduardo was added in a separate paragraph as being the most damaging version of what the Argentines might have been able to work out, attributed to an unidentified source in the Argentine police. Then, as agreed with Albert, he provided a brief version of how Aboukir had attempted to murder him in his flat, but that thanks to the timely intervention of Albert, he had been killed. He went into slightly more detail about the manner in which they had disposed of the body and the fact that they had been able to ensure that there could be no blowback to Frobisher's assignment. It had been agreed that there would be no mention of Sam's presence. Leandro thanked Charles for the support he'd provided through Albert. He presumed that Frobisher would now want him to continue with the assignment.

A first rapid reply asked him to do a full damage assessment as to the risks of the affair being traced back to Leandro and through him to Albert and Frobisher. With Albert they had already prepared something along those lines and he was quickly able to respond.

The next morning saw a reply.

> Assignment temporarily on hold. Thanks in part to your efforts, sufficient evidence now accumulated pointing to fact that Argentine government and Iranians are in serious discussions. Has enabled us to fulfil our mandate with client. Although Aboukir eliminated, Argentine government will now be on alert to any possible meddling. Given extreme reluctance of HMG to be found in any way interfering in Argentine affairs, it has been agreed that, until things calm down, we should curtail efforts in Argentina until further notice. As expression of sincere gratitude, cheque for £30,000 will be credited to your account. If any expenses, please send detailed statement and they will be reimbursed. Yours C.

The reply left Leandro with mixed feelings. Of course the cash was more than welcome and he would no doubt be expected to spend some of it on Sam. But also a feeling of frustration. However much he might, unwittingly, have come close to the action, he felt that he had in some measure simply been an accessory, rather than a true actor in the drama. He wondered - almost with a tinge of jealousy - whether Sam, in whatever she might be up to on behalf of Mossad, would not have found a way to become a more direct protagonist. Still, nobody could have accused him or Sam of being simple bystanders in Aboukir's final moments.

Thinking it over, he wondered where this feeling of frustration was coming from. Might he be acquiring a taste for the strange pace of life into which he had plunged ever since meeting Sam over a year ago? Could he ever reconcile himself once more to a life dictated by the whims of the markets and his country's erratic economic policies? The feeling was strangely exhilarating.

Neither he nor Albert had bothered to try and work out whose bullet had killed him. What did it matter, anyway? Between them, they had finished him off, which was the main thing. Leandro tried to avoid thinking about that moment when he had pulled the trigger. In some ways, at least as far as he was concerned, there was a benefit in having shared the execution with Albert. Rather like the man in a firing squad given a rifle with a blank, so that no one could be absolutely sure whether or not they had fired the terminal bullet.

In his reply, Leandro thanked Charles and confirmed that he stood ready to continue with his investigation whenever it suited Frobisher.

He picked up his cell phone and rang Sam.

"Where do you want to go for dinner?"

"Have they paid you?"

"Are you suggesting I only invite you when someone hands me a cheque?"

"That's the way it feels a lot of the time," came the reply, though the tone of voice made it clear that the reproach was far from serious.

"Bitch."

"Oh, by the way. I've got bad news for you."

"What's that?"

"Your Russian girlfriend has had to leave the country."

"What do you mean?"

"She rang me half an hour ago to say goodbye. Said that Viktor Alexievich had told her to leave. Apparently the ambassador was given something of a rough ride by the Ministry about the extracurricular activities of his house guests."

Sam laughed.

"She must have been pissed off," Leandro said.

"You bet she was. But she specifically asked me to pass on her love to you."

"Now you're lying, Sam."

"Maybe. Anyway, we can reminisce about her over dinner."

Sam put the phone down.

His landline was ringing.

"I'm beginning to have my doubts about that Arab girlfriend of yours,"

Elena's opening remark, the tone of voice clearly betraying unusual anger.

"Why now?"

"Did you know that she's lent her house in Punta del Este to the two girls?"

Leandro was silent. Sam had not mentioned it on her return from Uruguay.

"No, actually, I had no idea."

"Well, she has. And somehow, in my book, that's a step too far into our lives. Yours and mine."

"Oh dear. I'm sure she did it with the best of intentions."

He was less convinced than he sounded. Why had she hidden it from him?

"Well, I suggest you try and find out. Get some explanation. Alejandra's problems are for her to sort out. And if we can help, we will. But I'm not in favour of your latest love stepping into the ring."

Elena hung up without another word.

Dinner might turn out to be more complicated.

September 2008

Friday, 12 September 2008 (AM) – PASAJE DE LA PIEDAD, BUENOS AIRES

The elimination of Aboukir had restored confidence to the Argentine negotiating team. But not to the same degree to the Saudi side, so that their final meeting had been held the previous week on board White Lady anchored in front of one of the leading hotels on the Costa Smeralda. Much to the visible discomfort of the Argentine and Venezuelan delegates, the meetings had taken place after midnight, given that Ramadan had started some ten days earlier. Details of the shipment had been agreed, along with the upfront payment of the first instalment of the Prince's commission, in the form of a five million dollar transfer into a numbered account in Lichtenstein. The final contract had, at the request of the Prince and most irritatingly for the Argentines, gone into extensive detail as to what the insurance would and would not cover, and the respective liability of the two parties. Sam had been invited to attend, much to Leandro's disgust.

To be frank, in her absence, his attention had been focused elsewhere, as the relentless collapse of the new world economic order and US capitalism edged ever closer, the stock price of Lehmann Brothers – along with that of its Wall Street rivals - providing the surrogate for market sentiment. Freddie Mac and Fannie Mae, the two housing finance giants underpinning nearly half the US mortgage market, had been taken over by the Federal Reserve a week earlier. Only two months since Bernanke had assured everyone that they were fine!

When, without warning, Sam breezed into his flat, the demise of one of Wall Street's oldest names was only three days away.

"Bit of a change, after Rome and Geneva," she exclaimed, as she embraced Leandro.

"That's the downside of foreign travel. But you'll readjust fast enough. Don't worry."

"I know I will. As soon as you've taken me to wherever we can get the best steaks in town."

"Surely, with all the smart places you've been to in the last ten days, that'll be an anti-climax. Anyway, it's usually down to the one who's been travelling to bring presents to those who stayed at home."

"Funny you should say that."

She opened the diminutive pouch which, for Sam, usually served as a handbag.

"I hate handbags, they seem to imply that women need to carry around more than men to operate effectively," she had once explained.

She handed him a small rectangular parcel wrapped in brown paper.

"Sorry about the wrapping. Had to make it unobtrusive for our friends in customs," she apologised. "All the way from Geneva."

"Plain chocolate. The way to my heart," Leandro said, removing the wrapping.

Sam said nothing, an enigmatic look on her face.

"*Pucha*! You're crazy!"

Leandro was staring into an elegant, leather bound case containing an identical gold Rolex to the one he had lost that night at the bar. Even down to the black crocodile strap.

"My God! You meant it. I adore you. Come here."

"Of course I meant it. I always do. You should know that by now," she whispered and slipped between his arms.

"Where did you find it?"

"Passing through Geneva after Sardinia, I visited Antiquorum, the horology auctioneers. My father was one of their longest-standing clients, so its doors and vaults – as well as the arms of its Italian founder – just seemed to open for me. They soon found the model when I described it. The 18 carat gold Bubbleback Oyster Perpetual. Early 1940s vintage."

"It's identical to mine."

"The Prince was in very generous mood after we closed the deal," she said. "All in all a good trip."

For the time being, she saw no reason to tell Leandro anything about the meeting she had had with her Mossad case officer in Paris.

"So the deal's been signed?" the Israeli intelligence officer had asked, as they sat in a cafe in the Rue de Buci in the *6ème arrondissement.*

"Yes, two days ago. The shipment will be loaded in a small harbour close to Puerto Deseado at the end of the month. I'm afraid I don't have the name of the ship which the Prince will use. I'll try and find out, but it probably won't be easy."

"I understand. Although they're happy for you to sit in on some of the meetings, they obviously don't show you the correspondence. Don't do anything foolish, but if someone should mention it, we'd be very interested."

"After that, the ship will make its way across to South Africa, and then, apparently picking up small shipments along the east coast, carry on up towards the Gulf. They expect to get there around the end of October."

"And you say the shipment will include not only centrifuges but also uranium? Do you know how much of either?"

"All I heard was a reference to three or four 20-foot containers. One of them specifically for the yellow cake."

"In theory, that's quite a lot of yellow cake, but I suspect most of the space will be taken up with the cladding and other protection."

"So, do you want me to continue seeing the Prince?"

He looked at her quizzically.

"The Prince? Or the Princess?"

Sam was quite unfazed by the inelegant question.

"Both. Though I suspect that her appetite may generate more regular meetings."

He thought for a moment.

"That's fine with us. As I told you, we need to have a good window on what he's up to."

October 2008

Tuesday, 28 October 2008 – COMOROS, INDIAN OCEAN

In the last week of October, a small tramp steamer flying a Panamanian flag inexplicably sank in perfectly calm weather off the coast of Mozambique, at a point approximately 100 kilometres south of Mayotte. She had left the port of Maputo some five days earlier, having indicated that her next stop would be the port of Dar es Salaam in Tanzania.

This last voyage of a long, arduous career, spent shuttling up and down the coasts of some of the harsher continents of the world, had begun on a windswept, cold and rainy late-September night in Puerto San Julian, a small fishing port on the coast of Santa Cruz Province. The steamer had docked the night before alongside the only pier and, during daylight hours, had been draped with fishing nets and old canvas to break up her silhouette. With darkness, these had been removed. An hour later, four 20-foot containers had been delivered by truck to the end of the jetty and then loaded with great care into her refrigerated holds, under the supervision of a team of Argentines, who looked more at home in Buenos Aires than in this remote fishing port. Around and on top of the containers had been packed a façade of crates of fish, just in case someone took a cursory look during this first leg of the voyage.

Under cover of the darkness before dawn, the little red-hulled steamer had emerged into the grey waters of the south Atlantic, initially seeking the cover of an extended Spanish fishing fleet operating on the edge of the Argentine Sea. From there she had set a course east-north-east in the direction of South Africa.

At one point, a couple of RAF Typhoon fighters had flown some five kilometres south, plainly on a training exercise from Mount Pleasant on the Falkland Islands, taking no interest in the solitary steamer.

With some 7,500 kilometres separating her from Cape Town, the journey would last between twelve days and two weeks, depending on the weather and mechanical performance. On the latter score there was little to be feared, as underneath her battered exterior, the engine and guidance systems would have looked more at home in a vessel one tenth of her apparent vintage. Before leaving, a couple of Argentine engineers who had accompanied the containers had made a point of checking out the engine room and the bridge. The Filipino captain, given his command of Spanish, had been able to satisfy them on all counts.

After Cape Town, she had stopped off at Port Elizabeth and Durban before finally making it to Maputo on 20 October. Collecting cabotage at each stop usually meant a stay of a couple of days. Known only to the captain, a couple of Argentine backpackers had been trailing her up the coast to monitor her progress. Rios, anxious to get away from the mood of failure pervading Muñoz's team, had leaped at the chance to get out of the country. At each stop, a report went back to Buenos Aires.

At Maputo, where they had remained for three days, she had taken on a cargo of meat for delivery in Tanzania. The Argentine backpackers had checked out the ship as she lay alongside the dock near the ferry terminal. Rios had dropped into the Argentine consulate, ostensibly to collect any mail which might have been forwarded to them, using his visit to report to Buenos Aires that the vessel appeared to be on schedule. As if by chance, they had met the captain at a bar on Avenida Samora Machel, where he had confirmed that his next port of call would be Dar es Salaam. Estimated date of arrival 28 or 29 October. Another message was sent following her departure.

Rios and his companion arrived in Dar es Salaam on 28 October, where they waited for two days for the ship in vain. Finally, claiming that they had agreed arrangements with the captain back in Maputo for a cheap passage to Mayotte, they had made enquiries with the Dar es Salaam harbour authorities.

They were informed that a very short 'mayday' message had been received from the vessel some four days earlier, which had been picked up both in the Comoros and in Nacala. The message had indicated a position some sixty nautical miles southwest of the island of Mayotte. The message had only been received once. Another ship in the area had been diverted to the approximate position from which the message had come and had found only two inflatable life rafts, both empty and taking on water, as well as a certain amount of general debris, spread over a large area. An aircraft sent up from the airport at Pemba, roughly opposite where the ship had apparently gone down, had flown over the area, but had reported no sign of survivors.

Rios was in no hurry to seek instructions from Buenos Aires. A couple of days on the beach might serve to build up the necessary courage before returning to the office. Not that there had been anything that could have been done to prevent the catastrophe by two men on foot. But post-mortems in SIDE were not always guided by logic.

November 2008

Monday, 3 November 2008 (PM) – PLACE VENDÔME, PARIS

They were sitting in the bar of the Ritz in Paris. A wet, blustery late autumn afternoon, most of which Sam had spent with Farida in the sauna on the top floor of the Prince's beautiful *hôtel particulier* in the *7ème arrondissement*. She had flown in two days before from Buenos Aires in response to the now almost routine command to present herself in whatever capital or resort the Saudi couple might patronize. Since the meeting in Sardinia in September, she had been called once to London in the middle of the previous month. In intelligence terms, the few days spent there had added nothing to Mossad's brief, the Prince being away in the United States, apparently continuing his discussions with Raytheon.

So as to be able to arrive a day early and spend at least one evening with Sophie, she had concealed her actual date of arrival in Paris from the Princess. She had found her old friend tired and frailer than when they had last been together in May. Gauloises consumption however seemed unchanged, as also the clarity of her mind. As they had parted at the top of the spiral staircase outside Sophie's apartment, Sam had promised she would be back as soon as she could steal a chance to get away.

The session with Farida had in many ways been predictable and Sam was seriously wondering how long she could continue to respond to these house calls. Not that she had in any way betrayed this to Farida, who had rounded off the afternoon with a private show laid on by one of the leading Parisian fashion houses. To Sam's taste, far too conventional and, when the Princess had sought her views at the end, she had not hesitated to say so.

"What do you mean, Samira. They're so beautiful."

"Perhaps it's just me, Farida. I need something more exciting, more dramatic."

"What you mean is *plus sexy*," Farida had replied, the tone teasing and curious.

"Certainly. And, if I may say so, with your figure, they would suit you. And maybe also please your husband."

The Princess had laughed.

"It's easy for you to say that, Samira. But, for someone in my position, I have to be far more careful."

"You're right, but you also have your private moments. When you're alone with him."

The Princess had not replied, apparently thinking over what Sam had said.

The Prince turned to his wife.

"So my dear, how did you spend the afternoon? Profitably I hope."

Farida and Sam exchanged glances and smiled.

"Extremely, my dear. With Samira, what else would you expect?"

He turned to Sam.

"I'm glad you were able to get away at such short notice."

"I am always at your command, Your Highness."

"Yes. Of course."

"Samira is suggesting that I upgrade my style. *Que je change mon look…*"

The Prince looked at Sam.

"Oh yes? What had you in mind?"

"Something more sexy," Farida replied, giving Sam no time to reply.

The Prince took a quick look at Sam, as if to test what that might mean.

Sam was wearing a pale grey knitted sweater dress which fell in ample folds to just above the knee, fur trimmings on the sleeves. Over this, a wide knitted cape of a darker grey wool, its large hood framing her face. The soft ensemble from Les Copains, one of her favourite designers, the same she had worn for dinner with Leandro at Oviedo, a few days before her kidnap back in April. The picture completed tonight with shiny black leggings and grey stiletto heeled shoes.

The expression on the Prince's face suggested he would probably not get in the way of his wife's transformation.

"Well, my dear, I'll drink to that," the Prince laughed. "And while we're about it, let's also drink to the successful conclusion of our little piece of business."

Sam looked at him, trying to conceal her curiosity.

"I thought we'd already done that last month."

"Ah, that was only the overture. Now we're drinking to the finale, Samira. The curtain's come down. No more need to spend time with our Argentine friends. In fact, best avoided."

"So you won't be requiring my services anymore," Sam asked, looking at the Prince.

"Who said anything about that?"

He looked at Farida.

"Have you suggested that to her, my dear?"

"Quite the contrary," the Princess replied emphatically.

"Then that's settled. Now let's drink some of this delicious, what is it, Dom Perignon 1961. Don't they call it the Charles and Diana?" He turned to Sam. "Ironic to be drinking it in this hotel, don't you think?"

The look on her face betrayed she had not the slightest idea why.

"It was from here that Diana drove away that evening and was killed in the car crash by the Pont d'Alma. With Dodi Fayed."

Sam had been twenty years old. She could still remember the worldwide outpouring which greeted the death of the Princess of Wales. That being said, she had always harboured her own views on the subject of the British Princess.

The Prince turned again to his wife.

"Absent friends?"

Mohammed joined them.

"I bear good news, Your Royal Highness. Rothschilds in Geneva have paid. It's in our account."

"Fill the glasses, Mohammed. There's one for you there. The cheque should be more than sufficient to buy up the whole of the remaining stock ten times over," he added, almost as an afterthought. He smiled enigmatically at the Princess. She raised her glass.

"To our everlasting enemies. Long may they prosper."

How to interpret this strange exchange? A Jewish bank paying a Saudi Prince? And if the news was being shared with her, it presumably related to the Iranian question.

A couple of bottles of the champagne later, they rose to leave, with Sam as usual respectfully bringing up the rear with Mohammed. As she passed the bar, a man who had been discreetly studying her for some time, stopped her.

"That's from Les Copains, isn't it?"

"Yes it is. Do you like it?"

"I should. I've recently become a fashion consultant for them."

The French heavily accented with Italian. A strong, handsome face, receding short-cropped hair, sexily unshaven.

"Albino d'Amato's my name. You'll be hearing more of me."

"I already have. You've worked for Kenzo, haven't you?"

"Amongst others. But I'm interested in the detail you've added. What is your name?"

"Samira. Which detail?"

"The black latex leggings you're wearing. They set off the rest in a very striking fashion. I must remember it for a future collection. May I steal your idea?"

"Of course, I'm very flattered. Thank you. I agree with you. They give a girl a wonderful shape of leg."

"Exactly. Here, let me give you my card. If ever you come to Italy, Samira, let me know. Maybe you can work with me."

The Prince's party had paused at the door of the bar.

"My friends are waiting for me. I'm sorry, I must go. Thank you. Perhaps one day in Milan."

"*Arrivederci,* Samira."

They shook hands.

She caught up with the Prince and Farida.

"Everybody wants you, don't they, Samira," the Princess murmured in her ear.

Tuesday, 4 November 2008 (PM) – RUE DE JOUY, PARIS

Her Israeli case officer had met her for lunch in a little bistro in the Rue de Jouy. A few blocks away from the Shoah memorial.

"I wanted to pay my respects."

Sam reported the somewhat mysterious conversation in the bar of the Ritz.

"Sounds as though that little episode is closed. Things should be safer now."

Sam looked at him.

"Safer in what way?"

"I was thinking of what happened in Punta del Este back in July."

"Oh that? Yes, presumably it won't happen again."

"I wouldn't think so. Our sources suggest the Argentines still haven't worked out how the assassin died."

"I don't think anyone knows. The press dug around, but couldn't come up with an explanation. Most people put it down to SIDE having caught up with him."

He shook his head.

"We know *that* didn't happen. At one stage they identified him, but then they lost him. Until his corpse turned up."

Sam was not about to enlighten him further.

"Messy business. My man Leandro lost a good friend. Morales. They used to play rugby together in the old days."

Her case officer signalled to the waiter to bring the bill.

"Yes. I'm afraid we rather lost control towards the end," he murmured, almost as if talking to himself.

Sam just about managed to conceal her astonishment. Was he saying that Aboukir had in some way been operating on Mossad's behalf? A loss of control that had brought her to within inches of being garrotted on a kitchen table with an aubergine in her cunt? With Leandro shot into the bargain?

She bit back the staccato of questions flashing through her mind. She couldn't speak of that final session with Aboukir without revealing the role of Frobisher, of Albert and Leandro's connection.

Her fury faded almost as fast as it had come. She would ignore the remark. As if she hadn't heard it.

"Many thanks for lunch. The *coquilles St Jacques* were delicious."

Sophie's flat being only a few blocks away, Sam decided to walk. On the way, she tried to analyse the implications of her case officer's remark.

The conclusion must surely be that, in some way, Mossad had been controlling Aboukir. Presumably without his knowledge. From the little he had said in Leandro's kitchen, it seemed unlikely he would have been consciously working for the Israelis. Somehow, Mossad had been able to feed targets to him in a manner which could not be attributed to Tel Aviv. He had made some reference to a jihadist group in Baghdad. That must be the channel.

Yet, not content with that, the signs were that the Prince had also been working on behalf of the Israelis. In his case, consciously, given the payment he had just received. Her countrymen had thought they were being incredibly clever in working through a Saudi Prince to support Shia Iran, a channel so irrational, so incredible, that it must pass undetected. A classic case of *viveza criolla*. In their peculiar reasoning, Caballero and his team had seemingly discounted the risk that this might be a Sunni trap. In fact, it had actually been a Sunni – Israeli trap! She had read somewhere that the ties between Saudi and Israeli intelligence were far closer than anyone might suspect. Perhaps not surprising, with Iran as a common enemy.

Where did this leave her? Was it possible that the Prince had known of her links to Mossad? And by involving her, found a way to ensure that Mossad would retain its confidence in him? Hadn't her reporting back to Mossad done exactly that? Trying to work out all the variations was starting to make her head spin. Too much Muscadet at lunch.

At least she was still alive. And so was Leandro. However, somewhere in all of this lay a lesson in humility.

"Will do you good, Samira," she muttered to herself, as she pressed the buzzer to Sophie's flat.

Not for the first time, she had thought she was in control. Her near demise at the hands of Aboukir suggested otherwise. Wheels within wheels. How much of all of this to share with Leandro?

"Come up, Samira. What a lovely surprise. You can cheer me up."

Monday, 10 November 2008 (PM) – EDIFICIO MARTINEZ DE HOZ, BUENOS AIRES

The inexplicable disappearance of the little freighter was not without consequences back in the Argentine capital. The news had reached Buenos Aires at the beginning of the month and fallout had been rapid.

To Muñoz's ill-disguised satisfaction, his colleague from the Policía Federal had rung him that morning on his cell phone to announce that one of his officers in the Casa Rosada had reported seeing the young adviser packing his papers and taking a taxi at the side door on Balcarce.

"Failure on that scale doesn't go down well at the top, as you can imagine."

The news had also apparently swept away Caballero, who had packed his bags that morning and disappeared across to Uruguay. Another embarrassing problem for Muñoz, who had been tasked to watch the negotiator. Until his whereabouts could be established, there was little he could do about Caballero.

Muñoz could turn his attentions to other matters. Including his obsessive determination to open up Dávila's secret empire. Something which he could only undertake very discreetly, given the fact that, ever since Dávila's death, it had been decided at the highest level that further investigation into the man's secret world carried a potential risk of embarrassment to key figures in the present government. Were his investigation to get to the ears of his superiors, and in the worst case to those of Señor Cinco, as the head of La Casa was referred to, given the floor of the building on which his offices were located, Muñoz knew that he could find himself in serious trouble. For a member of SIDE to be caught making life difficult for the Kirchners, even indirectly, carried severe penalties.

He had been able to pull all the files on the case without attracting too much attention by going through one of his assistants, Francisco Flores, who had been involved in the investigation at the time. The young man had given him a quick guided tour.

"Dávila appears to have been a double agent, a member of the Montoneros also working for the military. Involved in a lot of betrayals and interrogations. Just after Malvinas, he seems to have gone to ground in Zürich, where he stayed until about six or seven years ago. Worked in finance, in two of the large banks, UBS and American Express. Came back here and caught up with a number of his old Montonero friends. The rest you already know, as he started to work here."

"And you say that he was running some kind of blackmail operation?"

"As far as we can see, it seems to have been extremely lucrative. Also very nasty. He seems to have been sexually very perverted, but also to make use of that in his blackmail operations. As a result, at least one of his victims seems to have committed suicide back in April. A businessman called Contreras. May have been a paedophile."

"And wasn't there something about a woman? Maybe Swiss."

"We tried to do some digging in Zürich, but of course we had to be very careful and we were very rapidly told to stop making any enquiries in that direction. As you can imagine, a number of people don't want to risk something going wrong. Especially any suggestion that our organisation might be running accounts there. Which, of course, we all know to be the case anyway."

"Along with practically every other intelligence service in the world," Muñoz commented with a smile. "But this woman? Do we know anything more?"

"Not much. Except a possible connection with the address in Uruguay."

"Show me those photographs again. The ones our team took of the Saudi Prince's villa."

Muñoz scanned through the telephoto shots of the house, including a couple showing the Prince seated with two women on the front terrace.

"Have we any idea who these women are?"

"The dark haired one was a member of the Saudi negotiating team. According to our people, who covered the only meeting which took place before the attack on Caballero, she was present at the negotiation. Gave her name as Samra Harari. We also think she may have been at the meeting in Tobago."

"And the blonde? What do we know about her?"

"Possibly spends time in Uruguay. Arrived in a Mercedes sports car with Uruguayan plates. And, interesting, also visited the clinic to see the Russian woman, Kalyagin, who was shot in the hotel by Aboukir. One of the Uruguayan policeman asked her some questions. Later told us that she had a Swiss passport. But they refused to give us her name."

"And you think she might be living in that villa off Calle 5? The one that Harari visited that night."

"Yes. It might be an idea to check it out."

"Okay, Matias. Leave me the files. I'll get them back to you as soon as possible. If I have any more questions, I'll let you know. Thanks, that's been useful."

"Just be careful, *patrón* . As you know, they don't want things stirred up in that direction."

"I know. Keep it to yourself."

After Matias had left his office, Muñoz continued to study the photographs. As he examined the images of Dávila encased in his rubber coffin, his features obliterated by a gasmask, Muñoz shook his head. To think that the presence of this sexual pervert had been tolerated at the heart of SIDE. In an organization which spent as much time watching itself as watching others, was it credible that Dávila's deviance – not to mention his blackmail operation – should have gone undetected? To what extent had there been complicity at the highest levels of the organization?

As he put the photos back in the folder, his eye was caught by a number of typewritten pages. A list of files, often with the name of a SIDE operation. Clearly someone had been trying to do a damage assessment on Dávila, by taking a look at any files which he might have pulled near the time of his death. Presumably in case one of them might provide a clue to his killer. He jotted down some of the names and file numbers. He would also take a look.

Sunday, 16 November 2008 (NOON) – DELTA

Spring had arrived and the late morning sun was blazing. The ardour of the *Argentinos*, especially their women, was relentlessly to soak up the sun at every opportunity in preparation for the beaches of Punta del Este. No right-minded *porteña* would arrive in anything other than the perfect shade of bronze!

Sam was no exception, although careful never to overdo it. The first warm weekend since she had returned from the chill of Paris.

Stretched out on a striped blue and white sun mattress, her hands clasped behind her head, her back arched, her body glistened from a combination of perspiration and sun oil, the minutest Brazilian string having abandoned any attempt at concealment.

From under his straw hat, seated in a deck chair at the far end of the veranda, Leandro studied her, The Economist he'd been reading abandoned beside him. The arch of her back, the thrust of her breasts, a posture brutally recalling the image of Sam at Aboukir's mercy. Now, without the drama, she seemed purely erotic. And he was sure she knew it.

"I've never asked you. Did you have your tits operated?"

Sam raised her head, pushing her sunglasses back onto her forehead

"What?"

"I know, sounds like a stupid question."

Sam rolled her eyes in disbelief.

"Has it really taken you eighteen months to ask that question?"

Leandro shrugged his shoulders.

"You really are a *boludo*, Leo. No! Of course not. With what I've got, why should I bother?"

She pulled her dark glasses down again and rolled over onto her stomach.

"Anyway, if you think they're that great, I'll have to start rationing you. Now, be a nice guy and put some more of that sun cream on my back. And my butt. You're bound to enjoy that."

She closed her eyes to switch on her other senses. The whisper of the light breeze in the *casuarinas* along the river bank, the cry of a *bicho feo* somewhere in the distance, the soft call of the little doves which fluttered in and out of the willows. A faint perfume in the air, occasionally overlaid with the scent of the *asado*. The caress of Leandro's fingers.

With the passing of the years, Leandro had allowed the plot of land surrounding the riverside house to develop naturally, most of the trees native to the Delta. In one corner, a jacaranda in full bloom. The tree which lit up the streets and parks of Buenos Aires at this time of the year with its cloak of blue flowers.

"When did they say they were going to arrive?" she murmured.

"Hopefully not too late, otherwise everything will be incinerated. When I've finished, can you check with Juanita how she's getting on with the salads?"

Having pulled a towel over her torso, Sam went inside.

"Juanita? Have you got everything you need?"

"Si, Señora. No problem. They should be ready soon."

Juanita had taken Leandro's transition from Elena to Sam in her stride. Hardly surprising, given the flexible social mores of the *isleños*. Sam wasn't even sure that Juanita would take offence at her nudity, but just in case.

Juanita followed Sam out onto the balcony, her crooked smile missing teeth. The *isleños* might live in a world of satellite dishes on corrugated iron roofs, but modern medicine or dentistry penetrated only occasionally. They seemed none the worse for it.

"How are the children, Juanita?" Sam asked. In truth, she had lost count of how many that might be.

"Fine, except Angela. She's now living with a man near Paraná de las Palmas. Not a good man. But then, she's seventeen. These young people have a mind of their own. Shall I prepare the table, Señora?"

Sam looked down towards the long trestle table and wooden benches, which Leandro and Carlitos had set up earlier in the morning in front of a large *eléctrico*, a willow native of the islands, its pale frizzed leaves giving the impression of having received a 500 volt charge.

"Just put out some plates, cutlery and glasses. I think there are some paper *servilletas* in the cupboard. Has Leandro prepared the wine?"

"Yes, Señora. I'll do that."

"That may be them," Leandro called, leaning over the railing and looking downstream.

The sound of a very large engine was slowly approaching. As Sam watched, the long, sleek lines of a scaled-down *cigarette,* a smaller version of the powerboats used for offshore racing, appeared between the trees from the direction of the Urión. The kind of craft least favoured by Leandro, whose carefully restored, mid-1960s wooden hull had been moored farther along the bank to make way for the new arrivals. In spite of its gleaming varnished wood and chrome fittings, far more discreet.

Alejandro Martinez, a good friend from their days together at Citibank, was waving from the rear cockpit, a slim, long-haired blonde by his side. Now running a very lucrative little asset management company.

Leandro pulled on a shirt and walked to the end of the short jetty, where he threw Alejandro a painter to allow him to tie up downstream.

"Don't worry, there's never any traffic up here. How are you, *che*? Good to see you."

"*Que tal*, Leo? This is Sol. Sol. Leandro."

Leandro helped Alejandro and Sol onto the jetty, before allowing the powerboat to stream down with the current.

Pulling on one of her favourite Harley Davidson T-shirts and a pair of black linen shorts, Sam joined them on the lawn in front of the house. They all kissed.

"Brought you some champagne," Alejandro held up a small, portable cool box.

"That's some boat you've got there," Leandro complimented Alejandro. "Fruit of a highly lucrative deal, no doubt?"

"No comment, *che*. Attorney privilege."

They laughed.

Alejandro undisguisedly studied Sam, before turning to Leandro.

"*Que chicas monas, che*. We're very lucky."

The two girls embraced. Sol was certainly good looking. Perhaps a trifle overdressed for the occasion, in her brown suede trousers and black silk blouse, under a light black PVC jacket. Leandro flashed a look at Sam to indicate that she should control her instinctive competitiveness. She smiled back. She would be a very good girl today. After all, Alejandro was one of Leo's best friends.

As she surveyed the scene, the look on Sol's face seemed to suggest she was used to being taken to rather more elegant places than this primitive hut hidden out of sight up a weed-clogged channel, where the audience for her elegance and good looks, her boyfriend and his powerboat, was almost non-existent.

Sam detected it at once. Her strategy today would be the reverse of the usual. Low key. Simple. Unspoiled.

"Don't you just love this place?" she asked.

A second's hesitation.

"Wonderful. So original."

Sol walked across the lawn to inspect the place more closely, positioning her smart black Tods carefully on the driest tussocks of the rye grass at every step.

Leandro sensed the trap Sam had set.

"How about some of your champagne. The *asado* still has about half an hour to go."

Sol leapt at the invitation, returning rapidly to Alejandro's welcoming embrace.

At that point Carlitos, having docked his ancient rowing boat at the steps of the jetty, called over to Leandro.

"Do you want me to finish the *asado* for you, Don Leandro?"

At the sight of Carlitos' face, with its long scar running down one cheek and the fearsome *facón* he was brandishing in one hand as he came up the steps, Sol edged even closer to Alex. Sam smiled, before walking up to Carlitos and depositing a large kiss on his unshaven cheek. This was by no means the first time, but it always caused him to blush under his stubble. She almost sensed Sol shuddering behind her.

"Fine, Carlitos, many thanks. Here's your bottle of red. Help yourself."

The *asador* always had the right to his own bottle as he tended the grill.

Turning to the rest, Leandro gestured to the balcony.

"Let's go up in the meantime. There are some more comfortable chairs for the ladies."

As they waited for the first offerings of *choripán* to be brought to them by Juanita, the conversation between two ex-bankers inevitably turned to the financial crisis shaking the world, since the day that Lehman Brothers had declared bankruptcy in the early hours of September 14th. The same day that Merrill Lynch had been pushed into the arms of Bank of America for a mere US$ 50 billion, half its market value even less than a year before. A couple of days later, the two investment banking giants, Morgan Stanley and Goldman Sachs, had been forced to give up their prized independent status to get access to Federal Reserve support. Then in that same week, the Fed had provided AIG with a US$ 85 billion loan, which had rapidly proved inadequate to cover its losses on its massive portfolio of credit default swaps, a further US$ 40 billion having to be poured into the ailing monster.

Since then, the saga had continued relentlessly, with more and more cash being unlocked to sustain the market.

Whilst Sol showed every sign of finding it hard to understand how it might affect her lifestyle, Sam displayed her usual fascination with current affairs, earning Alejandro's evident curiosity in the process.

"Have you worked in banking?" he finally asked.

"No," Sam laughed "Numbers bore me. But I'm interested in politics. It seems obvious to me that this crisis must be as much about inept politicians as about reckless bankers."

"That's enough, you two," said Leandro "I thought we were going to have a relaxed lunch. That subject is everything except relaxed. Especially for Alejandro."

Alejandro did not demur and Sol threw him a grateful look.

Carlitos was waving to them from the lunch table.

"Everything's ready."

Leandro led the way.

By the end of the lunch, having dispatched some four bottles of Catena Zapata's best merlot and several kilos of meat, Sam could see that Sol was beginning to relax and enjoy the surroundings. Alejandro was a good friend of Leo's and Sam had initially been disappointed by the apparent showiness and superficiality of his companion. Raised in the Grand' Bourg area of Buenos Aires, alongside Palermo Chico one of the most expensive and select in the Argentine capital, her predictable preference for talking about her summer holidays in Europe, dropping the names of expensive resorts on the Mediterranean and shopping expeditions on Faubourg St Honoré or Via Condotti, had, as she relaxed, finally given way to a more genuine interest in her hosts and their secret retreat. Not for the first time with pretty girls from that background, Sam detected that the veneer of little rich girl often concealed a more unspoiled personality.

The shape of the sleek black powerboat riding quietly alongside the jetty suggested that Alejandro was not above using even the most primitive pick-up techniques, which most Argentine girls would find hard to resist. Sam had little trouble in visualizing Sol, with her long blonde hair cascading down to her waist and the impeccable silhouette of most girls from her social background, draping herself carefully on the long nose of the launch. As such, she would only be one of a host of beautiful *porteñas* doing the same up here in the Delta during November and December, before setting off on the obligatory migration - for January and February – to Punta del Este.

The two men now sitting on the railing of the jetty, having predictably returned to the subject of the financial crisis, the two girls had adjourned to the rear platform of the powerboat to catch the afternoon rays of the sun. Sol, it emerged, had spent the last year at the Ecole des Beaux Arts in Paris, studying sculpture and now had her own studio in San Telmo, where she was preparing her first exhibition, planned for the autumn.

"I must call in and see what you do."

"Any time. Please do, Samira. I'd love you to come."

For Alejandro's sake, Sam was pleased that Sol had proven not to be the *botinera* she had initially seemed, that there had been much more to the girl than at first met the eye. Including a shared love of Paris. By the time the four had parted, plans had been laid to see more of each other.

"What did you make of Sol," Sam asked, as they stood on the end of the jetty and watched Alejandro and his girlfriend waving from the powerboat as it began to move out towards the main channel.

Leandro's reply was cautious. Jealousy was never totally absent from Sam's make up.

"Sweet girl, I thought."

"And not stupid," Sam added. "Not bad looking. Wouldn't you agree?"

She watched Leandro out of the corner of her eye.

"Certainly. The kind of girlfriend Alex always seemed to find. Some men have all the luck!"

"What the fuck is that supposed--"

But before she could finish her sentence, Leandro had spun her round and was kissing her.

The image of Sam that morning had haunted him all day. As the sun began to go down behind the *casuarinas*, they made love on the drawing room floor, the front door open to add an extra touch of drama.

Later, at the hour when the mosquitoes finally withdrew to rebuild their forces for the onslaught of the following evening, they returned to the verandah. Sam with a Campari, a foretaste of summer, Leandro with his usual whisky.

"Something I need to share with you."

From her tone, he detected it might be something serious.

"Go on."

"I learned something interesting in Paris. You'll never guess."

"I won't even bother to try."

"Now you're being lazy."

"No, but with you, guessing games are a waste of time."

"Have it your way. In a nutshell, it looks as though my friends at Mossad have been controlling everything."

"What do you mean by everything?"

"I mean everything. Everything I was involved in with the Saudis. And - wait for it - even possibly Aboukir."

Leandro whistled.

"You can't be serious. Why would they do that? And how?"

Sam drew a deep breath before continuing. It sounded almost like a sigh.

"In the case of the Saudis, given the fact that both Tel Aviv and Riyadh will go to any lengths to stop the Iranians, perhaps we shouldn't be surprised. And our dear government thought it was being so smart, so *vivo*. It looks as if all those efforts are now lying at the bottom of the ocean. The Indian Ocean, to be quite precise."

Leandro was staring at her.

"How do you know?"

"I haven't seen it in black and white, but I'm pretty sure that's what happened."

"And Aboukir? What makes you suspect that?"

Sam hesitated. If she told him, there was little doubt that it would constitute a serious breach of the rules as regards her Mossad connections. The kind of professional confidentiality she and Leandro had implicitly said they must respect. But, given the fact that Leandro had nearly lost his life - not to mention she hers - she'd come to the conclusion that she owed it to him.

"My Mossad case officer virtually said so. He implied that, in some way, they had been controlling Aboukir."

Leandro shook his head.

"But without Aboukir's knowledge, surely?"

"Almost certainly. Somehow, without his realising it, they must have been feeding him names. Presumably through the terrorist group which hired him."

Leandro drank half his whisky. He stared out at the darkening river. What the hell had he got himself into? What kind of world was he now moving in? Things had seemed bad enough at the end of the Dávila affair, when he had attracted the attention of SIDE, an organization widely suspected of having been granted almost unlimited powers by the Kirchners to maintain control. Not content with that, he now seemed to have added one of the world's most feared intelligence services to the list of agencies which had him in their sights. One which appeared to have set him up for assassination. Was there any going back?

"And you? As a matter of interest, do they actually know that you nearly got killed? Or for that matter, me? Are you saying they gave him my name? Or yours?"

Sam shook her head.

"I don't think they know anything more than SIDE as to how Aboukir died. But if they had set us up, my case officer would never have let on."

Now it was Leandro's turn to draw a deep breath.

"So where does this leave us?"

"I'm not sure."

"From you, I was expecting a rather more reassuring reply."

"It's just not that easy."

"But are you going to continue to work for them?"

"For the time being, it looks that way."

"Fuck that! I think you're crazy."

Sam stretched out her hand and touched his arm.

"You've known that all along."

"Not *that* crazy."

The look on Sam's face expressed concern.

"Does that mean you're not going to love me anymore?"

"To quote you, it's just not that easy."

She got up from her deck chair and went to sit on the railing, with her back to the river, looking down at him.

"I don't know about you, but, with what we went through, I love you even more. Surely we're not going to allow a minor assassin to get in the way of that?" she whispered.

Leandro shook his head again. Then he smiled.

"You're probably right. Not a minor assassin. Now, had it been a major one…"

"Give me some more Campari. I've told you before. You make the drinks too small."

Friday, 28 November 2008 (PM) – CALLE 5, LA BARRA,

"Madame Carla, you have a visitor," Naya announced.

It was the end of November. Punta del Este was showing all the signs of summer just around the corner. The flights from Buenos Aires and the ferries to Montevideo were beginning to witness the annual shuttle of Argentine owners sprucing up their flats and villas, hopeful of lucrative rentals during the brief summer season.

Carla, wearing a light jogging suit after an intense session of aerobics with Sam downstairs in the spa, was seated in the frame of the large picture window. She waved at Sam, who was lying naked on a mattress beside the horizon pool which stretched towards the pale blue line of the Atlantic Ocean. Sam blew her a kiss.

A year ago at about this time, she had met Sam at a party in the run-up to the Argentine Polo Open. They'd agreed to celebrate the anniversary together. An absence which Leandro had accepted with good grace.

"Don't forget Eduardo's getting married on the sixth."

"I'll be back long before. Don't worry, *mi amor*."

In many ways, Carla believed that their meeting had set in train the events leading to her ultimate liberation from Dávila. Since the events of that final night when Dávila had died, she had not been back to Argentina. As they had gathered for this year's Open, a number of her polo clients had called her, offering outrageous sums of money to join them, and one or two had even flown over to see her. But caution dictated that until further notice she should avoid returning to her homeland.

"Who is it?"

"He gave his name as Inspector Muñoz. Here's his card."

Division of Transnational Crime and International Terrorism. Servicio de Inteligencia del Estado. 11, Avenida 25 de Mayo, Capital Federal.

Carla didn't like the look of that at all. She hesitated a moment.

"I'll be with him in five minutes. I need a shower first. And go and warn Señorita Samira to get out of sight. Only then show him in."

She went to the bedroom to change, emerging a quarter of an hour later, impeccably turned out in a dark blue linen safari jacket and skirt over a blush pink blouse. Her mass of hair gathered in a pigtail. Make-up discrete.

She found Muñoz standing by the window admiring the view. She checked. No sign of Sam.

"Good afternoon, Inspector. I'm sorry to have kept you waiting."

"Not at all, Señora Bodmer. I should have announced my visit."

Not that that had even occurred to him. The visit was always meant to be a complete surprise. Otherwise this lady might have been tempted to disappear.

"Can I offer you some tea? Or a coffee?"

"A coffee, thank you."

"Please sit down," she said. "Unless you want to go outside."

"I can admire the view from here."

When Naya appeared, she ordered two coffees.

For a moment they sat there, neither saying a word. Finally Carla broke the silence.

"So, Inspector, how can I help you?"

"Thank you for receiving me."

Carla was too well brought up to suggest that she had not been given very much choice in the matter.

"I believe, Señora Bodmer, that you were here two months ago. At the time of the attack in the Mantra Hotel?"

"Yes," Carla said.

"In fact, I believe that one of the victims was known to you. Is that correct?"

"Tatyana Kalyagin? A friend of mine from Switzerland. She told me that she was visiting Punta del Este and most unfortunately got caught up in the attack. Luckily, her wound was relatively light. I've heard that she is now completely recovered."

Tatyana had sent her a photograph of herself in a Moscow night club. A selfie taken from under the table. Judging by her visible anatomy, recovery was definitely complete.

"So I'm told. She was very fortunate."

Muñoz paused to drink some of his coffee.

"You may have heard that we were able to catch the assassin. An impeccable operation."

Carla had reason to believe that this might be a flattering version.

"I hadn't heard. That's excellent news. Congratulations. But how can I be of assistance to you, Inspector?"

Muñoz stared hard at her.

"Am I right in thinking, Señora Bodmer, that you are of Argentine origin? But that you now have a Swiss passport?"

"That's correct. I changed my nationality in the 1980s. After the events, when I had taken up residence in Switzerland."

"Ah, of course, the events. You are referring to the period of the *dictadura*, no doubt."

"Yes."

"When you were detained?"

"Yes."

"And interrogated? Perhaps even tortured?"

"I'd be happier if we didn't discuss that."

The look on Carla's face was becoming increasingly hermetic. This certainly wasn't an area that she wanted to revisit in the company of someone from SIDE.

"I understand. But, unfortunately, I will have to ask you a few questions. Off the record, of course."

Carla had good cause to know that nothing was ever off the record with people like this.

"That would be preferable," she replied.

"The investigations relating to what happened during that period are ongoing. The statute of limitations does not apply in the case of crimes against humanity."

"Of course."

"Have you ever felt the need to contribute to this valuable effort? As you know, President Cristina Fernandez de Kirchner, like her husband before her, have been doing all within their power to bring the criminals to justice."

"That is an excellent thing."

"Exactly. Especially since there are many corners of what happened in those days which have yet to see the light of day. It's a painstaking task, but one which, thanks to the efforts of the present government, is making real progress."

"I understand."

"If so, would you be prepared to help, Señora Bodmer?"

Carla fell silent for a minute. She needed to be very careful. This was an area in which events could take sudden and unexpected turns. Damaging turns. She got up and walked over to the window, looking out towards the ocean. Muñoz came and stood beside her, not looking at her, but following her gaze.

"I believe it is a matter to which you should give serious consideration, Señora Bodmer," he said quietly.

She turned and looked at him.

"I will be very honest with you, Inspector Muñoz. For the last twenty-five years, I've been trying to put those events behind me. My memories are too painful. Certainly too painful to be stirred up again just like that."

She tried to detect a reaction, but he was giving nothing away.

"I would need to give it some thought. But I should warn you that my response is very likely to be unhelpful."

Muñoz was silent, studying her. He detected a powerful personality, one over which it would not be easy to gain the upper hand. The research they had been doing since the discovery of Dávila's body at the end of March had thrown up his connections with a Swiss woman. Also property that might have come into the possession of the woman standing beside him. A number of shell companies based in Panama appeared to have been behind the deal, which the Panamanian authorities seemed reluctant to open up.

What had been the link between Dávila and this woman?

And more recently, what was her connection with the Russian girl, who had got so close to Caballero? Given her link with the Saudi Prince, could it really be so innocuous? And Samra Harari, the Syrian? Part of the Saudi negotiation team. One of his men, watching the two women as they sat on the terrace, had reported discreet signs of intimacy between the two women, when left alone at one point by the Prince taking a phone call. Add to that Harari's nocturnal visit to this villa.

He suspected that at this moment, Carla was resisting his desire to dig up the past. Somewhere she did not want to go. Two areas of this woman's life interested Muñoz. He would see which would turn out to be the easier to unravel.

"This is a beautiful house, Señora Bodmer. How long have you lived here?"

"I spend most of my time in Switzerland. I only borrow this house from a friend. He kindly lets me use it pretty much as I wish."

"Rather out of season, wouldn't you say?"

"In fact I much prefer it. I'm not a great fan of the summer months. Too many people. But spring can be very beautiful here."

"I know what you mean. And Buenos Aires? Do you ever come back there? To visit relatives, perhaps?"

"I was there a couple of times last year. Before coming here last December. Since then, I haven't been back."

Her lightning visit to the river delta back in March, when Dávila had died, would have left no trace in the name of Señora Bodmer. Dávila had unwittingly made sure of that.

Muñoz nodded.

"No relatives?"

"I have a sister, but I broke with my family back in 1983. When I left."

Carla felt that the time had come to try and regain some of the initiative.

"Inspector Muñoz, if I may ask. Is there something in particular about which you wish to question me? One does not receive a visit from a representative of SIDE every day."

He needed to make up his mind which way to point his enquiry. Perhaps a direct question would provoke a reaction.

"Does the name Dávila mean anything to you?"

She had been expecting that one. Her gaze never wavered. She gave a look as if to indicate that she really didn't know what he was talking about.

"Dávila? They come from Salta, don't they? I've met one or two in the past. Man or woman?"

She had to be prepared for the possibility that they might have been spotted together, although she knew that Dávila had tried to be as discreet as possible in her company.

"Alberto Dávila."

She appeared to be digging into the past. A good act. But an act, nevertheless, he suspected.

"The name does seem familiar."

"No more?"

"No. I mean, I do seem to recall having met someone of that name in the past. What sort of age?"

"A man of about fifty. Or at least, he would have been."

"Remember that I left Argentina many years ago."

"Of course. But perhaps from somewhere else?"

Carla lowered her eyes, apparently scouring her memory.

"Perhaps in Switzerland?" Muñoz hinted.

She looked up.

"There was someone by that name in Zürich, now that you mention it."

Assuming they had done their research, they would know that she and Dávila had lived there at the same time.

"He worked there for some time," Muñoz added. "In finance. He was murdered earlier this year."

"I'm sorry. But I don't see how I can help you. Or at least, you haven't told me how I might."

Muñoz turned away. The seed had been sown. He was certain that she knew who he was talking about. Perhaps just another little detail would jog her memory.

"Is it possible that you might have met him at the time of the *militares*? During your detention?"

"As I said earlier, that's not a part of my life I'm keen to revisit. So please don't take me there."

"Of course, I'm sorry."

"If it's his murder that you're investigating, I really don't see how I can help you. I don't see why you think I can. Where was he murdered? In Switzerland?"

"No, in Argentina. But you're right. Things are not very clear. Our investigation is still at an early stage. The picture is confusing."

Muñoz seemed to be jumping from one topic to another. Was he interested in Dávila or the attack on Caballero?

"Forgive me, but perhaps not as confusing as you suggest. Sufficiently clear, it seems, for you to make the effort to come and see me."

Now it was his turn to come under pressure.

"All part of a routine enquiry."

She was not impressed by that one and said so.

"How routine are enquiries related to those events? And when they involve your organization?"

He hesitated before replying.

"You are right, of course. They never can be routine. For the time being, Señora Bodmer, perhaps you will think about what I asked you. You have my card. If you think that you can help, please call me."

"Of course. But I warn you that the answer may be no. Let me show you out, Inspector."

As they walked through the hall towards the front door, Muñoz glanced to one side down a corridor leading to other rooms in the villa. As he did so, one of the doors opened and a young woman, dressed in a black silk peignoir, her feet bare, stepped out, but, on catching sight of him, turned and went back into the room.

At the door, Muñoz shook Carla's hand, before walking towards his car. The driver was holding open the passenger door. He turned, as if suddenly remembering something, and walked back to Carla who was politely waiting for him to leave.

"I've just remembered, Señora Bodmer. Does the name Janet Williams mean anything to you?"

Carla's defences had almost been down, but not completely. For a tenth of a second, her eyes widened, before recovering the puzzled look which most of his questions had elicited earlier.

She shook her head.

"I don't think so. I don't know many people with English or American names."

"It was just a thought."

Muñoz returned to the car and, with a friendly wave of the hand, climbed into the back.

Carla returned his wave and watched the car drive away.

As he lit a cigarette, looking out towards the empty beaches which the car was passing on its way back into Punta del Este, Muñoz was in little doubt that Señora Bodmer had many of the answers he was looking for. Dávila. Janet Williams. She knew exactly who he meant.

Add to that the presence of the woman Harari. That profile and haircut were unmistakable. Harari? Another version of Haidar? In the months before his death, Dávila had run a trace on her. Connected traces had included a certain Leandro Flemming. A name which had also appeared in the little notebook found on Aboukir's body. Dávila had taken a close interest in the journalist, even to the extent of possibly placing an eavesdropping device in his flat. Muñoz wondered whether it might still be working. And in the same cluster of traces undertaken by Dávila, a young detective by the name of Eduardo Falcioni, from the

Comisaría 17a. The *Comisaría* suspected of running the trace on Aboukir.

But of Bodmer, no trace, no file. Perhaps because Dávila had known her so well that no trace was required.

In ways Muñoz could still not explain, he sensed the presence of Dávila in the Aboukir case. Perhaps no more than a coincidence. But a coincidence he would exploit.

As he looked down onto the brown waters of the River Plate below the aircraft, his mind was made up. To solve the riddle of Dávila, Bodmer, Harari and Flemming must become part of his undercover investigation.

GLOSSARY

AFIP	Administración Federal de Ingresos Públicos, Argentine tax authority
aguantar	put up with
alpargata	espadrille-style canvas or cloth shoe commonly worn by gauchos
Andate a la mierda!	*Go to hell!*
asado	barbecue
asado de tira	beef ribs
asador	person in charge of barbecue
Asesor	Adviser
bandoneón	small accordeon used in tango
barrio	urban precinct
bicho feo	great kiskadee, tyrant flycatcher
bife de chorizo	tenderloin steak
bife de lomo	sirloin steak
boina	beret, Basque style, often much larger, commonly worn by gauchos in the Province of Buenos Aires
boludo	idiot, pejorative, but largely meaningless nowadays
bombacha	long pleated gaucho trousers, possibly Turkish origin, buttoned at the ankle

botinera	"gold digger" or "bounty hunter", term often applied to the female companions of leading footballers
cacerolazo	popular anti-Government demonstration, banging of pots and pans
campo	generic word for Argentine countryside, also for farming community: also applied to a farming unit
Casa Rosada	Presidential Palace in Buenos Aires
chambre de bonne	maids rooms in old French houses or flats, often located under the roof
che	familiar name for other person, most often addressed to men
chimango	species of bird of prey in the Falconidae family, found in Argentina, Brazil, Chile, Paraguay and Uruguay
chinchulin	tripe
cholita	indigenous Aymara and Quechua women, easily identified by their distinctive outfits of multiple skirts and petticoats, shawl and bowler hat
choripán	chorizo sausage in grilled bread roll, common starter to any *asado*
colectivo	bus
Comisaría	police station
Coquilles St Jacques	scallops
cordero	lamb

cortado	coffee with hot milk
Dictadura	dictatorship, usually applied to the military government which ruled Argentina between 1976 and 1983
dorogoya moyá	(Russian) my dear (applied to a woman)
empanadas	savoury pasties
estanciero	landowner
facón	short one-sided dagger carried by gauchos
faja	broad rawhide belt worn by gauchos
Fuerza Aérea	Argentine Air Force
hijo de puta	son of a whore
hôtel particulier	French, private town house
isleños	islanders, inhabitants of river delta north west of Buenos Aires
lapacho	tree growing high in the Andes of the South American rainforest
maricón	homosexual (male) (pejorative)
mate	yerba mate leaves, herb tea, popular in Argentina, Paraguay and Uruguay
medialuna	croissant
medialuna de grasa	salty croissant
monte	stand of trees in the pampa
morcilla	blood sausage

mozo	waiter
ojo de bife	rib-eye steak
papas fritas	fried potatoes, chips
papas paille	thinly sliced chip potatoes
parrilla	grill for barbecue, restaurant specializing in grilled meat
pasaje	narrow side street, usually dead-end
porteño	inhabitant of Buenos Aires
portero	concierge, porter
potselui	kisses (Russian)
pucha!	Heck!
pueblo	town, village
Que boludo que sos!	You're such an idiot…
Que chicas monas!	What beautiful girls!
quebracho	*Schinopsis lorentzii*, hardwood tree known as red quebracho
quincho	outhouse, usually housing the barbecue and dining area
quinta	weekend residence in the Province of Buenos Aires, usually not far from the city
servilleta	napkin
SIDE	Servicio de Inteligencia del Estado, principal Argentine intelligence service

siloviki	Silovik is a Russian word for politicians from the security or military services, often the officers of the former KGB, GRU, FSB, SVR, the Federal Drug Control or other security services who came into power (Wikipedia)
taqiyah	in Islam, a legal dispensation whereby a believing individual can deny his faith or commit otherwise illegal or blasphemous acts while they are in fear or at risk of significant persecution: more generally applied to dissimulation
turco	slang term for immigrants from the ex-Ottoman empire
uno a uno	the period between 1 April 1991 and the 2001 Argentine financial crisis when, under the terms of the Convertibility Law, the US dollar – Argentine peso exchange rate had been pegged – and held – at 1 : 1
villa miseria	shanty town, Hispanic version of Brazilian *favela*
viveza criolla	superior intelligence (or wilyness) with which many Argentines believe themselves to be endowed: at times characterized by a certain reluctance to think through all the consequences and risks
vuelta y vuelta	seared, very rare (for steak)

TABLE OF CONTENTS

PROLOGUE

April 2008 2
May 2008 7
June 2008 82
July 2008 278
August 2008 503
September 2008 537
October 2008 542
November 2008 546

GLOSSARY
TABLE OF CONTENTS
DEEP WARS - Extract

DIRTY WARS

About Nicholas Brentano

Also by Nicolas Brentano

Extract from **D€€₱ WAR$**
appearing in 2017

Monday, 20 October 2008 – CASA ROSADA, BUENOS AIRES

"Señora Presidenta? You called?"

"Of course, *idiota*. That's what the buzzer's for…."

This new secretary wasn't going to last long at this rate. She hadn't seemed so stupid at her interview… There were days she dreamt it would have been wonderful to enjoy the services of the incomparable Isabel Ernst, Evita's German secretary…

"Bring me that Sotheby's catalogue which arrived yesterday from Geneva."

"At once, *Señora Presidenta*."

The girl carefully placed the elegant catalogue on the table beside her.

"That'll be all."

She began to leaf through the catalogue until she found the page which Geneva had marked.

Lot 62

A very important cushion-cut sapphire and diamond ring, Property of a Lady

Cushion-cut Kashmir sapphire weighing 45.68 carats, set in a platinum mount pavé, two-row border of circular diamonds.

Estimate: SFr.3.5 - 4.0 million / $2.9 – 3.3 million.

A whole-page photograph of the square ring on the opposite page. Beautiful against a blue background.

"Property of a Lady," the text said. The note accompanying the catalogue had been categorical. The lady in question was none other than Eva Peron. Geneva indicated that they had been able to check out the provenance and that there was no doubt that this was a piece which Evita had deposited in a Swiss bank during her 1947 visit. How did Geneva know? The blue of the sapphire and the white of the diamonds – the colours of Argentina. Maybe, but hardly conclusive. She had seen hundreds in similar combinations. Yet they must have it on good authority. You didn't throw information like that around without checking your sources. And certainly not if you were sending it to the reigning president of Argentina.

Date of the sale 20 November. A month away. Time to try and get further confirmation. The junta which had kicked out Perón in '56 had gone to great lengths to track down his bank accounts in Switzerland. Maybe someone was still around who knew about those attempts.

The President pressed one of the buttons on her large phone. Direct line to her head of security. The man with the best connections to SIDE and beyond.

"Vittorio. Are there any files still around about Peron's assets? Bank accounts in Switzerland. That kind of thing. As I recall, the junta tried to find them after they kicked him out. See what you can find. I need it by the end of the week at very latest."

Calling him Vittorio somehow sounded more sinister than plain Victor. It was also a signal to him that the subject was one of maximum discretion.

Dirty Wars
Appeared in 2014

Into a sinister world in which sex, crime and espionage overlap, Malvinas veteran and ex-banker Leandro Flemming, led on by Sam, his sexually audacious mistress, are drawn in pursuit of the murderer of an English polo 'groupie' in a Buenos Aires boutique hotel.

In the process, they uncover a bizarre relationship between interrogators and victims, born in the dark cells of the ESMA interrogation centre, blossoming, like some black orchid, more than 20 years later on the shores of Lake Zurich.

Did the 'dirty war' between the terrorists and the Argentine military dictatorship ever really end after the Malvinas war or have its protagonists re-emerged in new, dangerous guises in today's Argentina?

From the warmth and charms of Argentina's old-world capital city to the deviant strata which lies below the surface of Switzerland's financial centre, their investigation leads them into a milieu of erotic extremism, severely testing their own relationship.

About Nicolas Brentano

Nicolas Brentano is the pen name of a long-term observer – and lover – of Argentina, whose travels and professional activities in politics and finance have provided him with first-hand knowledge and insight into many of the settings and actions of this book – though perhaps not the more extreme!

Riding the switchback of Argentina's fortunes throughout the decades portrayed in this book, he shares the love of his main characters for the kindness and compassion of *los Argentinos*, who - in spite of all the hardships which successive governments have inflicted upon them – retain the confidence that one day their country will return to the world status it once enjoyed.

nicolasbrentano@sifpublishing.co.uk

info@sifipublishing.co.uk

SifiPublishing
WWW.SIFIPUBLISHING.CO.UK

htning Source UK Ltd.
lton Keynes UK
HW02f1504140818
27229UK00006B/268/P